Growing Up Amanda

DANIEL WRIGHT

Order this book online at www.trafford.com
or email orders@trafford.com

Most Trafford titles are also available at major online book retailers.

Printed in the United States of America.

ISBN: 978-1-4269-4772-8 (sc)
ISBN: 978-1-4269-4773-5 (e)

Trafford rev. 11/12/2010

 www.trafford.com

North America & international
toll-free: 1 888 232 4444 (USA & Canada)
phone: 250 383 6864 ♦ fax: 812 355 4082

Chapter 1 — Jack 1
Chapter 2 — My Family 4
Chapter 3 — The Theater 8
Chapter 4 — My Uncle Ken 12
Chapter 5 — My First Experience 16
Chapter 6 — A Virgin 21
Chapter 7 — Dad's Brew Drinking Buddy 24
Chapter 8 — Marianne and Chad 28
Chapter 9 — The Amanda Revue 35
Chapter 10 — Marianne Set Free 39
Chapter 11 — The Parade 43
Chapter 12 — Bargain Bob 48
Chapter 13 — Ty and Danny 52
Chapter 14 — Stories of Bargain Bob 57
Chapter 15 — Sam and Roy 59
Chapter 16 — Religion 63
Chapter 17 — Busted 65
Chapter 18 — Busted Once More 68
Chapter 19 — My Bus Driver 71
Chapter 20 — My Own Bus 75
Chapter 21 — Difficult Business Conditions 78
Chapter 22 — Shopping Plans 82
Chapter 23 — Shopping 85
Chapter 24 — My Good Will Store 88
Chapter 25 — Family Fun 92
Chapter 26 — A Business is Born 97
Chapter 27 — Bri 100
Chapter 28 — John's Birthday 104
Chapter 29 — Tyson (Don Juan) 109
Chapter 30 — The Party Has Ended 111
Chapter 31 — First Day in Business 114
Chapter 32 — Bird Day 119
Chapter 33 — Sam's 123
Chapter 34 — The Professional Trucker 130
Chapter 35 — Meeting Ebony 134
Chapter 36 — Sex Education 136
Chapter 37 — Party Bus in Place 139
Chapter 38 — Babysitting at the Sampson's 142
Chapter 39 — Using My Powers 147
Chapter 40 — Chad's Taxi 149
Chapter 41 — The Game and Sunny 152
Chapter 42 — Rainy Day Business 159
Chapter 43 — Josh's Birthday 163
Chapter 44 — Ty Busted 167
Chapter 45 — Conversation with Bargain Bob 169
Chapter 46 — Marianne's My Girl 173
Chapter 47 — Bwana Ron 176
Chapter 48 — A Talk With Dad 182
Chapter 49 — Beach Party Soon 186
Chapter 50 — Our Government 189
Chapter 51 — Ray Ray 192
Chapter 52 — Cadillac's and Uncle Bob 194
Chapter 53 — Sunny 201
Chapter 54 — Cookie Delivery 209
Chapter 55 — Sharing Sunny 214
Chapter 56 — Monopoly 218
Chapter 57 — Mr. Sampson 223

Growing Up Amanda

The Premise of My Story

Have you ever envisioned living life as the opposite sex? In that life, what would you do differently from what we observe and live with on a daily basis? What would you change if you were in that body? Family or no family? What would you do for recreation? Would you enjoy sports? Your love life, working habits and especially sexual attitudes would most likely change dramatically. Would you be more or less controlling? What kind of a leader would you be? As a female, if you became a male, would you be much more active sexually? Would you have many sexual partners or few? How would you live your life as the opposite sex? I suppose we each would have our own individual ideas, I certainly have mine.

I am a sixty-year old businessman with many businesses over the past forty years. Most have been successful. I became a self-made millionaire before I was forty. I have always been a controlling kind of person in my personal life as well as in my relationships. I have watched, studied, lived with, married, loved, hated, been in awe of, addicted to and lusted after the female population most of my sixty years.

Many times I have made the statement to beautiful women, some young, some not so young, that were struggling with life: "If I had your looks, your body, your personality and smile, I would control the world, or at least my immediate world." I sometimes ask myself in that position blessed with what they have, which of course, would also include some reasonable degree of intelligence, what would I do differently with my life? The first on my list would be control. I would never, under any circumstance, let men control my little world, let alone my life. Loving them, fine, I would always be positive this man deserved my love, and that I knew him well enough and was positive he would be a success in whatever he chooses to do. No lazy bastards in my little life. If I choose to have sex with whomever, for whatever reason, fine. I will be controlling the mood, not them. I would own the world of men!

In my observation, many of these women have no concept of what they possess or how it could be used to benefit them. This female could live the good life, new cars, beautiful homes, and travel. Many will find my vision in this story disgusting, who cares! I don't intend to please everyone. It's impossible. This is my vision and how I would handle life as the opposite sex, from very young to growing older. My experiences and personality have been projected to several of the characters in my story.

Are some women simply born with a sexual desire that most men simply take for granted? Is it always a matter of self-esteem? Is it possible some females are just simply born with an abnormally strong desire for sex? It happens with many men and no one questions it. Is it a matter of genes or chromosomes or maybe a hormone imbalance? Are one in a million females born with an abnormally strong desire, or are there many? I don't know if anyone really knows. Most women who fall into this category, I'm certain, don't begin to understand. Certainly Amanda doesn't know where it comes from. As I move on with my story you will understand what it has done to her and how she lives and learns to control her little world with what God given gifts she was born with. What she chooses to do with her gifts will shock some and repulse others. Follow Amanda through her journey as she begins learning how to put her gifts to use to benefit her life all while dealing with high school, family and her budding sexuality. Perhaps she has been given the soul of a male. But, why – How? Come along for the ride in *Growing Up Amanda*. I guarantee many shocking surprises as you laugh and cry while you get a glimpse inside Amanda's world in this coming-of-age tale.

Daniel Wright, *Author*

CHAPTER 1

Jack

My first erotic experience was the summer of 2008. It was a warm, muggy southern evening. I was walking down our gravel road as I quite often do with my German Shepherd, Bandit. Bandit's my buddy. He's four-years-old, large, dark and intimidating. I'm wearing super-tight spandex short shorts, pink lacy panties and a very tight white little top that shows my midriff. I'm wearing no bra, still quite shy in that area. I have perky nipples that protrude out through the tight white cotton material.

There is very little traffic on our short road. I didn't recognize the vehicle approaching me. The car stopped beside me, the driver looks at me and says, "Hello!" He was mid-aged, short, curly blond hair with a big friendly smile and a shiny new car. I gave him a returned, "Hi!" He asked me if I wanted a ride. Bandit was out in the field, so the gentleman didn't know I had company. I said with a smile, "No, I live right down the road." He smiled, "I'm Jack, what's your name?" "Amanda." "Nice to meet you Amanda. That's a really nice name." "Thank you." He continued to gaze at me. "You certainly are looking great this evening. I love those shorts." "Thank you," I answered with a smile. "How old are you?" "Jack, a gentleman never asks a lady's age!" He gave me another smile and a wink. I felt a tingle in my body. I loved standing in my road with this handsome man looking very closely at my short shorts and staring at my body. He looked me in the eye from across the road and said, "Would you like to make five dollars?" I rotate my legs back and forth, "What would I have to do?" "Nothing," he answered immedi-ately, "just answer one question." "What's the question?" I asked with a smile. He looked me in the eye, "What color are your panties?" I give him a big smile while

thinking to myself that here was a man who will pay me five dollars! That's a whole week's allowance, just to tell him the color of my panties. I could do that! I look directly at him, "Pink." He gives me a sexy look and reaches into his pocket and hands me a five-dollar bill out the window. I step across the gravel road to retrieve my pay. I take it from his hand and thank him. "I love pink panties," he replied, "would you like to make ten dollars more?" I smile, feeling a bit too comfortable. I was rotating my little hips from side to side and pressing my nipples that had become erect in my tight white cotton top. He couldn't take his eyes off my crotch and was gazing at my firm nipples. "What do I need to do?" He nodded with a smile, "I want to see your pink panties." God, I thought, I love my pink panties so much. I stand in my mirror at home and look at myself in them and get very excited. Here is a man who will pay me ten dollars to see them. I love showing my little friends for nothing! I smile and said, "OK." I turn sideways and pull the leg up to expose my lacy pink panty covered thigh. He stared at my thigh. "Amanda, for ten dollars I need to see them all. Pull your shorts down."

An erotic tingle shot through my body, an exciting rush. I didn't begin to understand, it was so exciting. I knew I could not do this standing in the road. Did I dare get in his car? I put my better judgment aside. "OK, but I need to have you drive me down the road one hundred yards. I'll show you where to pull off." He smiles and tells me to jump in. I look for Bandit; he was not around. I knew he would go back home soon. I slide in and point Jack to an isolated drive. He pulls in under a big tree where we could not be seen from the road. Excitement is running through my body. I love showing my panties to the boys when opportunities arise. Here is a real man who is going to pay to see them. How exciting is that! I slid to my door to get out. "Where are you going?" "I am going to model my panties for you." I close the door and go around the car to his window and give him a big smile while putting my thumbs on each side of my shorts and slide them to the ground and kick them off. It was so exciting watching him stare at my little pussy area. The passionate look on his face excited me even more. His face was so intense staring at my crotch looking up to my erect nipples and back again. "Turn around, please, Amanda, I need to get my ten dollars worth." I slowly turn around to show him my hot little ass. I rotate it back and forth. I knew I had to be driving Jack crazy. I felt my crotch tingle! A dampness, it was getting wet, I didn't care; it was so exciting to be driving this handsome man wild and myself as well!

I shake my buttocks back and forth two more times and reach for my shorts to put them back on. I look at Jack. He lifts his hand from down in front of him and reaches for a ten-dollar bill and hands it to me with such a passionate look. "Amanda, for another ten dollars will you let me touch them?" The thought made me tremble. To have this man's hands on my panties flashed back to the "Eensy Weensy Spider" and what a turn on it was for that boy to touch me. Now here is a man who is going to give me ten dollars! Oh my God, how could I say no? I was so aroused, while not even knowing where this tingling sensation was coming from. I pick up my shorts and slide back into his front seat. His hand immediately slid up

my leg to my thigh – God it felt so good. His hand then slid from my thigh up to my damp panties. He leans over and kisses my ear, "Your pussy is so wet." I moan. He slides his hand up and down my damp mound. I felt so good. He whispers in my ear, "Spread your legs." I obey. His hand moves up and down my pussy very quickly, "Let me touch the backside." To earn ten dollars a girl does what a girl has to do. I slid over on the seat, put my knees down and stuck my round little ass in the air. He slid both hands up and down my buttocks – Oh God! His hands went up and down between my legs, how could this feel so good! I found myself gently pumping my ass up and down and side to side. He buries his face between my legs and begins licking and slurping on my ass and my wet pussy. My new panties are soaked with juice. I did not know where it was coming from and didn't really care. I didn't know what was happening within me. As I look back, I know that day I came in my panties and all over Jack's face while he continued to suck harder and slurp louder. Oh my God! That moment I will never forget.

As I roll back upright on the car seat while reaching for my shorts, Jack is staring at me while rubbing his crotch with a slow up and down motion. "Now are you going to help me?" I wasn't sure what he meant, although deep in my mind I wanted to know. I continued fumbling with my shorts and slid them over my wet panties. I look at Jack one more time as he continues rubbing his hand up and down his gray slacks. I open the car door and got out of the car. "I have to go home now." Jack, looking rather disgruntled and breathing heavily managed to say, "Amanda, this was so much fun!" I smile. "Amanda, will you give me your cell phone number?" I was clutching my phone in my hand. Thoughts flashed through my mind, yes or no? Oh, why not? I gave him my number as he scrambled for paper and pen. I walked around the big tree and toward my road. I looked back. Jack was doing something, his hands were down; his head was pressed against the headrest. I heard a very loud moan. I wondered, is he OK? I kept walking. I hear the car start. Thank goodness he is alive was my thought as I walked down the road. Jack drove up to me and stopped. "Amanda you should get home and change those wet shorts." I smile as he drives away. He was right. My panties were soaked all around my little pussy and the crack of my rear. It felt so good as I walked home. I had twenty-five dollars in my hand. That was five weeks allowance in just thirty minutes of pure pleasure!

I crept into the house very carefully as not to be spotted in my wet shorts. I went to my bedroom and slid them off and lay on my bed thinking of what had just happened. It was so exciting and felt so good. Could there be something wrong with me? What was it that just happened? Was this sex? I didn't really understand . . . but I was happy. And, Jack had my phone number. I sure hoped he'd call soon!

CHAPTER 2

My Family

I live in a little rural town in the mid south. It has been a perfect summer...lots of sunshine and an occasional passing thunderstorm, some with the intensity that causes you to rush to the window and patiently wait for the next bolt of lightning as the rain pounds the lawn. My body and long legs glow with a beautiful tan. I love the sun and what it does to my already naturally dark skin. I know, "Those rays will wrinkle your body, Amanda," I hear it from Mom constantly – doesn't matter, I live for today. When I am old and my body is damaged, I'll be wealthy, I'll take care of it then. Right now I love my tan body. I am a teenager, who has the time to worry? A girl must feel good about herself and that I certainly do! I catch the men's eyes wandering over my body, I love the sensation I get deep inside as their eyes scour my shapely self. I don't really understand why, but I love the attention.

Mom, Dad, my two older brothers and I live in a very nice four-bedroom home. It's located on a one half-mile gravel cul-de-sac off a secondary two-lane highway. We have a beautiful well-kept lawn; between Dad and the boys it is manicured to perfection at all times. We have one neighbor at the very end of our short road. Stiley Ferris, who is exceptionally wealthy, is another neighbor that lives toward the highway. He owns the land that surrounds us. Stiley is a well respected local businessman. His wife, Norma, is a well-known model and travels extensively; she's very worldly. I see her in town occasionally. She's sexy and so gorgeous and she has an aura about her that a person can't help but take notice to.

It was a very hot summer afternoon and my brothers and I were invited to the Ferris's pool. My brothers care for their yard and gardens. The swimming pool is huge with fun floaty things everywhere and a giant waterslide as well. The grounds

around the pool are landscaped beautifully. It was great fun. We were told to call Mr. Ferris and his wife by their first names, Stiley and Norma. I could not take my eyes off her. Norma was five feet ten inches or so, very tan, long blonde hair and wore make-up even at the pool. I would guess her to be thirty-six years old, and Stiley in his forties. He smoked cigars and was a bit pudgy. Norma was so classy and so very well spoken as she talked of her world travels. I was totally in awe of her. Even at my age, I knew I would someday live in a house like this. I vowed I would somehow find a way to live like the Ferris's. How did Norma become so worldly? How could I make that happen in my life? I vowed I would get to know more about her and what it would take to become what she is. I wanted to learn from Norma Ferris. I wanted to know her and understand her.

My Mom is also attractive with long dark thick hair, five feet and seven inches tall, and long slender legs. Mom is a nurse. She works for the hospital and attends to patients in their homes. Occasionally, she is gone three to four days at a time. She is well liked and personable. She is also somewhat religious. Mom sent us to the Baptist Church when we were younger and when she wasn't working she would join us. I knew even at my young age that Church was not for me. I dreaded it! I listened to the stories of Jesus and God and was convinced they were really great guys and would do my best not to lie and cheat and be good. Certainly, I did not want to go to that Hell place.

My Dad is a very low-key good man. He's employed at a local factory. He's a dedicated worker – never late, never misses a day's work and always pays his debts on time. He preached that to my brothers and I constantly, those are three of the many important things I learned from my father. He does not believe in organized religion, period. He would read the bible occasionally, but felt most churchgoers were hypocrites and many needed the security of organized religion. Dad's problem is that he likes his cocktails on Friday evenings.

My oldest brother Joshua is tall with dark hair, extremely handsome and very athletic. He plays both football and basketball and is popular with many friends. My second older brother John has sandy colored hair, not quite as tall as Joshua. He hasn't much interest per se in contact sports, but is on the college cheerleading squad. Yes, he and one other boy along with six girls make up our local college squad. Their small college plays their games on Friday nights. Our high school dropped athletic sports many years ago with budget cuts. Hence, our high school and area follows our college team very closely.

As for me, most can't believe that I'm only a teenager. I'm not shy in any manner, opinionated, outspoken and extremely outgoing. I am five feet seven inches tall and have been told as pretty as any of the college cheerleading squad. I just love it, my legs are long and my butt is shapely.

It's mid summer, school will be starting in six weeks or so. I am so looking forward to school beginning. The bus will be picking me up every morning and returning me in the afternoon. Someday I may feel the need to have my own car. Though, at this time it's not important to me.

So far it has been a summer filled with fun, learning, and growing. I have had some experiences that I will never forget! I am learning a side of me I somehow love, but do not always understand. I have lived somewhat of a naive life I suppose. But God, am I catching up so quickly!

I remember back to when I was going into the second grade. My Mom got so upset with me. At that young age, I refused to wear the clothes she purchased for my second grade debut. She bought baggy blue jean shorts and skirts, baggy blouses, farmer shoes and cotton underwear. I insisted on clothes that fit. Even then I was quite tall for my age, with long legs and a nice round little butt. I loved the way my butt wiggled when I walked. I told Mom: "I want clothes that fit me properly, stylish shoes, and silky panties just like yours." I just loved her silky lingerie. Sometimes while Mom was working I would go through her dresser drawers and try them on. They were so silky and made me feel so good. Convincing Mom to return my clothes was a battle, however. Finally, Mom gave in and returned them all! She invited me to go shopping with her two days later. I was overjoyed.

Our shopping day arrived. Mom gave me a choice to go to Kohl's or Good Will. I cringed at Good Will, but as Mom went on she explained, "At Good Will you will buy items for ten to twenty percent of retail and many times you cannot tell from new. You can buy five to six times as much for the two hundred dollars we have to spend." She suggested we at least stop and look. It was on the way to Kohl's so I agreed. So off we go! Good Will was only one mile from our house. I did not expect to agree to shop there for myself! I must admit after walking the rows and rows of skirts, slacks, tee shirts, shorts, shoes, sweaters, and sundresses; I was pleasantly surprised. Many items were like new and only two dollars to four dollars each. I would have enough clothes to fill my drawers and my closets, and throw many old things away if I chose. We shopped and purchased so many tops, bottoms, shorts, shoes, it was so much fun! Only one problem, "Mom, do I have to wear someone else's panties?" She laughed and agreed we would save twenty-five dollars and go to Kohl's for my lingerie. I was so happy! I was elated the day was over! The clothes and panties from Kohl's were so perfect. I could not wait to get home and try them all on.

We went home with my new wardrobe. Mom was so pleased to see me so happy. I went directly to my room and lined up my wardrobe on my bed. I laid my panties out and quickly undressed. There were pinks, blacks, yellows, and whites, all with lots of lace. It made me tingle inside just looking at them.

Looking back at that age I didn't understand the way I felt, as I slid a pair of those sexy panties up my legs and pulled them over my round little butt. They felt so great and caused a tingle between my legs. I had no idea what it meant! Oh, my goodness, how it excited me. They all fit perfectly. I look in the mirror at my long legs and my cute little round butt as I twist and turn in my new silky panties. This is great! Now time to try on my clothes. My clothes looked awesome! No one would ever know they came from Good Will. Two of the little short skirts have me fantasizing about wearing them and letting them creep up just a little to show the boys my pink, white, blue and yellow panties. I could not wait until school time.

Second grade was great. I liked my teacher Mrs. Mieter so much. We learned to read, write and spell. I learned very quickly. I loved wearing my little silk panties under my skirts and my shorts. I loved it when I caught the little boys peeking at my bare legs. At seven years old, I had no idea what the excitement I was feeling meant. I found some boys rather shy and others very aggressive. I met two of the boys who just adored me. Both were named Dave. They sent me little love notes. On the playground I took turns letting them push me on the swing. Of course, my dress was positioned so they could peek under my skirt. The slide worked even better to really put on a show! They and others nearby always would enjoy my little show. Mom would constantly tell me I was her little extrovert. She had no idea how I loved being the little showgirl even in the second grade. Sometimes I would sneak away with just one Dave and we'd kiss just like I would see Mom and Dad do occasionally. It felt so good! Both Dave's just loved kissing me too.

On a rainy day me and my neighbor, as Mrs. Mieter called us, Jimmy, we're sitting at our desk, which are two seats side by side, singing a song called "Eensy Weensy Spider". You make your hands kind of walk like a spider while you sing. It was so much fun, Jimmy had his spider walk up one of my legs and under my little skirt, which had ridden quite high on my leg. That little spider climbed very slow and sensuously up my leg. It was so exciting, yet, I didn't know why. The spider got between my legs with one of his hands, and that one handed spider continued playing in my panties for several minutes. After the song was over I sat there and spread my legs a bit wider, oh how I loved that spider! It was the most exciting thing in my life at that time! Jimmy never saw or spoke to me again. I wanted him for my neighbor again so badly! I would wonder later, how could I make that happen again? What I learned then, sometimes you don't make things happen, they just come along. But how can I make them happen? I'm not very good at being patient. I would let many classmates as well as adults enjoy my leg and panty shows and my round little ass. I loved it when I would catch them gazing at my little body. It was very arousing to me even at age seven and eight.

CHAPTER 3

The Theatre

Later that summer, I felt a stirring and yearning within me. After my rendezvous with Jack I am constantly thinking of that deep tingling feeling I felt inside. I cannot stop thinking about the sensation I felt all through my body. I'm riding my bike, actually my brother's bike, into town. I love riding my brother's old bike. It gives me an option when I stop and talk to someone. If it's a female I stand up and straddle the bar. If it's an interesting male, I can do all sorts of provocative things with my stance over the support bar. I have my allowance and am off to Good Will. I'm wearing tight shorts with baggy legs and blue panties with a narrow crotch and a tight white tee shirt with no bra. As always my nipples are standing quite erect.

I arrive at Good Will and walk the rows of racks of clothing. I have ten dollars to spend. I pick out a pair of hot pink spandex shorts and a stretchy kind of light pink top that are both yellow tags, which is half off. My bill is three dollars and fifty cents plus tax. How I love getting a great deal! While I was paying for my clothes a very heavy set beautiful black lady told me I had very nice legs and was a very pretty young lady. I thanked her. I love it when people notice and compliment me. As I was getting ready to leave I noticed my tire was almost flat. I sighed, I was over a mile from home. I know! I'll call my brother. No, that won't work, they're both at work. I look around. There's a gas station down the street about a block. I start to pedal, it still works, just a little tougher. I ride in and, yes! There was an air pump. I peddled up to it. A teenage boy was pumping air in his tire. He smiles and looks up at me. "Hello," he said while looking down at my tire, "looks like we have a similar problem." I smile and nod. I had positioned my bicycle perfectly so while sitting on the seat I could drop one leg and turn myself to give him a nice look at

my silky lingerie, which I knew had to be partially exposed through my baggy legged short shorts. It worked! He looks up and gazes directly at my exposed panties and probably a peek at my hairy bush. He drops the air hose and fumbles to retrieve it. I smile at him as he attempts to compose himself. He quickly goes back to his air job. He finishes and looks up my little shorts. He stammers, "Ah, ah, could I help you with your tire?" I was still smiling and said, "Oh sure, thank you so much, my name is Amanda." "I'm Jason," as he stands up and pushes his bike aside. My bicycle was positioned so I didn't have to move. He grabs the air hose and gets down on one knee. My crotch was directly in front of his face. I twist on my seat and lower one leg just a little more. He was attempting to be cool and it was not working. He was having trouble getting the cap off the stem. I thought I better make some conversation. "Do you know my brothers Josh and John Shiels?" He stammers, "Yes, they both are a bit older than me." "Are you friends?" I ask. "No, they run in different circles than I do." He was doing his best to stay focused on my tire and not the Amanda show. He asks, "Why have I not seen you at school?" "Jason, you don't pay enough attention, I've see you several times!" "Hmm, I'll work on that," he answers.

"There," he said, as the tire was full with air. He did his best not to look at my exposed panties and pubic hairs. He looks back up to me! I catch him peeking and give him another big smile. He asks, "Where are you going?" Before I had a chance to thank him I said, "I'm going home." He looked at me, "I'm going to a show, want to come along?" "What show?" I ask. "There are some Star Trek reruns playing at the Capri." The Capri was a small theater down the street that shows reruns for cheap admission. I thought I would test him, "I don't have any money left after shopping." "I'll pay, it's OK." I look at my watch. It was only two o'clock p.m. Dad wouldn't be home until six o'clock and Mom was working a twenty-four hour shift. I'm not really a Trekkie, but oh well. "OK!" He smiles and climbs on his bike and I follow him. We lock up our bikes and walk in. It was a run-down place, but clean. Jason paid our admission. I think he paid my way with his popcorn money. He asks, "Do you want to share a coke?" I agree realizing that it was probably all the money he had in his pocket.

The show had already begun as we entered. It was very dark. We chose a seat right in the middle. I could not tell what row, it was much too dark. We took turns sipping our coke as our eyes adjusted. Jason was completely engrossed in the movie. I was looking around the show room. The theater is totally empty except for one man directly in front of us near the doorway where we had entered. I looked at the screen. I never cared for Star Trek and it did not look much more entertaining today.

I rearrange myself and let my left leg bump Jason's. He didn't appear to notice, his eyes were glued to the screen. My eyes had adjusted, I could see quite well. I look back toward the doorway. The gentleman in the row in front was looking over his seat and paying a lot of attention to me. I smile to myself. I adjust myself and lift my left leg up to the back of the seat in front of me, as I adjust my body to the right, my left shoulder rested on Jason's. He paid no attention.

The man in front was paying no attention to Captain Kirk. He had found a new star and was truly enjoying my show. I pretend to be watching the Captain as I casually spread my legs just a bit more. I was looking straight ahead, but could clearly see him with my side vision. He was totally engrossed with his star. He did not look away. He was staring directly at my crotch. I was uncertain just how much he could see, I loved it! He was licking his lips. My nipples started getting hard and were tingling against the soft cotton material. I take my leg slowly off the seat in front of me, lift it a bit and bring it slowly down and twist my body more to my right and spread them just a bit more. I wanted to show him some of my hairy bush and blue silk panties. Jason still had no idea what was happening! Amazing, he is a total Trekkie!

I was getting excited and brave as well. I look directly at him and smile while moving a finger to my erect nipples. I touch them very gently, God, it sent electricity through my body. My pussy is getting wet. I move my ass back and forth while moving my crotch up and down very slowly. It felt so exciting! I am so excited, so hot, so wet between my legs. I love the feeling. I feel it dripping down my thigh to the velvet seat. I look directly at him. His face says it all. He was as hot as me, that was apparent. I was just getting up the nerve to wave him over to the seat on my right when he got up from his seat. My heart sank. Crap! He was leaving! It was over! My heart skipped. NO! He was moving back to our row. He slid sideways down our row and sat beside me. My heart was pounding, my breath was short, and my legs were still spread. One finger is still on my nipple. I look at him. He was a rather handsome man, maybe forty or so with a well-trimmed beard and nicely pressed shirt and dress slacks.

Jason looks around and notices me with my legs spread and the guy who has found a new seat beside me. The man's hand immediately touches my knee, which I had leaning on his seat. I look straight ahead. God this is so exciting, although I am a bit nervous. The nervousness didn't last long as his gentle touch slowly moves up my thigh. Electricity shoots through my body one more time. Jason has come to life. His hand is clumsily touching my left thigh, God, a hand on each thigh moving slowly toward my panties and to my very hot crotch. Oh God, both hands arrive simultaneously. I slid my hand over to Jason's zipper. The area's very hard. I run my hand up and down his shorts, he is squirming and I feel him shudder. My hand was wet. It was an odor I did not know, a musty and unusual odor. Jason removes his hand from my crotch.

My new friend was massaging my pussy very gently with two fingers. I was slowly pumping myself up and down. I reach for his crotch area. His thing is out of his slacks. It's hard and so long. I had never touched one before. The skin is so soft. The head was round, spongy and very slippery. It felt good and excited me even more! He then stood up and faced me. Standing directly in front of my theater seat, he sticks his big long thing in my face. He gently rubs it over my cheeks and nose. It was wet, sticky and slimy and was so very exciting. In a deep voice he said, "Open your mouth." I couldn't. He continues to slide it around my face,

his juices covering my nose and cheeks. I was watching Jason from the corner of my eye. He is staring in amazement with his mouth wide open. The man suddenly moves sideways and slid it in and out of his open mouth. God he did not object! Jason's head was going up and down on his big sticky thing. I think he liked it. This went on for several seconds. He pulls it out and steps back in front of me. He steps forward to my face while stroking it wildly. He begins moaning very loudly. Something came squirting out. It was thick and white. In a low gruff voice he said, "Open your mouth." I was so caught up in the moment I did. His slimy thing squirts in my mouth, eyes, and my hair. What is happening, I had no idea and really didn't care! I was breathing heavily. It stopped. He started from the base of his shaft and squeezes it forward until the last gob emerges from the head. He sticks it in my mouth and said, "Lick it off." I did. It had an unusual taste, not good, not bad. He then stood back, put it back in his pants, while zipping up, he looks at me and said, "Thank you, you little tramp." Then he walks out.

I sat there unable to move. Finally I look at Jason with slimy stuff dripping down my face, my eyes burning. I try to wipe it out. Jason looks at me, "Don't you ever tell anyone I had a cock in my mouth." I look at him and ask, "Was that a cock?" I had heard that word but didn't know what it actually was.) He answers, "Yes, I will never tell anyone a stranger shot his cum all over your face and in your mouth." I ask, "What is cum?" He smiles, "You should know," as he ran his finger across my face. I think we have an understanding I will never tell a soul, but to be honest, I really didn't care if he tells his friends. I was loving the moment. I sat in my velvet theater chair with cum dripping down my face, still savoring that moment. The odor was growing on me. I touch my chin with my finger and slid a gob into my mouth and swallow, thinking that perhaps I am a little tramp. I whisper, "I've got to clean up my face." He smiles and said, "OK," and went back to being a Trekkie. I walk to the lobby to find a bathroom. I could not find it! I walk to the popcorn stand with my head down as much as possible and ask directions. The young blonde girl looks at me with her mouth wide open. I guess she knew what cum was. She gave me the directions with a smirky smile on her face. Soon after, I got on my bike and peddled home without saying good-bye to Jason.

What an afternoon! I'm riding my bike home, horns are beeping, and guys are turning heads and staring. Is it just one of those beautiful late afternoons, or do they know what I am feeling? Now I know what a cock is, I know how cum squirts. I'm smiling at the honking horns and letting my shorts ride as high as possible. What is cum for? Is it just for squirting all over, or for squirting in your pants like Jason's did? I peddled onto my road. The horns have stopped honking for this day.

CHAPTER 4

My Uncle Ken

It's late afternoon. I'm home. Dad won't be home for a couple of hours. I take my little Good Will bag and do some personal modeling. I take my baggy leg shorts off and slide my blue panties down and kick them aside. I slide my hot pink little short shorts over my butt. I look in the mirror. These are so hot. They fit my butt, and round it out so nicely. Old top off, new top on, oh, oh, oh, it is just as hot. I strut back and fourth for a few minutes. I look so good it is making me wet all over again. I finally crawl on my big bed and spread my legs and massage my titties and nipples as I think about the afternoon. It was so exciting spreading my legs while he was staring at me. Sticking his big cock in my face and shooting his cum all over. Oh my, I wonder to myself, why has Jack not called? It's been weeks now. Maybe that's how guys are. This guy who came on my face zipped up and walked away. Jack doesn't call. Jason came in his pants. I touch my new shorts. They are all wet with my juices. It felt so good as I fell off to sleep.

I awaken from my little nap to the rattling of pots and pans in the kitchen. I get up, brush my long wavy hair, put on some lip-gloss and go to the kitchen. Dad is home and fixing dinner. "Hi Daddy," he smiles and gives me a big hug. "What's for dinner?" "My world famous beef pot roast." Dad's really quite a good cook. He usually cooks simple dishes, usually a meat and potatoes kind, but always tasty. "Honey, would you set the table? The boys will be home at seven o'clock and we will have dinner at seven-thirty." I said of course and proceed with my job. "Honey you're going to be so excited, Uncle Ken is back home and will be spending Saturday night with us. He is going to start painting our house." Uncle Ken, Dad's step-brother, has been my favorite uncle since I was very little. I just love him. We

lways have so much fun. I used to set on his lap and he would read me stories, he's
he best! He tells me funny stories. Sometimes he wrestles and tickles me. It's always silly fun. I've been missing him. For four months he has been away on a
large construction job in another state. When he is home he comes by often. Uncle
Ken is very tall and muscular. I'm sure the muscles come from all the physical
labor he does where he works. He's just a happy guy. He has been divorced for
three years and never has a girlfriend. "Oh, goody! It will be so good to see Uncle
Ken again and have him spend a whole weekend with us!" I was so happy. I finish setting the table and go outside to let Bandit out for a walk. Bandit is also happy
to see me. He went right straight for my crotch with his wet tongue. I'm sure he
smelled my earlier excitement. He was making a mess of my new shorts with his
wet tongue. Weird, even through my shorts it felt good. I tell myself, "Amanda,
you're such a tramp!" I found one of Bandit's sticks and sent him to fetch, that
works. For now he forgot about my private area. We played fetch for a while. I got
his dinner and put him back in his pen.

The boys pull in. "Hi guys, how was your day?" "Good Amanda, how was yours?"
John asks. I smile and said, "Way too much fun!" Josh smiles, "Good girl, what did
you do?" I hesitate, "I've become a pretend Trekkie." They both laugh; they know
how I hate Star Trek. We head to the house. Thank goodness that conversation
ended. John eyed my new shorts, "Amanda those shorts are hot; how did your crotch
get wet?" Embarrassed, I point to Bandit. "Yes," continues John, "Bandit certainly
has good taste." I add, "Or, I taste good!" We all chuckle and go inside.

We gather around the dining room table for dinner. Mom, of course, will not be
home until Sunday evening. Dinner is great. Dad always does a great job. Dad tells
the boys that Uncle Ken is back home and will be staying Saturday night with us.
He is going to paint our house before fall. He is going to start Saturday morning."
Dad mentions that he will have to work Saturday on the evening shift at the factory.
It is double time and he couldn't turn it down. "Uncle Ken will be keeping track of
you guys. He will sleep in our bedroom." The boys chime in; Josh will be gone Saturday and Sunday to football camp. John said he was staying with one of his
friends. Both will be home on Sunday afternoon. Dad smiles and says, "Well,
Amanda is a hand full by herself." The boys laugh. Dinner finished, I help Dad
clean the table while the boys do the dishes. We move to the living room and turn
on the television, relaxing for the rest of the evening. It's fun with most of my family
sitting together. I miss my Mom. I got up. I'm calling it a night. It's been a long
day. We said our good nights and I retire to my bedroom.

Saturday morning seems to arrive so quickly. I awaken at eight-thirty a.m. I get
up, comb my hair, brush my teeth, and put lotion all over my legs and face after
taking a hot shower. I walk into the living room and see Uncle Ken's car in the
yard. He must be painting on the house. I look out the side window. Dad and
Uncle Ken are scraping the old paint. I hope it will be break time soon so I can see
my favorite uncle. I pour a bowl of cereal and a glass of milk. The door opens and
in come all four. Josh and John were helping paint as well. It was time for a break.

I was wearing only a short sheer housecoat. It was OK. I jump up and run to Uncl Ken and throw my arms around his waist. He picks me up and bounces me up and down in his arms with a huge smile on his friendly face, "Amanda, you've grow so much in the last few months, look at you." He was right. I had grown a coupl of inches, my hips had widened in a very positive way and I now have firm breasts "Honey, you are so beautiful, you look more like your Mom every day." "Oh than you Uncle Ken. I miss you so much when you leave us. I want you to quit takin; those long jobs. You need to stay closer to home." He agreed and said he did no see a job on the horizon that would keep him away in the near future. I finish m breakfast while we all talk about what had transpired the past months while Uncl Ken was away. They finish their coffee and went out to continue their project.

My phone rang. It was one of my best friends, Marianne. She's a blonde, ver pretty and an extrovert like me. She's bubbly, not quite as tall as myself and at tractive. "Hi Amanda, how are you?" "I haven't seen you in a week now," I saic "what's going on?" "Nothing exciting, just wanted to say hello and hoped we coul do something soon before school starts." Marianne did not go to my school, al though she lives only one mile away. She is in a different district. I met her at a lit tle lake back in the woods with her big brother two summers ago. We had so muc in common she became one of my very best friends. "Yes, we must plan somethin, before school starts," I said. More chit-chat and we said our goodbyes.

The boys, Dad and Uncle Ken finished scraping the house on Saturday. The would begin painting on Sunday. Uncle Ken would be painting alone. There wer activities on the agenda for the rest of the family. Uncle Ken, Dad and I had a early dinner before Dad left for his night shift. The boys had left earlier. We clea the table and did the dishes as Dad was leaving for work. Uncle Ken offers to hel I said I was just fine. "OK Honey, in that case I'm going to take a nap. It's goin, to be hard work keeping track of you tonight," he said with a grin on his face. smile back, "Yes, I'll make you earn your wages!" I finish the dishes and pick u the kitchen and dining area.

Thoughts race through my mind, "What should I wear?" I know we probably wi be sitting in front of the television watching some good stuff. I had already don my laundry after Bandit licked me all over, my new Good Will outfit will be pei fect. I go to my room, lie on my bed. I'm feeling lazy. I'm thinking, "Get u Amanda." I get up and go in the shower while fantasizing how I want to look fc my favorite uncle. I'm back in my room slipping on my favorite yellow panties They follow the curve of my shapely and rounded little butt. They cling just belo the lower cheek line and leave no panty line. I guess I could go with no panties, bt I love them so much. I pull my short spandex shorts over my little ass. I take a pee in the mirror; Oh, oh, oh! I love the look! They cling so perfectly. I slide the match ing stretchy top over my head. No need for a bra. My breasts seem to get bigge each day while my bush is sprouting new hair daily! I hear rattling in the kitchei Uncle Ken is up and about. This top is perfect. My nipples are very hard as I gaz at myself in one of my many mirrors. I run the brush through my thick hair dozen

f times. My hair is just over my shoulders. I love the length. I apply just a little mascara to my long eyelashes. They are so long and very lush. Just a touch of eye shadow, dark blue, and my shiny lip-gloss. I bought my cosmetics at the Dollar Store with my money from Jack. I try not to wear makeup when Mom is around. She doesn't approve. My skin is tan and perfect. There is no need for the little bottle of creamy foundation I purchased. I stand in front of the mirror and look at myself. I'm hot!

CHAPTER 5

My First Experience

I love Uncle Ken, and crave his attention. I want him to look at me as a beautiful woman and not as his niece. My day is coming soon. I can feel it! One more time I look in the mirror. I turn sideways, give my little ass a wiggle back and forth, look over my shoulder and smile. I feel hot! How I love what it's doing to me. My little pussy is getting damp just looking at my body. This is so great! I don't understand why, but I love it! I turn and open my bedroom door. Uncle Ken is on the sofa watching TV. It better not be a Star Trek rerun. I strut out of my bedroom. Uncle Ken looks at me and gasps, "Oh my God Amanda, look at you. You are so beautiful." It was music to my ears. Uncle Ken was always my big hero growing up and to hear him say those words was so perfect. I smile, "Thank you Uncle Ken," and slid to the other side of the sofa. "What are we watching?" "Oh I'm flipping through the channels." He tosses the remote to me, "Here Amanda, you choose." I begin flipping channels. The news, shopping network, The George Lopez Show, Uncle Ken stops me. "I really like George's wife. Her ass is as beautiful as yours." I look at him and roll my eyes. I had no idea who George Lopez was let alone his wife. Regardless, I stop flipping. I want to see this woman he is comparing to me. Angie, the wife, appears. She was an older lady with long dark hair, kind of noisy. She was wearing tight slacks, a tight top, and a luscious smile. She turned and I agreed. She did have a nice ass. I look at Uncle Ken and said "Yes, when I'm older I would be happy having her ass." Uncle Ken gave me a wink and a nod, "Amanda, I think you are well on your way!" I shrugged, I wasn't sure what that meant. I begin flipping channels again. I come to a Hannah Montana and Miley Cyrus concert and stop. I love Hannah, she is so straightforward, clean and

so outgoing. She is one of my many heroes. I tell how Uncle Ken how much I like her and he pretends to listen. I am at the opposite end of the sofa leaning back on the arm with one leg on the floor and the other on the sofa. I have his attention. I continue talking. "Hannah has no butt and she is not very tall. I love her smile and other people seem to love her. She has become one of my favorite stars." Uncle Ken smiles and agrees. "Amanda, I love you, but can we watch something different?" I continue flipping. Larry King . . . Chris Mathews . . . Discovery, "Is this boring TV night or what?"

I normally don't watch much TV. When I do, I usually know ahead of time what I am going to watch. I'm not giving up until I find something Uncle Ken and I both can enjoy. I found it! Bring it on! It's "Cheerleader Group Competition" with lots of hot girls to watch. I love this kind of show. I love watching the girls, how they look and act. I listen to what they say and watch them. I notice they are friendly, flirtatious, and sometimes nasty. I watch and learn. "Uncle Ken, how are you with my choice?" He nods approvingly. I rearrange the sofa pillow on the arm and lean into the corner while sliding my butt down the seat on a side angle facing the TV. My feet are about four inches from Uncle Ken's leg. The girls are doing their cheers and bending over to show their cheer panties. Cheer uniform panties are normally dull. Not the case here. One team has black sort of bikini type and the others wearing bright gold, silky and sexy. There is a story line to the show I guess. I am paying more attention to the beautiful girls showing their legs, butts and panties. Uncle Ken is watching the same. He hops up, "I need a beer," and heads to his car. He comes back with a small cooler and sets it down by the sofa. Mom normally does not allow alcohol in our house, so obviously Uncle Ken keeps his beer in his own possession.

He sits back down and runs a finger down my leg as he slides into his seat. I rub my bare foot up and down his leg as he pops the lid on his beer. I give him a sweet smile. "Which cheerleader is your favorite?" I ask. His eyes leave my long legs and curvy butt. He smiles at me and says, "Four different ones, but I especially like that one girl on the gold panty team. They seem to be picking on her. She has my kind of ass, nice and round and she looks hot. I think it's the fit of her panties that makes them so sexy." I understood exactly what he was saying; flashing back to Mom and my battle going into second grade. I smile to myself, "Yes, it's all in the fit." Uncle Ken chugs the first beer and starts on his second. "Uncle Ken, can I have a taste?" He hands me the can with no hesitation. I sat half way up and took the ice-cold can, sat sideways and took a sip. I had not tasted beer before. It was OK. Not good, not bad. Hmm, that was my same thought when I tasted cum a few days ago. Since then I knew I wanted more! Would I be reacting to beer the same way? I take another swallow and hand the can back. I rest my foot on the side of Uncle Ken's leg. I rub very slowly with my bare foot. He put his left hand on the top of my foot and very gently runs his fingers up and down in a circular motion. God! It felt good, such a gentle touch. It sent a hot chill through my body. He switches his half empty beer to his left hand and hands it to me. I lean forward and

take it from his hand. I take another swallow, then another and hand it back. Uncle Ken gulps down what remains and pops open another as we watch our cheering girls. I slide off the sofa and wobble a little as I stand up to go pee. I smile at him, "This is fun. I've had a few swallows and can't stand up." We both laugh. "I don't want to be a cheap drunk." I turn to walk but first wiggle my little ass back and forth, knowing my shorts had ridden into my rear and my panties were probably partially exposed. I knew I was rotating my little ass much more than I normally would. Was it those swallows of beer or was I just showing off? Either way I really didn't care.

I step into the bathroom and look back giving Uncle Ken another smile as I close the door. I look in the mirror, checking my long wavy hair. My eyes are big and dark brown. My Dollar Store mascara and eye shadow made them look even larger. I turn to see what kind of a show I had given Uncle Ken as I had walked away. As I thought, my panties were well below my shorts and my shorts were very tight into my crack. I look hot! Maybe it was the beer adding to the illusion. I finish my business and pull my panties up into my little pussy. I wash my hands and once more look in the mirror. My little nipples are standing straight up. I touch them both. A shot of pleasure shoots through my body.

I strut back to the sofa as Uncle Ken's eyes massage my body. He looks in my eyes and said in a very low voice, "Amanda, you are dangerous." I smile. I don't think either of us had any real idea, at the time, how dangerous I would be someday. I sat closer to him and reached for the beer he held in his hand, it was three quarters full. I smile and said, "Get your own, I'm taking this one over." He pops another. We went back to watching our Cheerleaders. I continue sipping on the beer. It tasted better with each sip. I am feeling more and more relaxed. I slide back to my original position on the sofa. I laid a bit more on my backside and spread my legs just a bit. I am getting braver. It must be the alcohol. I run my right foot up and down Uncle Ken's leg while putting the other on the floor. I had to be showing my yellow panties and probably a bit of my hairy bush. He takes my foot in both hands and very gently caresses it. For a working man, he had very soft hands and a very easy touch. I spread my legs a bit more as I softly groan with approval. He continues massaging my foot. It was pure ecstasy! He could not take his eyes off my partially exposed pussy. I love the passion in his eyes. I can feel the wetness running down my thigh. I wonder if he could see my pussy leaking. My question was soon answered. Uncle Ken reached over to my thigh with two fingers and ran it up toward my wet pussy. He slowly pulls his fingers back and licked them dry. He continues this several times. Oh my God! My body is trembling. I spread my legs wider, this has to be heaven. He lifts my foot to his mouth and gently licks and sucks my little toe. He moves on to the next and the next, while stopping to dart his tongue in and out between each toe and my big toe is now being passionately sucked and caressed by his hot mouth. I lift my left foot and slide it up his leg to his crotch. I feel for his hardness. My foot now between his legs, oh it was so hard. I want to see it, I want to feel it, I want to taste it. I want to feel his cum squirting in my face.

pull up my top and stroke my erect nipples, my crotch throbs. I didn't really understand why. I only knew of cum squirting in my face from a few days earlier. Why does my pussy feel this way? My nipples are so sensitive. I want to see and to feel his cock – now! He put my right foot down. Moving up my body, his mouth is on my nipples, first the left and then my right. He is so passionate. I spread my legs so wide as I feel his hardness still in his jeans. Rubbing between my legs, he slowly moves up and down on my wet panties and shorts. What is this? I don't really care. My mom always told me your body is your temple. My temple was on fire, and I loved it. I was going to let it burn. I was moving my hips up and down on his hardness.

Uncle Ken raises his body up and off myself. I'm hoping he has not cum in his pants like Jason. It doesn't seem to be the case. He pulls my shorts over my thighs and tosses them on the floor. He gazes into my eyes with such a passionate look. "Amanda, you are a wicked tramp aren't you?" I gasp passionately, "Yes, I am." He pulls my panties over my knees and rubs them in his face. I watch him lick them and kiss them. They are so wet and he loves it, I am beyond myself. Tossing my yellow panties aside he buries his face in my hairy pussy. I feel his hot tongue licking up and down between my legs. It reminded me of my first sexual experience at my Grandma's house. I spread my long legs even further. He is devouring my clit. He looks up at me with an astounding sigh and stammers, "Amanda, you are a virgin!" I was a bit taken back. His voice was so profound, I wasn't sure what that meant. A virgin? Uncle Ken rolls me over on the sofa. He puts me on my knees with my little ass in the air. He buries his mouth again between my legs. He's licking and sucking my asshole! It feels so amazing. His soft, wet tongue is licking up and down and wildly sucking my ass. This is amazing beyond any thoughts or fantasies I have ever had. Why would a man want to do this? I'm always so clean, but why would a man suck and kiss my ass? I didn't understand. Oh! It felt so good, the same position with my ass high in the air when Uncle Ken spits his saliva on my asshole. I feel a finger slide up and down my crack, then eases inside my butt hole. It was a very strange sensation. I like it. He slid it in and out very slowly. It felt quite good. I start rotating my butt. I start to pump on his finger. Soon it seems larger, I'm not sure what I am feeling. I look around at Uncle Ken and ask, "What are you doing?" He pats my ass and says, "Honey, relax, it's OK, I will show you." I relax a bit as he continues. I thought it must be two or three fingers in and out of me. It didn't feel good. It didn't feel bad. It was kind of like the cum and the beer earlier. His stroke was picking up, my ass was stroking his fingers. It was OK. He pulls his finger out. Why? I thought to myself, I am just beginning to enjoy it a little, don't quit now. I hear him spit again. His saliva was right on target. I felt it wet my stretched asshole. Oh my God! I felt Uncle Ken sliding his cock up and down my crack. God, it feels so good. It was so hard. I drop to my knees. Uncle Ken steps to the floor off the sofa. I raise my hand and grab his long cock. I lick its head; it was so soft and spongy. I slip the head into my mouth. Yum! I take as much as I could and pump my mouth up and down. I wanted to taste his cum so

badly. Uncle Ken was slowly pumping his cock in and out of my mouth. My crotch was on fire and no idea why. I wanted cum in my hot mouth and face. His cock wasn't near as juicy as the one earlier in the week at the theater, although it really felt great in my mouth.

Uncle Ken said, in a dominating voice, "Amanda get back on your knees." I did not want to move, but responded. I drop to my knees on the carpet, my little ass high in the air. Uncle Ken again rubs his cock up and down my crack. It felt so good as he very slowly continues sliding it up and down. I hear him spit again. When his cock would slide past my asshole, I wanted him to slide it in where his fingers were earlier. Finally, the head of his cock stopped right at my ass door. I felt pressure, uh, oh, more pressure, that's enough, it hurts! Uncle Ken says loudly, "Amanda, it's OK, relax." I tried to relax, oh how it hurt. He slowly slides his big cock inside me, and now in and out pumping it back and forth so very slowly. So many thoughts are racing through my mind. I love my Uncle Ken now even more with his big cock inside my body. He continued working it in and out very slowly. It was feeling better. It slid deeper and deeper and now did not hurt nearly as much. Uncle Ken continues, as I hear his passionate moans. God, it was feeling better and better. I pump with him. He is now slamming it in and out, as I pump back wildly. Suddenly Uncle Ken is groaning like the man at the theater. I feel hot juice squirting deep inside my body. Uncle Ken pulls it out. I feel the balance of his hot cum squirting all over my round little ass. Oh my God! I reach back, I want to feel it. I rub it all over my ass and lick my fingers. I slump to the carpet, Uncle Ken rolls to his back beside me. He let out a big sigh. "Amanda, that was fucking amazing. You are so fucking hot it's scary!" I sigh again.

CHAPTER 6

A Virgin

What a week it's been. After a slight pause I ask, "Uncle Ken, what did you mean when you said I was still a virgin?" "Amanda," he said, "when you have real sex it's in your pussy not your ass." I was confused. I knew there was no hole there for a cock. "You have skin over the opening called your hymen or as guys call it, your cherry. Some day someone will break that and put his cock inside. You will then no longer be a virgin. You can get pregnant and have babies. What we have done is at least safe in that regard. You cannot get pregnant sucking cock and getting your ass fucked." "I want to remain a virgin forever," I told Uncle Ken. "I want no babies. What I have experienced is fantastic." He smiles and said, "I hope you stand by that Amanda. You can control this world with what you have with those tall, long legs, your fantastic body, your total beauty. You should always be in charge. Most women never understand or they fall in love, at least what they believe to be love. Amanda, love is very overrated. It is really only a strong liking for someone. You will think about it constantly. It could totally dominate and consume you: Your heart and head goes wild, but Amanda, it normally only lasts a short time. There are exceptions, but not many. Many married couples stay together, but not only for love. The passion of love is mostly gone. There are the kids, financial security and for some only a security in itself. Amanda, avoid love as long as you can. Let them love you and believe me many will. Keep your heart and soul to yourself and keep that virginity just as long as you possibly can. I also want you to know what we have done here tonight, if anyone were to ever know, I would go to prison for the rest of my life." I gasped, "Why?" "You may be of age, but in this state I am your guardian tonight, this is not acceptable." "Oh, my God,"

I respond. "Uncle Ken, no one will ever know, I promise you." "I believe that." "Uncle Ken, why do people get married?" "Well, honey, for all the reasons we just discussed and many want a family. For that reason you need to be married." "Uncle Ken, I never want to be married and I certainly do not want a family." "That's fine Amanda, you are young and will likely see things differently some day. My advice, stay with the upscale world. Avoid the guys who insist on telling you about all that they have and how great they are. Normally, the ones that have to tell you have very little and normally are very insecure. Stay away from the thugs, the drug users. Be careful, you may not know, but they are in your school and around every corner. Many of who will want to love you. Stick with the go-getters. Choose your friends. Choose the intelligent, the worldly, and homely. They do not all have to be beautiful. You can learn something from all. Choose your friends so carefully, and learn from them as much as possible. We all think so differently. Analyze what they say – learn."

"Uncle Ken, do you think that there could be something wrong with me? I love showing my body. I love it when men look at me. I love wearing hot little clothes and I love the feel of cock, the taste of cum, and feel great about it. Is that terrible?" "Honey, when I was growing up in my teens it was unheard of for a girl to do these things. Times are changing. I'm sure some of your girlfriends are sucking cock and doing what you are doing and feeling what you are feeling. I'm sure you're not alone. Amanda, there are diseases you can get doing these things. There is something called a condom that goes over a cock so it doesn't squirt inside you. You should be using them." "Uncle Ken, I love the cum squirting everywhere. How could it be exciting without that? The smell, the taste, I love that." "Honey, I was just telling you there are things that can happen. I have never used them and have had many partners and never had a problem. But, the problem does exist." "I understand," I said, "and thank you for sharing with me. However I cannot imagine enjoying sex without the cum."

"Can I tell you a story about something that happened to me this week at that little theater in town?" "Of course." I didn't think I could ever tell anyone this. I continued. "I went to the theater with this boy I met. He was rather boring, so I started flirting with a man in the row in front of us. This man was the only other person in the whole theater and I spread my legs and showed him my panties and some of my bush. He immediately came back and sat beside us. He ran his hand up my leg and into my panties." I told Uncle Ken about how this stranger had rubbed his hard, slimy cock in my face and wanted me to suck on it. I couldn't and I'm not sure why. Then I told him how the boy I had come with had his mouth open and the man stuck his cock in his mouth. He slid it in and out a few times and then pulled it out. His cum was squirting out. He stuck it in my face and ordered me to swallow it. After calling me a tramp, he simply got up and left. I looked over from my pillow waiting for Uncle Ken to respond. He said nothing, but his cock was erect and standing straight up. Oh my God, I love it! Uncle Ken obviously appreciated my little story.

I rolled off my pillow, sliding my hand on to his erection. I was sliding my hand up and down very slowly. Uncle Ken took a deep breath. I ran my tongue up the full length of his shaft and licked at the little hole at the head. It was slightly sticky. I kept licking, the juices were a bit salty, and I liked that. I continue licking as it leaks on my tongue. I open my mouth wide and slide the head into my mouth. I took as much of the shaft as I possibly could down my throat. My mouth was slowly sliding up and down and more juices were now wetting my tongue. God, I love this salty goo. Uncle Ken was wildly pumping it in and out with my rhythm, up and down, up and down; my head was bobbing. He groaned: I knew what that meant. I could feel it squirting on my tongue and sliding down my throat. I wanted more! Oh God, it was so great! My mouth was full of his cum. I was ready to swallow my first load, when Uncle Ken pulled on my arm, "Amanda don't swallow it!" I was puzzled. Some had already oozed down my throat. "Pull your titties toward your mouth and let my cum drip over them." I open my mouth letting the balance of his cum drip down to my hard nipples while emptying my mouth. Uncle Ken's finger was stroking my nipples, first one then the other. My nipples have always been very sensitive. With his juicy cum all over them it multiplied the sensitivity times ten. I push his finger aside and lightly stroked them with my two fingers. Oh my God, it was so slippery and slimy it sent shivers straight to my pussy. My nipples were so erect, I continue stroking them. The feeling was indescribable. Uncle Ken put his head between my legs and was licking my pussy. I was pumping it in his face. I spread my legs, his face buried. I felt something stir so deep inside me. It was like a deep sneeze wanting to escape my body. It builds and builds, God it took my breath away. My whole body quivered and surges with pure pleasure, nothing like I have ever experienced. I crash to the floor, totally breathless. Uncle Ken rolls over and lies next to me. When I finally get my breath I ask Uncle Ken, "What was that?" I could feel him smiling, "Amanda, you had an orgasm." I ask, "What does that mean?" "Amanda, it's the same as when a man cums. I have never been with a virgin and I am certainly no expert," he confides, "but I've always believed a lady does not cum until she's had her cherry popped. Honey, after what I have experienced tonight, I've learned it's possible that one can cum without that happening!" It made me feel very good knowing that I could remain a virgin until I chose otherwise, and still totally have a ball with sex.

CHAPTER 7

Dad's Brew Drinking Buddy

Sunday morning I awaken to sunshine flooding through my window. I roll out of my big bed at nine a.m. and quickly do my bathroom duties. Now to the kitchen, I look out my window and notice Dad's car. He must be sleeping as he worked the night shift. Mom will be home this afternoon. I can't wait to see her. I miss her. The boys will be home as well.

I hear Uncle Ken, he is outside painting the house by himself. He taught me so much last night. He helped me understand so many things I will never forget. I have a light breakfast and walk out to visit Bandit. I open the gate, he dashes out of the pen and heads directly to Uncle Ken's ladder. I look up and shout, "Good morning Uncle Ken!" He smiles and says, "Good morning," and continues painting. I find Bandit's favorite stick and give it a toss. I feel a little awkward after last night, but I'll get past it. I wonder how Uncle Ken feels. Does he feel awkward as well? OK, it's another day. I'll push these thoughts out of my mind. I feel so relaxed and for some reason not having the sexual thoughts that normally control my mind.

I toss Bandit's stick again and tell him to fetch as he charges away. My mind drifts to family. I am so glad Mom will be home today. I'm sure we'll be having a nice family dinner at home this evening. I have always felt closer to my Dad than my Mom. I'm not sure why that is. Mom is kind of introverted, not much of a conversationalist like Dad. I don't think either one has ever told my brothers or myself verbally "I love you." I guess it doesn't really matter. There is much love. It is just not spoken. In fact, I have not told either of them as well. My Mom is so sexy

When she walks down the street I see heads turn. She is not as outgoing as myself. One of her sayings is, "Amanda, you are my little extrovert." She also says, "Amanda, your body is your temple, take good care of it." I have worn Bandit out and put him back in his pen.

I go back into the house and start the vacuuming and work on laundry. I like the house in perfect shape when Mom gets home. I love how it feels, floors vacuumed, tables dusted, kitchen floor scrubbed and both bathrooms all shiny.

Two o'clock rolls around and I go to my bedroom and pick out one of my little bikini bathing suits. The little bikini bottom is so hot. My little hairy bush pokes out both sides of the crotch. My Mother would absolutely insist I put on my boy shorts bathing suit if she were home. She sometimes would suggest I trim my bush. I refused. "Mom, I love it, I will never trim or shave that area." Mom just shakes her head and insists that I wear the boy short type suit. To keep her happy, I honor her wishes when she is around. I tie on my little string top. I look at my titties standing up in my top. They seem to be getting bigger by the day, like my bush, which continues to sprout new hairs daily. Oh well, what's a girl to do! I grab some lotion and a towel and head out the door.

The grass is getting so tall. The boys will probably mow this evening. I find a lounge chair and drag it to the side yard. I walk over and let Bandit out of his pen. He jumps to the yard and smiles a hello, and bounds off heading for Uncle Ken on the ladder out front. I'd forgotten he was still here. I walk over and ask how his project was progressing. "Moving right along," he said while wiping the perspiration off his forehead. "I would help, but I have to tan for a couple of hours." He smiles. "You've done your job. I watched you through the window tidying up for your Mom. You're a good girl Amanda." "Thank you Uncle Ken, you are a good uncle . . . in so many ways." I smile and walk back to my lounger.

I spread my towel over the lounge, grab my lotion, and cover my body thoroughly. I love the oily smell and how it makes my skin glisten. I have a dark complexion. A little sun always adds something. I get dark rather quickly. I love the look. As soon as I settled Bandit arrived with his stick. I toss it one last time and tell him, "Bandit that is it for a while." I think he smiled and said OK. The sun feels so good. It's eighty-two degrees. To me that's perfect. It will be cooling in the next few months. Our area normally receives very little snow, but some cool evenings. I am learning these days how weather patterns are quite different. I look forward to see what fall and winter bring this year.

As the suns rays warm my skin, thoughts begin racing through my mind. The experiences I've had over the summer. Wow, what more can there be? I believe I've done it all. Sold a look at my panties and let a man touch them and got paid all the while he was sucking and licking between my legs. Next, I had a man squirt his cum in my face and I swallowed gobs of it while sitting beside my friend who sucked his cock. I had so much fun Uncle Ken and I learned that I'm yet a virgin, wow! There can't be much more, can there? I've done it all! Bandit is back with his stick. "Bandit, I told you I was taking a break." He hung his head and laid down beside me.

Dad should be getting up soon. He probably had just gotten to bed as I was waking. The boys should also be home soon. Mom will be home around five o'clock or so. My mind is wandering again. Labor Day weekend, the big parade, I love the parade so much. Hmm, that is this Saturday. I get so excited thinking of life's simple pleasures.

A car is coming up our drive. Bandit bounds off and barks, maybe it's the boys. I turn in my chair. No, it's a guy getting out wearing jeans and a short sleeve shirt, a ball cap and a big mustache. He is walking toward the front door. I don't want him waking Dad ringing the doorbell, so I slide out of my chair and call to Bandit who seems to have found his best friend. He is supposed to be our guard dog, but he forgets and just wants to love everyone. I smile and say, "Hello." "You must be Amanda," he replies in a booming voice. I watch his eyes feel me up and down. He isn't missing a thing. "I am Ray Johnson, I work with your Dad. He told me to stop by this afternoon and we'd have a brew or two," he said with a big laugh. I smile back at him, "Yes, I am Amanda. Dad is still sleeping, but he should be up and about soon." "Oh, OK." "You are welcome to hang around, but I don't want to wake him quite yet." Ray chuckles, "OK, do you mind if I grab a brew?" I look at my watch not wanting to be rude to one of Dad's friends. "That would be fine." I walk back to my chair. Ray grabs his brew and meanders back in my direction. He sits down in the grass at my feet and again looks me up and down. He casually stares at my exposed pubic hairs and said, "Amanda, how old are you, around twenty two or twenty three?" "Ray, you're close, however, it is not polite to ask a lady her age." Ray rolls back on the grass and does a belly kind of laugh. "OK Amanda, you got me there." I smile as he chugs on his brew. Ray was not at all my kind of guy, but I still was getting a stirring feeling because of his seductive stares. Why does that excite me so much? I thought there must be something wrong with me. I love it and knew I would be in control, always! Ray, taking his eyes from my crotch, has moved up to my breasts. "What college do ya go to?" I smile and said, "State." He shakes his head up and down while his eyes remain glued to my breasts. He said, "What cha studying to be?" I look him directly in the eye, "A professional slut." That caught him off guard. I don't think he'd heard of that kind of course before. He didn't seem to have a come back, he just gulped. He stammers a bit and then said in a semi-serious tone, "I didn't know they taught that kind of thing at State." "Ray, it's a joke." Ray's eyes perk up, he jerks his head up and belly laughs again. "Ha, ha, ha, you got me," and starts to explain. I interrupt, "Ray, please don't explain it's OK." "Amanda, you got me, girl you're going places, I can tell."

I hear the front door open. Thank God, Dad to the rescue. Ray lifts himself off the grass, his eyes never leaving my crotch until he heads in Dad's direction. I relax in my chair soaking the rays after giving a wave to Dad. I lay out for another hour or so watching Ray periodically go back and forth for his and Dad's brews.

I went inside after putting Bandit away. I was wishing I could avoid the living room where Dad and Ray were, on my way to my bedroom, however, there was only one way. Dad gets up and gives me a big hug. Rays eyes are now caressing

ny round little ass. While kissing Dad's cheek I remind him that Mom and the boys vill be home soon. He smiles, he understood. I smile very cordially, "So nice to neet you Ray." And turn and strut towards my bedroom. I hear Dad excuse iimself to use the bathroom. I step into my bedroom, as Dad is walking toward the athroom I am feeling a bit promiscuous. I look back at Ray as I walk through my edroom door. I leave the door half open. I walk to my lingerie dresser and search or just the right panties. I lay them on the dresser all in full view of Ray sitting in he big chair. I can see him without turning my head in his direction through my ide vision. I feel his eyes all over my body. I turn myself slightly in his direction. am bad. I reach back and untie my little top with a quick pull. It drops to the floor. Ray's mouth drops wide open. I simply love what I am doing to him. His cock has o be rock hard. I smile to myself as I reach up with my hands and cup both of my itties and squeeze and tickle my nipples. I turn away from Ray and bend over eductively sliding my bikini bottoms slowly down over my knees exposing my airy pussy from behind. I spin around on one foot and look directly at Ray and mile. I slide one hand over my bush and slide one finger up and down and watch iis facial expression as I slowly close the door. I slide into my bed. In my mind, I gree with my theater stranger. I really am a tramp, and God how I'm loving it!

CHAPTER 8

Marianne & Chad

I awaken an hour later to the sound of pots and pans banging about the kitchen
I hear conversation. I skip to the bathroom, do my business, touch up my lips and
run the brush through my long locks. I go back to my room and slip on a warm up
suit and move towards the bustle. Mom, Dad and the boys are in the kitchen preparing dinner. I run to Mom with open arms. It was so good to see her. She gives me
a huge hug. "Mom I hate it when you are gone for so long." "Oh honey, I don't like
it either, but it's Mom's job." "What can I do to help?" "Set the table please, honey."
I turn to Josh and Johnny, "Good to have you home." "Thank you Amanda." Josh
gives me a big smile. "Dad, how was your night?" "Just another night on the job
Amanda, it was fine. Did Uncle Ken take good care of you last night?" "Oh, very
good . . . Where is Uncle Ken?" "He is finishing the north side of the house, and
then the scraping will be totally completed." "Will he be joining us for dinner?" I
ask Mom. "No, he has plans this evening." Mom was completing a beautiful tossed
salad as the oven buzzer rang. Mom opened the oven and pulls out her famous tuna
noodle casserole. It looks and smells scrumptious. Buttery cracker crumbs all over
the top. The aroma was incredible. We all sat down to the table. It was so good to
have us all together. I sit back and look at my family and smile. I was so happy.

I was scooping out my salad as Uncle Ken came walking through the door. Dad
asked Ken, "You sure you won't join us?" "No, I'm going to clean up and go on
home." "Big plans tonight?" Dad asks. "Sort of," Ken answers and heads toward
the bathroom. Josh says with a starved look, "Mom this salad is great! I can't wait
for that casserole to come my way," as John is scooping out an extra large helping
"Johnny you're an animal," Josh says, "the rest of us would like to eat as well."

Mom smiles, "Not to worry; it's a very large pan." "Mom, this casserole is delicious," I said. "Thanks so much," she responded.

"The holiday weekend is coming up, who has plans?" Mom asked. John spoke up, "Josh and I have our final softball tournament." It was odd, John normally did not do sports, but he loved to play softball. "We're going to win, right Josh?" "I think we've got a shot," he says. "I will be home for the weekend," Mom says. Dad shouted, "No work for me either!" I excitedly blurted, "I want to go to the parade on Saturday, would you like to go?" "Amanda honey, you enjoy the parade, Mom and I are all paraded out." I knew that. When I was little we always went together. These days it was just not important to them, which I guess was fine. My friend Marianne and I would have a perfect time. Dinner finishes. Dad sends the boys to mow the lawn and I ask, "When do you mow Ferris's lawn again?" "Monday," Josh replies, "we will miss Saturday, we both will be gone." Dad moves to the TV. I get up and help Mom with the dishes. It's so nice to have Mom home to chat with. We finish cleaning the kitchen and it's all shiny again.

Mom walks to her room as I sit down on the sofa with Dad. He peeks around the room being sure Mom was not within hearing distance and whispers in my direction, "Honey, what did you do to my buddy Ray this afternoon?" I attempt to look puzzled and ask with a bewildered look, "Why?" "I came back from the bathroom and his mouth was wide open and his shorts looked like a tent. He got up stammering and said, "Uh, uh, I have to go." I gave Dad a shy smile and said, "Daddy I have no idea, he must have had too many brews." I cross my legs and turn back to the TV. "Amanda, why on earth did you tell him you were going to school to become a professional slut? He believed you!" "Dad, I told him I was kidding! How could he be so naïve?" Dad sighs and said, "Honey, you know you scare me, you're not a typical teenage girl." If only he knew, I thought to myself.

It was a lovely evening being home with family and enjoying TV. Feeling tired, it was to be an early evening for me. I say my goodnights and head to my bedroom. I turn on my music and shower, washing all the lotion off my body. Coming back from the shower I ask if Bandit has been fed. Dad said he was good to go.

The week was flying by. I called Marianne on Tuesday to see if she wanted to come by on Wednesday and tan while we make our Saturday parade plans? She was so excited, she just loved parade day. We planned a one o'clock rendezvous. So many things I wanted to talk with her about. She was one of the few people I could confide in. Wednesday morning arrives. Mom and Dad are both working. I'm not sure where the boys have gone this early, probably working at the Ferris's. I shower and do my business in the bathroom, eat an early lunch and head back to my room to choose bathing attire. I have quite a collection, the Good Will is a godsend. Should I do my boy shorts or my bikini? I vote for the bikini, as Mom would not be home before six o'clock. I would be safe from a lengthy lecture on how disgusting my bush was for the public view. I slip on my smallest bikini. I'm looking good. My curly hairs are everywhere, I just love looking in the mirror, it excites me. Someday, I thought, I'm going to the beach just to show off. I brush my hair, add

mascara and lip-gloss and went to locate a perfect sunspot for Marianne and myself. I let Bandit out and pull a couple of chairs over to my sunspot, while giving Bandit's stick a toss. I walk back inside to grab towels, sun lotion and my cell phone. I then go back to our lounges, I toweled them both and spread oil top to bottom on my body. It felt great. My long legs shimmered as they always do after applying my oily sun block.

A car pulls in the drive. Marianne jumps out. Her brother is driving. He opens his door and walks over to my sunny area. He is blond, five feet nine inches or so, very chatty like Marianne and handsome. His name is Chad. He graduated last spring and is working as a security guard while going to community college. I jump up and give Marianne a big hug and Chad as well. I ask if he would like a chair, he answers no and sat on the grass as Marianne and I arrange ourselves. Marianne's bathing suit was cute, although not showy. She is much bustier than I. She did have a bit of a tan and it made her long blond hair look even blonder. Unlike me she likes to keep her bush trimmed with little or no pubic hair exposed. She looks so gorgeous. Chad was attempting to avoid eye contact. It is so fun listening to him chat while trying not to stare at my little show. I love watching him squirm on the grass. Marianne is putting oil on her legs, back and chest. I pick up my oil and reapplied it mainly for Chad's benefit. I lift my long legs, one at a time, and pretend not to notice his obvious stare. I love it! I try to picture just what he was seeing as I lift my leg high and twist one far to the left and slowly oiled it up and down rubbing oil to my thigh and all over my exposed hair. I couldn't be certain just how much of my bush was poking out of my bikini. I'm sure Marianne couldn't help but notice Chad's uncomfortable arousal. She was smiling, she knows what I'm like. Of course, Chad wasn't leaving yet. I was wondering if Marianne could possibly handle watching him stick his cock up my ass or watch me suck her big brother off. I am so bad! Just the thought was dampening my pussy. I slide my feet toward me on the lounge, my knees now in the air and my legs spread just a bit. I ask Chad "How is your new girlfriend I've heard rumors of?" He stutters as he peels his eyes away from my body. "Aaaaah, she's good." I give him a big smile as our eyes connect. I lick my lips just a bit. He moves his leg from side to side very slowly and I spot the big bulge in his silky long legged shorts. They were baggy, but the silky material made the large bulge very apparent. I could not let myself go any further with this flirtation with Marianne sitting beside me. Marianne and I began chatting about our parade plans. Chad took one more peek as I gently slide my hand over my bikini crotch and smile at him one more time. He rose to his feet attempting to move very quickly so his back would be to us. It didn't work, we caught him.

He was embarrassed knowing we were checking out his large bulge. He stuttered a "Bye-bye Amanda . . . call me Marianne when you need your ride." We watched him get in his car and drive away. Marianne and I laughed so hard while we high fived each other. "Amanda, my poor brother! You are so bad." "Marianne I just love it. I've got a story to tell you." She sucks her breath in, "I'm all ears, how can ya top what just happened?" "Oh," I said with a smile, "wait til you hear! "Oh, my

God!" Marianne said. Marianne is sitting cross-legged Indian style in the lounge chair beside me listening intently. I'm contemplating which juicy story to tell her first. I decide to go for the shock factor and tell the theater story.

I begin by telling her about the flat tire and meeting the boy. Then, going to the theater, being bored and doing my own little show for the man in front of us. Marianne chuckles, "Kinda like the one you just put on for my brother, right?" I giggle, "Exactly." She chuckles and leans in closer, "Then what happened?" I tell her all the sordid details about rubbing the boys cock and him cumming in his pants. "How could you tell?" she asks. The front of his pants got all sticky and damp," I answered. When I got to the part about the man sticking his cock in my face, sliding it up and down my cheeks and wanting to put it in my mouth, Marianne gasped. "Did you?" she shouted. "I just couldn't. I don't know why!" When I told her about my new friend sitting there, watching what was happening with his mouth hanging open. I told her the man stuck his cock in his open mouth and he began sucking on it. Marianne fell off her chair laughing. "Ohhhhh, my God!" she said almost breathless. She sat there on the lounger with her mouth open in amazement. I told her about the man pulling it out of my friends' mouth and ordering me to open my mouth while he shot his cum in my mouth. "My first taste of cum, Marianne! I decided at that moment I love the taste so much." "You spit it out, right?" I smile again, "No, I swallowed every drop." "What did the man do then?" I laugh out loud. "He zipped up his pants, called me a tramp and walked out!"

Marianne sat in amazement, "What did you do then?" she asked. "You'll love this. I go to the bathroom to clean the cum off my face and hair and I couldn't find the bathroom. I had to go to the girl at the soda area to ask. I'm sure she is still telling the story about me with cum everywhere." Marianne appears to be in shock. "Amanda," she blurts, "I fantasize about exciting exotic things with strangers. But, oh my God, you just do them! How?" I consider her question. "Sometimes they just happen. I guess I do encourage them. My feeling is why fantasize if you can possibly live them?" I ask Marianne, "If the situation arises would you live your fantasies or are you content to fantasize?" Marianne took a deep breath, "Hmmm, I'm not sure." I shook my head, "Well, if I can dream or fantasize and do it without harming anyone, why would I not live it? Marianne; do you think I am that different from you and our classmates?" Marianne looks at the sky, "I'm really not sure, Amanda we are teenagers, how do we really know?" I respond quickly, "I may be young, but I know I will always live my fantasies and dreams when possible, if I have to make them happen I will." Marianne leans sideways and gives me a big hug, "I love you, you are my best friend. I learn so much from you."

"Marianne, I don't understand, but I know what I know, and I think about sex constantly! I'm learning this year what it is all about. Marianne, there is more to tell you, but not today. I believe that last story was all you can handle for now." Marianne sighs, "You're right Amanda, enough of your sex stories for today."

Bandit walks to me wagging his tail. "Bring me your stick," I shout! He hunts it down and brings it to me with his big toothy smile. I give it a toss from my

lounger. "Marianne, I don't understand why I have these sexual desires or why I love to show off my body. It excites me to walk down the street and have heads turn, I smile at the men with my seductive smile . . . don't you enjoy those things?" "Yes, I do enjoy the young boys looking at me. I'm embarrassed when I see grown men gawking at my breasts, or checking out my ass and legs." I chime in, "Really? The men excite me the most. I would much rather play with them if I have the choice. The boys probably all cum in their pants like my theater buddy."

"Who was that guy?" Marianne asks. "I promised I wouldn't tell after watching him suck a cock." She smiles and shakes her head. "Marianne, do your panties ever get wet? Did you enjoy watching me drive your brother crazy?" "Yes, I sure did," she giggles. "Sometimes my panties do get wet, but I don't have the courage to show off as you do. Although," she continues, "it might be fun, after watching you drive my poor brother wild. I think I am going to put on a little show at my next opportunity and see what it feels like."

"I have never given those kind of things much thought Amanda. I believe you were born with something most of us may not feel, at least not as teenagers. Maybe it comes with age, I'm going to practice very soon so I'll be deadly when I'm grown," she giggles and taps my arm. "Marianne, if you choose to practice keep in mind as you walk down the street, down the hallway at school, and at the mall to smile and be happy (fake it if you have to). Always keep that happy and friendly look. It makes us much more approachable. You must be very approachable. None of this will work if you don't meet others. Also, your attire seems to make quite a difference. Of course, you know, I love tight, sexy and short." "Yes, I know," she says with a smile. "Normally you do wear that type of clothing. Doesn't it make you feel so good when you walk down the street and all the men turn their heads while the wives and girlfriends hate you?" Marianne hesitates, "I guess I really don't pay enough attention to the looks. But yes, I do love to look sexy. Although Mom and Dad have big trouble with my sexy attire." I shake my head, "Yes, I understand. I was blessed, Mom and Dad learned not to dictate my wardrobe in my early grade school years. Marianne, you should come to the Good Will with me some day. We'll buy some disgusting stuff you can keep hidden for a quick change at my house." Marianne smiles, "That is a great plan, but, Good Will?" "Oh, Marianne, let me show you before you get that attitude . . . Do you like the little sexy outfits I wear?" "Yes, I do." "Marianne, it's all Good Will. My Mom taught me in second grade, you stop with me and look. Sometimes for ten dollars I can buy five or six skirts or five or six tops, you'll see." "OK, we're going shopping soon Amanda."

We lounged and enjoyed the sun's rays as I tossed Bandit's stick a few more times. "Marianne, are you a virgin?" She looks away very quickly. I was puzzled. I assumed she was. "Marianne, are you going to answer me?" She looks back to me and sighs, "No, I am not." "Oh my God, I had no idea, I'm sorry I asked. It really is none of my business." "No, I'm glad you asked. There is no one I could ever talk to about it except you." I lay my hand on her as she continued, "When I was eleven my neighbor Andy, who was fourteen at the time was my sitter. When Mom and

Dad were away we would sometimes play around. Well, one thing led to another and we had sex one rainy evening." "Did you like it?" "It hurt quite a lot the first time and we got blood all over the sofa. No, the first time was not much fun." "So that means you did it again?" Marianne smiles, "Again and again and again." I was shocked! "Don't you worry about getting pregnant?" "Oh, he always uses a condom." "What is a condom like?" "It's a stretchy, lubricated thing like a balloon that he puts over his cock." "Wow, Marianne that is incredible, does it feel good?" "Oh God yes! I miss it so much when he doesn't come over for a couple of weeks. I should tell you the rest of the story." "What?" I gasped. After taking a very deep breath and letting it out Marianne continues, "One afternoon, when Mom and Dad were working, my brother walked in on us." "Oh, my God," I squeal! "Yaaaaaa," she continues. "We were on the sofa. Andy was on his back. I was riding his cock, sliding up and down; it was feeling so good. I started cumming, squealing and moaning wildly. When I opened my eyes there stood my brother watching every move." "Oh my God, Marianne." "He let out a disgusted breath and asked Andy to go home. Andy, of course, obliged. I was so embarrassed. Grabbing my clothes I went to my bedroom and slumped on my bed. Two minutes later my bedroom door opened and in he walked. I was lying on my back still totally naked. He took off his pants. I asked, 'What are you doing?' He looked at my wet pussy and said, 'Now it's my turn.' I said, 'Chad I can't do this.' 'Oh, you can't huh? I just watched you get fucked,' as he continued undressing. Again I insisted, 'Chad no, I can't, you're my brother.' He kicked his pants to the floor, with his erect cock pointed directly at my pussy. 'Either fuck me, or I tell Mom and Dad. You have been fucking this guy for some time, I know it!' 'Chad! You wouldn't,' I cried. 'Oh, but I could,' as he stroked his cock with his hand and climbed on my bed. "Amanda, I had no choice." I shook my head in total disgust. "He put on a condom, spread my legs and rammed his cock deep inside me. I might as well enjoy it, I decided. He pumped it in and out, in and out, it did feel good. It began to build deep inside. I spread my legs wider, it was building. I was fucking him back. Oh my God, Amanda, I came so hard. At the same time he pulled it out, took the condom off and slid up my body. I listened to him moan with pleasure as he shot his load all over my breasts, oh God it felt so good. He rubbed his cock in his cum, rubbing his cum, stroking my nipples. Amanda, I didn't know how sensitive my nipples were. I continued rubbing his gooey cum on my nipples, it was building again, deep inside me, building and building. My nipples were driving me wild. Suddenly, my hips moved up. I screamed wildly, I have never cum that intensely, it just kept cumming and cumming, oh my God. My body slumped to the bed. He climbed off, looked at me and said, 'Marianne, you are one hot bitch. Too bad you are my sister.' As he grabbed his clothes and walked out the door, I laid there. I had just cum like I had never experienced before. My sheets were soaked, my pussy was wet with my own cum. My tits still felt hot with his load spread all over them. Amanda, I felt so guilty, this is my brother that I love. How could I do this?" "Marianne, you had no choice! Your Mom and Dad would have disowned you! How are you with

it now after all this time?" She hesitated, "Amanda," another big sigh, "he comes to my bedroom and fucks me sometimes twice a week." "Oh my God," I shout! "Yes it does feel good, but the guilt I live with is horrible. I know someday Mom or Dad will catch us, it's inevitable." "Oh, Marianne, that is terrible. That's disgusting!"

We continue relaxing on our lounges not saying a word for several minutes "Marianne, do you want it to stop?" "Oh yes, so badly." "I'm going to make that happen within two weeks, I promise you." "Amanda, how?" "Girlfriend, leave it to me. It's going to be OK." "Amanda, you wouldn't shoot him?" I laugh, "No, it won't hurt a bit." We smile at each other and I gave her a hug. "Enough of this stuff. The parade is only three days away. I can't wait. How about you Marianne?" "Yes I'm excited too. You know how much I love parades." We make our final plans for Saturday morning and then she grabs her cell phone and calls Chad for a ride. She went in to use the bathroom while Bandit and I played. I look over my super tan. It is really looking good.

Chad arrived a few minutes later and drove Marianne away. Chad did not get out of his car, he simply honked as they drove off. I wonder if he'll fuck her on the way home. If he does, my bet was that it would be his last piece of Marianne. I whistle for Bandit and tell him this was his last trip to find his stick. He smiles and in his way said OK. I put him away and give him dinner.

I head to the bathroom and shower. I then went and tidied up the kitchen and set the table for Mom. She will be home soon, as well as the rest of the family. I pick up the newspaper, read the highlights of the news from top to bottom. I try to stay up on current events as much as possible. I really like knowing what is happening in the world, our town, and how our sports teams are doing. Just as I finished, Mom pulls in the drive. I greet her at the door and give her a big warm hug. She glances around the house and said, "Oh, Amanda, you are such a treasure. The house looks so nice and you set the table, thank you!" "Yes Mom, I spent most of the day shining it up just for you." I think she knew I was joking.

Dad arrived home and the boys soon after. We had a great family dinner and re tired to the living room and switched on the TV. We chit-chat with lots of family talk for a while and eventually eight thirty rolled around. I said my goodnights to all and head to my room. I was tired, not sure why. I realize I hadn't done much today, I un dress while checking myself out in the mirror. I love my body. My tan lines are looking so hot. I read somewhere that many ladies tan nude and have no tan lines I didn't understand that. I loved pulling my panties down and seeing white skin around my pussy and my rounded butt. My breasts are almost pure white. My shoul ders and chest are so dark. I love being tan. When I am rich, I will have my own tan ning bed. I swear my titties have gotten bigger just today. My hair looks great, long and dark, it is so thick, I love the natural waviness. I turn to check out my ass one more time. It is round and firm. I move from foot to foot just so I can watch it wig gle from side to side. I turn back around to the front side again and stare at my bush. It had gotten hairier today. I found the perfect pair of white silky panties, slip them on and climb into bed. I make a plan for tomorrow as I drift off to sleep.

CHAPTER 9

The Amanda Revue

I am awakened in the morning with a roar of thunder. The rain beating on my windows is what woke me. I jump out of bed and look outside. It was nine thirty and still so dark. A bolt of lightning flashed through the air. Wow, that was great! I love the rain and the storms and this is a great one. The rain continues to hammer on my window. Ew, Ew, Ew, I have to pee. I slip on a little top, open my bedroom door and head down the hallway to the bathroom. To my surprise, my brothers, Josh and John, are sitting in the living room. I smile as they caught me in my silky lacy panties and my little top. I felt a little embarrassed. I would not let them see that. I smile and said, "Good morning guys," as I strut toward the bathroom. I thought to myself, as I felt their eyes all over my ass, it's really no different than a bikini bathing suit and they've seen that a hundred times. Even though it was my brothers I still enjoyed their eyes ogling my body. I did my bathroom duties, brush my hair and now time for the return trip. I wonder if they would be polite, and go to the kitchen, their bedroom, go stand in the rain or just sit and wait for the show. My question was quickly answered, as I head down the hallway back to my bedroom. Well, they didn't go stand in the rain, they obviously heard the bathroom door open and all eyes were now on the Amanda show. My brothers were not going to give me a break! Fine, let's do a show! I refuse to let them know I was not very comfortable. I was much too proud. As I was passing by them I stop and look them right in the eye, put my hands on my hips, give a quick jerk of my neck backwards so my wavy locks fall with a flip behind my shoulders. I gave them a big smile and said, "Are you boys enjoying your little sister?" I was doing my best to turn the table, let the embarrassment be with them. Well, it didn't exactly work, Josh with

a very big smile said, "Amanda you might be a kid, but look at you. You could easily be an adult, you are beautiful." John pipes up, "Amanda, you've gone this far turn and model for your brothers." I give them a disgusting, but sexy smile, and said, "OK guys, you asked for it!" I turn very slowly and put my ass directly in their view, shake it back and forth three or four times, turn slowly to face them and put my head down. I lift my top over my head, shaking my head to settle my hair, while sliding my hands under my breasts and squeezing them upward toward my mouth I gently lick each nipple and then look back at them. The amazement in those four eyes. I wish I had a camera. That picture of my brothers so excited by their kid sister will be implanted in my brain forever. Were they embarrassed? That was my goal. Oh, I wasn't done, the Amanda show was not over. As disgusting as it is, my pussy was getting very damp. With my nipples very erect, I slid my hands downward as I'm thinking to myself, maybe now they will go stand in the rain and I can move on to my room. No, of course that didn't happen, they were thoroughly enjoying 'The Amanda Revue'. I'd gone this far I thought. I'm finishing this show with a grand finale. I slide my right hand down my belly to the top of my white lacy panties, I slide it under the waistband and down to my pussy. Oh, it is so wet. I wonder if they can see my wetness on my panties and on my leg. I can feel the wetness creeping down my thigh. It flashes through my brain, is this normal for every pussy to get so wet? I slide my fingers to my clit, ewwww, it sends a tremor through my body. I threw my head back with a guided flip (this part for show), it feels good, but now I do what it takes to perform a real show for my big brothers. I gently stroke my clit through my panties. I suddenly have a desire to show them my hairy pussy. I take both hands and slide my thumb under the waistband, I think to myself, way too late for them to go stand in the rain and I could still move on to my room, but no, that does not seem to be an option at this time. I slide my new white lacy panties down to my thighs, exposing my hairy pussy to my brothers. think they are in awe and have never seen such a hot hairy bush. I now slide my fingers over my clit and slowly move it to my mouth as I give my two fingers a lick I kick my panties toward them as I finish sliding them down my legs. I give them my best sisterly smile and move on to my room as I begin to close the door. finally give them one last smile, "Guys, enjoy the storm." I take a deep breath, God that was fun!

As I sat on my bed, I thought, Amanda, should you be ashamed of yourself. After some very serious thought I decided that in no way should I be ashamed. The boys enjoyed themselves and no one was harmed. I had an entertaining experience Although it was my big brothers, they certainly could have stopped me by saying "Amanda that is disgusting." Now that may have embarrassed me.

This exhibitionist fun had started two summers before. I spent awhile with my Grandma and Grandpa in the city one hour from our home. They lived four blocks from the downtown shopping area. I would love to take my savings and shop from store to store. I never really made friends. I'm not sure why, perhaps my smile was not just right and I was perhaps just not approachable. Of course, I would always

ear my Good Will tight little short tops and little skirts. My butt wasn't nearly as
und at that time and not much in the boob department. I'm sure I looked more
ke a kid. I, of course, got lots of looks on my four-block walk. Even at that age
ertain men would be watching all too close as I strutted my way up and down the
tore aisles.

One day on one of my journeys back to Grandma's a car pulled up beside me as
walked down the sidewalk. A man probably in his forties with a very happy smile
sked me where Sam's Club was from here. I did know the direction because I
ould go there with Grandpa occasionally. I stood by the passenger window and
ave him directions. He thanked me and then as he was putting his car into gear
aid, "Would you like to get a coke at the drive-in right up the street?" Well, this
as the first person I've spoken to all week, other than my grandparents and a new
iend would be great. I said, "OK." He unlocked the door and I slid in. He im-
ediately laid his right hand on my leg. I was not sure if I should allow that or not.
is two fingers were gently kind of tickling my bare leg. I decided that it was OK.
e chatted a little about the weather. He asked me what grade I was in and I told
im the tenth. He asked if I had a boyfriend as his hand and fingers were stroking
larger portion of my leg. I squirmed a little and know I should be moving my leg
way, but no, I slid it three to four inches closer to him. It made me want to sing
y "Eensy Weensy Spider" song. Now, being encouraged, he was getting even
raver, his hand slid up my little girl skirt and touched my pussy thru my panties
ith one finger. I spread my legs a few inches wider. Now with two fingers my
rotch started moving up and down very slowly with the stroke of his move, it felt
 good. He pulled the car into a vacant parking lot and shut off the ignition. I
new it was time I should leave, and said I had to go. Before I could move, his full
and was stroking between my legs, I could not move. He told me my panties were
 wet. I knew. I could feel the dampness. He looked at my face, I was whimpering
ith passion. I had no idea what was happening, but I knew I liked it. He whis-
ered in my ear, "I want to kiss your panties." Oh, God! He turned sideways and
ently pushed my head and body back on the seat. He lifted my little yellow skirt
nd buried his face in my panties. He was licking and sucking. I was pumping my
antied crotch in his face. He pulled the leg of them aside, his tongue was now
cking my exposed little pussy, and I was in awe. This stranger, his mouth, his
ngue, his face, buried between my legs, why would anyone put their face down
ere, I did not understand, but it felt so good! Suddenly he was groaning. I did not
now what was happening. He lifted his face off my pussy.

I sat up and rearranged my panties and pulled my skirt down and said, "Mister,
have to go." He was unzipping his pants and saying, "Honey, look what you've
one to me." I opened the door and quickly slid out.

I was ten blocks from Grandma's house. I needed a brisk walk to calm myself
own! That was kind of fun I thought while walking. He had his huge stick in his
and when I got out. Should I have stayed? I was uncertain as to why my panties
ere damp. Yes, his wet mouth, but some of it seemed to be from me. Anyway, it

felt good. My wet panties, my wet little crotch, my little skirt, maybe someone else would want to get a coke. As I walked home I received a few wild stares, but no new friends. I went directly to my room. I supposed I should shower, but was enjoying my wetness. What Grandma can't see won't hurt her. We had our dinner and I watched TV with Grandma. Grandpa was off doing other things, nine-thirty time to go to bed. I'd had a big day.

It was beginning to darken outside. I flipped on my bedroom light. I glanced at my window, which shown directly to the neighbor's house. A man was peeking at me through his window. It startled me at first, but I got a rush. My panties had dried but still felt good tucked in my little bush. I pretended not to notice him and went about my business doing this and that. I could see him from the corner of my eye watching me closely. My first exhibitionist experience was about to begin.

I stood at my bedside and pulled my yellow skirt down. He seemed to disappear. I watched his curtain moving, without looking directly, I knew he was watching. lifted my top over my head and shook my hair down, lifted my fingers and played with my erect nipples. I loved the feeling of being watched. I pulled my panties down to expose my little pussy. I then switched off the light very casually and slid into my bed. That was so fun. I slipped my hands to my crotch and tickled it just like my guy in the car. As I was drifting off, I hoped this would go on for the rest of my nights at Grandma's. Knowing I was being watched and putting on my show. Of course the night before I leave I would do a super show. I would slowly undress play with my titties, stroke my pussy until it was very wet and lick my finger several times. I would look directly at his face tucked behind that curtain, give him my hottest smile and throw him a kiss and shut the lights off. Oh, how I still enjoy being watched.

CHAPTER 10

Marianne Set Free

I am on a mission to free Marianne. The rain has stopped, I walk to the living room and the boys have gone. I am telling myself, "Amanda, you've got to be so up when you do see them." I will not show any discomfort or embarrassment in any way. I walk to the phone and ring Marianne's home number and big brother answers the phone. In my sweetest, sexiest voice, I say, "Hi Chad, this is Amanda." In return in his sexiest voice, "Hi Amanda, how are you this morning?" "Chad, I am very good, but could be so much better." He asks, "In what way?" "Chad, do you know how excited I got watching your cock get hard while you were checking out my hairy pussy?" I could feel him smiling, "I really want to see you." "When?" he asks. "Come see me this afternoon." "Where?" "That little drive off our road." "What time?" "Oh, let's say three-thirty." In a quick little raspy voice he answers, "I'll be there!" Step one: Plan in Play.

At two o'clock I close the door as I entered my room. I sort through my closet of slutty little outfits. I come across a white, little girl skirt, perfect. I was well aware if I chose to look twenty I could. Today I choose to look very young. I wore a little girl skirt. One that is very short and flared at the bottom, like little girls wear (of course). I found a yellow top with spaghetti straps. It was hot yellow, very soft cotton. I wanted my nipples to be so erotic and erect. I tried them both on. My mirrors told me yes! I found a perfect pair of panties with butterflies everywhere and pastel pink as well. Great! Now pink knee socks. Perfect! OK undress, time for a nice hot shower. I need to be so clean for the cock that was coming my way.

Back in my room I slid on my perfect attire. Brush, brush, brush my wavy long hair and add a little lip-gloss. Slide on my butterfly panties and my hot knee socks

and my bright white tennis shoes. I admire my hot thirteen-year-old look as I look in my mirror from all angles. There, perfect! Add a little orange flavor lollipop to complete my little girl look. Oh, yes! My little nipples are standing so tall; it excites even me. Now for my hair, I'll do a double ponytail. I pull my hair to each side and add a rubber band to each. Cute! It's almost three o'clock and I am getting excited. I will have a cock in my ass very soon. What is wrong? Why am I so excited? Is this a blessing or curse? I have no idea. Who cares, I tell myself. I am on a mission today. My panties are getting damp with the excitement coming my way. I sure hope Chad likes butterflies. I peek at my panties to be sure my wetness is not showing. The rain had stopped earlier. Still no sun, it is very muggy. I walk slowly up my drive to the road and walk toward my spot. Yes, his car is parked under the big tree. His windows are open and his car all shiny. I peek in the window with my big sexy smile, while licking my sucker, and say in my cute little girl voice, "Hi Chad." I open the door and slid in beside him while letting my little skirt ride very high. He immediately laid his hand on my thigh, leaned back in his seat and gave me a very cocky, "Hi." His hand is moving toward my pussy. I wasn't comfortable with the arrogant look on his face and his cockiness. I act submissive, I called him, and so I must really want his cock was his disgusting demeanor. I bit my tongue. I will play this game you arrogant asshole. Soon would own this disgusting bastard. His fingers are pressing at my panties to get into my pussy. He is staring between my legs. I ask in an all so sexy tone, "Chad, do you like butterflies?" He grunts, "I can take 'em or leave 'em." What an asshole! I was seeing a side of Chad I hadn't seen before. He was trying to force his fingers inside my pussy. He sat back and in a cocky voice, "I want to see that hairy pussy." I've got to have him, as I tolerate his disgusting arrogance. I pull my panties down and slide them over one leg, exposing my pussy. That excited Chad, he unzips his pants and pulls his already hard cock through the zipper opening. "Suck my cock," he commanded. I obey putting my head down in his lap and flicking my tongue over its head. His juices are leaking into my mouth, salty and tasty. His cock was big and so hard and tasted very good. I slide my tongue and then my mouth up and down his shaft, it was getting harder. I didn't want him to cum yet. I lift my mouth off and roll to the car seat and stick my hot little ass high in the air. He squeeze past the steering wheel and mounts me. I could feel his wet cock starting to slide up and down my pussy, it felt slimy and so good. He was pressing on my unopened hole and pushing much too hard, I slid my hand around behind me to his hard shaft and steered it to the proper hole. He seemed unhappy with that and guided it back to my pussy. In a very strong voice, I said, "Honey," as I slide it back to my ass, "this hole or no hole." Reluctantly he gave up and slid it into my hot ass. "Oh, yes! Fuck me!" I wailed. As he was slamming my ass he squeals, "I'm going to cum." quickly shout, "Chad, cum all over my pussy!" I pull his cock out of my ass and roll to my back and spread my legs as wide as the car would allow. It worked. Chad grabbed his long hard cock and jerked it twice and spewed his hot juice all over my hairy pussy. Awww, it was fantastic! It squirted and squirted. I ran my hand over

ny pussy it was so gooey. I rub my hand in his cum. Chad slides back behind the
steering wheel and tosses his head back. "Holy shit! That was great." I smile as I
pull my butterfly panties over his hot juice. I pull my skirt back down trying to be
lady-like.

I look at him, "Chad that was too much fun. Write your cell number down so I
can call you again." He quickly found a pen and scratches it on a scrap piece of
paper and hands it to me. "Anytime!" I tuck it away, open the car door and scoot
out, not saying a word. I walk to the road, slowing my pace the last few steps.

Behind me I heard the car start. I'm at the road walking home as his car pulls up
beside me. I step to his window. He still has that cocky womanizer look on his silly
face. I thought, I hope you enjoy that cockiness. I knew I was never going to see it
again. As I stoop down a little and look into his car, I plant both feet together and
said, "You arrogant prick!" His eyes blinked, a look of shock, "You slut!" he shrieks.
"Chad, if you ever put your hands on my best friend Marianne again you will live to
regret it." A shocked look over took him, "What do you mean?" he stammers. "You
bastard, you've been fucking your only sister for years. It stops now!"

The arrogant smile, "Bitch, you can't prove that." "Yeah, you are right, I can't, but
I can prove this. You just fucked perhaps an underage girl, knowingly!" He fires
back, "You can't prove that either." I give him my sexiest smile, as I run my hand
down my butterfly panties. "Ever heard of DNA? Well, Fuck Head, I've got yours!
It will be under lock and key, until I die, maybe longer!" (My joke!) I will decide
someday if you deserve getting them back, but for now you bastard, I own your ass."

Looking down he shakes his head with remorse, "Please don't tell my Mom and
Dad." I again use my sexiest smile, "Oh, no, I won't do that. This will go directly
to the law enforcement. Marianne may not testify, but, you son of a bitch, I got
your load right here in my cute little butterfly panties. I own your cocky ass! You
will never touch Marianne again, clear? Never smile or flirt with me either, you
arrogant bastard. If I need a fucked ass some evening, you will be here. It doesn't
matter where you are or what you are doing, you drop it. That is unless you want
to spend twenty-five years in prison. I will be your master. If I need a ride or want
the company of a sister fucking bastard, I will call you. The first time you don't
show or are not punctual, your sorry ass will go to prison. Am I clear! Questions,
spit them out now!" Silence. "Fine, go! Get out of here!"

I stood and quickly walk toward the house while he sat in stunned amazement.
I gave him no time to catch me and pull off the evidence. He was now my slave and
Marianne was free. I was shaking. I had never spoken to anyone that way. I don't
normally get upset. I surprised even myself. I certainly put the fear of God in him.
I laugh, he really has no idea if I'm of age or not! Who cares? It worked!

What he was doing to Marianne was disgusting. What got my insides churning
was his cocky attitude. Mr. Stud huh, he can use it on others. I will never tolerate
it again. He will be my taxi service. I knew I would never call a male for a fuck
again. I enjoy their lustful stares, not the attitudes!

I saw Chad's car turn toward the highway. I was somewhat concerned he may

have come after me. Without the cum-soaked panties I had as evidence, no slave. I breathed a sigh of relief as I walk up my drive. Well, another successful afternoon. I had a great fuck, released Marianne and have a taxi and slave when needed. I consider a car occasionally, who wants the extra expense now that I have my taxi service! I took the last few steps to my door. I could feel Chad's cum leaking down my legs from my panties. There was a slight hint of the aroma drifting to my nose. I went to my room after getting a plastic bag from the kitchen and a magic marker. I pull off my panties and put them in a zip locked bag and marked it D A H C. Chad spelled backwards.

I flop down on my bed. The boys would be home soon. I wonder if they will ever see me the same way after putting on my strip tease. I will force myself to act like the same sweet little sister. They will never know I am a bit uncomfortable. No problem! I can be a very good actress. I will never forget the facial expression as they watched the Amanda show live. I wonder, they are in college, are they still virgins?

I roll over and close my eyes. I awake and look at the clock, it is six-thirty. The family should be home. I pull my jogging suit on, brushed my hair and walk toward the bathroom. "Hi!" I said as I wave to the boys who were watching the news in the living room. I didn't look directly, I kept moving down the hallway. I did my duties, touch up my lips, walk back to the living room and sat in the big chair. I wave hi to Mom who was fixing dinner. I look at the boys and ask, "Where did you guys disappear to this morning?" Neither of them looked up at me. John replies, "Work to do at Ferris's." "Oh I thought that might be the case. Did you guys get it done?" I ask. "No, we will finish tomorrow and we're off for the weekend. Our big softball tournament . . ." "Well, good luck with the game. I wish it wasn't so far away. I'd love to be there." "I know," John answered. "We will keep Mom and Dad updated. We could play up to five games if we continue winning." "You guys will give it your best, I am sure of that." From the kitchen Mom shouts, "Amanda, come set the table please!" "OK. Where is Dad?" "He and Uncle Ken are painting on the house, please set an extra place for Uncle Ken, Amanda."

We finished a great dinner, I helped Mom clean up and Dad told the boys to get the lawn mowed tonight, as they would be gone on the weekend. Mom and I talked about various things. As we cleaned up I asked, "Mom, are you sure you don't want to go to the parade Saturday with Marianne and me?" Mom smiles, "No honey, but I do have to do some shopping in town. I'll drive you." "Oh, that would be great!" My plan was to call my taxi driver for his first run. I would save him for later.

CHAPTER 11

The Parade

Saturday morning came very quickly. The boys were gone by the time I got up. I stepped outside onto the deck. Uncle Ken and Dad were outside painting. What a beautiful morning! Not a cloud in the sky. There's lots of sunshine and seventy-three degrees already with no humidity. I stepped back inside and Mom asks, "Could I fix you some breakfast?" "No, I'll grab a bowl of cereal, what time does the parade start?" "It starts at eleven, so we'll leave around ten fifteen Amanda, is that OK?" "Sure, can we stop by and pick up Marianne?" "Of course honey."

I finish my cereal, put my dish in the sink and off to my room I went. Hmm, what would I wear today? Let's see, something showy and cute! That shouldn't be too difficult as most of my clothing is exactly that. Mom would have to critique my appearance, so forget super tight bottoms. I look through my closet. Oh perfect! I pick out a little schoolgirl pink skirt and a tiny yellow tank top. I hope my nipples don't stand up with Mom in the area. She will insist I wear a bra. The skirt is about four inches above my knees. I think that'll get past Mom. I look again, hot! I add white knee socks and yellow silky panties. Wow, just to be sure, I put on a long button up sweater over my top to get me past Mom. "OK, I'm ready." Out the door I go. I walk over to Uncle Ken and Dad to say good morning. They wish me a great day, I yell, "I'm letting Bandit out, keep an eye out please!" Dad acknowledges with a wave that it was fine.

Mom is in the car and ready to go, I hop in. It was a quick trip to pick up Marianne. We pulled in just as Marianne was coming out the door. She was wearing a rather sexy dark blue silky tight top with cleavage that looked so hot and light blue very tight shorts. She looked so perfect. We all said our greetings as she slid in beside me.

We arrive in town. Holy crap, cars are everywhere and streets were blocked off. "Wow, what a turnout. I'll leave you girls here, it's only three more blocks into town." We thanked her and slid out. "I'm going to the mall, call me later if you need a ride Amanda." "Thanks Mom, we will." Mom pulls away as I unbutton my long sweater and hang it on my arm.

Marianne looks me up and down and says with a big smile, "Amanda that outfit is disgustingly cute!" "Good Will," I said. "Wow, I am going shopping with you as soon as I get some money." "We'll work on that." We continue to walk down the street. There was an ever so nice light breeze. I love the feel of the air blowing under my skirt, causing it to just float. Sometimes having to hold it down. I certainly would not want anything showing. The breeze was flowing around my legs, thighs and my crotch. It felt so exhilarating!

We arrive at the parade route, there were so many people everywhere. "Marianne, we must be in front, let's find a perfect spot." It was difficult. There were hundreds of people in front of us. I was getting a bit concerned. We had to be in the front row. We looked and looked and finally found a place where the crowd wasn't quite so deep. We attempted to work our way forward through the crowd without causing too much commotion. We push, squeeze and turn excusing ourselves. The guys didn't seem to mind. It was the looks on the ladies faces. They were not appreciating our move toward the front. "Come on Marianne, only two more rows in front of us." She taps an older gentleman on the shoulder. "That's my Mom and Dad, up there. Do you mind if we get past you?" He checks her very quickly and said, "No, not at all," and lets us move in front. His wife was shaking her head as he let us slip in front of them. Now, one more row, how? To the right, there are two young guys in front of us. Marianne smiles so big and flirtatious, it amazes even me. "Guys," she said seductively, "could we stand in front of you? You are so tall!" They both look over and down at us and reply, "Of course, come right on up here and stand right in front of us." "Oh thank you guys, you are so sweet." We are in the perfect parade spot, now where's the parade? I look at my watch, ten fifty-five. We are away from the starting point so it will be a bit of a wait.

There are so many people, like sardines in a can. It's hard to stand strong just to keep our position. Marianne turns around to the guys who let us up front, "Hi, I'm Marianne and this is my sister Amanda." I'm thinking you go girl, as I turn and smile. "Hello, I'm Ty and this is Danny." "Hi guys, thank you so much for letting us sneak in front of you." "Well that had a dual purpose. The parade is thirty minutes or so away so we might as well allow some scenery in front of us." I thought that was a nice line. I turn to see who was speaking. It was Ty, who happens to be standing directly behind me and very close. He appears to be seventeen or eighteen. Probably the same age as his friend Danny, who was directly behind Marianne. Both were preppy looking with no ball caps, thank God, and quite handsome. Marianne and I continue small talk. Danny caught Marianne's attention and asks, "Where are you gals from?" "Aurora," she lied. "Geez, so far away." "Yes we love parades and love the drive down here." "Two sisters who both enjoy a parade and

drive an hour to get to it? That is awesome! Are you cheerleaders at Aurora High?" Marianne smiles, "No, Amanda and I graduated last year. We go to Aurora State." "Oh, that's awesome," says Ty. I'm listening, and can't believe Marianne can be such a bull-shitter. I've never seen this side of her. She continues, "Amanda just broke off her engagement and we decided to get away for the day." "Awesome," he repeats.

Now we can hear the parade in the distance, some bands and fire sirens. It is finally getting closer. I was thinking about, but couldn't ask our new friends, if they know my brothers. We are from Aurora. As the sounds get closer, Ty whispers in my ear, "How long were you engaged?" I answered, "Only six months." Still whispering in my ear, "What happened?" "I decided I am not the marrying kind." "That's cool. What do you do?" (I wanted to ask Marianne, but decided I must come up with my own story.) "I go to Aurora State, school starts in another week." He says, "Cool."

The parade is now passing us. There are high school bands, fire trucks and floats from many businesses. It is so beautiful. The crowd is clapping and cheering. I am crazy about this simple excitement. I love being twenty-something and going to Aurora State as well. It is so much fun, Marianne and I bull-shitting these guys. Wow, I love it! I'm enjoying one float after another. The body behind me is getting closer, and the crowd is very tight. It seems even tighter here, Ty has moved very close. I know that I should probably push back and tell him to knock it off, but what the heck. His closeness does feel very good, as he is massaging his semi-hardness against my ass. I can see a huge nineteen fifty-nine pink Cadillac next in our view. I've seen this car several times before, it belongs to a businessman in our capital city. They call him Bargain Bob. The car gets within our view, it has a huge banner on the side reading: "Cadillac's and our Miss Capitol City." It is a gorgeous pink Cadillac, with a rumble seat on the trunk, full of beautiful women. The gal in the rumble seat is wearing a crown. It is our new Miss Capitol City. She's gorgeous! Dark hair, beautiful eyes and an amazing smile. Her teeth were so white and perfect. I so wanted that to be me someday. I have read in our local paper that Bargain Bob had gotten a team together to bring a Miss Capitol City pageant to our city. It had been twenty years since they had a representative of our capital. I thought this has been a great and positive happening for our state. Bargain Bob is from here. He grew up locally and is very well-known. His pink Cadillac is always full of women. I always look them over one at a time. All are attractive, some young and some not so young. They always seem to be having so much fun. I was always amazed by them. The car was passing with Bob driving. He seemed to be kind of an unusual duck, tall, slim, and dark in his mid-forties. He is semi-handsome, always well dressed and does funny television commercials. Bargain Bob operates several furniture stores in towns around us. He is on television constantly, promoting his furniture stores. One particular commercial I remember and laugh about when I think to myself, who would respond to that type of advertising? He would be dressed perfectly, and then say to the world on TV: "If you're a slob and

don't have a job, you can still get credit with Bargain Bob." I guess it works! He has many stores and a pink nineteen fifty-nine Cadillac full of women that I am watching go by in our parade. People are waiving and yelling, "Hey Bargain Bob, I'm a slob, we love you Bob." I have heard he has a huge barn full of classic Cadillac's. He has been receiving a huge amount of press about a restaurant cabaret event center he has opened in our capital city. It is in a semi-rundown area of town and he has spent several million dollars renovating a huge older building with no city assistance. The project is talked about often on my favorite radio station. I haven't been there, but it's on my list to get Mom and Dad to Cadillac's on October fifteenth, which happens to be my birthday.

Ty's erection is now pressed against my ass and very gently sliding slowly up and down my rear. It has gotten very hard. I look at the parade goers around me. Everyone is engrossed in the parade and paying no attention to my little parade. Marianne looks at me and asked, "What's wrong?" She obviously has read my expressions. I whisper in her ear, "Ty has a hard on and is rubbing it up and down my ass. Don't look Marianne!" "Tell him to stop," she says. "Why? It feels good." She rolls her eyes and whispers back, "You are so bad," and giggles. Somehow the parade is not quite as important as he continues massaging my ass with his cock. At this point, I can't tell for sure if his crotch is under my nylon skirt or on top. Of course, it made little difference, I fantasize he was under my skirt rubbing my yellow panties, which are getting very damp. I was very gently pumping against his hardness. Eww, I feel a finger, gently sliding between my legs. I look around me. Thank goodness no one is paying any attention. He continues slipping his finger back and forth over my pussy. I am getting so hot. He must feel the dampness. His finger right in the midst of my wetness, he has to be as hot as myself. I know I need more. A flash goes to my head, what if he cums in his pants? I'm going to get left here with my wet pussy and have gotten nothing but a little finger pleasure. I must stop him before it's too late. I lean against him and whisper in his ear, "Ty, it feels much too good, let's take a ride after the parade, I want to enjoy a bit more of you." He gave me a smile and patted my yellow pantied ass and pulled his hand back. I slightly turn and from the corner of my eye I could see him sniffing my pussy juices from his finger. God, I love a good parade.

Marianne and Danny seem to be hitting it off quite nicely as well. The parade is winding down, the final float is passing, followed by policemen on horses. The four of us are moving through the crowd, "Let's get some lunch," Ty suggests. I wanted more than lunch, but it was a good start. Marianne said she was a bit hungry and ready for a burger. "Where to?" Danny asked. Of course us gals are not from town so we say nothing. "How about that drive-in burger place on the highway?" Ty asked. "Sure, that's perfect." I decide to take a chance knowing I could reverse gears if needed, "You guys want to take our car?" Marianne's mouth falls open and gasps as she rolls her eyes at my suggestion. "No, come ride with us." I agreed and Marianne recovered very quickly in a stern voice, "We just met these guys, maybe we should follow them!" I smile to myself, let's make them beg. "Yes,

you are probably right, we'll just follow you guys." "Girls, come on, there is no need, it would be great to chat and get to know each other, we are harmless." "All right, I guess it will be OK." We walked with them to their car and away we went.

It's mid afternoon, the weather is awesome. I sat close to Ty, and Marianne looked quite comfortable sitting next to Danny in the back seat. Ty laid his hand on my bare leg and rubbed it. I gave him an OK smile, of course his hands were on my pussy just a bit ago. We talked about school and chit-chat. Danny, from the back seat commented, "You two certainly do not look like sisters." "We have different fathers," stated Marianne, and the conversation moved on, rather dull, but the anticipation of what was to happen later on was certainly exciting!

CHAPTER 12

Bargain Bob

We pull into Burgers For U. It was an old fashioned drive-in, sit-in-your-car type of venue. It was a lovely setting. A young girl in a little uniform skirt came out to take our orders. She was smiley and bubbly. The menus are posted on big boards in the center. We placed our order of burgers, fries and shakes.

I look over two spaces to our right and the pink Cadillac from the parade is pulling in beside us. "Oh my God!" I blurted, "it's Bargain Bob's car." Bob wasn't driving. It was a very tall, thin black guy. In the back seat were two gorgeous gals and Bob smack in the middle of them, with two more beautiful girls in the rumble seat. I peaked around the driver, and I see Miss Capitol City in the middle and another light-skinned black guy on the passenger side. The whole group seemed to be having so much fun partying and laughing. Someone would say something and everyone would burst into laughter. We all stared at them, it made us want to laugh and join in their fun. I couldn't hear what was being said, every few minutes would come a very clear, "O'La Lay." We all shook our heads in amazement, I wanted to walk over to that pink Cadillac, tell Bob who I was, say "O'La Lay" and jump in the middle of the party. They didn't appear to be drinking alcohol, just having too much fun.

Our food arrived, we passed it around getting our orders straight. Our cute little waitress was now a big hit with Bob's group. We heard a huge "O'La Lay" as they welcomed her to the car. She was beaming. The driver had a huge smile on his face with big bright white teeth. He was a happy sort of guy, with a huge bubbling personality. I couldn't hear what he was saying, but the whole car and our little waitress was roaring with laughter. We couldn't help but stare and smile. I munch

on my fries while contemplating on how I was going to meet Bargain Bob.

Miss Capitol City and the rest of this happy group were my kind of people, very upscale and knew how to have fun. I wasn't sure how, but before we left, I vowed I would meet them. We finish our burgers while I excuse myself for a bathroom run. I knew I needed to get myself cleaned up, I knew I wanted to have Ty's cock before going home. I climb out of our car and caught the happy guy at the wheel checking me out immediately. Of course, my skirt was very short and difficult not to get a peek at my panties as I climb out. With big white teeth in a friendly way, "Hi, how are you?" he asked. I stood up, straightening my skirt, "I am just perfect, thank you." He looked me in the eye straight faced and said, "Yes, you sure are." He put his head down laughing with a woo - hoo and the whole car roared a funny and happy "O'La Lay." I shook my head and smiled and moved toward the bathroom. As I rounded the backside of the car, the light-skinned guy on the passenger side was saying, "Honey, when you come back, stop by and meet my friends." He had a very friendly smile and was almost too polite. I smiled again and kept walking with my little strut, I could feel all eyes on me. That always feels so good.

I do my duties, clean up, brush my hair, mascara, eye shadow, lip-gloss . . . I am looking hot. I walk around the corner of the building. I hear another "O'La Lay" as they tap their soft drinks together. The front passenger spotted me and insisted I come over and meet Tiffany, our new Miss Capitol City. I thought that was a good line, after all, who would not want to meet this beautiful girl? I had read all about the pageant in our local paper.

I walk to his door as he continued in his polite manner, with a friendly outgoing smile. "This is Tiffany, Miss Capitol City," as he waves his hand toward her, "and you are?" he asked. "I am Amanda," trying to duplicate his polite manner. She said, "Hello Amanda, so nice to meet you." I wanted to ask her so many questions, although I knew this was not the time. "I'm Tyson, this is "O'La Lay." He pointed to the driver. I looked a bit puzzled and asked, "Why do you call his name and constantly cheer?" They all roar. I was more puzzled. Bob from the back seat, with a very different mannerism, said in a kind sort of happy voice, "It's a very long story, when you have time, I personally will share it with you." He wasn't flirtatious, just a straightforward statement with a pleasant grin. I could tell he was a good guy.

I was just curious, "What does 'O'La Lay' mean?" Tyson looked me in the eye, with a very serious tone and said, "Only one person can tell you and he is right here." He pointed to the driver, "Walk around and ask him." I was surprised at the response, but obeyed. I slowly walked around in front of the car, all eyes watching my every move. I stepped to the door and waited for an answer. Tyson pipes up, 'Amanda you gotta ask him." I move from one foot to the other, look him in the eye, 'What does 'O'La Lay' mean?" He motioned with his little finger for me to come closer, I moved forward in a very serious manner, "I could tell you, but I would have to kill you." The whole group roared. I wasn't sure if he was serious or what that really meant. Obviously it was a family joke.

Bob again speaking in a calm voice, "I will explain that one as well Amanda.

O'La Lay!" "Amanda, have you personally met Bob?" Tyson asked. I shook my head and said, "No." He fires back to Bob, "You mean we found someone you don't know!" His head sorta bounces with a laugh. "Amanda, this is Bargain Bob. He also owns Cadillac's in town." "Hi, Bob." He pleasantly smiles and reaches over one of his gals, takes my hand, pulls it gently toward him and kisses the backside; "My pleasure, Amanda." He then introduced me to the rest of the ladies. They are all so pleasant. "What is your connection to each other?" I asked. The driver immediately responds, "Oh, we're all family, Bob's my Dad." Bob pipes up, "Tyson is my brother and the rest are all my favorite cousins, just one happy family." It was obvious they were just kidding around, jerking my chain. I smiled and said, "O'La Lay." How they loved that line. The whole car roared and did another loud "O'La Lay" that could be heard for blocks. The driver said very seriously, "Don't say it unless you mean it." They all roared with laughter again. Another "O'La Lay" broke out. Oh my goodness, they are all so crazy, I wasn't sure how, but I wanted to be part of this crazy happy family. "How does one become a cousin I inquired?" Bob looked me right in the eye in another very serious tone, "Amanda, it's hard work and it doesn't happen over night. You have to work very hard to become one of my cousins." They all laughed, as the girls all were nodding their heads.

I had no idea what all that meant, but I believed my chain was being yanked again. Bob could see the bewilderment in my body language. He pulled two cards out of his wallet and hands them to me, "Amanda, here are two complimentary dinners for you and a friend at Cadillac's. Come in some evening. We can talk and perhaps you could work at my club someday." I smile, "Thank you Bob, that is very kind and yes, perhaps I could be a 'Caddy Girl'," and then another, "O'La Lay."

I asked, "Bob, do you know my Uncle Ken Jones and Robert Shiels?" Bob thought for a second, "I went to school with a Ken Jones and Robert Shiels. I think they were a few years younger, I do remember them." Bob went on, "I didn't know them well. I used to see them watching us at football practice. I don't think they were old enough to play on the J.V. team." "That's right Bob, they said they knew of you." Tyson smiles and says, "Everyone says they know Bargain Bob. You can't always believe it to be true." I understood what he was telling me. If someone sees Bob out and about, or on TV, they feel they know him.

Geez, I've forgotten about my friends, how rude. I turn and introduce them all around. We get another big "O'La Lay," too much fun. Marianne came over, locked her arm in mine and walked me back to the car. "Come on Amanda, time to go." "OK," I answered, as I turned back to the pink car and thanked my new family to be for the great entertainment. Bob handed three business cards with Cadillac's on the front with a picture of him on it. "Give one of those cards to Ken and Robert and tell them to stop by. I would love to see them."

I seem to have an instant like for Bob, I'm really not certain why. He was just a straightforward and fun kind of guy. I wondered how he always stayed so tan? In

all of his commercials, I noticed his perfect tan. I would ask him that, along with a hundred other questions I was storing away. I am making a plan. Bargain Bob would surely be hearing from me. I wasn't certain that I could become a cousin, but that was my challenge. I bid my farewells and waved as they did one last "O'La Lay."

Chapter 13

Ty and Danny

I walked back to the car with a happy smile and slid in close to Ty. He smiled at me. "Amanda, you sure enjoyed that crazy gang didn't you?" I sighed, "Ya know Ty, they were crazy. I don't quite understand it all, but they were having big fun. I don't think we see that sort of thing enough . . . just a group of adults, still making time to be silly. I loved it . . . it was an experience I won't soon forget." I don't think Ty quite understood, but that's OK, I did. I vowed to have the life I just experienced. When I am in my forties, I want to still be having that much fun.

I look over my shoulder in the back seat at Marianne. Her new friend's hand is running up and down her leg. "O'La Lay!!" I shout. They all respond, "O'La Lay!" Ty's hand is stroking my leg, I rub my bare leg against his. I feel him breathe deeply. I slowly run my hand up his leg and under his baggy shorts. He started breathing deeply. I asked Marianne, "Is it time to go to our car Marianne?" She is kissing her new friend rather passionately. She answered, "No, it's only four o'clock." "OK. Ty, where are you taking us?" "For a ride," he answered, as he slipped his hand between my legs. I spread them just a bit as his finger massaged my pussy.

These guys seem a bit dull after leaving the pink Cadillac gang. Oh well, we do what we have to do. Ty turned the car onto a gravel road, I knew exactly where we were going. I'd heard my brothers talk about this particular area by the river. It was a great parking spot. I pretended not to know. "Where are we going?" His finger was trying to work its way inside me. I had to slow him down. I didn't want him to know quite this quickly that was not going to work. I pushed his hand back and slid my hand to his hardness under his shorts. I stroke my hand up and down

as I glance up at his eyes as he steered the vehicle. I lick my thick hot lips, while sucking in my breath. I need to get fucked, but my mind continued to drift back to the pink Cadillac group. I didn't understand why. It wasn't a sexual thing, but it somehow gave me a little high. Somewhere there was a connection.

Ty is so aroused. I love it so much when guys get so excited. Of course, my pussy is getting very damp, I knew I was in control. I am not certain why that seemed so important, but it was!!

I peek back at Marianne, she is fully dressed and on Danny's lap riding him up and down, with her mouth crushed to his. It was a hot picture. Ty pulled the car close to the river to a secluded area and shut off the ignition. He put his right arm around my shoulders and pulled me close. His lips pressed to my mouth as he passionately kissed me. He was already so hot and I certainly was getting there. He moved his mouth to my neck, one side and then the other, sucking on my skin. I whisper softly, "No hickeys please." He moved to my ear. Eww, it sent an electrical shock straight to my pussy, I stiffened. He knew he had found one of my many weaknesses. He moved to the other ear, the same pulsating shock. His hand was stroking my crotch very rapidly. I need his cock in my ass now. I slide his shorts partially down and expose his hardness, his cock wasn't huge, but it was so hard. I flicked my tongue over the head very slowly. He moaned, God I did not want him to cum so soon. I want his cock deep inside my hot ass. In one quick stroke, I yank his shorts all the way down. He kicks them off. I roll to my belly and push my pantied ass high in the air. I feel him move past the steering wheel and climb onto my backside and slide my panties down. His cock trying to find my pussy, I let him slide it back and forth with several strokes, I reach behind and guide it to my ass.

I'm not convinced he knows the difference, and am well aware it will not be the long fuck session I desire. I wet my fingers, reach behind me and slide my saliva over my ass. I do this a couple of times to get enough wetness for me to feel comfortable. He finds the target. He is pressing, more pressure. I am pushing . . .it begins to hurt. I know once it slides in, the pain will diminish. I moan, no pleasure yet! I'm sure he is clueless to the pain I am experiencing. I moan again, as he slides his long slim shaft deeper into my ass. Aww, it is feeling better. He moans loudly. Exactly as I thought! He shoots his load after two strokes!

I realize again why I like men so much more than these inexperienced boys. I feel his hot cum squirting deep in my ass. I moan with pleasured appreciation. He grunts as it slides out. He rolls back behind the steering wheel and collapses.

I look around to the back seat to check on Marianne. She is engaged in another passionate kiss. Her top is off and he is sucking her large firm breasts. Her panties remain on, I am not understanding, she's not a virgin. Does she not like this guy? He is pulling at her panties as they passionately kiss once more. I hear her whisper, "No Danny, you don't have a condom…" Poor Marianne is going to go without. Good for her, no condom, no pussy. I will talk with her and possibly teach her my ass trick. It may not be the same, but oh how I love my ass getting fucked.

It appears I'm going to have to take control here. I open my door, slide out and hop into the back seat. Danny's pants are down, his cock at attention. His cock is pointing directly at Marianne's mouth. She is rejecting it. I haven't asked her if she sucks cock, I supposed she had, at least for her jackass brother. Oh well.

I move around in front of Marianne's closed mouth and slide his hard cock into mine taking as much as I could slide down my throat. I roll my eyes and look up at Marianne, she seemed relieved. I've got to talk to this girl. I slide his cock in and out of my mouth. It is rock hard, I knew it would be shooting any second. Bingo! I took two huge squirts in my mouth. I pull it out, two more squirts in my face. Marianne's face is close to mine as I point it at her . . . squirt, squirt. She is gritting her teeth while grinning. I want to tell her so badly that it's all OK as it dribbles down her chin, nose and her cheeks. Thank goodness it missed her eyes! She relaxed a bit as Danny sank into the seat. I am still so turned on. I have a partial load in my mouth, cum dripping down my face, Marianne with cum covering her cheeks and nose. Looking to her, I have no control. I want her. I grab her head, pull her toward me and press my lips to hers. I force my tongue and his cum into her mouth. She accepted and returned my passion with a kiss, my tongue flirting with hers. She tastes the load that my mouth delivered. She sucked in my tongue as our tongues dance back and forth. I ran my mouth up her cheeks and cross her nose licking any excess cum that remained, clinging to her face.

My mouth now on hers, she sucks and licks the cum from my tongue. Oh, how I love her. I move my mouth ever so slowly down and began kissing her breasts. I am so fucking hot! I suck her nipples, first one then the other; she is so passionate! Is this real? Can this be happening, I ask myself? If it's a dream let's enjoy this eroticity!

I move down her body, my tongue making a path to her belly, in and out of her belly button. I cannot stop. I'm going down, down, as my thumbs slide Marianne's panties off. My God, I thought she had no pubic hair. I find a perfectly trimmed, blond bush. I suck in her arranged thick pubic hairs. Marianne is pushing it wildly in my face! I am so out of control. My tongue has located her wet hole, its wetness is driving me crazier. I ram my tongue deep inside her. Oh my God, how I love the taste of her juices. I am lapping them up as her pussy pounds my face. I look up to see Danny watching in awe, his look almost humorous. He's shocked. Has he never seen a woman suck pussy before! I smile to myself.

I hear the car door open behind me. I feel a hand lift my ass off the seat, I move to my knees, as I bury my face deeper into Marianne's blond pussy. Oh my God! I feel a cock slide into my ass. I don't look, it must be Ty. I continue ramming my tongue in and out of Marianne. She is moaning wildly. My ass is high in the air with a cock slamming in and out. This is my day! I raise my face and scream, "Yes, fuck me!" I can feel the overflow dripping between my legs.

Marianne is wildly grinding her pussy in my face. I feel her tremble. She grabs my hair with both hands, from the back of my head, and pulls my face deeper into her hot wet pussy. Her juices are flowing, she is cumming in my hot mouth. I lick and suck. I love this flavor, it tastes so much different than male cum, God, how I love Marianne's pussy.

I hear the door open. Danny slides out, going to take a break I suppose. I continue running my tongue in and out of Marianne's hot box not wanting to miss a drop. My ass still in the air, I feel hands caressing my cheeks. Oh my God, now Danny is ready for more. He rams his hard cock into my open juicy hole, pounds my ass four times and moans loudly. I feel his hot sperm squirt all over. I feel his cum dripping from my ass.

I continue sucking and licking Marianne. She pushes my face away and says, "Amanda, I love you, I need to kiss you." I move my mouth closer and we passionately kiss. We both take a deep breath as I hold her hand in mine. "Whatta Day . . . O'La Lay." We all settle back in our seats.

"Wow," I say aloud now relaxing in the back with Marianne on one side and now Danny on the other. Ty, who moved back to the front exclaims, "That was the best parade I've ever experienced." While shaking his head, Danny chimes in, "Wow, you girls are too hot, sure wish you lived closer!" This was great for now, but I have no desire to fuck you guys again. Once was more than enough. I enjoy men so much more than these young boys.

After catching our breath and composing ourselves, we went about retrieving panties, tops, skirts and slacks to get redressed. Ty started the car and we drove back to town. "When can we see you girls again?" Danny inquired. I spoke up, "I'll give you my cell number." Danny found a pen and jotted it down. Of course, I gave him a fictitious number. "Where is your car, Amanda?" "It's by that little strip mall just before the main street."

He pulls into the parking area, "Which car?" he asks. I could see Marianne's face grimacing. I look around and point, he pulled up beside a yellow convertible corvette. "Wow," Ty is taken back, "That is beautiful." "Yes, I enjoy it." "How do you afford that ride?" "A lady must work hard," I reply. They let us out and we give the boys a peck on the lips and say our goodbyes. As they are driving off, I am searching my purse for my keys. They turn the corner and Marianne literally jumps up and down. We do a high-five and laugh and laugh.

"Amanda, you are too cool!!" "Well, thank you Marianne, you did quite well yourself, I think we both have outdone ourselves." "Now, how do we get home?" "Call your brother!!" Marianne dials his number. "Hi Chad, can you come pick us up at the strip mall by town?" She listened, said, "OK," and hung the phone up. "He has a date and is already late, he can't." "Give me the phone." I push redial. Chad answers, "Chad, Amanda, we need a ride now, we'll be at the coffee shop in the strip mall." "OK," he replies obediently, "give me fifteen minutes." I hang up. "Marianne, let's go into the shop and get a coke, I'm really thirsty." "Amanda, how did you do that?" I look at her and smile, "It was my serious tone of voice." Marianne is totally baffled. I wasn't ready to tell her that story. In fact, I was uncertain that I ever would.

We ordered soft drinks and discuss our rendezvous with the boys. "Marianne," I whisper, "You have not sucked a cock, have you?" "No." "I just assumed between your brother and your neighbor, you had." "No, they never asked me. It never really came about. They just stick their cocks in me, cum and leave." I

understood. "Amanda, don't you worry about getting pregnant?" "You don't use a condom?" I sighed and whispered, "I'm still a virgin." Marianne sucked her breath in and gasped loudly in a shocked low voice, "Amanda, I watched you get fucked three times today!!" "Yes, I did Marianne, they fucked my ass. I won't get pregnant." "Oh my God, are you serious?" "Yes!" "It must hurt so much." "Only the first few times, after that, it's great!" "Well, you certainly were enjoying yourself, wasn't it messy?" "Marianne, when there is a possibility of a fucking, I spend extra time in the bathroom so I don't have a messy trip." "Wow, you're still a virgin, I wish I was." "Marianne, just because you're not, you don't have to let the guys fuck your pussy. You keep the count down. I can say, I have not had sex with guys. I don't consider what I do as true sex. Sex is getting your pussy fucked…I was very proud of you today. I could see how hot you were, and yet you stuck with no condom, no sex. You were in control, and once you learn to suck cock and take it in your ass, it opens a new world. Of course, I have no idea how it feels getting my pussy fucked. I enjoy what I do immensely. The guys are happy with my two holes, I'm saving my third."

Chad pulls up and toots his horn. We paid for our drinks, fly out the door and climb in. "Oh Chad, so nice of you to take time away from your busy schedule to pick us up." No answer, just a grunt. Marianne is still at a loss on this one. Chad drops me off and I thank him again. I walk up the drive. My panties are so slimy. I feel the wetness on my crotch and the air blowing up and under my little skirt. Geez, you'd think I'd had enough for one day, yet I am thinking of more. I touch the back of my panties, rub my fingers in the soggy wetness and stick them to my nose. I breathe in and smell the cum. It excites me too much.

CHAPTER 14

Stories of Bargain Bob

Bandit is barking a big, "Hello!" I go to the pen and let him loose. He likes my um soaked panties as well. I grab his stick and give it a toss, that always works. t's six-thirty, mom is in the kitchen, "How was the parade honey?" "Oh Mom, it vas so much fun, we had a great day." "Who drove you home?" "Marianne's rother." "Oh, that was nice of him." "Mom, where is Dad?" "He went to town to ave a beer or two. Uncle Ken is still painting…I'm sure he'll be in soon and we'll ave dinner." "OK Mom, I'm going to go take a shower and I'll set the table." "OK loney, dinner will be ready around seven."

I grab my robe and jump in the shower, take off my skirt and top and pull down ny panties. I could not help but sniff the cum stains. I take my shower and slip back) my room. I put on a little blue clingy top, white shorts and pink lacy panties. I rush my hair, touch up my face and skip back to the kitchen.

Uncle Ken is now in the house. I give him a hug and tell him all about the arade. "Hey, I have something for you," I tell Uncle Ken, as I finish setting the ble. Mom sets our dinner on the table, the aroma is causing my stomach to growl. Jmmmm, bean soup with ham, I am so hungry. I hand Bob's card to Uncle Ken, s we sat down. He smiled, "Where did you come across Bargain Bob?" As we pass e soup around, I told him about the parade, the diner and all of Bob's gang and eir "O'La Lay's." Uncle Ken laughs out loud with mom smiling. "Yes, Bob is one f a kind." Ken went on, "I think he's been married at least three times, left each ne and travels with quite the entourage. The 'O'La Lay' guy. I once sat in a bar ear his group, including his cousins, that group changes depending on who appens to be along. There are thirty or forty in his so-called family, as they call

each other, cousins, and brothers, on and on." I laugh out loud, "Uncle Ken, that is exactly what they were telling me. Of course, it's not true, right?" "No, but they are like family. They are just a good fun group. Anyway, the 'O'La Lay' guy, Bob, claims to have brought him here from some remote island in the Caribbean, in a canoe!" "Is that true?" "I doubt it, but they do tell it quite convincingly." "I told Bob I wanted to be a cousin." "He told you that you had to earn it, right?" "Yes, how did you know?" "I've watched Bob and his antics for years." "Oh, I didn't tell you one of the most important things, Miss Capitol City was with them and I met her. She is so beautiful and so nice, I hope I have the opportunity to really talk to her someday. I want to be just like her." "Amanda, she will be appearing at a lot of local events, you certainly could get that opportunity." "I hope so. Does Dad know Bob?" Mom answers, "Of course Amanda, most everyone knows Bob. Your Dad, like Ken, went to school with him." "Were his Mom and Dad wealthy?" "No," answers Uncle Ken, "he grew up dirt poor. I heard him tell the story one night. He knew at a very young age he would be a millionaire. He didn't know how he would make it happen. He was driven, most folks don't have that in them." Mom smiles, "Amanda, you remind me of him." I agree, "Mom, I'm not certain why, but I feel such a connection to him, it's so strange."

Mom quickly changes the subject. "Honey, are you ready for school on Tuesday?" Oh wow! I've been so busy; I'd forgotten how close it was. "Yes Mom, I'll be ready. Actually, I'm excited, I'm going to learn lots of stuff." "With that kind of language, you better learn some stuff Amanda! The bus picks you up at eight ten. You're the last pickup, that is good but you're the last off in the afternoon." I love my high school so much. Years ago our school had separate teachers for each class. Now one teacher teaches all subjects, more budget cuts! Oh well, it's OK. "Mom for my birthday, can we go to Cadillac's? Bob gave me a card for two free dinners." "We'll see Amanda." "Why haven't we been there Mom?" "I don't know, it's pretty far. When we go out, we normally stay in town." "Uncle Ken, have you been there?" "Yes, I have," he answered. "What is it like?" "Oh, it's beautiful, like Vegas, very elegant and great food." "Please, Mom, can we go for my birthday?" "We'll see honey." Dinner is finished and Uncle Ken said good night as I helped clean up. "When will Dad be home?" "Who knows, I don't expect him too early." I went off to feed Bandit and tuck him in for the night.

Wow, what a busy day, going to the parade, meeting Bob and his gang, getting fucked three times and licking Marianne's pussy. That was fun. And using my taxi service for the first time; what a day! I gave myself a big "O'La Lay," turned on my music and soon was drifting off as Jack passed through my mind, probably a dream. Why had I not heard from him?

Labor Day weekend flew by. The boys placed third in the tournament. Dad got home late Saturday night. He and Ken painted the house Sunday and Monday. I was about half finished.

CHAPTER 15

Sam and Roy

Tuesday morning, eight a.m. I'm waiting for the bus. The bus pulls up to a stop beside me. I climb the stairs onto the bus. Ray is our driver, same as last year. He is in his late forties, wears a ball cap and has a bit of a bulge in his belly area. "Hi Amanda, you've certainly grown over the summer," he said as he looked me up and down very carefully. I was wearing another little girl skirt with a tight top and no bra, of course. I counted thirteen others on the bus. I sat down by a boy named Roy. He had grown from spring as well.

"Hi Amanda, you are looking hot!" Roy's comment sounded stupid to me coming from his mouth as he seems like such a little squirt. Although he's my age, he's so naive and immature. "Thank you Roy." He is staring at my long legs. Of course, I didn't mind. "What did you do all summer?" he asked. "I kept very busy Roy, long stories that probably would bore you to tears." "Try me," he replies. What could I tell this kid to humor him? "OK, Saturday afternoon after the parade, a girlfriend and I stole a yellow corvette, picked up a guy, took him to the park and gave him a blow job." His eyes opened wide as his mouth fell open. "Wow, how in the world did you start the car?" he asked. "Someone left the keys in the ignition." "Do you still have it?" "Roy, if I still had it, would I be riding the bus?" "I guess not." "So, Amanda, do you like giving blow jobs?" he asked. "Oh, it's OK, I like the men to cum on my tits much better." "Holy crap Amanda," he chuckled, "that's awesome!" We arrive at school. I was ready for the bus ride to be over.

I walk down the hallway. Oh my goodness, there were pretty girls everywhere. How many had a summer like mine? How many were virgins? How many think of sex continuously? It was the first day and I already had so many questions,

before the year is over, I vowed, I would have some answers.

I took my seat in the front. I counted twenty-eight students in our class. Mr. Jackson introduced himself. He was new to the school, very handsome and well dressed. I would guess him to be around thirty. I see the beautiful female school-teachers on the news having sex with their male students, of course most of whom are much younger. I do wonder why are the male teachers not on the news as well? They don't fool around or they just don't get caught? I'll work on that one. I smile and crossed my legs. Mr. Jackson returned the smile.

The first day of school was going rather well. I think he will be good for our class. He basically told us what to expect of him and what he expected from us. He went over each subject one at a time and gave us an overview of what he would teach in the class. He was articulate, I liked that. We took turns around the room introducing ourselves. "Amanda," he said with a straight and formal voice, "what do you plan to get from your year in this class? Stand up and tell the class." I looked around the room, took a deep breath and stood up. "Well, first Mr. Jackson, I would like to say I am impressed on how articulate and organized you are. I really want to learn more of our U.S. history, mathematics, social studies, and world history. Hopefully, we can touch on sexual education." (The class laughs). "We all need more of an understanding in that area as well, including the need for birth control. I believe we will learn from you and you will probably learn something from us." The class applauded, wow! Mr. Jackson smiles, "Well thank you Amanda, very good." I felt good. I gave myself an "O'La Lay."

When class was over, several classmates came by to introduce themselves and some even congratulated me. I was happy. Mr. Jackson motions for me to come up to his desk. "Amanda," he said in matter of fact tone, "I can see you are not my normal student. I pride myself on reading my students quite well and you seem somehow to be blessed with something most will never understand. I'm not certain how deep that may be, of course, I only met you today. But Amanda, I encourage you to stay with whatever it is. Yes, I will learn from you and the others in this class. Much of this class will likely learn from you." "Thank you Mr. Jackson." I walked out of the room not fully understanding, but I knew I would figure it out someday soon.

The first day and no homework, that was good. The little bus is waiting out in front of the school. I climb on. Roy is waving and waving to me. "Hey Amanda, come sit with Sam and me." I hadn't noticed Sam before. He was a bit taller than Roy. I still had two inches on him. He had a big happy smile. "Hi Amanda, Roy told me all about you." I wondered what Roy had told him. "Did you really go joy riding in a yellow corvette?" "Of course, I certainly wouldn't lie." "I told ya!" Roy pipes up. "Wow, that is awesome! Do you really give blow jobs?" His straight forwardness was amazing. "Sometimes, if the right cock comes along." "Wow!" is all he could come up with. "Can I get a blow job?" "Sure, I'll pick you up in the yellow corvette when I borrow it again and I'll suck you off." "All right," he stammers, "you want my cell number?" "No, I'll just stop by your house, I'll want to meet your Mom and Dad." "Ohhhh, I don't know about that." "Well Sam, if I

an't meet your Mom and Dad, how could I suck your huge cock?" I smile to myself, this is too much fun. Sam did not have an answer. Roy jumps in, "Amanda, you bring the 'vette over to my house, you can meet my Mom and Dad." "Perfect, I'll let you know as soon as I have it again." "Awesome!" Roy seems to be happy now. I can't wait to meet Mom and Dad.

The bus stops at Sam's house. He stands up and moves to the aisle. "Amanda, it was really good to meet you, see you tomorrow." "Bye, bye." It's Roy and me. "Amanda, you are awesome." "Thank you Roy." I ran my hand over his trousers. "Why don't you show me your big cock?" "Amanda, I couldn't do that." "Why not Roy?" He breathes in very nervously, "I don't know, I just can't." "You do have one, right?" He stammers, "Ya . . . yes, it's not that big though." "Well OK, show me your little cock." I love watching the boy squirm and how I'm embarrassing him, this is way too much fun. We are pulling up in front of Roy's house. He jumps up and out. "Amanda, I'll see you tomorrow." I am so entertaining. I amaze myself.

My stop is next so I walk up by our bus driver Ray while waiting for my stop. I feel Ray's eyes on my ass and long legs. The bus stops and he pulls the door handle. "Have a nice night Amanda." "Bye Ray."

The night passes quickly and is pretty much uneventful. Up in the morning and I'm off to school, my bus is right on time. I slide between Roy and Sam. They seem a bit more relaxed today. Roy had obviously told Sam that I asked to see his cock. Sam touched my leg and said, "Amanda, I'll show you my cock." I smile, "Sam, save it for the ride home." I rub my hand over their jeans. Sam is a bit braver. He is rubbing two fingers on my bare leg. I roll my eyes and smile to myself, a girl does what a girl has to do. I let him tickle my leg. Soon Roy was tickling the other, it was good fun.

In my classroom, I settle into my desk. Mr. Jackson is a great teacher. He does not dwell on one subject. He makes us think about how the subjects relate to our world. We move to politics and how politicians function. I raise my hand. He points to me. I ask, "How on a bipartisan basis does anything ever become law or agreed upon when no two people in our universe seem to think exactly alike? How is anything ever really accomplished?" Mr. Jackson asks, "Does anyone have an answer?" He points at a boy in the back. "I think most people think pretty much the same way with similar ideas." Another hand up, "That's not true," she argues, "my Mom and I can't even get along!" (Lots of laughter in the class). My hand goes up again. "Yes, Amanda." "The Republicans and Democrats seldom agree on anything, how do we manage to get laws passed? Is there a connection as to why our state is broke and our economy is struggling? No one thinks alike, yet we make laws and deals that attempt to make everyone happy, but in the long run, never seem to work as well as planned." "Amanda, there is merit in what you are saying. Our politicians are made up mostly of judges, attorneys and doctors. They are an educated group, but know little about running a business. Our economy should be treated as a business. Most politicians have never had to pay payroll taxes and be profitable. They are very good spending our money with no returns, it is a very complex issue. We won't solve

it all today in this class. We should get back to our studies. Thank you, class for your insight and thoughts." We moved on to social studies.

School is out for another day and we are on the bus. I give Ray a little wink as I pass. I feel his eyes wander over my body. I slide to my seat between Roy and Sam at the back of the bus. "How was school Amanda?" Sam asked. They both are in my grade as well, although in a different class. "It was great! I just love my teacher. We talk about many subjects."

The bus is moving and both have a hand on each of my legs. I move a leg a bit closer to each, which encourages them to slide their hands a bit higher. The seats around us are empty. I pull my skirt up a bit more and expose my white lacy panties. They do like that. I slide down in the seat just a bit as they slide their fingers upward. They are tickling my pussy. I reach a hand to each of their crotches. Oh my, they are very hard. I stroke their hardness a bit faster running my hands up and down, up and down their jeans. Sam pulls his hand off my panties, stiffens his body and pushes my hand away. I look at his face. He has an embarrassed look. I am still stroking Roy. Suddenly, same reaction! I realize what's happening, these boys have cum in their pants. Oh well, it's fun watching them squirm. I put my hand on their wetness. "Guys, what is this?" I stick my finger under their noses, still, no answer. "Is this your cum guys?" No answer, they may not know what it is. A few weeks earlier, I hadn't known. I only learned this summer. "Wow, guys . . . it is your cum! If you cum in your pants again, I will not be sitting with you, OK?" I asked. "OK, Amanda," they answered in unison.

We pull to Sam's stop. He walks up the aisle covering his wet spots with his books. Roy whispers in my ear, "Amanda, will you help us, we don't know what to do and we want to have sex with you so bad!" "We'll work on that tomorrow," promised him. It is now his stop. "Bye Roy."

I moved up front and stood by Ray at the door. I face him and move my legs apart just a bit as I look directly at his eyes. He watches the road and gazes quickly to my direction. "How was your day, Ray?" "Very nice," he exclaimed as he took a deep breath. I reach down to scratch my leg, lifting my dress a couple of inches. Ewww...Ray liked that. "Better watch the road Ray," as the bus swerved a bit. We stop at my house. I jump down the stairs as Ray opens the door. I turn and wink. "Night Ray." I walk up my drive. My white panties are damp. Two little boys tickling my pussy and Ray ogling my body, I love that dampness between my legs.

Another relaxing night at home, I have dinner with the family, watch the news, read the daily paper, and talk with my brothers who see me in a whole different light. It's a good thing they don't see me as just that kid anymore. I am becoming a woman.

Time for bed, I say my goodnights, shower and turn on my music. Before going to bed, I give Marianne a call. We reminisce about the previous Saturday and laugh. School was good, and we would see each other very soon.

CHAPTER 16

⟨Religion⟩

Up in the morning, a quick breakfast and off to school. The bus is right on time.
I slide in between Roy and Sam. They seem a bit shy today. I must have really intimidated them. "Oh, come on guys, we had fun. I was too hard on you both, it's
OK." They smiled as some of the embarrassment eased. I put a hand on each leg
and promised them some fun on the trip home, that lightened the mood. "Give us
a clue Amanda, one little clue?" Sam asked. They were all ears. "I'm going to
teach you a new trick." Roy piped in an innocent tone, "Amanda, I don't like
magic." "You wait and see." We chatted about our teachers and classmates. The
bus arrives at school. Off we go for another day of learning.

Mr. Jackson greets me at the classroom door. "Good morning Amanda, you look
very nice today." The room was soon seated and we began our studies.

The lunch bell rang. I see Sam and Roy in the lunch area eating their lunch and
decide to join them. "Another clue, Amanda?" begged Sam. "Find a seat toward
the back of the bus with as few other students around as possible," I whisper. "OK,"
he whispers back.

Later that afternoon in class, I approached Mr. Jackson as he was standing by his
desk. "Mr. Jackson, my dad once told me, when you believe in someone, you should
let them know. These first few days of school, I've come to believe in you." "Thank
you Amanda." I walked back to my desk and sat down.

We cover many subjects and as usual, odd discussions arise from his teaching
style. We moved onto religion. Most students seem to have some interest. Mr.
Jackson made it clear this was class conversation and he was not condoning religion
in any way. Someone asked, "Why are there so many religions?" "Different peo-

ple interpret the same book in many different ways," Mr. Jackson answered. "As we discussed yesterday, no two people think exactly alike." I raised my hand, he pointed to me. "Why is it the Arab countries believe in a God while their children, at a very young age, are brought up to hate our God and to kill and hate Americans?" I go on, "Millions of people hate us, is it religion that caused this, or have we treated Arab countries unjustly?" "Amanda, I'm not going to attempt to answer that question. It is a very complex issue, we could debate it for days." I raise my hand again, "May I ask another question?" "Sure, go ahead Amanda." "Is organized religion something that is needed by certain people for security purposes or do some believe that our God actually is going to help them with their trivial problems as minuet as most are? Millions die each year of starvation, disease and common accidents. Many countries have storms, tsunamis, cyclones, and hurricanes that kill hundreds of thousands. In many of these countries, all many have are their families. They live in little shacks and huts. Many families lose their sons, daughters, moms and dads in these storms. Many do not even know of any God, why is this? And, Mr. Jackson why is it that there are certain books in the bible that we don't know who wrote them, including the Book of Revelations? The bible was written fifty years after these different stories occurred. Mr. Jackson, you and I can't remember factually what happened last month, let alone fifty years ago. Were they smarter than us, or had much better memories? I'm sorry Mr. Jackson, I could go on, but I'm going to stop." The room was completely silent. Mr. Jackson gazed at me wide-eyed. I think I had lost the majority of the class awhile ago. "Well," Mr. Jackson finally piped, "thank you for all the insight and yes, it's time to slow down. Truly, these are difficult questions. Class, any response?" No sound, the class was dead silent. I believe at this point all were certainly contemplating my questions. The bell rings, school is out for another day, now time for my trick on the bus.

"Amanda, come up here please." I walk to Mr. Jackson's desk. "You are a very bright student. Whatever your age, you ask questions far beyond. There are no simple answers, you have raised questions that I have not considered. Amanda, I'm not sure anyone really has the answers. You keep asking, hopefully you will find the answers. Please tell me when you do." "OK, see you tomorrow!" I walk away. He was a good teacher, but even he had no answers. Why was that?

CHAPTER 17

Busted

"Hi Ray!" I give him a sexy wink and stand directly beside him just behind the steering wheel. I love watching his eyes move down my body. I know he's fantasizing about peeking under my skirt.

Sam and Roy followed my directions very well. They have a seat, second from the back. Nine other passengers, all toward the front, perfect.

The newest passenger is a beautiful little girl that has not ridden our bus this year until today. I'm not sure what her story is; she seems more mature than the rest of us. I think she may be related to Ray. She rode this bus every two to three weeks last year as well. She has short dark hair, big blue eyes and beautiful long eyelashes. She wears glasses that are so cool…they are rectangular in shape, black rims with a red stripe across the top and a little red teardrop on the wide corners. I'm not normally a glasses kinda gal, but I would love to wear those any day.

As I pass her, I smile and give her a wink. I am so brave these days. She nods and smiles in return. She has a skirt that is shorter than mine. She is very busty with a white tee shirt in which I can see the outline of her lacy black bra. I catch her eyes checking out my body as I move past her seat.

My boys are excited as I slide between them. I realize I don't have much time. My goal is that they won't cum in their pants today. Ray is putting our bus in motion. I whisper in each of their ears, "Unzip your pants." They look at each other, I ordered again. You would've thought I said 'take this cyanide pill! Now, guys!' They obeyed. With each of my hands, I slid into their underwear while lifting my legs a bit. As my skirt slid up exposing my tiny crotchless panties, my bush poking through the open crotch, both their eyes riveted to my pussy hairs. I

doubt they had ever seen a hairy bush before. I spread my legs a bit more while feeling them getting hard. I was very careful, I didn't want any cum in their pants. I slide my body down the seat while watching Ray closely. He was paying no attention. Good. "Take your cocks out," I ordered. They looked bewildered. "Guys," I blurted, "I didn't say take cyanide, take out your dicks!" That worked, two little cocks standing at attention. I slide down in the seat a bit more. I slide up my dark-blue low top and expose my little titties and very erect nipples. I slide my hand to each cock and stroke them just a bit, we want no cum yet. I know it won't be long. I tug on their cocks and guide them toward each titty. I peek over the seat to check on Ray, we're OK. I guide their little pricks in my titty direction. Over the seat in front of us is my little dark haired girl from a few seats up. She gives me a smile that assures me it's OK. "I just want to watch," she whispers. I lick my lips at her smile and continue. Both cocks are pointed directly at my erect nipples. I pull their bodies two inches closer, their little cocks are touching each nipple. I let go of their cocks and find their hand and guide each to their hardness. They know what to do, both are simultaneously stroking. My hand is rubbing on my hot little titties. I look up at the girl, she has to be so hot! I wanted to kiss her mouth so badly. The boys stroke themselves a few times and wow, here it comes, first one and immediately the second, squirting their hot cum all over my erect nipples. The aroma of cum, the sensation as I massage my nipples, oh my God! My dark haired girl loves the show. I see the excitement in her eyes and the expression on her face.

The bus has stopped a routine stop, I suppose. I am rubbing their slimy loads all over my titties. I am having so much fun. The look on the girl's face makes it ever more erotic.

The bus is not moving. I look up away from my slimy titties. Standing in the aisle is Ray with his hands on each hip. "What the hell is going on here?" The boys zipped up their jeans, myself pulling down my dark-blue silky top. He shouts, "This is my bus, what the hell is this? You are disgusting, a disgrace, come with me," and points to the front. They both follow him to the front seat. "I will be talking to both your parents," as he drives away. He drops them both off at their stops while shouting, "Your parents will be hearing from me tonight!"

Well, at least the little girl was in no trouble, she was only a spectator. Next stop was hers. She smiled with a very sexy twist, as she walked to the door. "Amanda come sit up front!" shouts Ray. I slide out of my seat and to the right of Ray in front. "Amanda, I must take you to your home and have a talk with your Mom and Dad." He looks over his shoulder; my top is wet with cum stains. Around my titties was wetness showing all down my top. "Look at you," he quips as he stares at my cum-soaked top. I think I am in big trouble. Is there a way out? "Ray, please you cannot tell my Mom and Dad. We were only having a little fun." I uncross my legs and expose my skimpy panties. "I will do anything Ray, please," I whisper, "my life will be destroyed." Ray, while steering the bus, cannot take his eyes off of my exposed bush. "Ray," I say softly, "why don't you pull the bus in that little turn off up the road so we can talk." He licks his lips and glances repeatedly in my

lirection. He steers the bus to the turn off and stops under the big tree and swings ⊃ward me in his seat. Still sitting, he says, "Amanda, what am I going to do with ⁻ou?" I smile my sexiest smile as I touch my cum-soaked titties through my top. Ray, I'm sure we can think of something." He stood up and took a step toward me. Ie reaches to his crotch and grabs himself. "Can I help with that?" I ask, as I con-ˈnue massaging my nipples. "Yes, you can," he said in a low raspy voice. He un-ipped his pants, slid his hand through his zipper and pulled out his erect cock. You asked for it, Amanda . . . get on your knees." I smile and obey. His cock was ᴏ very long and so big around with a huge head. I flick my tongue over the head, ᴇ groaned. I kissed it slowly, it was so juicy. I flick my tongue over the head, his ⅃ices leaking, it tasted so good. "Put it in your mouth," he commanded. I open my ɪouth as wide as I could. I could only get the huge head inside. "Open up bitch!" ᴇ commands. I stretched, he pressed. I am choking. I could not take any more. ⁻he more excited he became, his cock seemed to grow. It was so hard and was etting yet harder. It is now like a rock in my mouth. He is calling me his eautiful cocksucker. I love his talk. He screams, "Take it you bitch!" He groans ꜱ his head fell backward. His juices are squirting and squirting in my mouth. He ulls it out. It continues to squirt in my face and all over my hair. I feel his slime ᵣipping down my face. Wow, so much cum!

He slumped back in the driver's seat, zipped his pants and looked at me. Amanda, you are my beautiful cocksucker." I took in my breath, "You'll never tell ɪy Mom and Dad, right?" "Honey, as long as you take care of me, they will 'never' now." "Thank you Ray." I straighten myself. "Ray, it's not that far, I can walk from ᴇre." He opened the door, "OK Amanda, see you tomorrow."

CHAPTER 18

Busted Once More

I open the door. Dad is sitting at the kitchen table. Oh my God, why is he home? "Hi Amanda." I'm dead! I was still completely covered in cum from Ray and the boys. I hunch down quickly. "Amanda, are you all right?" I try to avoid him. I quickly look down. "Amanda, what is in your hair?" Oh God, Dad walks to me and runs his fingers through my hair, he feels and then sniffs. "It's cum, Amanda, what is going on, what is this?" "Nothing Dad," I said as I crash into a chair with my head down. He notices my top with wetness from my tits to my navel. He takes a deep breath, he starts to get upset. "Where have you been, have you been raped?" "No Dad, please!" "Please what?" he asks. "Don't ask," I plead. "Amanda, you must talk to me now." Tears running from my eyes down my cheeks. "Dad, I did not have sex." Dad rolls his eyes and shouts, "Amanda, look at you, cum in your hair all over your top." "Dad, I did not have sex!" "Amanda, you're not Bill Clinton." (The thought flashes through my mind, Bill explained it away and got away with it now can I?) I stop my tears. "Dad, I let two boys cum on me on the bus. I enjoyed it, so did they." "And you walked past Ray with cum everywhere and he was totally oblivious?" Dad got out of his seat, "I'm going to go have a talk with Ray, as well as the principal." "No Dad, please sit down." Another very deep breath. "Ray did catch me with the boys in the back of the bus. He was bringing me home to tell you and Mom. I offered him anything to secure his silence. I let him cum in my face." "What? That son of a bitch," he says as he is getting out of his chair for the second time and moving toward the door. "No!" I shout. "Dad, I enticed him. I showed him my tits, I told him what he could do to me, it's not Ray's fault, I enticed him, am at blame!" Dad took a deep breath as he stood by the door. "Why on earth

would you let a man do this to you?" "Dad, it's not sex, I am a virgin and I promise you I will remain that way. I encouraged all three to have fun with me." "You call this fun Amanda?" "Dad, I need to tell you the truth, please sit down." Dad moved to his chair and sat down and looked at me so intensely. He was shaking, I could tell he was shocked. "Dad, I have sexual thoughts, fantasies and desires that control my mind. I think of sexual fun continuously. Perhaps they are wrong, but I don't want them to go away ever. It may be demons, I may be possessed, but Dad, I love it so much!"

A solemn silent look comes over Dad. He calmed down. He stared at me for what felt like a very long time. "Amanda, I have to tell you something concerning your Mother. What you're feeling, I'm afraid, you have been born with." Now I was the one taken aback. I listened intently as Dad continued. "She experienced many of these same sexual feelings and desires when she was growing up. I hoped her ways in her early days would not be passed along. We believed they hadn't. We didn't think there was any way that they would pass to our daughter. Your Grandmother sent your Mom to doctors, psychiatrists and many counselors when she was very young. They would explain why and how she was the way she was, very complex issues, of course. It was a waste of her time and their money. Mom does admit that. I relate exactly to what you have just shared. Mom loved the thoughts, the feelings, the pleasure of fooling around with the little neighbor boys. This was when she was twelve and younger. She was quite cautious and smart. When your Mom was twelve, her mother caught her with her shorts down with a neighbor boy. Her mom was very upset and sent her again to multitudes of doctors, counselors and psychiatrists."

"Your Mom got a bit wiser after that experience. She let her Mom believe it would never happen again. That worked, although she continued fooling around. She could not stop. She does not know to this day why those desires never left her while she was young. She believes she was possessed. I believe it to be perhaps a hormone imbalance which some are born with Amanda. It's not a terrible thing, although you must learn to control it. Don't let it control you! Your Mom handled it so well until her early twenties, then her life changed. Someday, she may tell you that story. You must never harm anyone with your sexuality. Amanda, with your beauty and your desires, wow! You will be dangerous to the men of this world. You will break hearts while crushing minds and souls. Your Mom was blessed with beautiful looks, that smile and her personality. Amanda, do your best to control your emotions, be honest and more often than not, the problems from the heart will belong with your suitors and their emotions. Try not to mislead people, always be honest." I listened obediently. I wanted to hear more.

"Well young lady, this is all we can say for now. I think it best if we don't share this with your Mom. She will tell you of where these things took her in her own time, I suppose." "Oh Dad, thank you so much for sharing this story, I have a much better understanding. I could never have begun to understand on my own." I gave Dad a hug and he sent me to shower.

As I stood in the shower with the hot water spraying over my body, my conversation with Dad played over and over in my mind. I had somewhat more of an understanding. Was this a curse or blessing? I wasn't certain, when the time comes, Mom will help me. Am I really a danger to men? Was my Mom? That was not likely. I must always remain in control. I felt I was capable. Do I need counseling? I do love what I know of my sexuality so much, I don't want it to change. Thank God Dad made the decision not to inform Mom, let her choose the time to tell me of "her" early sexuality! Perhaps, she could not handle knowing her only daughter has her early-uncontrolled desires. Is it simply a hormonal imbalance or are these issues much more complex?

Somehow my mind has eased knowing there are others with my desires. I see no reason to adjust my life. I can and will handle it. Look out men, dangerous or not, Amanda is on the prowl. God, if Dad or Mom ever knew what this summer has brought to my life, can this obsession with sexual activity all come from Mom, or is there much more to this? I suppose time will tell! Out of the shower, I put it all out of mind as I get dressed.

I decide to take Bandit for a run. As we walk down the road, my mind flashes back to Jack. Why has he not called? Maybe he has lost my number. Oh well, not much I can do about that. Bandit found a giant stick. Oh geez, it's a flipping log! "Bandit, I can't lift this one, let's find something I can toss." We play toss the stick and I put Bandit back in his pen and serve him his dinner. Mom and the boys are home. We have dinner, watch the news and then I head off to my room. For me, it's been another day of learning and growing. I drift off while wondering…how much more is there to learn and understand? I have difficulty believing my sexuality can be blamed on Mom's genes and chromosomes! Can it be that simple?

CHAPTER 19

My Bus Driver

Getting on the bus, Ray gives me an overly friendly "good morning" and a look that I don't really care for. His eyes roam over my body, I smile. Hmm, is it just me? The look on his face is a cocky arrogance that reminds me of Chad. He's had my mouth, now he thinks I'm his. Yeah, it's probably just me I decide as I move to my seat.

My dark haired girl waves me to her seat. She's as gorgeous as ever. She is wearing a little short skirt, a hot low cleavage top showing her every contour. She's so busty. I love her hot look.

She is so excited. "Hi Amanda! You were so hot yesterday. I went home, went right to my room and got myself off. You were amazing with what you did with those boys. You had them do exactly as you wanted. You are too damn hot." I gave her a big smile. I really had no idea what to expect from this girl. "I'm Bri. What's your name?" "I'm Amanda. I'm glad you enjoyed the show!"

"Bri, just curious, why do you ride this bus?" "Ray is a very good friend of my Aunt's, who I stay with occasionally. I go to a private school and he lets me ride his bus. Did you know those boys got kicked off the bus for two weeks? I'm quite surprised to see you here. How did you mange that?"

I took a deep breath, do I tell her the truth? What if she tells her Aunt? I didn't know if she is one of those gabby girls, she certainly didn't appear to be. She appears much beyond her years. "Bri, can you keep a secret?" She rolls her eyes, "Yes, of course!" I hesitate, but I wanted to tell someone other than Dad and Marianne of my antics. "I gave him a blow job," I whisper. "You what? You're kidding me, right?" "No, I'm not." "Wow . . ." She turned and slams her back hard against

the seat. "Ray always was a horny bastard, he ogles me continuously . . . wow, you sucked Ray's cock, did he cum?" "Yes of course." "Did you swallow?" "About half, the rest was on my face and in my hair."

She laughed and held her hand up to high-five me. I slapped her hand. "Amanda, we are going to be great friends! That sounds like something I would do to shut him up. Here, take my cell number and give me yours." "Do you have a boyfriend?" She smiled, "Three or four, they all want me." "I certainly understand that. You are pretty Bri." She thanked me. "Look at you girl, you look older than me in some of those hot outfits you wear." "Where do you shop?" She asked. "My mom travels, she shops all over the world for me." I'm such a liar. "I'm not surprised, many of the clothes I have seen you wear, I don't see in local shops." The bus pulls to my school. "Bye Bri, call me!" "I will." Ray still has that cocky look as I jump off the bus - oh well.

In the classroom I give Mr. Jackson a quick peek at my upper legs and turquoise cotton panties as I slide into my seat. He takes a quick peek and gives me a smile. I take that as a thank you. No exciting subjects, just routine schooling.

The lunch bell rings. I grab my lunch and head for Sam and Roy. "Are you guys OK?" as I sit down at their table. "Nooo," Sam groans. My parents grounded me for thirty days and no bus for two weeks." Roy is nodding his head, "Yeah, only two weeks grounding for me and no bus as well . . . You know, Amanda, I don't care, it was worth it, thank you." Roy says, "Yeah, it was," Sam agrees, "but thirty days at home? Mom has to drive me to school each day, she is not happy." "I am so sorry guys." "What did you get Amanda?" I smiled, "I worked it out with Ray." "How'd you do that?" demands Sam. "A long story. Give me a couple of days, I'll try to get you guys back on the bus." "How could you possibly do that?" "I'm not sure, you'll just have to trust me guys." I give a big smile. "OK Amanda."

Back in class, Mr. Jackson is waiting for his panty peek. I didn't disappoint him. We cover several subjects. Mr. Jackson was explaining global warming, greenhouse gasses, CO_2, temperatures are getting warmer and warmer, ice caps are melting, Florida and other areas will flood, etc. etc. I raise my hand. "Yes, Amanda?" "Mr. Jackson, I believe there are two sides to this issue." "I don't think so, Amanda." "May I be direct and to the point Mr. Jackson?" "Of course." "I think you have been listening to Al Gore. He is getting rich off this issue along with thousands of others. Our median temperature has risen one degree in the last forty years. In the last ten years, we have emitted three hundred twenty-seven more gasses into the air than ever before while temperatures have not risen. I believe global warming is a non-issue." Several hands shot up, many agreed with me, as well as with Mr. Jackson. I love a good debate!

The bell rings, Mr. Jackson motions me to his desk. I may be getting a bit too brave. I walk behind his desk, lean on the back corner, cock one leg aside to let my skirt ride up just a bit and give him my cutest smile. He is so polite. He tries desperately not to look. I can read him. It was a battle for him not to stare. "You love a debate, don't you?" "Only if I have something to debate." "This global warming

situation is a very important issue. With your input, I'm not certain the class is grasping that." "Mr. Jackson, it's a non-issue, which is what the class should grasp. I believe there are two sides to most subjects. When I'm able to bring that to your class, I would think you would be a bit more appreciative." "OK Amanda, I do thank you for your input. I've been teaching for only four years, I certainly have room to learn." He touched my chin with his knuckle and says, "I know we'll be friends." I smile and walk to my bus.

Ray opens the door, licking his lips and eyeing my pussy. "Thought you were walking?" "No Ray, I would miss you." None of my friends were on board, I slide into a seat by myself. Ray drops off one student after another. I see his eyes in his big mirror keeping a close watch on me. He wouldn't know that I noticed. One more stop and then it would be mine.

"Amanda, come sit up here." Hmmm, I thought as I move to the front. Ray looks over his right shoulder while steering the bus. "Honey, lift up that skirt, show me those pretty little panties. You're my girl," he snickered. I so badly wanted to tell him: fuck you, I told my Dad, you frickin' pervert, but I had other plans for Rayby. I very seductively slid my skirt up and let him peek at my turquoise panties. He liked that. "Lift your top, I want to see those titties, did you wash them off? Hahahaha." That was his joke. I lifted my top to expose my hard nipples. Amazingly, they were hard, although I was repulsed. He pulled the bus under the big tree and turned the ignition off, turned in his seat and stood up rubbing his hand up and down his crotch.

He stood directly in front of me and put both hands on my titties and flicked my nipples. It did feel good as he continued. He stuck three of his fingers in his mouth and rubbed them across my breasts. His saliva made my nipples harder yet. He smiled. "Amanda, likes that," he said with a disgusting voice. His green work pants were looking like a circus tent. "Get on your knees," he commanded. I slid off my seat to my knees. He pulled my head to his tent. He slid his crotch up and down, while rotating my head around. God, it was so hard. I was getting excited - it was OK - I would play his game — for now. "Unzip my pants," he ordered. I reached for his zipper and slide it down. "Take my cock out." I obliged. I worked it through the open zipper. I do love his cock, such a huge head. "Take my balls out bitch." Somehow I was enjoying his smutty language. His balls are huge. "Suck my balls." I drop my mouth under his cock, stuffing one of his testicles into my mouth. "Yeah, suck on it little bitch." I had never had a ball in my mouth before. I sucked at his ball and attempt to engulf the second one. No go, much too large. I let one go and move my mouth to the second and sucked it in. It was exciting! I suck one while massaging the other. "Yeah, now suck my cock." I move his cock to my mouth. It was dripping with his slimy juices. I lick them off before inserting the head inside my mouth. My mouth stretched as I attempt to ram the head deeper inside my open mouth. Ray is holding the back of my head forcing it deeper. "Suck that cock you slut, tell me you like it." "Oh yes, I love your cock Ray." "Tell me you're my cock sucking whore." "Ray, Ray, I'm your cock sucking whore." I like

the dirty talk, it's exciting! He pounds his cock in and out of my stretched mouth. "Ray, Ray, fuck me," I begged. He immediately pulled it out, pulled me off my knees, turned me around and bent me over the bus seat. He pulls my panties to my knees, his cock is sliding over my pussy and ass. God, his big, slimy cock felt so good moving over my hairy pussy. He is trying to force it inside me. I reach my hand to his cock and guide it to my ass. The head is at my back door. Pressing, pressing, pressing, I realize there's no way his huge head is going to slide inside me. I turn and stroke his cock with my hand, it is getting even harder. I know he must be very close. "Ray, cum all over my ass and my pussy, I want to feel your hot cum squirting all over me." I didn't have to beg. He grabs his cock, as I lean on the seat and stick my ass high in the air. A huge moan - whoa! I feel it squirting, squirting, squirting on my ass crack and my pussy. I could smell his cum; God, it was so hot. "Rub your cock all over Ray." He quickly obliged.

He stepped back as I stood up while pulling my panties over my cum soaked ass. I was so wet. I arrange my skirt and top. I pull the bus door handle and bid Ray bye, "See ya tomorrow." I felt somewhat repulsed as I walk to my drive. My panties soaked in his cum felt so good on my ass. The aroma of cum was overwhelmingly sweet.

At least Dad should not be home today. I go to the kitchen and grab a zip lock bag and a marker. When in my room, I pull my panties down while soaking up every drop of his cum. I open my bag and slide them in, lock it up and mark YAR Bus. My plan is now in play. I lie on my bed and turn on my music while rubbing my hands over my wet ass and pussy. It is so wet and slimy even though I stole most of his juices for my bag. I rub my hairy bush. I could cum, but no, not fantasizing about that son of a bitch. I'll take a rest and deal with him tomorrow. I close my eyes and drift away.

A bit later, the family is home, noises are coming from the kitchen. I slip on my robe and head for the shower. I say my hello's as I pass. I hate to wash the cum off my ass, the aroma is yet so scintillating. Oh well, there's always more somewhere. Back to my room, slip on my jogging suit and out to help Mom. We chat about everyone's day. It was a great dinner as always. I finish the dishes, play with Bandit, read the news, watch some TV and bid my goodnights. I am exhausted, not certain why. I crash without my music.

Amanda, it's your bus." In a low, defeated voice Ray repeated the line. "Also, when I want your big cock, I will let you know and Ray, I will want it occasionally. I have your home number from the phone book. I will be calling. I also will be doing a little shopping for myself and may occasionally need just a little help financially, I'll let you know. So please Rayby, start putting just a little bit aside. Oh, and one more thing, tonight, you contact Sam and Roy's parents. I want them back on the bus tomorrow and their grounding rescinded. Tell their Mom and Dad you overreacted. Really, I don't care what you tell them, get it handled. Bye-bye for now Ray, it is so nice doing business with you!"

I open the bus door and strut toward home while wiping his cum from my face. Gosh, that was just too much fun. Now, I have a taxi man and my own bus and can do whatever I choose with it, plus some extra shopping money when needed. I've saved Marianne from being molested by her big brother and most likely will have Sam and Roy riding the bus and ungrounded while I get to enjoy hot cum squirting everywhere - how grand! Could this be what they were referring to when I was called 'dangerous?' I doubt it - oh well. Oh yes, how could I forget...I also have two guys I can call anytime I want or need a quick pick me up fuck and a bus service along with my taxicab. Who needs a car and all the expense of upkeep, gas and repairs! Life is just so perfect. "O'La Lay."

Back to the house, into the shower, time to get rid of Ray's cum. All cleaned up, I turn on my music and slide on shorts and a top. Time to go play sticks with my Bandit. On the way through the house, I tidy up a bit and shine up the kitchen. Mom, Dad, and the boys will be home soon. A family dinner tonight at seven o'clock is written on the pad lying on the counter - oh perfect!

CHAPTER 21

Difficult Business Conditions

"Hey Bandit, where is your stick?" Bandit runs over with his stick, I give it a toss, "Go get it boy!" Why is it dogs love to chase a stick? I'm not sure. Bandit certainly does enjoy it. I notice the lawn needs mowing, I would guess tomorrow - or perhaps tonight?

Everyone is sitting down to Mom's beautiful spaghetti dinner. Not my favorite, but when you're hungry, it's great. Mom has to work the weekend out of town. The boys work Saturday at the Ferris's and will mow our lawn this evening. Dad and Uncle Ken will be painting the house. What will I be up to? Hmm . . . no plans yet.

As we finish dinner, Mom reminded us we have three birthdays coming up soon - John's, September eighteenth, Josh's, the twenty-sixth, and mine, October fifteenth. "Boys, do you have any plans yet?" "No, not really," was the response. "Josh, would you like all of us to go out to dinner to celebrate yours?" "That would be great, Mom." "What's your choice?" I jump in quickly, "Oh Josh, can we go to Cadillac's? I have two free dinner passes." "You let Josh decide, Amanda," Mom suggests. "I haven't been there," says Josh. "I hear about Cadillac's all the time, I would love that. Great idea Amanda!" "Oh goody, I'll make a reservation, how many, Mom?" "Five for sure, Uncle Ken may want to join us, let's plan on six." I was so excited. Finally, I will visit Cadillac's. Maybe I'll see Bargain Bob and some of his Cadillac buddies. I told Dad that story one night. He got a chuckle out of it. He also had some Bob stories he shared with me.

Dinner is finished and the boys go out to the yard. Dad is going to paint. I help

Mom clean up. After finishing, I study the daily paper while watching the news channel. I'm off to my room to call Marianne and my new friend Bri. We tell a few stories and laugh. Bri will be riding our bus again next week. I'm anxious to see them both.

The next morning I can't wait to catch my bus. "Good morning Ray, how are you this morning?" He doesn't acknowledge me. I lean toward him and whisper, "Ray, in case anyone should ask, whose bus is this?" A headshake, "It's yours Amanda." "Oh Ray, thank you, you're so sweet." I pat his arm. Oh my gosh, I look toward the back of the bus, to my surprise, Roy and Sam have saved me a seat. "Guys, you're back, what happened?" Sam shakes his head, "The darndest thing, we don't know. We are both ungrounded." "Amanda," Roy asks, "how did you do it?" I smiled. "I had a heart to heart talk with Ray and I think he understood." They both laughed and high-five me as Ray peeked through his mirror. "We'll behave for a while," I whisper to the boys. It was such a happy reunion.

Walking into my classroom I wish a "good morning" to Mr. Jackson. He really doesn't appear to be a womanizer although his eyes check me out closer by the day. I, of course, would never encourage such a thing. Today seems to be filled with slow boring subjects although I am learning. Just ordinary reoccurring stuff mostly. I love learning about real life situations. I find no debates this morning.

At lunchtime, I meander through the lunch line and join my two buddies. "Amanda, can we steal a car sometime?" whispers Sam. "No, why are you thinking of such a thing? You let the pros do those things. You boys behave yourselves. You go to jail for that kind of stuff." "But you did!" "Honey, I learned from the best. I'm more in tune to that lifestyle. You guys learn and practice thinking. You don't need my help to learn and think. You're not cut out to be car thieves. You both are too smart to think of having that lifestyle. Leave that kind of stuff to me, OK guys?"

That afternoon in class Mr. Jackson took us into the business world immediately. He tells us how the stock exchange works and that most of us would someday own stocks. He was explaining what they were and how prices fluctuated from minute to minute and day to day. Our economy is in a boom period. The exchange had made record highs three or four times in the past few weeks. As he was teaching and telling of our booming U.S. economy, I raised my hand. "Yes Amanda?" "I do understand that the markets are making record highs recently, I watch the reports at night. But Mr. Jackson, I also listen to my Dad. Many companies are laying employees off as we speak. My Dad is working no overtime like he was a year ago. His factory has laid many workers off. Several area factories have closed. Our local unemployment is very high. Maybe we should be thinking beyond the obvious. The picture may be much bigger?" Mr. Jackson smiled. "Yes, there is relevance, the big picture is the New York exchange, that is huge!" I raise my hand again. "Yes?" "Perhaps there is a major disconnect to the big picture in what we are experiencing right here at home. Several of my Dad's friends are losing their homes. They received mortgages called 'adjustable rate.' Obviously, they were not aware of what that meant or maybe didn't care at the time and were happy to own

their own home. Today, those same people are losing them." "Yes, it seems to be just in our area at this time." "There must be others in our country that at some point will have these same problems. And besides that, our home values are shrinking while our property taxes move up. I, for one, have trouble believing in your booming economy theory Mr. Jackson. There is without question a major disconnect."

Many hands go up. Other students tell of their families and friends losing homes and job. Mr. Jackson, my favorite teacher, doesn't seem to understand. Of course, he probably rents a little apartment. He is a teacher and teachers can learn also. My future plan is to debate and teach the world, I am just practicing on Mr. Jackson.

The bell rings and I scoot out of my seat. Mr. Jackson again waves me over. I take a seat on the back corner of his desk. I lean in and cock my legs just right. He cannot help but notice my show if he is at all human. "Amanda, you do enjoy a good debate . . . Is it just with myself or is it your prerogative with anyone?" "I guess I'm not certain. When I hear an issue, whether in your class or walking down the street that I don't agree with, quite often I likely would voice my opinion if possible." He sighs. "Sometimes I believe you should be teaching this class." "Are you being sarcastic?" "No, not at all. How you can have such a positive input and force me to rethink what I believe. I was amazed at today's conversation. Yes, I understand your Dad is working in a shop with layoffs and overtime is a thing of the past. And I agree the A.R.M.s have gotten many homeowners in trouble. Why do you believe the average local business is troubled with our economy?" A deep breath. (I must bullshit a bit). "Bargain Bob is a friend of mine, he calls me his cousin. His furniture stores are struggling, his restaurant Cadillac's is on difficult times." "Really Amanda, you know Bargain Bob?" "Yes!" "Amanda, he is a legend in this area. Times are difficult for his businesses?" "Yes, they are." "Amanda, could you ask Bob to visit our classroom, tell his story and help the class understand what is happening with our local economy? It would be so informative." "Sure, I could do that." "Great, Amanda, that would be inspiring for at least a few of the students." "Mr. Jackson, by Christmas, I will make that happen." I am so full of shit. Mr. Jackson is so elated, it's made my week. Have I bit off more than I can chew? Not likely, I know I will be a cousin soon. Bargain Bob will be addressing my class, no doubt in my mind.

I arrange my body, cross one leg over the other to give Mr. Jackson a full view of my narrow crotch white mesh panties. I'm sure my hairy bush is poking out from the sides. I have no plans with my teacher for now, but I do love his lustful gaze. As I maintain my touch of lustful mystery, I slide my legs together. I leave out the door and down the hallway to go catch my bus.

What must be in Mr. Jackson's mind right this minute? Our economy, Bargain Bob addressing the class, or is he perhaps stroking his cock after staring at my partially exposed pussy? My bet goes to number three.

"Oh, thank you for waiting Ray. If I'm ever not going to be riding my bus, I will send word, OK? Also, Ray," I lean down to whisper in his ear, "I'll be needing fifty dollars today or in the morning. I need to buy some new panties, mine have cum

stains that just won't come out. You can pass it on to me when I get off the bus or run it over to me in the morning." I gently pat his arm. "And Ray, I won't be needing my bus this weekend, just keep it parked in your yard." I move back to join my boys. "Hi Amanda," as I slide between them. "What did you talk to Ray about?" Roy asks. "Oh, personal stuff." "Oh," he replies. "How was class?" As I take each of their hands and place them on my leg. "Amanda, we can't do this anymore." "Roy, we can do as we please. This is my bus, I have new rules." Two mouths drop wide open. "What are you talking about Amanda?" says Sam. "Guys, trust me, nothing terrible, I won't have you cumming on my titties for a while but everything else is just fine, Ray OK'd it." I gently guide their hands closer to my crotch. I love how the mystery of it all has them totally puzzled! A quick brush between my legs, a light massage, and we are at Sam's stop. He gives me a peck on my cheek and whispers, "Amanda, you are amazing, I love you." I smile as he walks down the aisle. I have one of my guys' hands gently pulling and twisting my pubic hairs. What a great sensation!

"Tell me Roy, do you like my hairy bush?" "Are you kidding Amanda, I love to touch and feel you. You have taught us so much. You are so beautiful in so many ways. I will be your friend forever," as he continues massaging my fun spot. The bus is in front of Roy's house. He gives me a peck. "See you next week Roy."

Ray pulls my bus to my drive. I walk up the aisle and stand facing him. He hands me a folded bill. I pull my skirt up and run two fingers over my damp panties. Ray may be pissed, but he doesn't turn his eyes away. I gently rub my sticky fingers on his lower lips. He runs his tongue over them. "Thank you so much Ray. I promise I will not make a habit of requesting money but, Ray," (I wink) "I'll make it up to you, I'm a fair little girl." I pull my skirt down and open the door. "See ya Monday Ray. And please, wash my bus over the weekend, it is getting quite dusty." As I strut up the drive to my house, I think once I get Ray trained he will be one of my buddies.

CHAPTER 22

Shopping Plans

In my room, I turn on my music and flop on my bed. It's Friday night. What does a young lady do to prevent boredom from taking over her world? My eyes close and I let sleep carry me away.

I am awakened by family voices. I jump up and walk out of my bedroom rubbing my eyes. Josh and John are fixing a sandwich. "No dinner tonight, Amanda?" "I guess not." Dad's not home and Mom is gone until Sunday evening. "You guys have plans tonight?" "Yeah, we're going to the mall and a show with the guys." "What are you going to see?" "Haven't decided yet," answered John. "Would you like to come along?" "No, but thank you, I'm going shopping tomorrow, I'll take it easy tonight, I must save my energy." They both smile.

I walk back to my room and call Marianne. "Hi Marianne, what are you up to this weekend?" "Oh, hello Amanda, nothing important." "Would you like to go shopping with me tomorrow?" "That sounds great Amanda, is noon OK?" "Yes, perfect! Is Chad around?" Yes, he's in the kitchen." "Would you ask him to give us a ride or should I?" Marianne hesitated. "You have better luck than I. He hasn't been himself with me." "Get him for me Marianne." "Chad, phone for you." I can hear Chad in the background excited about his phone call, I wonder how long that excitement will last. "Hello?" "Hi Chad, how are you?" No answer. "We'll be needing a ride to go shopping tomorrow at noon." "Amanda, I have to get this lawn mowed tomorrow." "Chad, honey, you just shut your little mower off at eleven-fifty and take a little break. While you're taking that break, you grab Marianne and be here at twelve o'clock sharp." He hung up. My phone rings. It was Marianne calling back. "Hello Marianne." "Amanda, Chad says he will drive wherever we'd

like to go." "Great Marianne. " "Amanda, Chad has been acting so different lately, what did you do to him? Oh, we had a chat Marianne." "Amanda, you must tell me about how you have transformed him! I can't wait for our shopping trip! I'll see you tomorrow!"

Dad comes in as the boys are leaving. Dad stops me and gives me a big hug. "Amanda, how are you, really?" He gives me a serious and concerned look as he sits in his chair and turned on the TV. "Dad, I am fine. I love my first week of school. My teacher is fabulous. We have learned many things this week." "We, as in the class?" asks Dad. "Yes, I don't always agree with Mr. Jackson on certain issues." "There are normally two sides to most situations, Amanda." "Yes, I do see that Dad. However, I have made a commitment to him I'm not sure I will be able keep." "Honey, what did you commit to?" "We were discussing our local economy and I told Mr. Jackson I would bring Bargain Bob in to discuss the local business conditions with the class." Dad chuckled, "Amanda, I understand you met Bob this past weekend, you should be careful committing to something you may not be able to provide." "Yes, I know Dad, sometimes I get a bit too arrogant." "Honey, I am sure you are safe. Bob is a good guy, I'm sure he'll enjoy addressing your class. I haven't seen you in action Amanda, but I feel that you are capable of accomplishing anything you put your mind to. You're only young once. Use your youthful energy to accomplish things that are meaningful and lasting, you seem to be working on just that. You know Amanda, Bob can be quite the center of attention and somehow things happen when he's around."

"How well do you know him Dad?" "Oh, not that well. He was between Ken and I in high school. It was odd how even then he got along with all the different clicks in school. The athletes, the intellectuals, even the nerdy guys, they were all his buddies. Most of the teachers liked him, although he would drive them crazy." "How?" "He loved to disagree. It didn't matter what the subject was, he would take the opposite side. I wasn't in his class, of course, I would hear those stories from students as well as overhearing teachers chatting amongst themselves." "When we go to Cadillac's for Josh's birthday, I will ask him to fulfill my commitment." "Good Amanda, again, be careful making commitments. Honey, anytime you need to talk about anything in your life, I'm always here for you." With that, Dad excused himself and walked to his room.

One day soon, I knew that I would have a conversation with Bob and pick his brain. So many questions I have for him. He was the only wealthy person I knew of with the exception of the Ferris's and someday I hoped to know Norma as well.

The evening news started to repeat itself so I decided to go check on Bandit. "Go get your stick!" Away he charges. Why has Jack not yet called? It haunts me. I fantasize sometimes about him sitting in the car, paying me to show him my panties. God, that was fun! Most men, I'm sure, want to peek under my shorts or skirt. If more would only ask! Oh well.

Bandit and I play for a while. Dad is waving goodbye. "Where you going Dad?" "Going to town for a cocktail or two. I'll be home in a couple of hours. Ken and I

will be painting tomorrow." "OK Dad, bye!"

I can't wait to see Bri next week. She seems to be my kind of gal, different than Marianne, who is a bit more reserved although I am going to work on those things with her. Shopping will be so much fun tomorrow. It's nine o'clock. I undress, lie on my bed and drift off for the evening.

Morning arrives, I've had twelve hours sleep and am rejuvenated, my music was still blaring in the background. Perhaps that was the reason I slept so well. I take my shower. I must always be clean and prepared for what life may bring my way. I eat a light breakfast as usual. It's another beautiful summer morning.

I go out and let Bandit run. "Good morning, Uncle Ken! I see Dad has you hard at work." "Oh yes, your Dad is a slave driver." "I'd help you, but I must do some shopping." "Priorities come first Amanda," quips Dad with a smile. "OK Bandit, I see you've got your stick, go get it," as he flies off. "Do you need a ride honey?" asks Dad. I wanted to say no, I called my taxi. I bit my lip, just a simple, "No Dad, I'm fine. The lawn looks beautiful. The boys are doing such a great job keeping it up, aren't they?" "Yes Amanda, they do. The Ferris's taught them great yard grooming." I toss Bandit's stick a dozen times before re-caging my dog. Now back to the house to prepare for my shopping adventure. It will be great fun spending my hard earned fifty dollars.

CHAPTER 23

Shopping

At twelve-noon sharp, my taxi arrived. "Bye Dad and Uncle Ken, I'll see you later." Marianne jumped out and gave me a big hug. "Amanda, I've missed you. I wish we went to the same school." I agreed. "I've missed you too." She was dressed in a little girl skirt, white, almost see through. I could see an outline of blue panties through the cotton material. She wore a tight fitting yellow stretchy top. I could see the outline of her bra with her nipples leaving a large impression in the stretchy top. We were in reverse this week. I was wearing skintight pink nylon paisley-print shorts. The ass fit was perfect. I let the back of my black panties ride just below my cheek line and wore a little blue top with no bra, of course. My breasts weren't as large as Marianne's, although my nipples protrude so beautifully.

"Hello Chad, thanks for giving us a ride, that is so nice," as we slam the doors closed. Chad wasn't talking, I don't know why. "Where ya going?" he asked. "Let's go to Jay Burg." That got his attention. That is a large mall north of us about a hundred miles away. I laughed, "Chad, be sweet, it's a joke." "Ha ha," he grumbled. "OK, let's go to Value Land." Value Land was a giant outlet like TJ Max, although much larger in size. Ten minutes later, we're at our destination. "Thanks Chad, you want to shop with us?" He declines. "OK, we'll call you when we're shopped out." He sped away.

Marianne puts her hand in mine as we strut across the street. "Amanda how is it that you got Chad to drive us?" "He's just a good boy Marianne." I chuckle. She whispers in my ear, "He hasn't been to my bedroom for a week. That has not happened in years. What did you say to him?" she asked. "Marianne, I told you I would handle it and I did. Can we just leave it at that?" Marianne takes a deep

breath, "I guess so for now. What are you shopping for today Amanda?" "I need some new panties. I will look at skirts and shorts, but I like to save money and shop at Good Will for those items." "Yes, Amanda, that's what I am shopping for myself. Maybe we can stop at Good Will and you can show me all those deals." "OK," I agreed.

I wander over to the lingerie department as Marianne walks to the junior's area. Oh, so much to choose from! All colors, shapes, name brands - Henson, Vanity Fair, Olga . . . all two and three dollars a pair. I sort through them and have collected eight pairs and two hot skimpy bras. I know the department stores don't like you trying lingerie on, but I must! If the fit isn't perfect, I will not wear them. I'm not wasting my hard earned money, God, how I hate returning things. I find the fitting area. I'm amazed how quiet the store is, not many customers for a Saturday. Is it the economy or just a coincidence?

A man is sitting in a high-backed chair. I suppose he was waiting for his wife's fitting session to end. I walk to the large fitting room. The booth is comfortable, with a rod and curtain for a door with mirrors on all three walls. I look at myself in the large mirror on the wall at the end of the aisle. I look hot! It made my nipples tingle. I turn to work the curtain down the rod. The man in the chair is watching my every move. Oooh, this could be fun. There is still no one around. His wife must have a boatload of clothes, she has not appeared. I smile at him as I slide the curtain halfway closed. I turn and placed my new selection on the shelf. I look directly at him as I pull my shorts down in his full view. God, how I love the look on the faces as I shock them, it's shock and awe. I just love it!

I reach up and pull my top over my head - if I had a camera!! My little titties pointed directly at his face. I squeeze my nipples just a bit. He is rubbing his hand over his crotch. I'm slowly sliding my panties down, out comes his wife from the other end and does not see me. "Jim, are you OK, you look like you've seen a ghost." "Uh, oh yes honey," stammering, "I'm fine. My stomach is bothering me a bit, I'll be fine dear, you go ahead and shop, I'll just wait here for you." "OK, see you in a while dear."

I reopen my curtain and pull my panties down and kick them off. He is livid. His hand is moving up and down his crotch. I love it! I slide my right hand very gently over my hairy pussy. I turn and pick up a lacy pink thong, bend over and pull it over and tuck it between my cheeks and wiggle my backside toward him. I'm so brave! I step into the aisle and look at myself in the big mirror. I am hot! I turn around for him again. Oh my God, he has a fifty-dollar bill in his hand and is waving it back and forth very slowly. I step back into my booth and motion him with my finger. He walks to my booth, looking all around and over his shoulder. It appears wifey is still busy with her shopping. He steps in and closes the curtain. He leans against the mirrored wall. "The fifty is yours, I want your mouth for two minutes." I took the bill. He unzipped his pants and I dropped to my knees. It was very long and very hard, not terribly big around. I covered my teeth with my lips and opened my mouth. He drove it in and out, and in and out. "Don't move," he

whispered. "I just want to fuck your mouth." He was pounding my open mouth - a muffled groan. "Oh, Ooh, Ahh . . ." Cum began to fill my mouth, I feel it gushing against my tonsils and dripping down my chin. He pulled it out and squeezed the shaft as I lick off the last glob. He zipped his slacks and walked away. I wondered if his stomach was any better? What a nice load. I licked my lips and got to my feet.

My lingerie all fit perfectly, how great! The poor guy would have no idea. I would have sucked him off for pleasure. I'm seeing how this works and wow, fifty extra dollars! Wait until I tell Marianne. I go to find her. "How goes the shopping Marianne?" "OK," she answers. "Did you find your panties?" "Yes and two little bras." "Amanda, you don't wear them." "I'm planning ahead, soon Mom will insist and I should be prepared." I held my fifty-dollar bill up. "Look what I found." "Seriously, you found it?" "Well, sort of, I was putting on a show for a man at the changing booth and he gave it to me." "Amanda, you are soo bad!" "He came into my booth and I sucked him off." She gasped, "How do these things happen to you? Forget it Amanda, that's a stupid question. You make things happen. You do amaze me! I want to learn some of your tricks, would you help me Amanda?" "Of course I will. So, have you found anything you like?" She showed me four items, the prices were reasonable but the clothes were kind of Marianne-boring. The price tags read twelve to nineteen dollars for each piece.

"Come on Marianne, let's walk to Good Will, it's only ten or twelve blocks." She agrees, and off we go. Marianne in her little girl skirt and bulging breasts, myself with my hot tight body shorts with black lace panties riding below the legs. We strut our stuff down the street.

CHAPTER 24

My Good Will Store

We are off to my favorite Good Will shop. Oh my goodness, the attention we are getting! There are cars beeping and trucks honking. Marianne was enjoying the attention as much, if not more, than I. "Is this dangerous Amanda?" "Why?" I asked. "Look at us." "Honey, we can take care of ourselves. We are the danger." We laughed and high-fived each other.

A car pulls left to a side street we are about to cross. The driver stops and in a friendly manner, waves. "Hi girls, where are you going?" "On the way home," I shout to him. "Want a lift?" he asks. "No, we enjoy the walk." "I'm Tom." "So, why do we care?" Marianne responds. "Are you girls stuck up?" "Yes, it's true!" He wasn't giving up quite yet. "I love stuck up ladies." His car pulled away. We smile to one another. As we walk to the next block, his car is across the street and is facing us. "Where you coming from?" "We are going home from work." "You work at the mall?" "No," Marianne replies, "we work at Roma's." "You two are dancers?" "Yes," says Marianne. "Oh wow, you both are so beautiful. I stop in there often and haven't seen either of you." "Oh, we just started two days ago." "I'd pay anything to see either of you dance." "We'll be on the stage tomorrow night Tom, come see us." "I have to work, but I could take a sick day." I walk up to his car. "Tommy, we would love to dance for you," as I run my hand up my crotch over my tight shorts. "Then honey, I'm definitely going to be sick tomorrow. What time is your shift?" "Eight." "I'll be there," he says with a happy smile.

We strut on toward our Good Will store. Marianne and I laugh. "Do you suppose he'll be there tomorrow?" "Marianne, what those jerks tell you really doesn't mean a damn thing. Who knows, who really cares? It was fun jerking his silly chain."

I open the door to the Good Will store. There was a big sign that read: fifty percent off orange tags. I point it out to Marianne. There were large racks of clothes everywhere, all very neat and clean. Marianne headed to the tops and blouse area. I grab a cart. "Oh Amanda, some of these tops are so hot, three dollars, forty nine cents and many have orange tags. This is great! Thank you for bringing me." There were hot tops, skirts, shorts and even a little bikini bathing suit. We both found so many perfect outfits. There was no need to try them on there. Most of them were small and very body tight stretchy material. I couldn't wait to try on my wardrobe at home.

Two hours and tons of fun later, we were at the checkout. "Any discounts?" the clerk asked. "I've heard you give a ten percent discount to customers over fifty-five." The little clerk looked at me and rolled her eyes. "It's just a joke." She seemed to get it after my explanation and gave me a smile. The total will be thirty-nine dollar ladies. I hand her my hard earned fifty-dollar bill. Marianne is digging in her purse. "No, Marianne, I'm using my Value Land tip, I'm buying!" She was so excited, she gave me a big hug and kiss.

I called our taxi just before the checkout lane. Chad should be arriving any second. Walking out the door our timing was perfect. Our taxi was pulling up to the curb. I slid in and Marianne closed the door. "What are you two doing at Good Will?" "It's my favorite store." "Amanda, you may be thrifty but come on!" "Chad, do you normally like my attire?" "Of course, it's all very hot and seductive." "Well, it all comes from here." "Are you kidding?" "No, Chad, this one time, I'm very serious. Marianne, let's show him some of our pieces." Marianne opens the bag and holds up our selections, piece after piece. Chad is shaking his head and staring at the thirty-nine dollar receipt. "Wow, sixteen pieces!" I think we had Chad sold. "I've seen at least two that would cost forty-nine dollars by themselves. The next time I am shopping for my girlfriend, I certainly will check it out." "Amanda, try that one on," Chad suggests. It was a long fitted top or maybe a short dress with a long pointed triangular shape on one side with a split, short on the other side up to my upper leg. It is pink, blue and light with green angular stripes. It is stretchy and very silky. "Oh, that one is Marianne's. Try it on Marianne," I say with a smile. She hesitated. "Why not?" I'm certain she has decided that Chad has seen all that she has. "OK." She kicks off her shoes, lifts her bottom off the seat and pulls off her skirt. Her little white lacy panties pulled tight into her blond bush totally arouse me. I just want to run my hand up her soft, tan legs and touch her blond pussy. I take a deep breath. Amanda, self control girl. My hand does not move, nor do my eyes. I cannot take them away from her hairy bush. Her bright white silky panties are ever so slightly tucked into her pussy. I so badly want to taste and kiss that little mound. "Quit it, Amanda," I tell myself sternly. She reaches for her top and slides it over her head and long blond hair. Again, why am I getting so hot? Her large breasts are standing straight and so firm, they certainly do not need the support of her flimsy see through bra. And her nipples, God, I just want to bury my face in her cleavage and lick and suck them so badly. She reaches for the silky top and leans forward to

pull it over her head. Her tits bounce as she leans forward. She pulls the silky soft material over her head and chest and pulls it downward, even sitting down; she looks so damn hot in it. "Chad, pull in here, pull up to that big tree over there so Marianne can model for us." "Sure," he says as he pulls off the road right up to my favorite tree.

"Open the door Marianne, and stand up for us," I say as I continue trying to fight my overwhelming urges. She opens the door, puts her feet on the grass and stands up while at the same time, arranging it into place. On the long side, it comes six inches below her cheeks, forming a triangle shape. On the short side, it comes about two inches below. It clings to her body. She takes a few steps away from the car. Her beautiful ass wiggles like Jello in the soft, clingy silk material. It looks so hot. She continues walking forward and then turns back toward us. Her tits bounce as she steps forward. "Marianne, you are so hot. Chad, don't you look," I command. Marianne knows this is the hottest top or skirt she has ever worn. I know she can feel the passion erupting inside me. It shows in her eyes as she struts toward me. I get out and put my arms around her. I've now lost control. I move my hands to her beautiful ass and squeeze her cheeks gently. I put my mouth on hers, we kiss passionately. She slides her tongue in my mouth. How I love her hot mouth. Her passion matches mine. I move my tongue and mouth to her ear. "Marianne, I love you and want you so much." She pulls my mouth back to hers, our tongues are interlocked. I suck her mouth and tongue. I'm going to explode. Her mouth is on my ear. "Oh Amanda, make me cum, please make me cum." I guide her body to the front seat pushing her gently on her back as I climb on and passionately kiss her mouth. She is guiding my head downward. Her breasts are so beautiful. I devour her nipple, she squeals. That excites me all the more. Her passion, I can feel it. She is as hot as I! How can this be happening? God, I do love cock, but how I also love the passion I'm feeling with my best friend.

The next nipple, they are both so hard and erect, like little cocks. I suck and suck. Marianne is squealing with pleasure. My pussy is dripping wetness down my legs. Marianne is gently pushing my head downward. Oh God, I am fantasizing about her thick hairy pussy, sliding my tongue in and out, sucking her juices. I reach her firm belly. My tongue is passionately sucking and licking her button. She is wild. I have found her hot spot. I suck it and lick with such passion. "Oh Amanda, I love you, you make me so hot, I love you." Her blond bush is pumping wildly. Oh how I want it. She gently nudges my head. I feel what she wants and I am so there. God, how I love looking at her thick blond hairy crotch.

My passion rises as I stare at her beauty. "Slow down Amanda," I tell myself. I want this to last. I want to feel the impression of my passion on Marianne forever. I will not forget this moment. I gently lick and suck on her blond bush. I want her to beg for my tongue. I continue kissing, mouthing and sucking her thick blond pubic hairs. "Amanda, please, I need more!" she screams. That is my cue. That was what I am waiting for. I bury my face in her wet pussy. I press my tongue so deeply and suck and lick with all that I have. She pounds her crotch on my face and

screams, "Oh Amanda, suck it, I love your mouth, I love you." God, how that turns me, I'm so fucking hot. My tongue is sliding deeper and deeper, is it growing? I'm not sure. It is so deep inside her, her juices are flowing down my chin, she is so wet! I'm swallowing all that I can grab with my open mouth; she is pounding harder and harder, moaning louder and louder. "Oh my God Amanda, I love, oh oh, oh, I'm cumming, I'm cumming, I'm cumming!" Oh, I love her cum. I'm licking and sucking and swallowing all that I can trap in my open mouth. My ass is high in the air.

I raise my head and yell, "Chad, where 'da fuck are you?" His door opens, the jerk is just watching. "Pull my panties down you fucking jerk." His mouth is now sucking and licking my ass cheeks. "Suck my asshole." It's like I'm on drugs. I want more now. His tongue is buried in my ass. I'm licking Marianne's excess cum. I lift my eyes. She is watching her big brother attacking my hot ass. "Deeper you whore," I command. He presses his finger between my legs. "Uh, uh, it is good . . . enough, I need your cock now." My mouth continues soaking up Marianne's juices. I hear his pants fall to the ground. His hardness is sliding up and down my crack. He hits home. The pressure, a bit of pleasurable pain, the head is in. His shaft slides deeper inside me. Oh God, he is pounding my ass with his hard cock. Chad moans, moans, moans, "Jesus!" he screams, "I'm cumming, I'm filling your ass with my cum. Oh sweet Jesus Amanda, I love your ass, I love your ass." I feel his passion squirting and squirting. God, how I love shopping at the Good Will.

CHAPTER 25

Family Fun

I am awakened Sunday morning with a crash of thunder and rain pounding on my windows. Oh, how I love thunderstorms. I lay and listen to the storm, so peaceful. I am so relaxed lying motionless in my bed. What is happening to me? I love cock. I love cum and oh, how I love Marianne's pussy. Is this normal? I have no idea. Loving cock is OK I guess, but Marianne turns me on so much, and now I find myself fantasizing about Bri. I don't understand, but if it's pleasurable for all, should it matter? I'm not certain at this time. The rain continues pounding my windows as lightning strikes once more. Where did all this start? My Mother's lingerie drawer flashes back. I didn't know what it was about. I loved putting on her panties, her nylons and thigh highs so much! Trying to walk in her high heel shoes, not knowing what I was feeling. It was all so very good. I was only five or so. I remember all the boys in school, and playing 'spider' in my panties. I remember the thrill it gave me. I remember the man at Grandma's house and the thrills of being in his front seat. I was so excited, stripping for Grandma's neighbor. God, it's only gotten better and I still don't understand. Will I ever?

Marianne is on my mind. Her blond bush I love so much, her hot mouth, her tongue, and letting my slave have a free fuck. You must take care of your slaves, I read that somewhere. Marianne decided to take her sleazy attire home. My slave would help her get in and out of the house dressed provocatively. I still haven't tried on my new wardrobe, I will soon. The thunder continues to rumble, rain still pounding against my windows. It would probably be a quiet day with the TV, who knows? I slip on my robe and head down the hall, its ten fifteen in the morning. "Good morning," I greet all three guys in front of the TV. "We thought you'd sleep all day,"

Dad said as he smiled. "Heck I would have, but that darn thunder wouldn't quit. So here I am!"

After my shower I comb and brush my hair until it shines and looks perfect. I put on just a bit of mascara, some eye shadow and lip-gloss. I always try to look pretty for my family. I smile in the mirror.

Out in the kitchen I hear lots of chatter. "Guess you all got rained out today ay?" "Oh well, rain is good." "I hope it passes," Josh says, "I would like to finish the Ferris's lawn. I've got football practice." "Dad, John's birthday is on a Thursday, will we be celebrating on that day or Saturday?" "Thursday is fine. Your Mom may be gone on the weekend." "Is a seven o'clock reservation OK Dad?" "That would be perfect. Uncle Ken will be joining us as well." "Would it be OK to invite Marianne?" "Certainly honey." I enjoy my bowl of cereal while I finish reading the local newspaper. I read an article telling of yet another local business closing. It's so sad.

Back in my room, the rain is still pounding at my windows. I'm looking forward to trying on some of my Good Will finds. God, that little top or short dress that Marianne tried on was so damn hot. That material looked amazing. How it clung to her skin and showed every movement of her shapely body. I need some more clothes, silky nylon only! I did buy a little skirt of that material, dark blue. I slip it on. Yes! Beautiful! Now a little silky pink top, perfect! It's only my family at home, but a girl must always look good. I walk back out to the living room. "Amanda that skirt and top I'd say is cute, but wow, it is totally hot. Are you going to a party?" John asked. "No, got to look good for my guys." They smile. "Is it new?" "Yes and no. It's from Good Will." "No kidding Amanda, do you still shop there?" "When a girl's on a budget, a girl must be thrifty." They laugh. "Only you would know Amanda. You're clothes are always perfect." "Thanks Dad."

Into the kitchen as I do some cleaning and shining, many thoughts are racing through my mind. I must find a way to make some money. I have collected one hundred and twenty-five dollars over the last few weeks. Questions will soon be asked. I could baby sit I suppose. But that would be what they call chump change. I could ride my bike around and pick up soda and beer containers to cash in for deposit money, more chump change. I need a business. I must work on that very soon.

Dad gets up from his chair. "I'm going to run over to Ken's for a while." He slips out the door. I plop down in Dad's big chair. "What are we watching?" "Some silly show," replies John. "Can we watch CNN news, guys?" "Yeah, OK." John switches to CNN. The boys seem to be becoming a little uneasy. They're doing their best not to be too obvious. They're having trouble keeping their eyes off my little skirt and how much its shortness is exposing. I break the ice. I can be so forward sometimes that I astound even myself. "Have you guys ever had sex?" I laugh inside, as their mouths drop open. "Amanda!" Josh tries to shut me up. "Josh, it's a simple question, why the discomfort?" "No sister, especially no little sister, asks those kind of questions!" "Guys, in case you hadn't noticed I am not the typical

little sister." John smiles and acknowledges, "Yes we have figured that out. After your little show a week ago, I can't get sexual thoughts out of my brain. I think you've turned me into a pervert. Every girl I look at I can't help but wonder, what is under that skirt and top?" I laugh. "I love your honesty John. Of course, Josh has had lots of pussy, right Josh?" "Amanda, I can't believe you talk that way." I give him a huge smile. "Well, do you fuck your little girlfriends?" "Amanda where do you hear, or know, talk like that?" I laugh. "Guys, it comes naturally." "You're a kid," John snips. "So? I still get around." "I suppose the next thing you're going to tell me is that you do your boyfriends." "No guys, of course not, I'm still a virgin and will be for many years. Although, there is more than one way to skin a cat." "And what the hell does that mean?" Josh demands. I love getting a rise out of my oldest brother. Johnny, with a big smile, is taking it all in. "Josh knock it off. You're a virgin just like I am. I have a hunch Amanda knows more about sex than the two of us. Tell me the show she put on for us hasn't haunted you." I cross my legs and look directly at Josh. I can't believe it, he's squirming on the sofa; he's so embarrassed! "You need a beer to relax yourself!" "How would you know Amanda?" he rolls his eyes, "I suppose you drink beer as well." I smile as I raise both my feet to my chair and let my skirt slide upward. A girl does what a girl has to do.

Johnny speaks up. "Amanda, please don't sit like that. I'm going to embarrass myself." "Why? Is your cock getting hard?" He looks down. "Oh my God Amanda as a matter of fact it is! You're my sister; I should not be looking at you like this." "Johnny, it's OK, I'm a little tramp. It's OK to look. I will remain a virgin. If I can help you guys learn, it's OK." "Geez thanks for that, Amanda. How are you so worldly?" he asked. "Guys don't ask. How many times have you jerked off since I did my strip show for you, Josh?" No answer. "Johnny, how about you?" "One hundred and eighty-seven," he answers somewhat sarcastically. Josh adds, "Yeah Amanda, you totally turned me on as well. I do jerk off and think about your long legs and your hairy pussy. That makes me feel so bad and disgusting." "You're not bad or disgusting, you're human. I did that to you. That would be a whole different situation if you came to my room and forced me. I encouraged you guys, I'm to blame. I'm an over-sexed little tramp. You guys might as well enjoy it. I love to have men watch me. It's not some terrible thing!" I put my feet to the floor, stood up and turned around, letting my yellow lacey panties shine. I then walked to Josh and grabbed the remote, clicked off CNN and turned the radio to music. I move to the center of the room and move my body slowly to the beat. Oh, do I have their attention! I'm aware it's going to be a difficult challenge to top CNN. I turn my backside to their eyes. I know exactly what this little silky skirt is doing. Now I flash back to what Marianne did to me yesterday. I let my body bounce to the beat. I feel my body jiggling through the sheer nylon material. I slide my hands up to show off my yellow panties. I turn to face them with the beat, my body gyrating. It is quite apparent they are so aroused. I slide my skirt to the floor and kick it off with my foot. "Unzip your pants, both of you." Johnny grabs his zipper and zipped it down. Josh glared at John and then slid his zipper down as well. "Take your cocks out boys."

ohnny obeyed. He pulled it out – it was standing at attention. Josh took a very deep breath and dug his out as well. Two cocks standing at attention and erotically feeling my moves. How fun is this? I pull my top over my head tossing it aside. I slide each hand under my titties pushing them slowly to my mouth. I tongued my right erect nipple and then my left and now tickled my nipples with my saliva. God, it felt so good.

My brothers are in ecstasy. Not that they had any idea what the term actually meant, I did! They are both stroking their cocks with me dancing to the beat of my music. I slowly begin to slide down my yellow panties. I stop, showing only a third of my bush. "Do my brothers want to see more?" "Oh please, yes!" Johnny begs, "Amanda, I fantasize about your hairy pussy continuously. You are so hot. How will I ever find a girl like you? Please, I want to see it again." I continue my slide. My panties are now at my feet. I kick them toward the boys. They land on Josh's lap. Oh God I cannot believe it! He picks them up smells, licks, and kisses them so passionately, rubbing them in his face. That totally turns me on. I've never seen a male loving my panties while they were not on my body. I'm so hot! My juices are seeping down my leg. I dance slowly back to my chair and slide onto it. "Guys, I want your cum. Squirt it all over me, now! I want it right now!" I didn't have to ask twice. They are both in front of me, jerking their shafts. I am sitting back in my hair with my legs spread widely. "God, I want your cum. wet my pussy." My passion has taken me over. I drop to my knees, one hand on each shaft. I squeeze them both into my mouth. What a rush! I am forcing two cocks into my wet hot mouth. My mouth is stretched painfully to the limit. Two cocks, no room for stroking. I force their heads to make them fit. "Oh . . . oh!" Groaning, it took only seconds. Two loads squirting simultaneously on my tongue, my tonsils, my fillings, and my teeth. Wow. It was running – not dribbling, but streaming down my face and my body, cum everywhere. What a rush! My brothers moaning with pleasure, knowing this was their first blowjob, and their little sister was there to help. It made it all the more exciting for me. They step back, now for the Amanda show.

My mouth is full, as they slump back on the sofa, totally exhausted for the moment. I look at them. I can't smile. I reach my right hand for my titty, pull it upward, and let a few dribbles onto my already wet titty. And now, the left gets the same attention. I close my mouth to hold the balance for the grand finale. I caress my titties with their slimy juices. Oh my God, my brothers' cum on my titties is so exciting. I rub it all over my nipples. I am about to explode I am so turned on. The boys are beyond erotically amazed at what they are experiencing. I move my body back and forth and moan with pleasure. I spread my legs wider exposing my pussy lips and my clit. I bend my head forward, take aim, and drop the final gobs of cum to my pussy slit. Right on target, my right hand grabs it before it slides away. I wildly rub it all over my hairy pussy, my crack, and my clit. Oh my God, I am about to explode! The boys are now back off the sofa, both cocks erect and moving quickly to my chair. "Ah boys, give me more cum." They quickly squirt a second load all over my pussy, my titties, and in my face. It's heaven. My hand is wildly rubbing my

cum soaked pussy, I moan, with no control. I scream, "I'm cumming! Oh my God! I'm cumming!" I continue rubbing my pussy with my hand, the pleasure continues, I spread my legs to the fullest. God, I'm squirting, I'm squirting. The boys stare in amazement. I have no idea what is happening. Four times I squirt liquid into the air. I don't know what just happened, I don't even care!!

I fall back in my chair totally out of breath my heart pounding wildly. "Wow," I say out loud. "I gotta quit this. I may have a heart attack." I smile to myself and look over at my brothers. They are exhausted as well, besides being totally limp. "Well guys, way too much fun, best part, we're all still virgins! Did you like our practice session?" Finally, Josh speaks. "Amanda, you are a Sex Goddess. You are amazing." He is shaking his head side to side while staring at my limp body. "Guys, for my own purposes I will remain a virgin. I'm sure that will not be the case for you guys. Would you like me to help you with that?" "If you're not going to give up your virginity how could you help?" Johnny asked. "Brothers, I'm not the only fish in the sea." "Do you believe you actually could make that happen Amanda?" "I'm more capable than you could ever imagine."

I pick up my panties, skirt and top. I stand up very straight, shoulders back, titties pointing directly at them. I put my hands on my sides and give a sexy shake of my hips, moving my hairy bush from side to side. "Guys, do you want some help or not?" "Amanda, you are our Goddess. If you help us out with that, you will be our favorite sister." We all laugh. "Well perhaps you'll get lucky on your own, but before Christmas your virgin status will be eradicated." I drop my clothes, clinging to my yellow lacey panties and slowly slide them up my legs to cover my pussy. I again pick up my skirt and top and strut to my room. I lay on my bed. Wow, what was that? Watery liquid had actually squirted from my pussy. Where does it come from? That had never happened before. Each time it squirted my body shuddered. Wow, whatever happened, please God, bring it back. I've never felt this relaxed. I better call the carpet cleaners, or at least clean up my wet pussy juices before I drift off.

Four o'clock, I awaken from my nap to the sound of my music. The sun is shining so beautiful and the sky so blue. I open my window, oh, the smell of clean fresh air with just a hint of fall. It feels so refreshing. My life is so perfect, I love to be alive I do have my concerns, but I'm learning and understanding so much.

The cum has dried and my panties are glued to my skin. It's time for a quick shower. I wonder how long the sun has been shining. Dad and Uncle Ken are both outside spreading paint. The boys are probably at the Ferris's I suppose. All showered and my hair perfect, I throw on shorts and a top and out the door I go. I clean what juices are left from the carpet very quickly and go outside.

"Where is your stick Bandit? Go on go find it. Hi Dad, hello Uncle Ken. Is it not too wet to paint?" "No, the sun dries it pretty quick," Dad responds. Their choice of colors was disappointing, although it certainly does look better. "Go get it Bandit!" I give his stick a toss.

CHAPTER 26

A Business is Born

There's not a cloud in the sky, only blue as far as eyes can see. Mom should be along soon. "Dad, keep an eye on Bandit please, I'm going to clean up the house before Mom arrives." "OK, Honey." I turn on the news while I polish, dust and vacuum. "Hey!" Oh my gosh, there's Bargain Bob saying, "If you got a job, you have credit with Bargain Bob," as he goes on showing sofas, mattresses and bedrooms. He waves his hands and talks fast, but speaks clearly. If I were short on credit I would go to one of his stores. I intend to be a cousin very soon. I can't wait for John's birthday next Thursday evening. In fact, I will pick up the phone and make our reservations right now while I'm thinking about it!

I finish my housekeeping and Mom arrives home soon after. "Good to have you home, Mom, I miss you." "Oh thank you honey. I'm so tired, would you please order pizza for dinner?" "Of course, would pizza at seven o'clock be OK Mom?" "Yes Amanda, that would be perfect, thank you." She heads to the bedroom, "Amanda the house looks great honey," and closes her door. Well at least she will have a couple days off. Poor Mom! She works so hard.

The following morning I awaken to another lovely day. My bus arrived right on time. "Good morning Ray. The bus looks great. Did you or the rain wash it?" "I did," he grunted, "before the rain arrived." "Good job Ray, you're a good bus washer. Maybe you should start a bus washing service right from your house and make bunches of money." He didn't seem to find that nearly as humorous as I did. Oh well. I slide into my seat between the boys, they tell me how they have missed me. Each has a hand quickly sliding up my legs and soon tickling my pussy. I spread my legs just a little, so there was plenty of room for both hands. Someday, I will have

a load of cum in my panties and see if they realize what they're feeling, so wet and sticky. Not sure how I'll work that one out, just food for thought. "You guys are making my pussy feel too good this morning. Don't you dare make me cum, you bad little boys." I'm not even near that horny this morning. I had all I needed for at least a day from my big brothers plus Marianne and her brother. Whew . . . I was a very busy little tramp over the weekend!

Another normal day at school, there were no debates with Mr. Jackson today, just some boring class stuff. I gave him his usual daily panty shot. I think he is appreciating me more and more. He seems to be gazing my way much more often. I think perhaps he may be avoiding subjects that could be debatable. That's good because I'm just not up to it today. Back on the bus I slide between my two boys. I sure hope Bri comes along soon. I need something new. The boys find no time for boredom as their hands slide up my skirt and tickle my pink panties. The bus ride came and went. "Bye Ray, I'll see you tomorrow." "Bye Amanda."

"Oh, Mom, you're looking so much better. I felt so sorry for you last night. You barely nibbled on your pizza." "Oh thank you Amanda, I was whipped. I do feel so much better today." "Dinner smells so good Mom." "We're having one of your favorites tonight, lasagna. I know you don't like red sauce so I made it in a white sauce." "Oh, thanks Mom, that's sounds perfect." "Dinner will be ready at seven." "I'm going to run into town to pick up a few groceries." "Can I come along, Mom? I want to go to the Dollar Store." "Of course honey." "What do you need at the Dollar Store?" "I buy my lip-gloss and hand and body lotion there. It's a very good deal." "It's nice you're so thrifty. Remember our first trip to Good Will?" "Of course Mom, I will never forget. Now it's one of my favorite places. I have Marianne shopping there now." She laughed, "That's great!"

At the Dollar Store I pick up mascara, lip-gloss, hot pink lipstick and eye shadow. I love to browse the aisles. There are so many things…glasses, dishes, soaps, hangers, cookies. I stop dead in my tracks. Look at all the cookies! There are dozens of different kinds and brands. I look closer. Oh my God!! I am so excited I run for a cart. I grab different kinds of wafers, butterscotch, chocolate covered, oatmeal, and chocolate chip. Yes, chocolate chip! Wow! There are twenty-four cookies in a bag for a dollar. Perfect! I find some small boxes. Yes, perfect, four rectangular boxes for a dollar. Excellent! I get ten bags of cookies, five packages of four boxes, equals twenty. Yes! I pay the cashier and haul my inventory to the car.

I am so excited! Should I tell Mom? No, not quite yet, let me get organized. This is almost as exciting as sex. I can't wait! I locate Mom and push the cart for her. I am beaming. "Amanda, what is it?" "I can't tell you Mom." I wanted to jump up and down. Control yourself Amanda, I tell myself. Mom pays the cashier, I load the trunk with groceries and off we go. "What are in your bags Amanda?" "Can I tell you later Mom?" "Girl, you better tell me now. Why are you so excited?" "Mom, I bought chocolate chip cookies and some cute little boxes." "Sooo?" Mom questions. "Amanda, what, are you talking about?" She was getting a bit agitated. "Mom, it's my new business. I know I have to make my own money." "And what is your

point Amanda?" "I'm going to sell cookies, twelve for five dollars." "Who will buy your Dollar Store boring cookies?" "Mom, it's got to be my salesmanship. They won't know how bad they are until I'm gone. I'm not looking for repeat customers. If I can sell a box to every fourth house, that's a lot of five-dollar bills and four dollars and twenty-five cent profit each time I sell one dozen. Isn't it great?" Mom was smiling and shaking her head. "Amanda, I don't know where you get it from. Not Dad or I, that's for certain." "Mom, let me practice on you. 'Would you like to buy a dozen homemade chocolate chip cookies? It's my famous recipe. I'm raising money to go to cheerleader camp. Please Mrs. Shiels, I really want to go to camp very badly. It would help me so much with my cheerleading skills. I could cheer our college athletes to victory, and the cookies are so tasty! I was up all night slaving over my oven . . . please help me! I've baked them to perfection!'" "Amanda, you scare me! I've heard enough. Yes, give me two-dozen!" We laugh.

"Dad and Uncle Ken are next. I must box them up soon, and the Ferris's!" "Amanda, I think you should stay with people you don't know. For fifty cents a dozen they can't be that tasty." I think I have Mom sold on my new business. She never has to really know just how many boxes I sell. It will cover any extra money should I ever need to explain where it's coming from. Such a good plan!

CHAPTER 27

"Bri"

As always, Ray is right on time with our bus. The boys are waiting, same ritual, it feels good, although getting a bit old. Regular class again, no lecturing or class discussion, just listening and learning. When the day is over I get on the bus. "Hi Ray." "Evenin' Amanda." Oh my God! I fly to the back of the bus, "Bri, I'm so excited. It's so good to see you!" We exchange hugs. I smile at my boys. "I've got to catch up with Bri guys." Disappointed, they understood. "Bri, you look so hot." Her glasses are so cool. She has one little miniature diamond on her nose. Her makeup is flawless. Not too much, just enough. Bri has red lips, long extended eyelashes, perfect bright white teeth, and a gorgeous smile. She wore a short skirt, a hot tight top with lots of cleavage, white knee socks and white tennis shoes. Bri has it all! I would die for her huge, firm titties. God I want to just grab a hold of her. She is so bubbly and so cool. I think the glasses help with that coolness.

"Amanda, I must tell you. The last time I watched you do those two boys right here on this bus, I can't get that picture out of my mind. How you controlled the whole scenario. You seemed so calm and controlling. I like that in a person. That was amazing. I'm getting excited thinking of it." "Bri, on the way to school in the morning, pick one of my boys. We'll set him between us and have some cool fun." "But Ray must be watching you very closely." "Bri, this is my bus. Ray will never bother me. I do what I please." "How?" she asked. "We've become good buddies. Ray and I have decided that this is now my bus." "What? What does that mean exactly?" "It basically means I do what I choose." I slide my hand up her leg, she sighs. "Amanda, be careful, I'm so horny." I took that as my cue. I try to control myself. I must be cool. I want her so badly. My hand reaches her panty line. I

gently slide it toward her pubic area, her legs spread a bit. I'm now tickling her pussy, just like the boys do to me. I know just how it feels, especially the first time, with a new hand. She is so hot. Her panties are damp. I slide my fingers under her panties. I so badly want my finger inside of her. Her bush is so thick, much more hairy than mine. It's so curly. I slide my hand up a bit. The hair gets yet thicker above her panty line. My arm will reach no further. I want to see it so badly. I look around. Only the boys are paying attention. I do own the bus, but I do try to keep a somewhat low profile. I point my finger at the boys, telling them with my finger to stay where they are for today. I slide down the seat and drop to my knees. Her head leans back against the bus seat. I gently spread her legs a bit wider. She had silky red panties with pubic hairs one inch down her leg on each side of her panties, it's a monster bush. My tongue moves up her leg, kissing and licking her baby soft skin. I can't get to her bush quickly enough. I want to deprive myself; her legs are so soft. God, if we just had more time. The bus will be at her stop soon. Bri's hands are now on the back of my head, gently pulling it toward her monster bush. I let her guide my wet mouth. I grab a mouthful of pubic hair below her panty line. She doesn't let me slow and really enjoy. She is nudging my mouth toward her wet pussy. I bury my face in her wet panties. She moans loudly, much too loud. I was so afraid we would have the five or six remaining students back here for the show. I decide I don't really care at this point.

My tongue is licking and sucking her juicy red panties, her hands are pulling my face tighter to her crotch. She pumps it in my face. I want to pull her panties off, but that'd be too much work and too little time. I pull her stretchy panty crotch aside. I ram my face and then my tongue into her hairy hole. It's so wet. God, it tastes so good. I continue lapping up her juices, my tongue wildly flicking her large clit. She is wild with pleasure. I wish I could see her face. The boys will give me a report soon. She spreads her legs even wider, purring quietly with pleasure, my tongue is going wild. She pulls my head tighter. "Uh . . . Oh . . . Oh God, oh my God, oh my God Amanda! I'm cumming . . . I'm cumming all over your face. I love your hot mouth. I love you." She now let her breath out with a big sigh. I'm still on my knees. "Amanda, I have never cum that hard. You are so beautiful!" That was like music to my ears. She's so wet. I have never experienced so much wetness. It sprayed out. I'm still swallowing all I can as I lick and suck on her legs. Her red panties are soaked. I squeeze out from between her legs and sit back up my seat. My face is covered in her wetness. She puts her arms around my neck, her mouth kissing and licking all over my face. She puts her lips to mine. We engage in the most passionate kiss. Her thick lips devour my tongue, sucking it deep into her mouth. I love her tongue. Her mouth is fresh like mint gum. Now I understand why she always has gum in her mouth. I love her mouth almost as much as her pussy. I peek out the window. We're at Bri's stop. Ray is watching us through his big mirror. "Come on girls, party's over." Bri and I arrange ourselves. "Amanda, thank you. I would like to go down on you right this second." "That's OK, Bri, I'll just take my little horny pussy home." "I feel so bad," Bri whimpered. "Let me fill you in on a little secret

Bri. I love it when my pussy is hot. I like it this way. I'm perfect." She gives me a kiss and walks up the aisle of the bus. "I'll call you tonight Amanda."

Bri stops by Ray at the door. "That was a hot ride, Ray. By the way, whose bus is this?" Ray rolls his eyes and shook his head. "It's Amanda's." "Ray, you're so sweet. How can I get my own bus?" As she slides her skirt up and runs her hand over her soaked red panties. "Do you like hairy pussies Ray?" Ray kept his mouth shut, he knew my rules. It was fun to watch him squirm. "Bye, Ray, since you're not talking." Away Bri went, next was my stop. "Thank you, Ray. You handled that very well. Don't you dare be looking too closely at the girls without my permission." His cock was so hard, his slacks forming a tent. "Ray, if you will be real good I may let you fuck her someday." "Do you mean that Amanda? I would do whatever you asked. She has the hairiest pussy I've seen in years." "You be a good boy now Ray." I opened my door and strutted away.

I lay on my bed thinking about how excited I was by her. Her hot mouth was so passionate. Her pussy had turned me on. I loved the way she spread her legs and how she held my head so tightly between them, her sweet juices all over me. Was it all cum? It didn't really make any difference – I loved it. Would she fuck Ray while I watch? I wondered. The thought of Ray's big cock in her pussy was driving me wild. I run my hand between my legs and think of her as I fantasized. I started cumming. I continued cumming. I sighed as my body went limp. After all that excitement, it was time for a nap.

An hour later my cell phone awakens me. "Hello?" "Hi Amanda, it's Bri." "Oooh Hi!" "Amanda, you are so amazing. What you did to me, I will never forget. That was amazing and right on your bus! Ray told me it really is your bus. I won't ask any more for now, that has to be a great story." "Yes, I watched you taunting Ray, you little tramp." She laughed. "He wouldn't talk to me. Is he shy in that kind of situation?" "No Bri, it's one of my Ray rules. He can't look at school girls without m permission." "Wow, great rule. He did look at my panties and pubic hairs." "Bri, you stuck them in his face, I can't count that." "That's true." "Would you fuck him Bri?" She hesitated, "In a horny state maybe." "Bri, he has a huge cock. The head is three or four inches in diameter and squirts a huge load of cum." "Well, it is sounding better." "Bri, I would love to watch while you get fucked." I could feel her smiling. "I would love to have you watch. We are so bad!" "No Bri, we're very good little tramps!" "Yesss," she answered. "Maybe next week we can live our little fantasy." "You must come to my house some night, Bri. Do you know my brothers?" "Of course, they are so cool. They never have paid me any attention, of course they graduated a while ago." "You are too hot, you are intimidating to many guys." "I'm sure." "I'll try to have them at home when you visit." "That would be great. Amanda, you just are full of great ideas and so much fun. I am blessed to have found you! You know, I'm thinking of getting a tattoo, whadda ya think? Would you want to get one?" "Bri! No way! Don't you dare tattoo your beautiful body! I will divorce you." Laughing, "Well, I don't want that. Scratch the tattoo!"

"Tomorrow morning Bri, should we each take a boy or go two on one?" "Let's do

some two on one and if time allows we'll have a little fun with Roy as well . . . sounds like way too much fun, Amanda. Someone is at the door, see you in the morning."

I leave my room and see who is out and about. Mom is cooking dinner, Dad was painting and the boys are watching television. "How are you Mom?" I wrap my arms around her and give her a big hug. "Just fine, would you set the table please?" "Sure, and Mom, you're right, I will not sell cookies to family or friends. It's like begging, I guess." "That's a very good decision." "What is hiding in the oven Mom?" "A pork roast." "It smells yummy. Dinner is at seven, right Mom?" "Affirmative," she replies. I approach my brothers. "How was practice guys?" "Good," answers Josh. "Are you ready for partying Thursday night birthday boy?" "I'm ready to rock and roll." "Marianne is coming with us." "Cool! It's always great to have her join us, she's a sweetheart." "Can we pick her up Mom?" "Sure, it's right on the way."

We had a nice quiet evening. I turn to go to my room for the night. "Goodnight all."

The next morning I board the bus as usual. "Good Morning Ray." "Morning Amanda, how are you?" "Just perfect." I slide beside Bri toward the back and give her a cheek kiss. She's so beautiful it amazes me. "Call Sam, Amanda!" "Hey Sammy, come sit with us." I was so happy to see Bri that I had ignored them as I passed. Sam slid between us. He couldn't take his eyes off Bri. That seems to be how guys are, they love you until the next one comes along. Oh well. Bri sees who is getting his attention. She lays his hand on her leg. That was all Sam needed. His hand is moving toward her panties. I could go sit with Roy, but I really love watching. His hand is rubbing her crotch as she spreads her legs for him. I grab his cock, it was hard. I stroke it up and down. He moans, "Oh oh oh," as the wet spot on his slacks gets wider and wider. His hand left Bri, it was over. Bri smiled and pecked his cheek. "Send your partner back to us. Better clean up that wet spot." He looked down with embarrassment written over his face.

Roy slid between us. "You girls are so hot!" "Yes we know that Roy. Can you last longer than your buddy?" Bri asked. He shrugged. It was only about ten minutes to school. Bri took over. "Get on your knees Boy." He obeyed. She grabbed the back of his head. She slid down in the seat just a bit and pulled up her skirt and exposed her white bikini panties with bushy hair running well below the panty lines. God I love seeing her monster bush again. She pulls his head between her legs. "Lick it boy." He was awkwardly doing his best. Bri pulled her pantied crotch aside. "I want to feel your tongue, little boy." I watch his tongue move in and out, she was leaking heavily. He tried to pull his head back. "You drink it pussy sucker." He tried, but was now choking. She pulled him by his hair. He looked up. "You're not done yet little boy." Pushing his head back down and pumping her hairy pussy in his face, rubbing it up and down. He was attempting to do the things Bri demanded. "You little boys must learn to suck pussy or you're not doing me again." She continued rubbing it in his face. He was safe, the school bus stops. Bri let him crawl out. His face was so wet. So was I. How I love watching her handle my boys, way too much fun.

CHAPTER 28

John's Birthday

The next couple of days passed quickly. I boxed cookies for my upcoming business. They looked quite good, almost a home baked appearance. I couldn't try one, it would have left me short one for my dozen. I decided when I left on my sales trip I would microwave them all to loosen them and give that home baked appearance. I was very excited about my upcoming adventure.

John's birthday has finally arrived! The family climbs into our van and we are on our way to pick up Marianne. John was in birthday spirits it seemed, as was Josh. Mom and Dad had gotten him a computer for his room, noting that Josh would have use of it as well. We hadn't had one before. Fortunately, we had become quite computer literate with teachings at school. It was a great gift.

We arrive at Marianne's. She slides between Josh and I. She was wearing a little short girly skirt and tight top from Good Will, not a word from me. I was wearing a very similar outfit. Marianne gave me a hug and a kiss, wished John a "Happy Birthday" and chatted with all. She was as excited as me. I loved seeing Josh check out Marianne's firm breasts and exposed legs. I couldn't blame him. I was having trouble not staring.

As we arrive at Cadillac's I look up to see a big Moet bottle on top of a large building with Cadillac's in neon letters on the bottle. How cool is that? A pink front of a Cadillac sticking out over large brass and glass double doors, although the gray and maroon exterior is rather boring. We park across the street. Through the double doors we walk onto beautiful marble floors. I look up at extraordinary brass ceilings and then down a long, wide burgundy hallway straight ahead of us. The hostess greets us immediately. "Good Evening, welcome to Cadillac's." She made

s feel so welcome. Her name is Stephanie. "Do you have reservations with us this evening?" "Yes," Mom answers. "It would be under Shiels." "Yes, of course, here you are." She grabs our menus and escorts us to our table. As we walked by I noticed a beautiful bar. It was large, very detailed and only seven people cocktailing and sitting at the beautiful brass bar stools. There was a full size pink Cadillac to our left that had been converted into a beautiful buffet. How cool is that? It is filled with all sorts of entrées. There is a happy face black guy singing with a microphone in his hand on stage. Two couples are on the dance floor dancing to the slow music. The atmosphere is filled with a Vegas presence like I have dreamed about and seen on television. There is also a pink Cadillac that set up high behind the dance floor that appears to be a D.J. booth. Life size figures of Elvis Presley, Marilyn Monroe, and the Rat Pak are set up high around the stage. Old, beautiful, Cadillac's are everywhere. There is an oak railing with brass insets and a large dance floor, the detailing is amazing.

We are seated and promptly greeted by our server. He's young with a long ponytail. He welcomes us all. "Good Evening, my name is Cody. Is this a special occasion or simply out for a relaxing dinner?" "Our son John, we're celebrating his birthday night," Dad answers. "Happy Birthday John." We all clap our hands along with Cody. "Can I get you a free cocktail John? At Cadillac's we sell liquor to anyone." He waits for a reaction and quickly adds, "Just kidding, of course." We all laugh. "But later I will bring you one of our wonderful homemade desserts compliments of Cadillac's." Cody goes over the specials and tells the club history. He told how Bargain Bob designed and built it to his dream and specifications. He also spoke of his obsession for classic Cadillac cars. The restaurant was so professionally done. I was proud to think that I soon will be a cousin.

We order drinks and are deciding on menu entrées or the beautiful Cadillac buffet. All the while the musician continued to play. He's very good. 'Ray Potter and the Music Machine' the sign read. He came to our table singing "What a Wonderful World." What a beautiful song, I thought to myself.

All eyes are wandering about, there was so much to see. If the food is half as good as the atmosphere, it will be a winner tonight. As I am looking around I spot "O'La Lay" sitting at the bar. I nudge Marianne. "Come with me. Dad, that's one of Bob's friends, we're going over to say hello." "I'm going to have the buffet," Marianne tells me. "Me too, I whisper."

We walk up to his left side, he's on the phone. He spots us and cut his conversation short. "Amanda!" he says with his huge smile. I was amazed he remembered me. He jumps up and put his arms around me like we were Bosom Buddies. "So good to see you," his eyes look us both up and down. "You two are lookin' good," he drawled. "This is Marianne, Mr. 'O'La Lay'" "Drop the Mister," as he rocks in laughter. "Let me buy you ladies a drink." "We're OK, we have them at our table. Where is Bob?" "He comes in about seven thirty or so." "Ty, is he here?" "He's here working, maybe in the kitchen. He'll be along soon."

No sooner said than Ty arrives. "Amanda, you are looking so good," as his eyes

totally massage our bodies. His tag says 'Night Manager.' "Oh you work here?" "Yes Amanda; part time. I help Bob out as much as I possibly can. He is such a true friend . . . having a celebration tonight?" "Yes, it's my brother's birthday." "Great," Ty says with a huge friendly smile. He asks several questions, some a bit personal. I think that's Ty's personality. I read a big sign at the Bar, 'Free Birthday 'O'La Lays.' "Mr. 'O'La Lay,' you even have a drink named after you?" He beamed "Yes." "Now, what does it mean?" "Honey, we covered that one," he says in a low sexy voice. "Don't make me tell you again." He rolls with laughter. We all break out in laughter, too much fun. "Let's meet your family, shall we?" Ray Potter, on a break, has now joined the festivities while I make introductions. He asked for requests while bidding a happy birthday to John. Other tables around us are all watching. Hopefully we were not disturbing them. Ty has ordered a round or Cadillac's for our table. Man, how I'd love a beer, oh well. "O'La Lay" has engrossed Marianne in conversation. He is quite a character I'm learning. Ty can't take his eyes off my long legs and my very short skirt. He chats about many things a different approach than "O'La Lay." Ty hones right in on you and always has a smile even while he is politely chatting. Hors d'oeuvres arrive. I tell Dad Marianne and I are having the buffet. "No, no, come, come," Dad says, "we're all sharing here." Ty continues, I could feel it…he wants to put his hand on my leg. If the family wasn't here, I'm sure his hand would be wandering under my skirt.

"What's your favorite restaurant?" he asks very intently. I think to myself, decide to try out my best theatrics. "I love this place west of town. It's so great, the atmosphere is very warehouse-y, that's the new look." "Yes," he agreed. "They have little stations with a chef at each one preparing each exotic offering right in front of you. They then serve you right at each station." "The chef serves?" he inquires. "Oh, yes, white suits, chef hats, all are so friendly. You stroll from station to station until you can eat no more. I just love it and, this is the best part (he is looking very puzzled) you pay twenty-five bucks to join, and that's all for the year! It's all free once you sign up." "Where is this place?" "I forget what street, but west of here. It's called Sam's." "Amanda, I've lived here all my life and go out all the time, I've no heard of it." "You must try it." Ty's eyes now roam over my body one more time. "Let me take you there." I hesitate. "Sure, that would be fun." "How about Saturday?" I have to work my business on Saturday." "What business are you in?" he asks in a continued super-friendly tone, with that big smile. "I bake and sell chocolate chip cookies." "Really?" "Yes." "Are you doing well with that?" "Yes, it is profitable and the cookies are the best." "What kind?" "Chocolate chip." "My favorite." He smiles again. I realized he was quite a bull-shitter, whatever kind I said would have been his favorite. "May I ask, how much do you get for them?" "They are only five dollars a dozen or four-dozen for twenty dollars." "That's a great deal. I want two dozen." "Great Ty, I will get them to you very soon. In fact, how about if we go to Sam's Sunday afternoon, about three o'clock?" "Great," he beams. "Give me you address." "Ah no, I'm engaged, I don't want Mom and Dad talking. Pick me up at that truck rest stop on the highway." "OK, that's great." "O'La Lay," Ty raises hi

glass. We are teaching the family how "O'La Lay" works. The hors d'oeuvres are simply fantastic. I nibble during our conversation. Our dinners are now being served.

I drag Marianne away from "O'La Lay" and we walk to our Cadillac buffet. From the eyes in the back of my head, I could feel eyes crawling over our bodies. I hear a big, "O'La Lay," behind us. My whole family "O'La Lay's." Too much fun! It's great to see Mom and Dad actually having drinks together, this is quite rare. I like this place and all its choices. "We're both on diets." It's something I say just for fun; something I often tell people just to get a rise out of them. We're not really on diets, and probably never will be. But the reaction it gets is quite often fun. We fill our plates. Marianne does mostly salad and I skip my salad and go for food, real meat, all kinds, and so beautifully presented.

Slipping back to our chairs, our little fan club has left, thank God. I need a little break. Our dinner is beautiful. Our server Cody has been great. Robert is clearing empty plates, they are so efficient; I'm amazed. I look up and coming through the front door is Bargain Bob. The hostess greets him with a big hug. Bob's eyes are everywhere. He is pointing down the long hall at something he doesn't like, that's very apparent. He waves down the bartender and is pointing at the lights, which are very bright. Suddenly the dining room lights dim. The ambiance now feels perfect. He does an 'OK' sign to the bartender. He shakes hands and chats with a group of people at the end of the large bar. Ty strolls up to him. Bob whispers something in his ear and points at Ray Potter, our singer. Ty immediately heads for Ray. The music level suddenly drops and the sound level is now perfect. Wow, I am in awe just watching him. Many more customers walk up to Bob and shake his hand. There's lots of conversation. Bob responds in a very serious manner. Another customer is waiting to shake hands and then more conversation. I wonder what they talk about. Everybody is smiling. Bob, apparently, does not smile often. I can see that he is sort of a serious sort, and somewhat intimidating to many.

I finish my dinner while trying to figure out the best way of getting Bob's attention. I decide I have plenty of time. Mom and Dad are on the dance floor. That is so sweet. I have never seen that before. That does my heart good. Of course, where does one go in this area for dinner that has music to dance to and a beautiful dance floor? Only at Cadillac's! I'm enjoying my entrée, which is fish in some sort of delicious heavy cream sauce. I finish it and go back to the Cadillac buffet to get one more little piece. Ty catches me at the buffet. "Amanda," with that eye twinkle and courteous smile. "Enjoying the buffet?" I compliment him as his eyes devour my now erect nipples. He is a very handsome man, I must admit. I wouldn't take serious too many of his complimentary flirtations. He tells that to them all I'm sure. I feel it as strongly as I feel his eyes continuously roaming over my body.

My eyes scan back to Bob who is still chatting and yet more people coming and going. I watch him move down the bar to "O'La Lay's" area. A huge "O'La Lay" rings out from the back of the bar. Bob taps his fist on drinks, as he appears not to be drinking. Ty is watching me gazing in Bob's direction. "Does Bob know you're

here?" "No. I'm sure he won't remember me." "Oh," he says, "Bob doesn't forget anything." I assumed as much. I will catch him when his customers disappear. I excuse myself and walked back to the table with my creamy fish. Back at our table, Ray Potter is looking for volunteers. He needs men on the dance floor. He has three and is pleading with Dad and Uncle Ken to join them. Finally Mom is encouraging them to help with Ray's little skit. They give in and move to join the row on the dance floor. Ray's music begins; it's the Jackson Five playing the song, "ABC".

The five, led by Ray standing in front of them begins the wild Jackson Five moves, following Ray's lead. Ray is a great dancer and very theatrical, he's a true entertainer. This group of five including my Dad and Uncle Ken trying to imitate Ray doing the Jackson's moves is hilarious. Their heads and necks turn side to side quickly and back. Their arms shoot straight out, a full turn, and then they shake their hips while cupping their private areas with their hands. It has the house roaring with laughter. I've never seen Mom and my brothers laugh so hard. Seeing her laugh out loud is so moving, it nearly brings tears to my eyes. This place is so great for my family. I wish I had a camera to capture this moment: Dad, Uncle Ken, Mom and my brothers all laughing so hard is something I've never seen in my life! This memory I will cherish forever. I wipe my tear away with my napkin. The crowd, some standing, applauds as the song finishes. Ray shakes all the guys' hands. Uncle Ken and Dad are grinning from ear to ear. Mom gets up and gives Dad a big hug. It was so precious! Where is my camera?

The birthday boy and Josh both hop up and give them both a big hug. "You guys are the entertainment tonight. That was too much fun," John tells them with a huge smile. "Thanks Dad, we are having so much fun and dinner was great!" Cody is sweeping our dishes away. Uncle Ken orders another round. God, a beer sure would be so fun. Oh well, I'll just pretend with my Mountain Dew. "O'La Lay" is back and conversing with Marianne and Josh. She seems to be enjoying him. Maybe I could go chat with Bob. I look toward the bar. He's alone, chatting with Stephanie the hostess. I turn to walk in that direction. A portly older gentleman walks in the door and heads for Bob, he gives him a big hug and they shake hands. Another couple walks in, a very tall handsome dark-haired gentleman with a moustache, and a tall, short-haired blond. She is stunning with her tight top and short blue jean skirt. Bob leaves his conversation and greets the blond and gives her a huge hug. Her face just shines as she smiles at him. Bob gives the gentleman a big hug and shakes his hand and interacts in conversation. Why is it all these people just seem to love this guy? I wonder what is it about him, and here I am sort of stalking him myself. I missed my chance I guess. I could plainly see this is not the place to have a meaningful conversation with Mr. Bob, at least not likely tonight. This is Thursday, what must it be on Friday or Saturday night? I will come up with something. I've got until Christmas to drag him to my school.

CHAPTER 29

Tyson (Don Juan)

It's so heartwarming to see Mom and Dad and Uncle Ken laughing together and having such a nice evening! I'd excuse myself to the ladies' room, but everyone is occupied, so I wander down the hallway toward the bathrooms. The hallway walls are covered with photos, many of Bob, and multitudes of high profile people. I suppose mostly customers. God, there is the mayor, the governor, pro ball players by the dozen. Oh, my gosh, it's Bob and Miss America and Miss Capitol City who just met. There are lots of beautiful young girls, dozens, probably cousins. I have a feeling my photo will be hanging there soon, but not tonight. I turn to Ty's smiling face as he moves very close behind me. My mind flashes, is Ty my ticket to catch up with Bob? I'm such a tramp. I inch back just a bit, he is very close already. My little round ass touches him slightly. He puts his hands on my shoulders in a very casual way. "Yes, I love these pictures," he says with a smile. He points out many of the athletes, telling who they were as he gently ran his hand over my bare shoulders. I was close enough that I could feel his cock hardening. This was not a scene for public view. I could certainly feel what was happening. I wasn't sure, but I felt it might be the early stages of a seduction by Mr. Don Juan. It was OK. He was very handsome and so manly and black. I'd not fucked a black guy. I'm sure this sort of thing is not allowed at Cadillac's. Let's see where Don Juan takes this.

"Well, Don, I mean Ty, I must borrow the ladies' room." I scooted away down the hallway. I take care of business as quickly as possible, wash my hands, do my hair and freshen up my lips; there, perfect. I step back out into the hallway. Don Juan is taking a sip from the water fountain. He turns and reaches for my hand. "Would you like to see the rest of the club?" "Sure!" He takes my hand, opens a door to the

right of the water fountain and leads me in. What? It's a mop room, with stacks of glasses and plates. He leads me across the room and turns to the left. It's another storage room, but much darker. He leans on a tall stack of boxes and pulls me close to him. His hands cup my ass. His hands are strong as he squeezes gently. He pulls my mouth to his. What a passionate kisser, although I've heard all Don Juan's are.

Our passion is rising. He gently massages my crotch, attempting to prove his passion for only me. I'm certain that is yet another great Don Juan move. I rotate my hips ever so slowly. It feels so good. His hands are on my ass, his cock rubbing against the front of my little skirt. His mouth is all over my face. "Amanda, you are so beautiful," he whispers in my ear while he passionately sucks and licks one and moves to the other. I'm so excited and he feels it. He drops his hands, reaches for his zipper and slides it down and pulls out his cock. He pushes my head down. I oblige and drop to my knees and go down on his large cock. I wish there was some light. Is his cock black? I could not tell. It's pitch dark. I slide the head into my mouth, he slides it deeper. "You like that Amanda?" he asks. I stop and look up, "Yes, Don, I do." "Honey I'm Ty." I return to sucking. "You want my load Amanda?" "Yes, cum all over my ass and pussy." I stood up and leaned over a tall bench. He yanked my panties down and tried to ram it in my pussy. I guide it to the proper hole. I reach back with the other hand with my saliva and lubricate my ass. I had soaped it in the restroom. Lubricated well, he rammed it in, pumped it a few times and I repeated, "Don, squirt it on my ass." He obliges, it begins to squirt and squirt. I massage his slimy jizz all over my ass and my pussy. He zips up quickly. "Amanda, have to get back to work. I will see you Sunday. I'm excited about checking out Sam's Restaurant." I stand up and compose myself, pull my panties over my cum-soaked ass and pussy. The strong aroma fills the room. I hope no one notices my new perfume. I will tell them it's called Donjn (for Don Juan) if I'm asked. I brush my hair and freshen my lip-gloss in the dark room.

I walk out the door and down the hallway. I find Marianne. "Amanda, where have you been?" "Why, are Mom and Dad looking for me?" "No, they're dancing. It's just me looking." I smile. "You little tramp you! It follows you doesn't it?" I give her an "O'La Lay" and she laughs. "Where is 'O'La Lay?'" "I'm not sure, he's a wanderer, he knows everyone. He is so much fun to talk to. He has lots of stories and listens to me as well. This has been so much fun tonight. Thank you so much for asking me along. I love you Amanda."

CHAPTER 30
The Party Has Ended

My eyes wander looking for Bob. He's on the backside of the bar with three Filipino girls and a long-haired beautiful blond, all doing an "O'La Lay." It's now ten o'clock. Bob has a cocktail in his hand. Their whole group is roaring with laughter again. I want to be part of the fun so badly! Maybe I'm too young. I can be as adult and perhaps as much fun as anyone else for Bob's family. However, tonight is not looking so good. Ty will perhaps be my salvation. Marianne and I walk back to our table. Mom and Dad are dancing slowly, it's so great! They seldom have fun, but tonight is the exception. The dining room is mostly empty. A gentleman in a black coat is sitting chatting with Uncle Ken. Marianne and I slide into our chairs. The gentleman quickly jumps up and says, "Hi, I'm Telly. I'm the Executive Chef here at Cadillac's. Did you enjoy your dinner?" "Oh yes, it was fabulous." "What did you order?" "The buffet, it was just perfect." "So glad you enjoyed it." "Where do your recipes come from?" "Bob gives them to me. I season them up and cook them to perfection." He has such a friendly smile, it makes Marianne and I both smile "Have you dined with us before?" "No, this is our first time, we will be back soon Chef Telly." He beams. "Glad you enjoyed yourselves. Have you met Bob?" "Yes, I have a couple weeks ago. He was in his pink Cadillac." Telly asks, "Which one?" with a huge smile. "I'm not sure, I know that it was pink." "Have you talked to him tonight?" "No, he's been very busy." "Oh, Bob is like a brother. He is always busy, you have to barge right on up." "My Uncle and Dad went to school with him." "Really? I'm going to let Bob know you're here," he walks toward the bar. Marianne says, "Amanda, he is such a nice guy! Chefs can be a pain in the ass. My uncle has a restaurant in Iowa and I've heard chef stories for years. This place is blessed to

have a chef like that, and to come out here and socialize. That is amazing. If I told my uncle he would attempt to steal that guy." We laugh. I turn to Uncle Ken and ask, "How are you doing?" "Just great. 'O'La Lay!'" We raise our sodas and clink together.

"Marianne, can you smell my perfume?" "Yes," she answers quickly. "Amanda, you smell like cum." "Why didn't you tell me?" "I didn't want to embarrass you." I got up and shot to the bathroom, pulled my panties off, wiped up what cum I could and stuffed them in my purse. I wet some paper towels, jump in a stall and clean myself up. I really didn't think anyone would smell my aroma. Oh well, it should be better now.

I walk back to the table panty-less. I turn the corner and Chef Telly is back at the table with Bob and chatting with Uncle Ken and Dad. What do I do now? Will I get an opportunity to say hello? They are engrossed in conversation, all standing, smiling, and telling stories. I wish Bob were like Ty and "O'La Lay." I wouldn't have this silly little problem. Of course, if he were the same I wouldn't be so intrigued.

"Bob," Dad asks, "have you met my daughter Amanda and her friend Marianne?" Bob gazes our way. "Yes, I believe I have," he said with a smile. "It was after the Labor Day parade. You promised you would use your dinner passes and here you are. Amanda, I want you to come back again." He reaches in his pocket. "Here are two more dinner passes. It worked once, you can make it happen again." He hands them to me while taking my other hand and kissing the topside. I really like him and I couldn't begin to understand why. He was not an average sort of man. I could see his complexity watching him with my Dad and Uncle Ken. Somehow this guy intimidated even them. Why, I wondered? This would be a challenge. I wanted to know and attempt to understand. I want to learn so much more about life and I believe this is my ticket.

Chef Telly steps back to our chairs. "Isn't Bob great? He's changed my life. I love this job, I have never been so happy in my life. I owe it all to Bob. He has taught me so much in my two years at Cadillac's." He went on and on. Why would this intelligent, handsome, personable guy go on like this? It was beyond belief. I cannot imagine talking about anyone like that. Are they serving bad water here at Cadillac's? Is Bob a cult leader? I will someday, somehow, get to the bottom of this. I want to understand it all so badly right now. I need Bob to show up at my class before Christmas, not a good night to make that happen.

Mom, Dad and Uncle Ken are getting out of their chairs and shaking hands with Bob and Chef Telly. Ray Potter breaks from singing and dancing and puts down his microphone and thanks them for celebrating John's birthday. With a glow on his face, he asks them to become part of his Jackson Five Group. Ray comes to Marianne and me and thanks us as well. I think he may be Ty's brother, same smile, same personality, and same roving eyes. I am so bad. I wish I were sitting so I could give the handsome devil a peek at my panty-less crotch. That will not be tonight. We bid our farewells and Bob turns from the end of our table. "Amanda, I'm

counting on you to use those passes." I considered a flirting comeback, I voted against it. He has flirtatious cousins everywhere. I didn't feel it would work in this case. We meander towards the door. Ty, "O'La Lay", the tall blond and gentleman and the Filipino girls are all having big fun at the bar. I hear a huge, "O'La Lay!" We all smile and Uncle Ken fires back, "O'La Lay!" Ty and "O'La Lay" come over and shake hands and give Marianne and I big hugs. Ty whispers, "See you Sunday." "I can't wait." "Don't forget to bring my cookies," he says with his happy smile. He pokes "O'La Lay's" arm, "Amanda bakes and sells chocolate chip cookies." "O'La Lay!" he shouts. He then looks directly at me very seriously and says, "Bring me a truck load!" He roars as the gang all follows with laughter. He ordered two-dozen. I was a little nervous. Maybe my cookies are really bad. I still didn't know. I didn't want to waste even one by tasting!

In the car on the way home Mom says, "I have not had so much fun since I can't remember when!" Dad was smiling so much he was elated. He certainly had enjoyed himself as well. But to see Mom relax and enjoy herself so much was a beautiful thing. It brought tears to my eyes just thinking about the pleasant evening. How grateful I am for this wonderful night with my family. Marianne enjoyed herself so much. She continued her thanks as she climbed out her door. "I'll talk to you soon Marianne."

We are home again. Everyone is all smiles. Mom, Dad and the boys walk toward the house. Uncle Ken is leaving, "Happy Birthday John and thanks for tonight. Without you this night would not have happened." Johnny looks back. "Uncle Ken I am all partied out. What a fun night! You're the best Uncle!"

Ken whispers in my ear, "Were you being naughty this evening little girl? I think you had quite a celebration yourself this evening didn't you?" How in the world did he figure that out? I am amazed! I wink. "A girl can't tell all her secrets Uncle Ken." He climbed in his car. I went straight to my room after grabbing a plastic Ziploc and pull my panties out of my purse and scroll YT, just in case it's ever needed. I crawl in and snuggle in my big bed.

CHAPTER 31

First Day in Business

Friday at school came and went quickly. That evening I called a friend of Dad's by the name of Linda who works at Sam's Club. I told her I needed a favor, and explained to her that she was to describe me and my guest to whoever was working the main entrance on Sunday at three-fifteen. I told her what I'd like them to say and how to greet me, and then asked her to solicit all your friends who pass out samples to help me as well. I explained in detail what my plan was. She was smiling. "Amanda, he is going to know better." "Well maybe, but I want him to at least believe that I don't. I'm auditioning for a movie." "Oh you are? What movie?" "Linda, it's just a joke. There's no movie, I'm just having a little fun, OK?" "Oh I get it." "OK, I'm with you now. Amanda, I will handle it, not to worry. Sunday three-fifteen?" "Yes, that is correct Linda."

After a nice family dinner I tell Mom, "Almost as good as Cadillac's, but not as good as Sam's." They all laugh. I told them what I was going to attempt to pull off with Ty. "Mom, it's not a date. I'm working on my theatrical abilities. A girl must keep them perfectly honed." She shook her head, she knew she wasn't going to win. "Amanda, where do you get these antics from?"

I go to my room and box up cookies for my business debut tomorrow. I put four-dozen aside for Ty and "O'La Lay." That leaves me sixteen-dozen. If I can sell half on Saturday it will be a good start. I'll need a very good night's sleep, got to work tomorrow. I fall asleep with my music playing.

I'm up at nine a.m. sharp. A perfect time for a business girl who does not like early mornings to start her busy day! It's a beautiful Saturday morning. The cookies look so good in their little white boxes. Perfect, all baked! Let's see, what

to wear for a first day on the job? This may be my most difficult decision of all. Should it be a skirt, sexy slacks, or little hottie shorts? I can certainly eliminate the jogging suit. How does a young cheerleader want to present herself?

Hmm...let's decide whom I want to appeal to. Moms who have little kiddies? Perhaps some, they most likely have little money and probably cook their own cookies and may not care if this hot little girl goes to camp or not. Maybe handicap folks who are in wheelchairs, no, probably not that many around. Possibly target little old men or women? Some perhaps, but I think I am leaning more toward ages thirty-two to forty-five. I would target men first, women second and I would work primarily in nice upscale neighborhoods. OK, so now what to wear? Ultimately I do have a profile of my clientele, that's for certain.

I try on skirts, shorts, tight slacks, hot tops, baggy tops, knee socks, trouser socks, and knee-highs. This is quite difficult! How to decide? Great product, great sales pitch, great attire. Come on Amanda, put something on and go! I'm going with what I feel comfortable in. I'll know much better after my first day on the job. My tight pink spandex shorts with very short legs. My favorite saying: if you have great legs, show as much of them as possible. I read that somewhere. I put on a hot white stretchy cotton top with frilly lace around the arms. A bra is a must. I must look professional for my first day. Sure glad I bought those little sleazy bras the other day. I look in the mirror, perfect. I want to buy cookies from myself! White knee socks, white tennis shoes. I look like a traveling sales girl. OK, now bag up my product. Eight boxes in each bag.

I'm going to use my bike today. I don't want a tire problem, not on my first day. I jump on my bike after telling Dad and Uncle Ken I'm leaving. I fly down the highway. I've decided on a subdivision half a mile the opposite direction of town from our road. I get an occasional honk or beep, it's great. I wave occasionally as I pedal my product toward my first customers. I'm so excited. I may be the next cookie queen. After all, Bargain Bob is known as the mattress king. He had to start somewhere. There appears to be maybe eighty or ninety houses in this subdivision, all very nice, with well-kept lawns, sidewalks and gutters. I ride my bike up to the first house. A perfect choice I decide as I walk up to my first customer.

I ring the doorbell. I ring it again and again. Darn, no one home. I push my bike to the next house. I repeat the same procedure, wow, no one home again. This is frustrating! OK, next customer. Ring! Yes, the door opens. A very old man peers at me. "Hello sir. I am selling home baked cookies to help send . . ." the door slams right in my face. Oh my God! How rude! I want to ring it again and tell him how rude he is. I regain my composure. OK, I push my bike to the next house. Ring, ring, the door opens and an early thirties attractive lady with a baby in her arms says, "Hello." "Hello ma'am. I'm selling cookies to go to . . ." She cuts me off. "Honey, we bake our own. Thank you for coming by," and closes the door. I take a very deep breath. What am I doing wrong? This is too frustrating! I should jump on my bike and pedal home. I could tell Mom I sold them all, no one would ever know. No, this is my new business; I will not be defeated on my first day!

I push my bike to my next prospect. Ring, ring, a fortyish man opens the door. "Well hello." "Hello sir," I say in my sweetest voice. "I'm Amanda, I am selling chocolate chip cookies that I bake myself so I can go to cheerleader camp over Christmas vacation. They're only five dollars a dozen, and they are delicious." He smiles. "Amanda that's great, a young lady that gets up on a Saturday morning and gets out to raise her own money. Young people don't do those things anymore. Yes, I would like two dozen." "Oh thank you sir!" "Honey, wait right here." He returns with a ten-dollar bill and I give him two boxes. "Amanda, you keep up the good work," as he closed the door.

Sweet! Now I am on fire. My first sale! To think, I almost gave up. I can do this! My heart is pounding. I couldn't believe how great I felt. My first sale! I push my bike so fast to the next house I left rubber bike tracks on the sidewalk. Ring, ring, ring, a middle-aged lady, fiftyish opens the door. "Good morning young lady." I give the same speech using my name, I'm feeling this is very important. "Yes darling, give me one-dozen." I'm smiling as she goes for my five dollars. I thank her so much as she closes the door.

Wow, this is great! I push my bike quickly before I lose my touch to the next house. A man is finishing mowing his lawn. He has just shut off his lawn mower. He is a handsome man probably in his mid-forties. "Hello," he says before I can park my bike. "Hi, I'm Amanda." I give him my story. He says, "Sure, come on in. I'll get myself a glass of water and take a dozen." I smile. He is looking me over quite closely. I follow him through his front door and wait just inside as he disappears. "Amanda, would you like a soda or a glass of water?" After peddling to here and forgetting to bring my drink I was quite thirsty. "Yes, a soda would be perfect." He came around the corner with a glass of water and a bottle of Mountain Dew. "Gosh, that's my favorite." "Come in and sit down while I find some money." I sat in a chair in the large living room. He handed me a five as I sipped on my Dew. I pull the cookies out of my bag. "What school do you attend?" I told him, and I also told him how much I loved school. "You certainly are beautiful. Do you do any modeling?" "Yes, I do." "I'm not surprised with those beautiful legs. Would you model for me?" His eyes roam over my body and legs. "I'd pay ten bucks to have you walk through the living room and let me enjoy watching your beautiful legs." Why not, I thought. "I'd love to," I say with a sexy smile. I slowly stand, put my hands on my hips, and slowly strut past him and across the room. I knew he was going wild watching my ass. I knew exactly how to rotate my hips as I walk. I turn quickly and look directly at him from across the room. How he liked that. I slowly walk back and stood directly in front of him. He handed me ten dollars. "I sometimes model my panties for my friends. I usually charge them ten dollars." He dug into his pocket and pulled out a wad of money and quickly handed me a ten-dollar bill. I slowly took one step backward, put a thumb on each side, and slowly slip my shorts down. God, this is as much fun as my first sale. I love exciting the men so much! I was wearing soft Henson brand, very low cut with lace on the top and around the legs. I knew he could see the outline of my hairy pussy thru the silky material. I kicked my shorts

toward him, they land in his lap. I wiggled back and forth, turned and ran my hands up and down my buttocks. My head was turned looking at him over my shoulder. He rubbed my shorts on his crotch, which excited me. I face him again and ran my two fingers over my pussy. He rubs my shorts faster, over his private parts. He moves them to his face. He begins kissing them. I love it. "For ten dollars more I'll sit on your lap." He quickly laid ten dollars on the coffee table. I slowly move toward him around the table. I spread my legs and slide onto his lap. He is so hard. I rock side to side on his hardness. It felt so good. I slowly rock back and forth, he is pumping me with my rhythm. His mouth touches one of my titties. "OK, I hate to be difficult, but I need ten dollars a piece, or two for twenty to kiss my titties." My math was very good. He pulled out a twenty, as it fell to the floor he pulled my top over my head and then lifted my little bra over my titties. He squeezed each one slowly while admiring his catch. He sucked one in. It filled his mouth. I'm riding his hardness faster. It feels so good. I love my sensitive titties sucked and licked so much. He went from one to another, sucking them in and then licking my erect nipples. It felt awesome. How I love men's hands all over my body. I'm hot! I lift my ass off his lap.

"Take your cock out. No charge." He smiled, unzipped his shorts and pulled it out. I slide back on his lap and rode up and down on his bare cock. It was pure pleasure feeling his soft skin and hardness rubbing all over my wet panties. "Your panties are so wet," he gasps in my ear. "Yes, look what you do to me!" I gasp! "Can I fuck you?" "No sir, probably not." "Please Amanda; I need to get my load off. Come on, honey. We keep this up and your panties will be soaked with my cum." "You'll be fine," as I smile at him. "Please Amanda; let me lick your pussy?" "Ooh maybe. Cheerleading school is very expensive." "What do you need Amanda?" "I don't want to take advantage sir, let me make you a special deal. I've got twelve boxes of cookies left, buy the rest of my delicious, homemade chocolate chip cookies," as I slide his cock through the leg of my panties. My pubic hairs are rubbing over his erectness very slowly. He is looking at what I am doing, he can't take his eyes off my hairy area. "That's only sixty dollars. I'm going to lie on my back, spread my legs so wide, while you suck the hairiest pussy you've had in a long time. And then, you're going to squirt your cum all over that hairy bush. Now tell me if that is not a great bargain. Let me get you some cookies to sample," I start to climb off. "No no no, honey, I believe you. I believe you." He pulls me back down and massages my titties with his mouth. I am being very careful with his rock hard cock. If he cums now I have cookies to sell. "So . . . do we have a bargain?" "Yes, of course, Amanda, yes." I roll to the floor; he drops to his knees. "Come take my panties down you bad boy." He rips them off. I spread my legs as wide as I could. His face is buried immediately. "Ohh that is so good," I moan. He is lapping and sucking my pussy. He grabs a mouthful of hair and licks my wild pubic hairs. I love it when men love my bush so much. He pulls up, jerks only twice. His cum is flying on my belly, in my belly button, squirting all over my pussy. He moans wildly, cum continues flying, it's so damn erotic. I am so blessed to be a cookie sales lady.

He finished, takes a deep breath and climbs to his feet. "Amanda, you are something! Amazing, that was amazing! You are truly every man's fantasy. Thank you so much Amanda." I pull my panties over my hips and wet pussy. I loved that 'just cummed on' feeling in my panties. He hands me sixty dollars. I dress and pick up the money that had fallen to the floor. "Amanda, if I like your cookies could I call for more?" "No, give me a name and number, I'll call you one day." He smiles and grabs a notepad. "I'll get the rest of the cookies from my bicycle." At the door he hands me a piece of paper as I hand him his bag of cookies. "Good doing business with you," I glance at the piece of paper, "George, I'll be calling when I do some more baking."

I hop on my bike and pedal down the street. Wow, I sold out and have a repeat customer, excellent. Could I sell just cookies? Yes, I believe I could make a business of that. Yes, I can force myself to handle rejection as difficult as it is. Sometimes no one will be home and I'll get doors slammed in my face, you can't possibly please them all. Why not continue with the more profitable side? Yes, cookies are a great concept and could work. I do love this other side of cookie sales. Was George just a fluke? I doubt that. What if someone harmed me with my antics? No, not likely, as long as I stay in neighborhoods with others close. Anyone too aggressive, I only have to make a phone call and someone goes to jail. It'll be a great working tool. Of course, someone could kill me I suppose. I don't see me letting that happen; I'm quite savvy. I have to go with the money side of this picture. Like Mom always said, 'your body is your temple.' I love to have fun inside my temple! I wonder if this excitement ever goes away. I know I would miss it so much. How I love men's hands, eyes, mouth, and tongues all over my body. It is continuously on my mind. I can't get enough of the stares and the thrill it creates within me. Do most girls notice this attention and are simply not interested, or don't really care, or perhaps find it disgusting? I only talk to two girls, Marianne and Bri. Bri is like me and loves it. Marianne I think likes the attention, but certainly is not near as aggressive. Bri and I make things happen, we know how to work things our way and make something happen. Is that control maybe?

I love my new business, Mom will be so proud. Sixteen-dozen sold, more on hold. I have money in my pocket and received a nice big tip. I will get back soon to the Dollar Store for more inventory. I fly into the yard on my bicycle. I am feeling very business like as I walk in the door. Mom is in the kitchen. "Amanda, I didn't expect you before four o'clock or so. How is the cookie business?" "Mom, I sold out!" "Oh my goodness." She runs to give me a hug. "I'm so proud of you!" I wave my money in the air. "Tell me some stories." "Well, it was not all that easy. Mom, I'm learning to accept rejection. Not everyone needs cookies you know." "Yes, I understand that." "But, Mom you cannot give up if you want to be successful in the cookie business." Mom gave me another hug. "You'll always do well Amanda." It felt so good knowing Mom believed in me.

"Is there anything I can do to help Mom?" "No thank you, dinner will be at seven as usual. You can set the table later." "OK Mom. I'm going to play with Bandit and I may take a little nap. It's been a long day."

CHAPTER 32

Bird Day

"Go get your stick Bandit! Get your stick boy." He sat. I got on my knees. He wagged his tail as he walked to me, licked me all over my face, and gave me his toothy smile. He wanted my attention. I put my arms around him and kissed his ear. God, I love him so much! He is my dog. I remember four years ago when Dad brought Bandit home, a tiny little puppy. I fell in love immediately. "Amanda, he is yours, you take care of him and he will take care of you." He has. Yes, he is my dog. We play for a while and he is ready to chase his stick. "Go get it, Bandit."

I go back to my room after setting the table on the way through. I put my money away and flop on my big bed. My music playing, my mind is on my new business. This could perhaps really be important. I must consider getting very serious about it. Working it three to four evenings a week, ten to fifteen hours a week or so, I could make some very good money! Amanda you must take control and make this little venture prosper. I am preparing myself to get very serious.

Suddenly, BAM! I leap up and run to my window. What on earth was that? I looked around, but didn't see a thing except for a feathery spot in the center of the window. I looked over to the grass. Oh, my gosh! A large red male cardinal had flown into my window and was now laying on the grass. One wing was fluttering just a bit. His eyes were open, his head was moving slowly and the red puff on his head was standing straight. Oh, my gosh, Mrs. Bird is sitting on a limb watching him. He is looking back. She is bobbing up and down on the little branch, softly tweeting to him. He tweets softly, she flies to his side. I can't believe what I'm seeing! The two birds peck their beaks together. I can hear her making gentle bird noises to him. She pushes his head gently with her beak. They gaze at each other.

Oh my God, is he is dying? Tears begin running down my eyes. I feel it, they are saying their last goodbyes. His eyes close. She is gently rubbing her head on his. He's gone. She nestles in the grass closer to him and puts her head on his. How can this happen? I begin to cry. This is the saddest thing I've ever witnessed. My day is totally destroyed. Oh, my God no, a cat appears. He wants Mr. Bird. Mrs. Bird is peeping and fluttering her wings. The cat doesn't care. I see her continue to beg. "Please don't take my husband away. Let me be with him just a bit longer. Please, a few peaceful moments with my best friend and mate. I am begging, please!" The cat has him and is now carrying him away. Mrs. Bird is flying after him begging, "Please, please, just a few more minutes with him," to no avail as he carries him away. I am sobbing uncontrollably. I watch Mrs. Bird fly back to her limb. She just sits, not a movement. Her head is down. What must she be thinking? She has lost her mate forever. She knew she would never see him again. Is this life? Oh my gosh, this could happen to anyone so very quickly.

I seldom have cried in my life. I fall to my bed crying and sobbing. What if Mom or Dad, my brothers, Uncle Ken, Marianne, or Bri were to die? I would want to die. Poor Mrs. Bird, I can't bring myself to look back out the window. I've lost it; I'm totally out of control. My door opens. Mom comes running to my side, I'm so embarrassed. I can't quit sobbing. "Amanda, what on earth is wrong?" She puts her arm around me. "Honey, tell me what has happened?" "Oh Mom, I love you so much." "And I love you Amanda." I continue sobbing. I'm now shaking. "Amanda tell me please, what has happened to you?" "Mom, I can't tell you right now." Mom is now lying by my side with her arms wrapped around me. She is holding me so tight and tears are forming in her eyes. "Honey, please tell me, what is it?" "Mom, someday you are going to die and so is Dad. I couldn't live, please promise you'll never die." Mom is hugging me so tightly. We're crying together, she feels my pain. I love her so much. I have never before appreciated the love I have for my family. This bird has shown me something so important in my life. I will be a different person. I will appreciate my family so much more after this day. It feels so nice to have Mom here lying at my side. I need her so much at this moment. I wrap my arms around her as the relentless tears continue. I attempt to control myself. My mind flashes back to Mrs. Bird begging the cat, knowing he is leaving forever. It was like lowering Mom into her grave, gone forever, never to be seen, never to hold me again as she is now. Death is so unfair. I just couldn't imagine continuing on without Mom in my life. What will happen to my lonely Mrs. Bird? What would happen to me? Oh God, why do these things happen? I close my eyes; I feel my body go limp as I drift off to a very deep sleep.

I awake to Mom gently shaking my arm. "Honey, I have dinner ready. Come on and eat...come on honey, let's get up." "Mom, I can't, I'm not at all hungry. I'm so sorry, I just want to be alone." "Are you sure honey? "Yes Mom. I'll be OK." "All right, I will check on you a little later...I'll save you a plate." "OK Mom." She closes the door. I don't want to even think right now. I am exhausted. I fall back to sleep.

Several hours later Mom is softly running her hands on my face. "Amanda do you

want me to bring you your dinner honey?" "No Mom, I'm not hungry." "Mom, would you ask Dad if first thing in the morning he would clean my window?" "Of course I will dear, but why?" "Dad will understand. This may be a positive thing once I get past it. Mom, I am not going to be selfish ever again. I want our family to change. I want us to let each other know how much we care about each other. I want us to be a loving, caring family. I will lead the way. Mom, I love you and Dad so much. I will tell you, Dad and the boys every day. My bird day has changed my life." Mom was puzzled. I did not want to totally break down again. I kissed Mom. "Tell Dad and the boys I love them Mom. I would like to be alone now." "OK, I love you hon." She slipped out the door.

Dad and the boys are in the living room, the TV is not on. I could hear their conversation as my bedroom door was slightly open. "Mom, is she OK?" asked Josh in a concerned voice. "I'm not sure," shaking her head. Dad asked, "What is the problem Anita?" "I wish I had an answer. She told me to tell each of you she loved you and that she wants our family to be more loving," shrugging her shoulders. "And, Robert, she would like you to clean her window in the morning." "What?" "I'm not sure why, but she said you would understand in the morning." John immediately said, "I'm going to get a flashlight and see what's going on." "No, you'll scare her to death shining a light at her window. She did call it her bird day and said her life has changed today." "What the heck does that mean Anita?" "I wish I knew. I have never seen anyone so upset. I was crying right along with her. I have no idea what has happened to cause this. It was so intense. I'm sure someday we will all understand Amanda's bird day."

"Amanda is always so strong. This is so shocking. I am so worried. If anything happened to Mom we would be devastated," said John. "I think we need to let her know how we feel Mom." "As she was crying, she was saying she could not handle her life if anything happened to any of us." "What in the world brought all this on?" asked Josh shaking his head with concern, "she came home today and was so excited. She sold all of her cookies and was on this huge high."

"I'm going to turn in. Robert, are you going to stay up for a while?" "No, I'm turning in as well." "Boys, I love you both," she says with tears welling up in her eyes. "I'm learning from Amanda. She insists she will tell each of us every day of her love for us. She is so right, I'm not sure where she gets it from, but I continue to learn from my teenage daughter." Dad smiled. "I love you boys. Anita. I love you. We had so much fun with all of you Thursday night. I'm proud of you all for so many reasons. Sleep well, we'll see you in the morning."

It was a partly cloudy Sunday morning as Dad brewed a pot of coffee and immediately grabbed a bottle of Windex and a towel and walked around the house with a small step stool. Looking at my two windows he spotted the red bird feathers in the center of her picture window. Quickly stepping up to clean the pane and then back to the coffee pot. "Robert, what did you find?" as she walked from the hallway tying her robe. "A bird hit her window that's all I know." "Was the bird still there?" "No bird, I'm totally puzzled. That doesn't help us solve anything."

"What are the options here?" "I couldn't even begin to guess," Dad replied. "Perhaps this morning she will share." "Hopefully her normal self will return." Dad poured Mom's coffee and handed it across the table. The boys came into the kitchen asking expected questions and were updated. I stayed in my room. At nine-fifteen, after their breakfast was over, I fully opened my door and left the bedroom. I walked to the bathroom with my head down. I did my business and headed to the kitchen. I was so depressed. I was still feeling so sorry for Mr. and Mrs. Bird. I could tell my eyes were red and swollen from tears. "Thank you Dad for cleaning the window. I love you all so much. I didn't mean to make a fool of myself. I just kinda lost it and I am so sorry. I never want to worry any of you. I am attempting to get my head back to normal. I know you all would like to know what has happened in my room to make me react this way." A sigh, "I wish I could tell you, I can't. I do not want to fall back into that state of mind. Speaking of it would certainly bring those thoughts back. Trust me this is a story I will someday tell not only my family, but also the world. I'm not ready at this time. Yesterday will go on my calendar as bird day. That's all on that subject for now, my family."

"Again, I love you all so much and I hope we will all let one another know how much we care. Any one of us could be gone any day. My bird day has shown me that we would be so terribly saddened if something happened to any one of us. I want us to let our love be known for one another daily. Do you think we could do that? I may not be making sense right now. I'm done talking for now. I will show you, my promise to you all forever."

I went around and hugged each of them. When I got to my Mom I was tearing up again. "Mom, I've never felt so close to you, thank you so much." She hugged me back as she took her Kleenex to her eyes.

CHAPTER 33

Sam's

The time has come for my "date" to my favorite restaurant. I'm not in the mood at all after yesterday's heart wrenching experience. But, I did make a commitment, and it must be honored. I need to brush up on my theatrics. I gaze into the mirror and geez, I need to do something with those eyes! Visine and some other serious eye restorer hopefully will remedy the situation. Now, what to wear? I need to ride my bike down the highway to the rest area. Yes, my little red capris. They fall just below the knee with a little tie thing on each leg and a little split at the knee that ties together. They really are very hot looking and the fit is so perfect. Now I'll put on a little red and white silky striped top. The fit makes my little titties look huge, well at least larger. It's perfect for my favorite restaurant and Tyson as well. It allows me to ride my bicycle without showing off my panties as a skirt would. OK, my wardrobe is all laid out. I'll slip on some shorts and go find Bandit.

Come on, my best dog buddy. I give him a big hug, put my arms around his neck, look into his eyes, "I love you Bandit." His tail is wagging as he looks at me with that toothy smile. I love it when he smiles. It's his love smile. I talked it over with him and he promised he is changing and will be more loving along with the rest of the family. He is starting today. "Go get your stick boy!" He charges off.

Uncle Ken pulls in the drive. I walked toward his car. "Good Morning, Amanda." I put my arms around his waist. "I love you. You're my best uncle." "Well Amanda, I love you too. To what do I owe this show of affection?" "Uncle Ken, you must change right along with the rest of this family. When you love someone you must let them know, one of us could be gone tomorrow." "OK Amanda, I will work on that, right now I'm going to love painting your house." As he walked toward his

ladder I heard him say to Dad, "Is Amanda OK?" "She is fine Ken. I love you." "Well, Robert, what the heck are you smoking? I want some." Dad laughed. They were talking and I'm certain they discussed life and what was happening a bit earlier.

"Go get your stick, Bandit!" I gave it a big toss. I look at my watch and see that I still have several hours. I drag my chaise lounge to a sunny spot and go back to put on my bathing suit. I grab my lotion and towel . . . perfect. "Go get it Bandit." I love him so much, he's my buddy. I rub lotion all over. It's one of those perfect days with just a few passing clouds. A little sun is just the ticket today.

Eventually it's time to get into the Sam's mode. As the sun warms my body I am thinking that my goal is to convince Tyson as we pull up to Sam's Club that this is my favorite restaurant. Now, it's up to my theatrical abilities and me. I'm honing them daily. Convincing Tyson how great these silly free handouts are and these little folks that work for a few dollars an hour are true exotic chefs, passing out exotic entrées. Tyson is a bright guy. He could easily laugh in my face. If he does, I lose, and man, how I hate to lose. He must be convinced that I love this place and the exotic food. Can I accomplish this little scam? We'll see where I take it, it's all up to me. Of course, Linda will be a godsend. Without her helping set the trap this could not be possible. I sent her money for chef hats, chef badges and getting all our little chefs on board with their stories. Today is meatball day at Sam's. This whole weekend, of all times, Sam's is passing out eight different types of damn meatballs. Hope Tyson is ready for exotic gourmet meatballs! If I am able to pull this off I will give up my cookie business and become a movie star, although cookies are working out quite well right now. If my project fails we'll have enjoyed some lovely Sam's Club meatballs, I'll collect my ten dollars for two-dozen cookies and have had a great bicycle ride. So "O'La Lay" to that!

The sun feels so good. I wish Marianne were lying beside me. If I weren't going to my favorite restaurant, I would've invited her. I can't even begin to tell her about bird day, but I can tell her I love her. I decide to give her a quick call. "Hello, Marianne, how are you?" "Oh Amanda, I'm so glad you called!" "I miss you Marianne, I love you and thank you for being my friend." I could feel her smile. "I'm lying in the sun." "You didn't invite me?" I laugh. "I have a date with Tyson this afternoon." I told her the whole story, she was laughing so hard. "Amanda if anyone can pull this off it's you." "O'La Lay," I fired back. "I'll give you a report." She "O'La Lay's" me and we said goodbye.

I eventually go inside. I shower, dress and pedal myself to the rest stop. I must be punctual to a fault, that is my motto. This little red outfit is hot. I love my look. It shapes my rear so perfectly. I'm glad I'm not a man in my little world. I would be in serious trouble.

I arrive at the rest stop. I park my bicycle on the big truck side and walk to the car side. I feel a little strange just hanging around the rest stop. I sit on a bench, that's a bit more comfortable. Great, I see Tyson's big smile as he pulls up in his beautiful Cutlass Classic. It's vintage, the top is down. Oh, God, what it will do to my hair. I slide in, he hands me a scarf. He's so smart, I wrap my hair and we say our hellos.

I give him general directions and we're off. He chats about various subjects. "What's in the bag Amanda?" "Oh Tyson, it's your cookies." "Great!" He has my ten dollars in his shirt pocket and hands it to me. "Open 'em up," he requests. "OK." I had microwaved them as I walked out the door so they were still quite soft. I held the box in front of him and he grabbed and munched one down. "Amanda, they are delicious." "Yes, they are good. Do you mind if I have one?" "Of course not," he answered. "When a box is open I devour them," I explain. "I try to avoid an open box. I must stay on my diet. I know what these beauties can do, you can't eat just one." "Yes, you're right," as he continues munching on cookies. "Tyson, you should save your appetite." "OK you're right, they are so delicious. I can't quit." I lock the box up. I peek first, only four left. I finally get a taste and they weren't so bad, I'm glad Tyson liked them. At least I've scored in the cookie department.

"I'm amazed I've never heard of this place." "You know, the best is that it's only twenty-five dollars a year and all you can eat." "That is so amazing." "And Tyson guess what…today is meatball day!" "What does that mean?" he questions. "The chef's are making exotic meatballs from all over the world." He sighs. "I didn't realize meatballs were exotic." Uh oh, this may be a tougher sell than I had expected. Amanda, dig deep. "You'll see very soon Ty." "I'm excited," he replied. "I know by listening and watching, you know what's going on in this world." "Yes I do," I answered. "Ty, the chefs all interact so well with the customers." "They make you feel so welcome. They also love compliments very much. Be sure you let them know, OK?" "Of course I will. I'm a chef myself, I know how important that is."

We make the turn and pull into the parking lot. "Amanda, this is Sam's Club!" "That's what I told you, Sam's — Sam's Club." "I've been here many times and have never seen a gourmet restaurant." "Oh yes, it's way in the back. I'm not sure how you could have missed it Tyson." "I haven't been a member in a couple of years." "I've only came here for a year and a half myself, perhaps it's new." "That may be the case," he agreed. We walk to the door. "Tyson we are so fortunate to be here on gourmet meatball weekend. Are you excited?" "Oh yes, very," as he gave me that big smile. I wave my Sam's card at the doorman. "Amanda, how are you? So good to see you…are you here for an early dinner?" "Yes, Bob, I'd like you to meet my friend Tyson." They shake hands. "Did you make a reservation?" "I called the maitre d' and he told me if we came this early we would be fine." "Beat the rush," Bob said as he grinned. "Amanda, did you realize it's exotic meatball weekend?" "Oh yes, I am very excited!" "I sure wish I could join you guys, but I gotta work. Life's a real pain sometimes to miss exotic meatball day." "You're right Bob, but life goes on." "Yes," he replies with his head hanging down. "Come on, Tyson, we're not going to miss it." We scurry across Sam's Club.

Our first gourmet station, here we go! "Chef Audrey, how are you?" "Oh my goodness Amanda, it's so good to see you, welcome to my station." She is wearing a tall chef hat, compliments of Linda. "Where have you been?" "Oh you know, busy, busy, busy." "Were you aware its exotic meatball weekend?" she asks. "Oh yes, when I attempted to make reservations they informed me. Chef Audrey, this is

Tyson. He works at Cadillac's." "Oh, I've heard of that place. But ya know what, their meatballs don't compare to what you'll dine on today." She has her little frying pan loaded. "Amanda and Tyson, I have prepared Russian glazed honey meatballs for you today." I snap up a tooth picked exotic Russian ball. I nibble a bit; "My goodness, Audrey, you are the best! Is this your creation?" She beams, "Yes Amanda, it is." "Oh, Tyson these are to die for!" Tyson stuffs the whole meatball in his mouth. Audrey puts her hand on her mouth and gasps. "Tyson, I certainly wouldn't want to embarrass you, but you must tongue them, not chew. Here try another one." Tyson looks at me and rolls his eyes. "Tyson it's true, it's like an oyster. You tongue them. You glide an exotic meatball down your throat a morsel at a time." He nibbles a small morsel from his toothpick, slowly rolls it around his mouth, his tongue slowly pressuring his exotic Russian ball to his mouth roof. "Wow, it does make a difference!!" He nibbles again, rolls and pressures and swallows. "Here Amanda, have another." "Oh no, we've got seven more stations to visit." "Tyson, would you like another?" "Yes, I'd love another one chef," says Tyson. "I need this recipe for Cadillac's." They laugh. "Wow," as he continues nibbling and rolling his Russian ball, "wow, that's amazing." He shakes Audrey's hand. She is beaming with pride. "Good job Audrey," I whisper as we walk away.

We move to our next station, "Amanda you look great today, came in early to beat the rush, ay?" "Hello, and yes, Chef Jerry. How I hate those long lines. Another hour and they'll be lined up fifty people deep on meatball day. Yes, thank God we don't have to deal with that. What is your recipe today, Chef?" "I have prepared Bavarian balls Amanda, prime beef mixed with Bavarian cheeses, one of my many winners." "This is Tyson; he's from Cadillac's." "Oh I love that place, only place in town that keeps up the quality like we do here at Sam's Club." Tyson smiles. "Come on Tyson, don't be shy!" He picks up a speared ball, we've got him trained! He nibbles and tongues a small morsel off his tooth picked Bavarian ball. I'm trying to tongue mine. I chew when Tyson's head is turned. "Chef, Chef, Chef, these are amazing. Would this be your creation?" I ask. "Yes," with a proud smile, answers Jerry, "it is." "So Tyson, what do you think?" He has barely finished tonguing his first morsel. Yes, he is ecstatic. "Chef Jerry, how many cheeses do you use?" "Three," Jerry says with pride. Tyson guesses, "Is it Parmesan, cheddar and wild goat?" Chef Jerry sighs, "You got one right." "Is it the Parmesan?" "Nope, it's the wild goat." Tyson looks down at his feet, "Damn, I thought I had that one. What are the other two?" Chef Jerry whispers in Tyson's ear, "I could tell you, but I'd have to kill you." "Ha, ha, ha," he roars. "I learned that from your 'O'La Lay' guy." "Come on Tyson time to go to the next station." I whisper in Jerry's ear, "Wild goat cheese, where did that come from?" He winks and says, "Wild goats I suppose." He roars, "Gotcha!" He whispers back, "I've never heard of such a thing – sounds good doesn't it?" I shook my head and think who could believe this little man could be so silly? I love it. Linda has outdone herself!

We go to the next station and everything is in disarray. There are pallets lying on their side and tables in odd places. Some items are upside down, but the chef

station is intact, it's Bob, our greeter and now in chef attire. Tyson smiles as he welcomes us again. "Oh, Amanda you are in for a treat today — my smoked Laredo style balls." He is smiling. He looks rather handsome, his dark Texas skin, with his tall white chef hat on his head. "I didn't realize you were a chef as well as a greeter," Tyson queried. Bob hung his head in shame, "I got demoted." "A chef is a demotion?" "Oh yes," answered the new Chef Bob. "That job at the front door of Sam's Club is premium. All the employees fight for it. We get to stand there all day and greet all of our wonderful guests and welcome many to dinner, of course. It's a great honor and it pays twenty-five cents an hour more than chef pay. I feel very bad at this demotion." "What did you do Chef, to cause this?" He again is hanging his head. "I made a big mistake. A huge lady and her four obese children come in continually for dinner. I must admit I find it disgusting. I don't want Sam's Club to go broke, they eat so much! I told her today if she didn't have a reservation I couldn't let her in. She was so upset. She found our manager and demanded her membership fee be returned at once and would never dine at Sam's Club again. My manager was furious as he returned her fee. He called me to his office and explained, 'Bob, we don't treat our guests that way. You are a valued employee, but I'm demoting you to chef. Never treat our valued customers in a negative manor again.' I told him my concerns. I wouldn't want Sam's to close," Bob shakes his head. "He assured me that would not happen. So…here I am. I enjoy being a chef, but God, I'll miss my greeting job." Tyson shook his head, he understood. I am rolling my eyes. Oh my word, how could little Texas Bob come up with a story like that? Wow. I now have a new respect for this man.

"Amanda, how are the Laredo balls, scrumptious?" "Oh yes, Bob this is definitely your calling." Tyson was still on his first meatball, third morsel, tonguing every small bite around his mouth. He snaps up another pick and begins tonguing, now shaking his head and asks, "What is that tangy flavor? The smoky flavor is perfect. I can't quite pick it out." Bob smiles with pride. "It's my famous splash of Worcestershire." "Yes, that's it. Great job Chef, these are superb." I ask Chef Bob, "Why is everything in such disarray at your station?" "Oh, you won't believe this Amanda." Tyson stops his tonguing and gives Bob his total attention. Chef Bob whispers in my ear, "They are getting ready to redo the floors. Sshhhhh." He continues with a grim look while looking Tyson in the eye, "Last night was my night off. I saw it on TV 6 News at eleven p.m.– a riot at Sam's Club." "Wow," as I play along. I couldn't imagine where this was going. "The line was two-wide for my smoked Laredo meatballs, it was as long as Cadillac's Chili Cook-off line. It was incredible. A huge fight broke out in the center of this long line. They were fighting for a premium spot in our line. Suddenly, fists were flying, women were screaming and children were running away with their moms. It was a very scary situation." "Wow, I find that amazing, but I do understand what these Laredo balls could do to people," says Tyson, as he continues tonguing his Laredo balls. "How did they break it up?" he asks. "Oh, the police riot squad was called immediately and guess what…they had to arrest Joe the greeter at the front door." "Why?" Ty

asks with a shocked look "He would not let them in." "Why," Tyson inquires, "would he not admit them?" "They didn't have a Sam's Club card. The greeter tried to explain store policy. They put the poor guy in cuffs and put him in their wagon and barged right on in. I'm not sure what I would have done in that situation myself. We must follow policy. I learned that today with a demotion." Tyson is mulling over the over the whole story. I can see he is hooked on Laredo balls. He now is on his seventh one. I caught him chewing one and frowned at him, he got the message and put his tongue back to work. "I think I would have broken store policy and let them in and took my chances with management," he finally surmised. "Well," Bob went on, "just because ten guys show up with uniforms, guns, clubs and badges, there's no way to know positively who these people are. They could be imposters. You'd be amazed the length people go just gain entrance on a busy Saturday night when it's meatball weekend. You can't be too careful." "Yes, I do see your dilemma," Tyson replied. "The greeter of course had no knowledge of the riot in the Laredo ball area," Chef Bob continues, "it's hard to say what you would do until you're faced with a serious situation like that. Knowing what we greeters have to deal with here at Sam's."

"Tyson are you ready for the next station? You are eating all of Bob's balls. You're embarrassing me, slow down a bit." "Oh Amanda, I'm so sorry, but you have me addicted. Where are my manners?" He grabs Bob's hand and shakes it. "You're awesome Bob. It's great to have you as a chef again. If you ever need a job I'm always looking for quality chefs at Cadillac's. Come see me." He hands Bob a business card as we wander away.

Tyson whispers in my ear, "I'm getting full." "Tyson, we must go to Linda's station." "Of course, but do you mind if I go back and get just a couple more with that wild goat cheese? I can't get them out of my mind." "Of course, there is Linda's station. I'll meet you there." Chef Linda greets me. "Amanda, you look so beautiful — oh that outfit. You've gotten so tall, look at you. So good to have you come by." "Linda, you have totally outdone yourself. The hats are perfect. The chef badges, wow! And Linda, the stories I'm hearing, oh my God! Did you come up with those scenarios?" "I wish I could say yes," she answers, "I explained what you were doing. They all loved it and all promised to have fun right along with you. Is it working?" "Oh my God, wait until you hear what has been said and so straightforward and with such honesty. This could have been a theatre today. I could never have dreamt the things I've heard. There was even a riot here last night!" Linda looks at me, "I didn't hear about that." "Linda, it's your buddy Bob's story!" "Ohhh, I get it, ha, ha, ha," she laughs aloud. "What are you serving, Chef Linda?" "These are Caribbean sweet melon balls." I picked one up, I can chew, Tyson's not watching. "These are very nice, Linda." "Yes, I just love them." "Although, I can't get caught eating one, I'd lose my job," as she quickly pokes one in her mouth. "They are so delicious. I just can't help but sneak one occasionally. Where is your friend?" "He went back to the goat cheese balls for another sample." "I've not heard of those." "Linda there is no such thing. That is just what the chef told him." "Oh I get it, ha, ha, ha. That's why I missed them."

Here comes Tyson. "Are you ready Chef Linda?" "I think so." "Tyson, Chef Linda, a good friend of mine. Her Caribbean balls in sweet melon sauce are fantastic." "All right, thank God I'm back, Amanda. You should see those pigs over in the goat ball station. They are pigs. They're all popping and chewing, no manners, mouths wide open while they chew on those goat cheese balls. I had to leave, they are total pigs." He now takes a pick to his mouth and gently tongues a small morsel. Linda is watching him too carefully as he tongues a second morsel. Linda blurts, "Why doesn't he just eat it?" Tyson looks at Linda and smiles. "She thinks she's going to catch me doesn't she Amanda?" "Yes," I jump in "Linda has her fun. If she thought she could convince you to chew on one it would make her day. Linda you pick on a different customer, not Tyson." Linda looks at my face and sucks in her breath. I think she got the message as I gently massaged and tongued my Caribbean ball with Linda carefully scrutinizing. "Linda, Caribbean sweet melon, it is very unusual," Tyson says as he bounces his tongue up and down against the roof of his mouth. "Yes, that melon flavor is beautiful. What kind of melons, Chef Linda?" "Caribbean," Linda fires back. "I understand that — there are many types of melons, you being a chef, I supposed you knew." "No," Linda says, "this is not Cadillac's. I just order 'em and serve 'em. I'm like an Applebee's chef I guess." "Ah Tyson we should move on to another station." I must get Tyson away. Linda is not as theatrical as the rest of her gang. She may blow my cover if she continues to talk. "Linda, so good to see you." "Bye, Amanda. Bye, Tyson." "Excuse me, Chef Linda, let me grab one more melon ball." He takes a nibble and his tongue is on the move, I love it. Linda is still staring in disbelief. She is not used to meatball tonguing customers I suppose.

"Amanda, I'm stuffed." "Yes, Tyson I've had enough myself, we can leave. There are three more ball stations, but I think we've already gotten our money's worth, I'm fine if you are." We wander toward the exit.

"Thank you so much Amanda," as we drive toward my 'car.' "I have learned a lot." "Wasn't it great Tyson? I knew you would enjoy it." "Yes, it was an experience. And a riot there last night, it's so hard to believe." "I missed the news." "I would have loved to hear what the TV-6 reporters had to say…I wonder if the greeter checked TV-6's Sam's cards." "Hmmm, I don't know Tyson, that is a very good question." "Chef Telly will get a charge when I tell him about their amazing exotic meatballs. I'll bring him over some night. You want to come with us?" "Tyson, I would love to." "We'll see what Chef Telly thinks and go from there." "OK, yeah that's great." We pull into the rest stop. Tyson starts getting a little frisky with my leg. I look at my watch. "Tyson no time, my fiancé is picking me up in an hour. I need to get home." He rubs his groin. "Can't you help me out Amanda?" "No time Tyson, I will see you soon." I peck his cheek and slide out the door.

"Thanks for a fantastic dinner, Amanda." I threw him a kiss as I walked toward my invisible car. He drove away. Good, somehow I had no interest in sex with Tyson. Not sure why, I was in the mood, just not with him today. I went to the ladies room. Who knows what a girl might find riding her bike home. Amanda must always be prepared!

CHAPTER 34

The Professional Trucker

I step out of the stall and over to the mirror, touch up my lips and pull my hair into a ponytail. It was cute, I must say. I check myself out again in the mirror, yes my ass was looking very good and my nipples erect. I walk out the door toward my bicycle for my ride home. "Hello young lady, ya need some help with that there bike?" I turned, a tall man appearing to be in his early thirties with a moustache, green t-shirt, and jeans is standing in front of me. "No, my bike is running quite well." "Great day ay?" "Yes it is." "Where ya goin honey?" "Home." "What cha doin here?" "Just hanging out." "At the rest stop?" he asks. "Yes, I do that. I amuse quite easily." He laughs out loud. "Am I amusing you?" "Not yet." "Ever seen a big rig, honey?" "No I haven't." He pointed behind him, a huge bright red semi-truck with a huge tall top and large trailer. "That's ma' rig right there." "Looks beautiful." I answer. "Ya she's a beaut. I love her like family. Wanna take a peek inside? It's just like home." "No, I should get home." "Ya may never get a chance to see a beaut like this one again." I never have seen a big truck on the inside. I suppose I could handle this guy if needed. I could broaden my horizon I suppose. If I go home to my room my bird day will haunt me. Let me entertain myself just a bit longer. "I'll take ya for a ride if ya'd like." "No, that's fine." His eyes wandering my body, as I listen to his southern slang.

He continued to prod me with his southern drawl. I finally agreed to take a peek. He jumped in the driver's side, slid over and opened my door. Wow, it was quite a climb. Pulling myself up the little steps holding onto the rails, I slid in and closed the door. It was really something, all leather, pleated seats, gauges everywhere; immaculate and leathery smells. "Is it new?" I asked. "Yup, she's brand new. Thirty

days ago. She's my world." I looked behind me, there was a huge king sized bed — Velvet curtains and bedspread with little velvet pillows. "Yup, I sleep in her a lotta nights. What're ya really doin' at the rest stop?" "Oh, sometimes I make some extra money," I reply. "What do you do?" he asks. "Oh, lots of things." "Like what?" "It's my secret, Mr. Trucker." "Well ya got any hair on your pussy yet?" I hesitate. "Maybe a few." "I don't believe ya little girl." Maybe he doesn't believe me, but his eyes do like what they are seeing, that is apparent. "Let me count 'em for ya honey." I laugh out loud. "Mr. Trucker, how high can you count?" "That's a silly question deary. I'm a professional truck driver." "Oh yes, I read somewhere they can really count, big time." He looked at me, not quite certain what that meant. "Mr. Trucker, you a dealin' man?" "Ya I am." "You put up a hundred dollars, if you can count my pussy hairs in five full minutes I'm going to suck your cock. If you haven't finished in five minutes I'm going to take your hundred dollars and go home." "How we gonna know how many ya got?" "Mr. Trucker, my boyfriend counted them last night, so I know exactly how many I have." "Oh, I got it," he replies. "Give me a pencil and paper, I'll write that number down so we'll be fair." "Ya I git' it. Honey, you got a deal." "Lay your hundred right there, Mr. Trucker." He dug in his wallet and pulled out a hundred-dollar bill and laid it on the dash. He handed me a pen and pad of paper. I scratched five thousand seven hundred and two and folded it. I thought, what a nice round number, this should be fun. I was looking forward to lying on my back on his velvet spread with my legs hanging to the floor and letting him pull my panties down. These days it's well worth a hundred dollars to check out a teenager's pussy. So I certainly wasn't taking advantage. Of course, I never do.

I love coming up with fun ways just to show off my bush. This is perfect for me to broaden my horizon. "OK, money out and pussy hair count written down." "Honey, ya gonna git on my bed." I slide out of my leather seat and move to his bed. I lay on my back, my legs hanging to the floor. "Mr. Trucker, take my knee highs down." He smiles while licking his lips. His hand grabs each side of my stretchy red slacks and slides them down. He pulls off my shoes and tosses them aside. His eyes almost pop out of their sockets. He can see my hairy bush outline and hairs wildly hanging out the panty legs. He doesn't move his eyes, just staring at my white panties and contemplating the tough job that lies ahead. It's time for him to bite the bullet. He puts a finger on my panty waistline and goes for the gusto. He slowly slides them down to my knees and over my feet. God, the look on his face was priceless. I would have paid him! The looks make my heart pound. The excitement, showing him my womanhood – what a thrill! I lift my feet to the velvet and spread my legs for him. I announce, "Your five minutes start now." I check my watch, he has his pencil in his hand. I watch him attempting to separate one pubic hair from another. I see his mouth moving fifteen, sixteen, seventeen, eighteen, this is obviously a great joke, although he hasn't figured that out yet. He really believes he's going to count them, I know better. It is a tangled jungle down there. Yet his pencil is attempting to untangle one after another, he is at one hundred sixty-seven now. "It's been two minutes and thirty seconds," I announce. "Honey,

are you sure?" he asks. "Mr. Trucker, you're wasting time, back to work." Two hundred one, two, three and on and on. I know five thousand seven hundred and two is far away. An extra hundred dollars is always good. A gal has expenses.

"Mr. Trucker, five minutes is up." I move my legs together. He looks at me and sighs with a shrug. "OK, you win. I'm only at three hundred and sixty-seven. I barely got started. Honey, you have more hair on your bush than I've ever seen. How old are you?" "I'm nine," as I smile to myself. "Oh my God, how is that possible?" He is shaking his head in disbelief. He is staring at my hairy mass. Just to antagonize him after his attempted counting session, I spread my legs a bit. "Honey, I want to kiss it." "Well Mr. Trucker, for twenty dollars more it would be OK." He pulls out a twenty and lays it on the dash with my earlier winnings. His mouth is wet massaging my pussy. It feels nice. I spread my legs wider, I must give him some value. I pump my bush in his face, he likes that. I feel his drool as he tastes my wetness. I feel it leaking, he's sucking in every drop. It's fun driving my professional trucker wild. How do I end this? What if he wants more? I feel that could possibly happen. I decide to just relax and enjoy his passion. I'm covered. I do have a backup plan. He unzips his pants. "Mr. Trucker, that is not part of our deal." "Honey, I got to have some of that hairy pussy." "For twenty more you can squirt you're cum all over my bush." "Honey, I want to fuck you." "No, Mr. Trucker. That will not happen." He is rubbing his cock all over and pressing it on my crotch. "MS162816472," I shout. That got a reaction. "How do you know that number, honey?" "I'm not as dumb as I look," I answer. He attempts to digest that one. His aggressiveness is subdued. He digs out twenty, lays it on the dash, and goes back to whacking on his hardness. It only takes seconds. His hot sperm is squirting all over my bush. I have spread my legs so widely just for him. My trucker must get his money's worth. He sighs and rubs his final dribble on my pussy and zips his pants. I locate my white panties and pull them over my wetness and then pull on my red knee-highs. "Mr. Trucker, you're just too much fun." "Honey, how do you know my Mississippi State registration number?" I looked puzzled. "I don't." "Well you told it to me." "Oh, was that the right number? Wow. Mr. Trucker, I just don't understand how I did that." I pick up my fun money and climb down the ladder, unlock my bike, and pedal away.

My mind is racing as I pedal. That was close. I did memorize his number, so I had a plan. That was good. It did make me a bit nervous that I had to implement my plan. Without that my virginity could have easily been lost to a professional trucker. A good lesson learned – you can't be too careful. His wetness feels good between my legs as I pedal my bike toward home.

I arrive at home, it's six-thirty. Mom, Dad and the boys are all home. Mom is fixing dinner and Dad and the boys are watching the news. "Amanda, how was your Sam's debut?" Mom asks with a smile. I give each a hug. "It was way too much fun. If Ty knew that it was a joke he certainly did not let on. I believe myself and Linda's gang convinced him." They all laughed. Mom had obviously told them of my humorous scam. "How in the world could you possibly convince someone of

such a thing?" Josh asks. "The detail, Josh, was incredible. All wore chef's hats and told amazing stories of Sam's Club meatballs. Most of them were very tasty. You would have to have been there to begin to understand," I explain. "Come on Josh and John, I'll take you to dinner. There are some exotic meatballs remaining!" "No, no, no, Amanda." We all laugh. I could see they were all so happy to see me bouncing back from bird day. It turned out to be perfect timing, my pro-trucker eased my tension. I dread going to my room but I must change my panties. I don't want anyone to detect my professional trucker odor.

CHAPTER 35

Meeting Ebony

Showered and changed for dinner I sit down with the family and nibble on a small salad. My stomach is so full of Sam's Balls. "Oh yea it's time for Birthday boy, next Friday! Josh, do we have a plan?" "Yes," Mom adds, "I'm home next weekend. Robert, are you working nights?" "No, no, I'm right here…OK Josh, what are we doing? Or maybe you have plans?" There's a brief pause. Simultaneously we all remember the game. "Gosh, I'm sorry, it's your big game Friday night! Silly me. What night is best for you son?" "Can we go back to Cadillac's Dad? I love that place." "Sure Josh that's great. Is Saturday night best or Thursday?" "Saturday is fine." It's music to my ears, and I didn't have to press nor suggest. "I'll make reservations for seven, Dad." "Yes very good." "I looked in the 'What's On' local entertainment guide, it shows an Elvis impersonator for entertainment on that weekend." "Oh, I love Elvis so much!" says Mom. She is very happy with our choice. "Dad, how soon before the house is finished being painted?" "Honey, I'm not sure. We don't spend too much time on it these days, we still have all the trim before it gets colder." "How are the Ferris's guys?" "Very well, Stiley complains his business is very slow and Norma is as worldly and gorgeous as ever." "Do you suppose we'll be invited to the pool next summer?" "I'm going to make that happen Amanda," Josh says.

School tomorrow, time to retire for the night. I hug my family and tell them I love them, then I'm off to my room. I slide into my bed. My music is singing. What a weekend. Wow, my life amazes even myself. Does everyone have so much happening? I guess one wouldn't know, most people looking at me wouldn't know I have just dealt with the most life-changing incident. My cookie business is booming. I let a trucker count my pubic hairs. I put together the most elaborate

prank in the city. I had a great party with a cookie customer, and also made several hundred dollars that I have hidden away along with my marked panties. I have been brought to the realization how much I love my family and how great life really is.

I did add George's sperm to my collection, not sure why, but why not? I have his DNA. I might as well keep it. There is a tap, tap, tap on my door. "Yes?" Mom opens it. "Amanda, Mr. Sampson is asking if you could baby sit his two children Wednesday evening, seven to eleven or so." "Sure, Mom. Will he pick me up?" "Yes, he said he would." "Sounds fine, I can use some extra cash." Mom smiled and closed the door. It's chump change, but I must keep up appearances. I drift off to the sounds of my music.

I awake to a cloudy morning. It looks like possible rain. The house is empty as I leave to catch my bus. "Morning Ray, how was your weekend?" "All good, all good." My boys already on board and they're all smiles. I slide between them, two hands immediately massaging my legs. "Did you have a good weekend boys?" "This is the most fun I've had since last week," Sam said with a smile. "God, Amanda, I love your legs, your body, and you, so much." Wow, did he have a bird day or is he just horny this morning? It's so fun sharing my legs and crotch with my boys. Both have a hand in my panties, massaging my pussy. It does feel good. I massage their slacks, I don't want them cumming in their blue jeans. I'm being careful, it must be embarrassing to walk with that gooey wet spot, I suppose. Some days the boy's playing with me does get a bit boring. It feels good, not near as exciting as it once was. I realize I need to find new situations continuously to humor myself. Someday will all that become dull and boring as well? I hope to find and create lively situations. It shouldn't be that difficult. I'm controlling my world while planning my destiny. I wonder if Sam and Roy and the pretty girls at school plan exciting and entertaining things. It doesn't seem so, but how would I know?

"Good Morning, Mr. Jackson. How was your weekend?" "Great, and yours Amanda?" "If I told you, you would not believe it." I smile and slide into my front row desk. We cover our morning subjects and then off to lunch. I sat down with my boys and we chat of school.

A tall black girl walks to our table, a person I did not recognize. "Do you mind if I join you?" "Of course, please do. I'm Amanda, this is Sam and Roy." "Thank you. I'm Ebony. This is my first day at your school." "Welcome," as I smile. "Are you in Sam and Roy's class?" "Yes I am." "Yeah, I saw you today. Where are you from?" Roy asked. "Ohio. My dad was transferred here. He manages the K-Mart here in town." "Good to have you in our school and city. A bit dull sometimes, but Amanda can show you how to change that!" says Sam. She smiled. Amazingly, she was taller than me and so pretty, and darn, her boobs were much larger than mine. "Have you always lived here?" she asks. Her voice is so soft and kind. "Yes, all three of us are locals, I guess you could say," Sam said. "Where do you live Ebony? Such a pretty name by the way." "Thank you. I live on the M-46 highway just south of town." We all explain where we live as well. The bell rings. "See you around Ebony," I say with a happy smile.

CHAPTER 36

Sex Education

I sat in my seat and let my skirt slide up my leg. I slowly cross and then uncross my legs for Mr. Jackson's benefit. I had not flashed him in some time. As he spoke, his eyes ran up my leg and stop on my sheer white panties. A rush shot through my body. He stammered on his words and quickly looked away. I'm quite certain he got a view of my pussy hairs through the sheer silk material. "What subject would the class like to discuss this afternoon?" No hands. I raise mine. He pointed to me. "Yes, Mr. Jackson, sex education?" The class laughed, many yes's and ya's. A buzz in the classroom, he took a deep breath. "I guess we could discuss the aspects of safe sex and diseases, including HIV which is very rampant these days. Not to mention you girls are aware what a pregnancy could do to your lives. Your world would change overnight and never again be the same. The best way is to refrain and have no sex until marriage. Not too popular these days, although that is the safest. Guys, gals, condoms are a must if you are or choose to be sexually active at anytime. Many STDs will not kill, but are very painful. HIV and AIDS, you die, it is out there. Yes, Amanda?" "Mr. Jackson, how many people do you know in this world, approximately?" "Oh, three hundred perhaps." "How many are HIV positive?" "None that I know of." "May I address the class?" "Yes of course." "Does anyone in the class know anyone with HIV?" Jacob raises his hand. Mr. Jackson points to him. "I don't know him, only of him. On the news one night it discussed Magic Johnson. He has HIV." "Yes Jacob that is correct, very good." I spoke up again. "Yes, he's had it for many, many years and he's alive. Why?" I ask. "That is an interesting question. He is an exception. A very wealthy man can afford the expensive drugs that control its spread to his immune system." "OK, granted," I answer, "here we

have almost thirty people and the only HIV case any of us know of is someone from television. If it is so rampant, why doesn't each of us know of three or four cases?" Mr. Jackson is shaking his head. I continue, "Is it possible that large corporations are making millions selling our population preventatives, doctor checkups, blood tests and a multitude of other things, because we believe it is everywhere?" "Amanda, you may have a valid point. However we must be careful, let's leave it at that. For the multitudes of STDs, the best answer is no sex. Second, always use protection or remain with one person you know is safe. Yes, Amanda?" "When we do become sexually active and enjoy the thrill and the sensation, why would any of us use it with only one person? If we're using protection, why not share and have fun and enjoyment with many partners?" "Amanda, it's not the way we are brought up. Ladies are called tramps that do those things." "Mr. Jackson, many guys go from woman to woman. It makes them a big wheel, a stud, Mr. Cool. No one calls him a tramp or a whore. He's the king. Is there a disconnect in this area? Please explain to the class." "Yes, what you are saying is true. There seems to be a double standard, it's always been there." "But why, is my question? Why do we accept it and live by it? If sex is that great, why can't we be like the boys and enjoy it without being labeled a tramp? I think it's time for the ladies of this world to say 'enough.'" "Amanda, that is not likely to happen. But you work on it as I imagine you probably will." The class stood and clapped. That made my day, I was happy to see someone agreed with what I was seeing around me in my little world.

The bell rings. "Amanda, come see me." I walk to the corner of Mr. Jackson's desk and lean as the class files out. I lift one leg a bit to show off. "Amanda, you always amaze me. How do you know these things to ask such relevant questions? I really do not have good answers, I'm not certain that anyone does. You do bring up some valid points on HIV: Why do I know no one with it? Is it a conspiracy? Maybe . . . the corporations do seem to control our world. But Amanda, you be careful, you obviously are an exhibitionist and God, I enjoy looking at you." He stares at my panties. I smile, "Mr. Jackson, I love your eyes wondering over my body." I peek around, it was safe. I pull my skirt up and run my hand over my pussy. I slide closer to his chair. I take his hand and guide it up my leg to my damp crotch. He sighs and slides his fingers up and down my crack. "How I enjoy the feel of you, your hairy bush could drive a man wild! Amanda, I fantasize about you continuously. You must stop this!" "Mr. Jackson, that's not likely, it's difficult to stop an exhibitionist you know." He smiled as he gave me one more finger touch as I stood up. "Mr. Jackson, you make my pussy much too hot. I need to find someone to take care of business." I walk away with his mouth hanging open. That was too much fun, seeing him aroused and walking away leaving him that excited. Awesome!

"Thanks for keeping my bus waiting Ray, you're a wonderful bus driver." He nods his head. My boys are waiting. "Amanda, where you been?" asks Roy. "I was showing my pussy to my teacher." "Seriously? Oh my goodness! Did you really Amanda?" "Yes. It's part of my job." "Did he like it?" asked Sam. "No, he loved it.

Feel my panties boys." They both respond instantly. "Oh Amanda, they're so wet!" "Boys, I love the way he stared at it. I let him run his fingers over my panties, it was so much fun." "Amanda, you're a wild woman." "Yes Sam, I am." "Isn't Ebony beautiful Amanda?" asks Roy. "Heavens, yes! Perfect skin and so tall. Boys, how can we seduce her?" Roy and Sam laugh so hard. "Amanda, you are unbelievable."

"Guys, you must learn to think for yourselves. Don't depend on someone else. I want you guys to plan. Step up! Make things happen! Don't be wimps. You hear me? You go guys!" They laugh at each other. "She's right, why can't we be like Amanda?" says Roy. Sam thinks a bit. "I guess we have to want to first, and I sure as hell do. Let's practice on Ebony, OK? Let's see what we can make happen. Amanda, if we get stuck, will you mentor us?" "You're my boys, of course!"

CHAPTER 37

Party Bus in Place

Roy and Sam have exited the bus so I decide to play with Ray for a minute. I move to the front. "Hi Ray," I move my hips side to side. "I'm going to need my bus October fifteenth for my birthday." "You know I can't take this bus from my yard!" "Oh I'm sure you can somehow find a way Mr. Ray. Be at my house by eleven a.m. that Saturday." "They'll fire me if they find out." "Well honey, you'll be in prison if my bus does not arrive on time. The jails are open on Saturday my Ray Ray. Be sure it's clean. I don't want to be embarrassed with a dirty bus, Ray Ray. We will be going to the beach on the big lake, so bring some gas money. It's going to be so much fun. Are you excited? Oh, bring your swimming suit, Ray Ray. I want you to swim and tan with my cousins." He's shaking his head. "What do I tell my wife?" "Honey, would you rather tell her you're leaving for prison? With my deal you're home in six hours or so. The other deal, you'll be home in say, twenty-five years. You decide, Ray Ray. You are just too much fun today." I get a sudden reflection of my bird day. "Ray, I do like you." I give him a little kiss. "Oh Ray Ray, I'm home. See you in the morning you handsome devil." Down my drive I strut. "Come Bandit, where is your stick?" I give him a big hug, he is so happy to see his best girl. "Get your stick!" I give it a toss.

Relaxing on my big bed listening to my music I realize it has been another great day. I have my bus lined up for my beach party. Now, I need to get my guest list together. What if the weather does not cooperate? I need to have a back-up plan. Hmmm . . . Roller Skating? Bowling? Take them all shopping at Good Will? Go to Sam's for meatball day? I'm being so silly. Oh well, I will find a plan, I'm sure. Mr. Jackson, hmm, I would love to do him. I doubt he would be that stupid. Then

again, what I'm learning of men is that it's not their intelligence that rules them, it's what's between their legs. That's what controls their lives. How many girls take advantage of that? My bet is not many. I could be the first I suppose. Oh well. A girl does what a girl has to do. "O'La Lay" to that!

My mind flashes back to Bob. I feel he understands these things. I'm not sure why, perhaps it's his look. He is not your typical man. Once I get to know him, I may say that I have wasted my thoughts, we'll see. That is, if he ever has time for me. It's my little challenge. Some girls do love a challenge. "O'La Lay!" Will I ever know what "O'La Lay" means?

I hear noises outside my room. I open the door. "Dad, good to have you home." I give him a hug. "I love you Dad." "I love you Amanda. Are you OK?" "Yes Dad. I'm fine. Will Mom be home soon?" "Yes, she will." "Would you like to talk about bird day, Amanda?" "Yes, Dad, I would love to eventually, but it still hurts too much. I'm not ready, OK?" "Honey, you know your Mom and I are here. We're very concerned." "Thank you Dad. Knowing you're here is enough for the time being." Josh and John are in the driveway. "Hello, my favorite brothers. You both ready for the big game on Friday?" "Yes we are. We will cheer them to a victory. Without the cheer squad, there is no chance of a win, we'll be there! It will be a victory." "Sounds good to me." "Maybe I'll stay home and celebrate my birthday," says Josh. "No no! You should at least show up." They laugh. "Are you excited Josh? Big game and the birthday party Saturday night." "Oh yes, who could ask for anything more?" "Dad, is it OK to invite Marianne again?" "Yes, that would be great."

"Amanda, Marianne is so hot. Does she have a boyfriend?" asks Josh. "No, she does fight them off. She and I have a pact to drive the boys wild." "Right," pipes up John. "You certainly do that," he gives me a wink. "Do you boys know my new friend Brianna Coats?" "Oh my God, Amanda, she is beautiful. Yes we know who she is. I believe she is out of our league." I smile. "That's exactly what she said about you guys. I believe you people don't understand your own presence. You need to talk to her. She is not out of your league as you say. Get yourselves out of that mode right this minute! There is no one that is out of your league, got that boys?" They smile. "It's shyness I suppose. We don't have your pizzazz and confidence. You were born with something very special," says Josh. "Dad, how did you do that for Amanda?" "I was drunk when she was conceived." We all laugh. "I love you guys. I am blessed to be part of this family. Dad, could you get drunk and bring me a sister?" That got a very big laugh. "No way, that party is over. I have my hands full with you three. Two Amanda's? I shiver to think! This world is not large enough Sweetie." I knew that statement was all too true. Mom is coming in the door. "Hi Mom, you look tired," I put my arms around her and squeeze a big hug. "Yes, I guess I am a little." "Would you like me to order pizza tonight Mom? I would like to buy to celebrate my first day in business and treat the family with some of my profits." "Amanda you don't have to do that, but it would be so nice. I'm not up to fixing dinner." "Mom, pizza it is."

Home from school Wednesday afternoon, I have had a couple of quiet days. I

played with my bus boys, picked on Ray and played leg-sy with Mr. Jackson. He avoided class discussion subjects. He did ask if Bargain Bob would be visiting the class. I assured him, before Christmas it would happen. He's looking forward to meeting him. Mom is back to her normal self, thank goodness, our new loving family is perfect. Bandit had his run and is smiling that toothy smile I love so much. He's so cute!

CHAPTER 38

Babysitting at the Sampson's

Six forty-five, Mr. Sampson pulls in the drive. It's time to make some chump change. "Hello Mr. Sampson," I said as I slide in the front seat. "Hello, Amanda, thank you for helping us out tonight. Babysitters are difficult to locate these days. Most of the girls have other interests, why is that?" "I'm not sure Mr. Sampson. I guess videos, TV, homework and laziness." "There you go, that's probably close!" Mr. Sampson was a handsome man probably in his early forties with a nice tan. He had gold rings, a Rolex watch and was driving a black Cadillac with burgundy leather seats. It smells brand new. "Your car is beautiful." "Thanks, Amanda, I just got it, she's my pride and joy. I love my Cadillacs." "Have you been to Cadillac's Mr. Sampson?" "Ya know, I haven't. I hear about it often." "I can't believe that Mr. Sampson, you being a Cadillac man, you must go. Cadillacs are everywhere, all classics and all so shiny, like yours. The food is amazing, and great entertainment, it's well worth the drive." "I'll have to do that soon." As we chat, I see his head turn slightly and peek at my long, tan legs. "Where are you going this evening?" I ask. "An open house for one of my large vendors, a computer software show." "Oh that should be fun." "Yes, lots of cocktails and hopefully some super deals on inventory."

Mr. Sampson owns a large computer warehouse type of business in town. People come from all over to purchase surveillance equipment, computers, and software. He's having a bit of trouble keeping his eyes off my legs. I cross them slowly in his direction. "Amanda, I'm sorry, but I can't help but notice your legs.

They are beautiful." "Thank you for the compliment." "They are so dark." "Yeah, I sun as much as possible. Mr. Sampson I don't want to be too forward, but if you would bring me a beer for on the way home, I would be so grateful." With some people I could never make such a request, but I believe I'm reading him quite well. He turned and looked at me for a second. "What brand honey?" "I like Mic Ultra, long necks. No cans, please." "The drive home should be interesting," he said with a wink. I give him a shy smile. We pull into his driveway. It is huge brick home with beautiful tall glass windows, a veranda across the front, two stories and a beautiful yard.

I'm wearing a white little girl skirt and a pink top with my little bra. I must be responsible today. Sandy and Andy greet me at the door. "Hi Amanda!" I had baby-sat for them a few times before about six months ago. They were nice kids, well mannered. "Hello, Mrs. Sampson, you look stunning this evening." "Thank you Amanda, my my, how you've grown. You have turned into a beautiful young lady. Thank you so much for helping us tonight. We lost our regular sitter, her family moved west. Would you be interested in sitting occasionally?" "If I'm available, I would love to, Mrs. Sampson." "The kids are to be in bed at eight-thirty. They've had dinner and baths so keep them in line." "No problem, they're good twins. At least they were." "Oh, they still are. Here's my cell number if you would need us. We should be home before eleven." "Very good. We'll be waiting!" I wanted so badly to remind Mr. Sampson about my Mic Ultra. I bit my tongue. "See you in the morning Sandy and Andy, behave yourselves." Out the door they went. "Well kids, what do you want to do?" "Amanda, can we play Clue?" "Sure, set up the board." It was so much fun. They loved Clue. I played mostly stupid and let Sandy and Andy each win a game. A tie, they were very happy with that outcome. "Can we play one game of Old Maid?" "OK, one game and then bedtime. Who will be the old maid?" They point at each other. "We'll see soon!" The game went back and forth and then; "Ha ha Amanda, you're the old maid!" "Oh no! How could that happen? Andy, did you cheat again?" "No, I really didn't Amanda!" "Well, OK, fine. I'm the old maid. Time for bed kiddies." "Oh do we have to?" "Yes, its eight forty-five, we're already a little late. Come on, I'll tuck you both in." I shut off the lights and we say our goodnights as I put the games away.

I turn on the TV and wander through the huge house. The tall ceilings enhanced the beautifully furnished home so tastefully decorated. I open the door just past the master bedroom. Wow! There were computers, screens, cameras, a sofa, a small bed, several large chairs, and a chaise lounge. Cameras are mounted all around the room. Hmm…interesting! There was a large screen covering one wall. They must show movies to clients I suppose. Oh well. I'm such a snoop! I step into their bedroom. It's so big! There's a king size bed, much bigger than my queen size. There's also a large screen television setting inside a huge wooden dresser. Very impressive! The whole house is immaculate. I could easily live like this. I wonder what Bob's house is like. I've heard several people mention how large it is. I'll know someday.

I walk back to see what is on television. I check to see what's happening in the world. CNN, MSNBC, Larry King, hmm, nothing much happening in the world it

seems. I see lights flash past the front window at ten fifty-five. Yes, my night of sitting is ending!

"How were the kids Amanda?" "They were perfect. We played Clue and Old Maid. We had a very big time. They are so well mannered, you must be very proud." "Yes, we certainly are. Amanda, you have cleaned up the kitchen, thank you. Sammy, pay her extra tonight." "Mrs. Sampson?" "Please call me Jen." "Jen, that is not necessary." "Hopefully you'll be seeing us again soon." "Thank you, Jen, it was fun."

As we leave I notice Mr. Sampson appears to have had a few cocktails, he is weaving a bit on our way to the car. "Are you OK?" "I'm fine Amanda," he opens his door. I slide to the middle of the seat. He looks toward his front door, then reaches over the front seat and pulls a bag to the front. "Here you go, just what you ordered Amanda." He pulls his car around the circle drive. As he drives down the road he pulls out a six-pack of Ultra. "Good boy, Sammy." He smiles while popping off my top and then his. I take a sip. God, it was good. It's been a while since I'd sipped a beer. "Honey, do you mind if I lay my hand on one of those beautiful legs?" "I guess that would be OK." He lays his hand quite high on my bare leg. As always, I do like a man's hands touching my body. He is being a total gentleman and simply running his fingers back and forth very gently. "Do you have a boyfriend?" "Three," I answered. "Good for you." "I need one more, four is such a nice round number. You know what I mean Sammy?" He smiles, "I think I do." The beer is great. In fact, perfect, as I take a big swallow. "I want to warn you Sammy, when I drink beer I sometimes feel a little frisky." "That's a good thing!" he says as he slides his hand a bit higher. I slide away from him a bit, pull my shoe and my knee sock off and put my left foot in his lap. "Sammy, would you put your beer down and massage my foot please?" He quickly found a cup holder and slid his beer into it and carefully pulled my foot to the center of his lap. My right foot is on the floor. I lean to the corner of the leather seat. He is peering at my yellow panties and massaging my bare foot. "Oh Sammy, that feels heavenly. You're much too good at this." He continues massaging my foot while driving and weaving a bit. He has no hand for his beer. I continue sipping on mine. "I'll show you where you can stop if you'd like when we get to my road, so you could sip on your beer." That was music to his ears. "That would be great Amanda." I guide him to my big tree. Sammy puts the windows down and shuts off the motor. "One more beer, Sam, please." He screws off the lid and hands it my way. We exchange bottles. I move my right leg to the seat, bend my knee and put my right foot on the seat edge. I slide my finger over my yellow panties as I massage his crotch with my left foot. Now I'm doing the massaging. "How is that?" "Good Amanda, very good." I continue sipping my Ultra, pressing harder with my foot while moving my finger a bit faster. "I'm very wet Sammy, why are you making me so wet?" His eyes are focused on my panties. "Show me your cock Sammy." He hesitates briefly, then unzips and pulls it out. I'm rearranging my foot. "Rub your cock on my foot Sammy." He obliges and massages my foot with his hardness. "That is feeling very nice Sam." "Oh God," he moans.

"Amanda, you are amazing. What you do to a man. I will fantasize about my cock foot massage all night Amanda." My full hand is rubbing my panties. They are soaked with my wetness. It feels so good.

Babysitting isn't so bad, if it just paid a bit more! I may work on that next time. I may have a good customer here. I would like his cock in my ass, not tonight. I want him to want me. I want to have my pussy on his mind daily. This kind of a guy, if he doesn't get it, it will drive him wild. Once I fuck him the party will slow for a bit. I certainly could be wrong but that is my assessment for now. "Sammy, I need some lotion on my foot please." "Oh Amanda, I don't have any." "Honey, yes you do." I rub my toes up and down his hardness, he caught my meaning. He begins wildly jerking his cock while rubbing it over my foot. "Oh Amanda, I want your pussy." I pull my panties aside to expose what he would not be getting tonight. "Oh God Amanda, let me kiss it," he attempts to move my foot off his lap. My foot pushes him back down. "Sammy, lotion please." He got the picture. No pussy tonight. I could feel his penis head wiping goo on my foot, it was very slippery and how my foot loved it. "Oh sweet geezis I'm cumming! I'm cumming!" I watch his sperm coat my toes and the top of my foot and my ankle. It was too much fun. He sighed as he slid his head back and his cock went limp. Now, let's give him the Amanda show.

I slowly pull my cum soaked left foot toward me. I put my empty beer bottle in the holder. I pull it close to my face with my right hand. I ran my fingers across the top of my foot and scooped up a nice heavy gob of Sammy's cum. He's watching closely. I let my foot loose and pull my panties aside and expose my furry jungle. I move my gob of his cum to my clit and slowly rub it over my entire pussy. It slides so nicely. It's so slippery. I rub it slowly over my pussy. Oh, Sammy loves my show. I rub a bit faster. I pump my crotch to my beat, oh wow, does that feel awesome. I pump my hips faster and faster. Oooh my God, I am cumming, and cumming. I amaze myself as juices squirt once, now twice, onto his leather seat. Wow. I am totally out of breath. It has taken my breath away! I must have a good finish. I pull my foot to my mouth and slowly lick the balance of his cum from my foot. It's so tasty. "Wow Sammy, that was a great load." Oh my goodness, his cock is hard again. "Amanda that was the hottest thing I've ever witnessed. Please let me fuck you." "No Sammy, be a good boy and put it back in its pen." "Let me cum on your pussy." "Sammy, put it back in its pen. Your wife will be very horny when you tell her of our little adventure." "Yeah right," he sneers. "Please, let me get off again," he begs. "Honey, put it away and run me home like a good boy." He finally gives up and puts big boy away. He opens a beer while I arrange myself. Wow, I'd squirted that juice once again. Was I OK? It certainly felt good. I was a bit concerned, all this wet stuff all over the seat. "Sammy, you certainly got me wet. You big bad boy." He smiled. "Wow that was something. I've only seen women squirting in porno movies. That was something! Amanda, next time I want it in my face. I want to taste you so badly." "Sam, could I watch one of those squirting movies with you sometime?" He smiled. "I will arrange that just for you, because you're my favorite babysitter."

Oh, he was so cute. The car is in my drive. Sammy hands me a fifty-dollar bill. "Honey, that is not enough." "But it's all I have." "This was worth ten times that. Oh well, I understand. Bye, bye Sammy, thanks for the beer. And Sam, you either wipe up or lick my juices off your pretty leather seat." I close my door and strut to my house. I wish I could follow him. My bet is he will go back to my tree and lick my juices off the seat and squirt that last load. His wife will not likely be getting any action tonight.

CHAPTER 39

Using My Powers

I wish I had the energy to sneak back to my tree to watch the Sammy show, it's already twelve twenty as I slip into bed. I have to remember to call Marianne tomorrow to ask her about Saturday night. I almost forgot. I need to remember to call Bri as well to see if she would like to go to Josh's game with me. That would be great. I need to get to the Dollar Store. I haven't gotten a chance to get there.

All these things are running through my mind. All that wetness that shot out of me, wow; that has happened only once before. Who do I talk to about such a thing? I assume it's OK, Sammy seemed to understand. And Jack, why in the world has he still not called? That is where all this excitement began. I flash back to all I learned and experienced that day. I don't know why my mind dwells on a call and meeting with Jack. Oh well. My mind refuses to slow down. Why would anyone save sexual pleasure for only one person? That totally puzzles me. I can't imagine one person for sexual pleasure? How? Why? Am I out of control? I don't think of one man as I fantasize. I think of men, several at a time, and the boys my age, it's fun to humor and pleasure them, but it's not like a man. A real man knows what he wants and how to get it, or attempt to get it at least. I really enjoyed tonight. I would have loved to sit in front of that steering wheel and ride his cock. I would have loved to slide it deep inside me. I controlled myself, and now could probably control him. He will want Amanda. At what point do I give it to him? I will think about that, perhaps never. I will just play with him for a while. I believe I'm learning to use my God given powers. I wonder, do most girls deal with sexual situations similarly? I have no idea, not that I really care as long as it works for me. I believe it's called controlling my destiny.

Bird day is on my mind. I try to block it out as often as I can. Will I ever be able to explain to Mom without breaking down? I don't know. My grades are good. My family is great. Yet sex remains on my mind continuously! Is that a bad thing? Is it unhealthy? God, I love so much how it feels and what I do for men! Perhaps someday it will fade away. God, I would miss it so much! So many questions! I need to shut it down and get some rest!

Thursday has come and I'm back home after a usual day of flirting with Mr. Jackson. I played leg-sy with my boys and reminded Ray Ray of my beach party in October. I invited my boys. I must catch the rest of the gang. I'll call Marianne and Bri in a bit, and Chad. I must go to the Dollar Store. It's eight o'clock, a nice dinner with the family earlier, we've come a long way since the weekend. We've been letting each other know we care. I love that so much. It took one small thing to change something that is so important. We are all so blessed. I need to get my calls made. I'm getting so tired. Last night was very restless. Bri was so glad to hear from me, next week she is on my bus again. Good, good. The Friday night football game is perfect, so I have my date for Friday. Marianne is good for Josh's birthday and Chad was very excited about a Dollar Store run with me. Of course, he had to piss and moan a bit, but he somehow managed to come around. I told Chad it had to be right after school as I was very busy. He is so great. He worked it all out. Four-thirty, he would be in my drive – perfect. Now, time for a good night's sleep. My music sings me away.

CHAPTER 40

Chad's Taxi

After all the tossing and turning last night, I finally get a good night's sleep. I wake up raring to go. "Good morning, Ray, you look sharp today. Is that a new shirt? It looks great." My boys are waiting, I slide in. "Amanda, we can go to your beach party. We're so excited." "Good guys, we have room for thirty on my bus, if you want to invite a friend it's OK." "Wow, we may do that." I love it when I make my boys happy. "Who else is coming Amanda?" "You know Bri, my friend Marianne, and our new friend Ebony. I haven't asked them yet, but I will soon. Ray will be partying with us too." "Bus driver Ray?" Sam asks. "Yes, he is driving the bus." "This bus?" "Yes. Guys, isn't that sweet of him to offer?" "Ah, ya it is. I'm asking no more questions," Roy smiles.

We're off the bus and to our classrooms. "Good Morning Mr. Jackson. You are looking very dapper today." "Thank you Amanda." There is little classroom discussion again today. I miss that stuff. The day passes quickly and before long the bell rings, it's time to go home.

I move to the desk corner and smile down as Mr. Jackson leans back in his chair. I move in close with my stance, my legs apart. "Are you going to the game tonight Mr. Jackson?" "Yes, Amanda, I am." "Great. Hopefully I'll see you. My brother is going to win the game tonight with the team's help to celebrate his birthday. My other brother will cheer him and the team on." "The Shiels boys?" "Yes." "I hadn't connected that, yes, your brothers. I look forward to seeing you at the game." "Bye bye," I strut out the door to my bus.

Our high school has no athletic program, budget cuts years ago. Our high school and the towns' population follow our local college team. They are part of a

conference of small colleges that play Friday nights. Most of the schools in our conference are in our state.

I have the best plan for Mr. Jackson tonight. I might just blow his little mind. I'm so excited. I give myself an "O'La Lay." "See you Monday Ray." I get off the bus.

I let Bandit out to play for a bit, and prepare myself for my run to the Dollar Store with my taxi service. "Go get your stick boy. Oh my word, Bandit, a log again? That will not work buddy. I can't lift it off the ground. Here is a much better choice, go get it!" He flies away.

Shortly after, Chad's car appears. "Hello Chad," as I slide in his door. "How is your world?" "I'm fine, although you don't help it much." "Honey, I don't bother you much, just in emergencies." "Oh, and the Dollar Store is an emergency?" "Yes, Chad, it really is. You see my business depends on inventory to survive, and my inventory has gotten very low. So Chad, honey, just quit your crying and be a good boy. It seems I've taken very good care of your little teeny weensy." I squeeze his crotch. He found no humor. Oh well. "What inventory are we purchasing Amanda? At the Dollar Store of all places?" "Honey, if you really want to know I will tell you. I don't want to bore ya." "Tell me Amanda." "I sell chocolate chip cookies." He laughs, "Ya right." "It's true Chad! Five dollars a dozen, profit is four dollars, twenty-five cents a dozen." "You actually find buyers?" "I sold out last Saturday, twenty-dozen. That's just short of a hundred dollars profit." "That's more than I make in three days. I get the picture," as he smiles. "You could sell that shit, but people would laugh at me knocking on their door." He laughs. "Amanda, you are something. Who would come up with such a thing? I suppose you tell folks you baked them?" "Yes, although I do. My microwave has a bake mode. Doesn't yours?" "Amanda, Amanda," he shakes his head with a big smile.

I quickly run into the store and purchase my cookies and boxes. I load my inventory in the car and off we go. I slide close to Chad. I would feel guilty not paying him somehow, and a cock in my mouth would be perfect. I rub my hands on his teensy weensy while pulling my skirt above my thighs, just for effect of course. He runs his hand up my leg while I fumble with his zipper. "You watch the road Chad." He helps me get it out. It's semi-hard, let's see what we can do here. I slide the head into my mouth and massage it with my tongue. That works, it's growing up quite nicely. I love the feel of a cock hardening in my open mouth. It gets harder and harder, it's rock hard, I know that feeling; it will be blowing any second. I'm pumping my mouth very quickly up and down, managing not to bump the steering wheel. I feel the deep jerking as his load pumps up. "Oh Amanda, oh my God." It shoots and shoots. I'm swallowing every drop. We want no messes. It's empty, I look straight at it and ask, "You got any more down there?" I smile and squeeze out the last gob and suck it down. I should have tongued it, oh well, too late. "Chad you're just way too much fun. I'm guessing there will be no fucking your little girlfriend tonight!" "Thank you Amanda, driving you isn't so bad." I grab my inventory and lug it to the house.

The boys are both home. "Happy Birthday Josh!" I give him and Johnny each a

hug. "Ready for the game guys?" "Yes we are!" "Amanda, was that Chad driving you?" "Yes it was." "Why and how?" "He's my buddy. He likes to drive for me. He says he's my taxi service. I think he may be practicing for a new career when he moves to New York City." "I didn't hear he was moving," says Josh. "I'm not sure either, but it does sound good right?" The boys' shake their heads. "Amanda, we will ask no more."

I busily get my cookies boxed and ready, not sure if I'll have time tomorrow morning, I will call George to let him know my oven is warming. "Your game is at seven, right, Josh?" "Yes. We're leaving shortly." "Good luck guys! Happy Birthday!"

Mom and Dad arrive soon after. "Hi honey, how was your day?" "Just great Mom!" "I see you're ready for business tomorrow." "Oh yes, I'll sell out early I hope. I want to be ready for Josh's birthday celebration." I give Mom and Dad a hug. "I love you both very much. Thank you for our trip to celebrate tomorrow night. It will be so much fun! Mom, I'm going to try and fix Marianne up with Josh. What do you think?" "Oh, she is such a nice young lady and so attractive. Sounds like a perfect plan Amanda." "Dad, will you drop me at the game at six-thirty?" "Of course honey."

CHAPTER 41

The Game and Sunny

It's almost game time as I hop out of the car. Dad and I did chat a bit during our drive. "Dad, there are some things I would like to talk to you about some day soon, when the family is away." "We'll do that honey, as soon as you are ready we will find the opportunity."

I hop out of the car. "Bye Dad, thank you so much!" I walk across the lot. I find Bri. She's so beautiful. She's wearing a tight blue skirt and a light-blue top that shows it all. As always, her makeup is perfect. And those glasses, so cool! That look always amazes me. We hug each other. "I've missed you Amanda. I'm so glad we could do the game tonight." "Me too Bri, and it's Josh's birthday today as well. He's going to win it for us!"

"Amanda, you look so hot. Look at you! That dress is wow, perfect." "We are a team, a two lady team. Let's go to the concession and get some food. I didn't get a chance to eat." "Yes, I could eat a little dinner myself." We walk through the crowd, we turn so many heads it's amazing. It's so funny as I watch wives slapping their husband's arms and scolding them. I love it. I can't imagine myself ever doing that to a man. We women are made to be adored and watched, we dress for that. If my man didn't look, I'd toss him away. I'm certainly not the only attractive lady. I think it must be an insecurity issue with many women. I'll never have that curse. A hot dog for Bri, a rare burger for me, and sodas, we are just perfect. Best burger I've ever had! Of course, when you're hungry they all taste good.

As I'm swallowing my last bite a hand taps me on the shoulder. I turn. It's a blond attractive girl I didn't recognize. "Hi, remember me?" "No, I'm sorry I don't." "I saw you at the Capri Theater a few weeks ago." Oh my God, should I be

embarrassed? I take a deep breath. Who would have ever imagined this girl would remember me? I had to ask. "How would you possibly remember me?" She smiled. "You have such a unique look and such beautiful features I doubt anyone forgets you." I poked Bri with my elbow. "The last time this girl saw me, I had cum in my hair, in my eyes, and dripping down my face." How this girl loved me 'fessing up, Bri's mouth fell open. "Oh my God Amanda, where were you?" "At the Capri," Blondie smiled. "My name is Samantha, my friends call me Sunny." "Nice to meet you Sunny." We both introduced ourselves. I told the girls my story, it was a hoot, they loved it so much. "You know Amanda I'm glad I found you. I always wondered where the cum came from. The older guy who left before you or the boy you were with, what a great story."

"Sunny, would you like to hang with us for a while?" "Sure, why not?" She was dressed in tight, showy, white stretchy slacks and a purple blouse. She was very busty. She wore sexy strappy shoes with high-rise heels, which made her taller than me. Today her blond hair was over her shoulders with just a bit of makeup. Sunny had a very happy smile and bright white teeth. As we stepped through the crowd, I could see the outline of her firm buttocks, which totally filled her hot white slacks. Wow, her ass may be rounder than Bri's or my own, with no panty lines. She wore either thongs or no underwear at all. What a strut on our Sunny. I can't believe I'm undressing her in my mind. Her and Bri chat, they both attend the same private school. They had seen one another although had never met.

It's getting near seven, we're going to stand on the sidelines, it has been decided. As we weave our way through the crowd, Sunny is in front. Again, I can't take my eyes off her ass as she walked. I wanted her. Why am I like this? Her perfect ass would not leave my mind. I kept envisioning Sunny on her hands and knees, me slowly sliding those white slacks down and just kissing and licking that round, beautiful ass. I was imagining her pussy, was it hairy or shaved? I needed to taste her. Amanda, knock it off! Control your fantasies for now. I attempt to obey my command. I was happy to see the guys gawking as well at us three musketeers.

Kick off time. We are receiving. A short kick, oh my God, Josh, my birthday boy has picked up the ball, he's headed for the sidelines. A missed tackle! He stiff-arms the next. Oh! A big tackler flying at him from his side! Josh somehow stops dead in his tracks, the big tackler tumbles into the sideline and runs over the crowd. Josh cuts back toward center field…it's wide open! He's gone! Oh my God he scored! I went crazy. This was unbelievable…the first play and my brother scores. We girls are ecstatic. "Sunny, that's my brother." "Josh is your brother?" "Yes." She is all the more excited. OK, extra point time. They hike the ball, the kick. No, no kick! Josh has the ball around the side, very wide. He is wide open! It's a total fake out. Two more points, wow! Who would ever guess on the first two plays, two scores and both my brother? This is so far the best ever! The crowd is roaring, standing and cheering, it is wild, the score is eight to zero!

Sunny and Bri are chatting with other classmates and introducing me as we walk toward the centerline. We finally make it to the centerline. Sunny is standing

directly in front of me. My eyes will not leave her beautiful round ass. The curve, the roundness, she has the absolute perfect derriere. It's driving me wild. I want so badly to drop to my knees and lick it, caress it, and slide those stretchy white slacks to her knees. I lightly brush my hand over her tight slacks, she has me so excited. I again, so very gently, brush my hand over her beautiful ass. I know what the guy from the parade earlier was experiencing. So much tension, will I get slapped? I wish I knew her a bit better. If it were Bri I was lusting after, it would be no problem. At this moment it wasn't Bri I wanted, I needed this blond with the beautiful ass! A hormone imbalance, is that me? I'm lusting as I have heard men do. I brush my hand against her again. She certainly felt it that time. She turns, my heart is pounding; I'm busted! She gives me the most beautiful smile. Oh my God, she licks her lips. Was that intentional or coincidence? I didn't know. Oooh God, do I dare brush my hand again? I have no control, my hand is on her ass slowly moving over her round cheeks. I feel her breath deepen while turning her head slightly toward me. She reaches back and gently touches my hand. Electricity is shooting through my body. She slides her hand into mine. I gently squeeze her soft fingers. My right hand drops to her white slacks; I touch her firm roundness. I want to drop to my knees and pull her slacks down so badly! I don't care who is watching. My passion is rising uncontrollably. I want her now. I've forgotten about the game, the crowd is cheering, Bri standing beside Sunny is jumping up and down. Josh is running with the ball, he has intercepted. Touchdown! Oh my God! The crowd is ecstatic, people jumping up and down, cheering, applauding; a wild scene as my brother scores the second touchdown. The extra point is good. The score is now fifteen to zero! The game is off to a very good start.

Thank you God, get me away from my lustful thoughts for now. They kick off, take down at the twenty-two-yard line. This team is not giving up as they march past centerfield, now immediately in front of us. I find my hand uncontrollably, but gently sliding over Sammy's round ass again. I'm so wet. She's slowly moving from one leg to the other. I squeeze gently. She pushes her little round ass into me. I'm moving both hands, circling and massaging so slow and gently. Oh my God, I believe she is as hot as me. I slide my hand between her legs, she's spreading them just a bit. I'm sliding it back and forth, she moans out loud. Bri looks directly in her face. "Are you OK Sunny?" "I had a little chest pain. I'm fine." "Amanda, what a game! Josh is having a perfect birthday!" "Yes he is." Where do I take this girl? I must have her. She is rubbing her ass into me again. I move my hands to her and continue massaging her pussy and ass. She is getting damp. I can't help myself as I lick my finger after pulling it from between her legs. It tastes so good. Just knowing where it came from. Halftime finally arrives, the score remains fifteen to zero. Great! "Let's get a coke," says Bri. "Yes!" We all three walk toward the concession area. "Hey guys look! It's my teacher Mr. Jackson. Come meet him."

"Hello Mr. Jackson," I say as I gave him a hug. "This is my cousin Bri and her friend Sunny. They work at Cadillac's." "It's so nice to meet you girls. You all three look ravishing tonight." Bri and Sunny follow my lead, there was no need for him

to know they were not twenty-one. Who knows where things go? You can't be too careful. "Are you servers at Cadillac's?" he inquired. "No, we bar-tend." "Wow, they are fortunate to have you two," he says. "The tips you two must rake in." "Yes we do very well." "Going to school?" "Yes, we are sophomores here." "What is your major?" You'd expect a teacher to ask those kinds of questions, I suppose. "Haven't really decided," was their answer. It probably would change many times. "Let's get smart and then make a decision," Sunny added. "I'm so tired of standing. Where can we find a seat guys? Mr. Jackson, care to come sit with us?" "Gosh, my van is parked right over there." He points. "Want to listen to some music during half time?" "That would be great. I need to sit," I answered. We follow him to his van. It was a huge shiny conversion outfit. He pulled the sliding door, Sunny jumped in, me right behind her. It had lush beautiful bench seats in back and big lush captain's chairs in front. Bri moved to the front captain chair. Mr. Jackson closed the sliding door and moved around to the front and turned on the music.

I was sitting very close to Sunny; I laid my hand on her leg. She gave me the most beautiful smile. I now know and understand why she was called Sunny, her face just shined. Take this slow, I want to savor every moment. Bri has turned in her seat, in fact she has rotated her swivel chair and is facing Mr. Jackson. "What a great van, what do you have to drink?" "Oh girls, I wish I could help. I know Amanda's under-age, I doubt you two are twenty-one." That's true but close. "Sorry to disappoint, but no alcohol tonight." "That's fine," smiled Bri. "A girl must try." She crosses her legs for Mr. Jackson's benefit. He is attempting not to stare. Bri leans back in her captain's chair and puts her feet on the front edge. Now, Mr. Jackson can't help but stare. She's so brave as she looks right at him, "You like that Jack?" She spreads her legs a few inches. I'm at an odd angle, and I can see her thick bush one inch below her panty line. I do love her pussy so much. I'm engrossed in the Bri show. I need to get back to Sunny.

I squeeze her hand gently, which is rubbing up and down the top of my fingers. I wanted to passionately kiss her mouth so badly. Slow it down girl, I run my hand up and down the leg of her silky slacks, she is ever so gently moaning, she is so exciting. My eyes staring at her breasts, I reach over and unbutton two buttons and separate her blouse. She was wearing a very seductive low cut lacy bra, her breasts ooze out at me. She had that sunny smile, loving my aggressiveness.

Bri is massaging her massive hairy area while licking her lips, staring at Mr. Jackson. "Do you like hairy pussy Jack?" "Yes." "Come and take a closer look". He dropped to his knees. "Jack no touching, just look and watch." She continued her personal massage slowly moving one finger up and down her white silky panties. Mr. Jackson was mumbling to himself, "Bri, do you mind if I unzip my pants?" "No, Jack, you wouldn't want to offend my cousin, would you?" She was playing with poor Jack. "Bri can I kiss your panties," he begs. "Jack, if I had a beer I get very romantic, without I just like to play with my pussy." I couldn't help but smile. She is so cool. I don't know which show I'm enjoying the most, Sunny, Bri, Jack or my raging passion. I slowly slide my hand to Sunny's private area. She

spreads her legs, I rub my hand a bit faster. She has thrown her head against the headrest. She opens her legs wider for my touch. I look back at Bri; she has pulled her panties aside, her pussy fully exposed. Two fingers slide up and down, she is groaning; Jack is rubbing his crotch wildly. "Please Bri, let me taste it." She gives him her sexiest smile, and sticks two fingers deep inside her wet hole. She slowly pulls them out, "Jackie, open your mouth." She slides her two wet fingers into his mouth. It's so passionate, his mouth wildly sucking her fingers and her hand.

I move my right leg over Sunny and slide onto her lap. We wrap our arms around each other. I kiss, lick, and suck her neck. The passion grips me. I want to leave my mark. I suck in the skin of her neck passionately. It feels so good, her soft sweet skin in my mouth. She wants to have her neck branded. She knows exactly what I'm doing. She wants my passion to show on her body. I let her skin go, I move to her ear. My wet tongue probing in and out, she's pumping her pussy wildly, I'm pumping back. I can take no more. I crush my mouth to hers, I'm licking, sucking and tasting her hot mouth. She pulls away and whispers in my ear, "I love this, Amanda, don't ever stop." Our mouths again suck each other passionately; I am squeezing her firm hot tits. I unhook her black bra, slide it off and look over my shoulder; Jack is still on his knees licking Bri's wet fingers and hands. I toss him Sunny's bra. He is quickly mouthing it and smelling it in a fit of passion. My mouth is on her nipples, while caressing them so gently. I rip her blouse open, buttons fly, I don't care, her breasts are so perfect. They are huge and so firm. "My God, Amanda, I want you now!" She pushes me off her lap, pushes my back to the seat, pulls up my skirt, rips off my panties and buries her face in my pussy. My passion has risen to limits one cannot begin to imagine. Her tongue is flicking my clit wildly, she realizes her tongue is not sliding inside. She is sucking and licking my pussy hairs, mouthful after mouthful of my pussy hairs and back to my clit. She pushes my leg forward, her tongue is sliding into my ass, in and out, wow! I attempt to control my passion, I do not want to cum. I want to save it. What if I squirt all over Jacks' velvet seats? I push her away gently and lay her down in the opposite direction. Bri continues her antics. Will she eventually fuck him? My poor teacher!

Sunny on her back, her huge firm breasts are bouncing side to side. I unzip her slacks, and pull them gently off her body. She is wearing a tiny thong. I slide it off. I'm so sweet, I hand them to Jack. He devours them. Licking, sucking, and stuffing the crotch into his mouth. My teacher is out of control. I watch him as I stare in awe. Who cares? I look back at Sunny. Her pussy is totally shaved. I have not seen that before although Mom has told me that is the way of today. I bury my face in her sweet wetness, it's so soft, and her pussy is like a baby's skin. I kiss it. I love it. I suck it and bury my tongue deep inside, ramming it in and out. I find her clit. She is going wild, pumping it up and down all over my face. Her pussy has had cock, it's wide open. She is moaning and pumping her passion, she spreads her legs so wide and is screaming, "I am cumming, I am cumming!" I continue to lick her juices, they are so sweet and wet. What a football game! Oh God, the game, I'd forgotten. Oh well, I'll get the score soon enough.

I climb out from between her legs. She lies motionless. Bri is pushing Jack towards the driver's chair and is pulling me. She guides me to my knees. She pushes a button and her swivel seat slides toward the passenger door. She drops to her knees and pushes me toward my teacher. I'm on my hands and knees with my head in Jack's lap. Bri is licking and kissing my pussy, and my once licked ass. Jack drops Sunny's panties and gently rubs his hands over my head and strokes my long wavy hair. He is pulling my head towards his tent like slacks. I kiss his hardness. Bri is sucking me wildly, I am pushing my ass and pussy in her face. "Oh, Bri make me cum!" Her tongue moves faster, I point my ass so tall and unzip Jack's slacks. His cock is loose, he rams it in my open mouth, it is so hard, I know he will blow any second. "Amanda, I want your cum, give me your cum." I love it. Bri is begging, what if I squirt? Whatever! Jack is pounding my mouth with his cock. It feels so good knowing any second I'll be swallowing my teacher's cum. All the while Bri had been working her magic on me. I could no longer contain myself. "Oh Bri, oh my God it's yours, open your mouth!" I squirt into the air. "Oh Bri, drink it Bri, drink it, swallow it." Bri is moaning and attempting to swallow every drop, much of which I know is soaking the carpet. Jack shouts, "Oh my God Amanda, eat my cum!" "Yes Jack yes," it squirts, he's moaning. Bri is sucking and swallowing, what passion! God, what a football game!

I'm sure we won. Cars are leaving, folks are talking loudly. Spirits are high, we must have won. We quickly get dressed. I find Sunny's saliva soaked panties, as I turn to give Bri a passionate kiss, "I love you Bri." Sunny is recovering. I put my mouth on hers, she looks in my eyes. "I loved that Amanda! What you did for me tonight, wow, you are my girl." She is so sweet. She meant every word, she is family. "Mr. Jackson, thank you for entertaining us tonight." He smiled. "Amanda, you will never cease to amaze me." We all climb out of our little room. "Sir, what was the final score?" "The score was fifteen to nothing!" said the man. "That Josh Shiels scored all the points. What a defense! That was amazing."

Oh my gosh! We didn't miss a score and had too much fun. I haven't arranged for a ride home, too busy I suppose. "Mr. Jackson, could you drop me home? I'm only a mile or so." "Of course Amanda. I'm going to run to the john, I'll be right back." "Bri, why didn't you fuck poor Mr. Jackson?" She gave me a sinister little smile. "Girls, I have as much fun driving these men crazy as fucking them. I love making them beg while watching their facial expressions while they drive themselves to a frenzy." How I related, Sammy, the other night, exactly! Yes it was entertaining.

"Girls, we must get together more often." I told them of my beach day for my birthday. They were very excited. It was a plan. Mr. Jackson returns. I give my girls a hug and passionate kisses. I love them both. A quick ride home, Mr. Jackson pulls into my drive. "Thank you so much, tonight was a night to remember," he said as he shakes his head. "Yes, it certainly was." I answer. "Your girls, wow. I'm glad they live out of town, too much for an old guy! That Bri certainly is an amazing girl, and Sunny, oh my god, the most beautiful ass, almost as fine as yours, Amanda." I

kiss his cheek and walk to my house. I quickly write a note to the boys. Congratulations to them both for a job well done, and happy birthday as well. Mom and Dad are in bed sound asleep as I peek through the open door.

I turn on my music and climb into bed. It's only ten o'clock. I'll dial George's number to let him know I'll be up all night baking cookies. No answer, I'll try again in the morning. I drift off to sleep thinking of tonight's events smiling, knowing I had a made a new friend. Isn't it amazing how things happen? My popcorn girl from the Capri, how wild is that?

CHAPTER 42

Rainy Day Business

It's nine o'clock in the morning and I'm up and getting myself in business mode. Oh no, it's raining. Oh boohoo - now what? All showered, time to make a new plan. I'll call George again. "Hello, George please." "This is he." "This is Amanda, the cookie girl." "Oh I'm so glad you called Amanda, your cookies are a big hit. I passed them out to my customers, they were elated. I told one of my neighbors all about you and he would like some cookies as well." "Wow, George that is fantastic. I baked all night long and now it's raining. It's a long bicycle ride on a rainy day." "Honey, we'll come pick them up if that's OK." "Hmmmm, I could make that work. How many would you like?" "Ten-dozen for me and ten-dozen for my neighbor would be great Amanda, and a fifty-dollar tip from each of us. May I be direct and to the point Amanda?" "Of course you can George." "We each want to borrow your mouth for only five minutes." "I can help you with that order George." I give him directions to my big tree for a twelve o'clock delivery.

That went well, I was very excited. All twenty dozen sold again. I switched the two-dozen for "O'La Lay" to George's order. We couldn't have "O'La Lay" with stale Amanda cookies. I walk into the kitchen, "Morning Mom and Dad." I hugged them both. "I love you so much." "Thank you Amanda, we love you." "Wasn't the game great? Fifteen to nothing, and our Josh scored all fifteen." Dad smiled, "Yes, we are very proud." "Where are they?" "They both had inside work to do at the Ferris's." "What do you do with this pile of cookies on a rainy Saturday?" I play stupid, "What do you mean Mom?" "Honey, it's raining." "Mom, do you stay home when it rains?" "No of course I don't, why would I?" "Amanda, don't tell me you're riding your bicycle in the rain to sell your cookies," Dad quipped. "Yeah, Dad, I've

been wet before, so what? Business is always first, I'm just like the mailman, rain or shine and of course you have taught me, we don't miss work, right Dad?" He shakes his head. "You learn much too well my daughter."

I go to my room and get dressed in my yellow bikini panties, my pink sparkly shorts and my pale-blue spandex top. I throw on my raincoat, a rain hat and rubber boots, I'm such a trooper. Thank God I'm only going one hundred yards, not likely I would pedal my bike up and down the road in this rain if I didn't have my sale. No need to microwave today, they probably will be giving them away. Ten-dozen in each bag, there, perfect. "Bye Mom and Dad." "Good luck honey, see you later."

Thank God it was only drizzling a bit at this time and very warm and muggy. I pedaled to my tree. George and my new customer were waiting. I hop off my bicycle. The windows were open. "Hi George." "Hello Amanda, this is Thomas." "Hi Tom." He was a very clean-cut sort of guy, mid-thirties I would guess. The rain has stopped and has transformed into a mist and muggy air. I toss my hat to the grass, unzip my rain jacket and toss it to the ground. I took the two bags of cookies and hand them through the car window. Tom put them in the back seat and thanked me. "You are more beautiful than George described." "Thank you Tom," as I rub my nipples with my fingers. Both are unzipping their shorts and a pair of cocks quickly appear, both standing at serious attention. A warm rush flows through my body. God how I love the sight of a hard cock and here are two, begging for my attention. Thomas opens his door. I turn my back and wiggle my ass for them. I peek over my shoulder watching them stroke their erections, what a turn on. How I love the things I seem to find. I gently slide my pink shorts to the grass and give them a tossing kick. I face them again and pull my top over my head. I shake my wavy hair back in place. I knew Thomas was going to get more than my mouth. I needed to get fucked today. It has been a few days. I walk to the open car door. Tom's facial expression is total awe. I could tell he has never experienced what I am about to provide today. I gaze at his rock hard erection. My pussy is so very wet. I need to go for a ride and I know who will be driving deep into my jungle. I slide onto Tom's lap - OHHHHH. His cock feels so good as I slowly caress his hardness with my pussy and ass. He pulls my mouth to his, God, the passion. I have no words to express the thrill. His mouth is all over my lips, our tongues licking and sucking one another. His cock is sliding up and down my panties, I feel his wetness. God, I need this cock now. I slide my panties aside while licking my fingers and rubbing my saliva on my opening. It's slippery and wet. I guide his hardness to my hole. I spot it perfectly, and press down very gently. I pressure his head through the opening. He attempts to ram it deep. Slow it down Tommy, slow it down. This cookie customer may cum too quickly. I can't have that. I control the pace. I put a bit of pressure and let it slide one centimeter at a time, slowly, deeper, deeper. It passes through my private jungle and deep into its depths. His mouth is sucking my tongue. I love his passion. His hands on my titties, wow, his hot wet mouth licking my nipples...eww so sensitive. I'm losing control while wildly riding his long hard shaft. God, it's so deep inside me. I feel my intestines groaning with pleasure as I

ride him up and down. Tom is growing yet harder, deep inside me. I know what that means. I get ready for his love juice shooting deep inside my body. "OHHHHH, Amanda, oh my God Amanda - oh my God - oh my Gaa...oh I'm cumming!" It continues to squirt. He's screaming! Oh how I love cum deep inside, as he collapses to the seat. His cock still erect inside me, I continue sliding up and down slowly, feeling the juicy cum my customer has provided my little ass. He shouts, "Amanda, you have to quit - my cock can't take any more!" He kisses my lips.

Oh crap, I forgot about Mr. George who is taking all this pleasure in. No x-rated movie could ever top this. "You two were amazing. If I had a camera, we would be wealthy." I climb off Tommy and move my mouth to George's hard cock. I pull the head to my mouth and suck off the slimy liquid, it's so tasty. I massage its large head with my tongue, why do I love cock in my mouth? I have no answer. I slide down the shaft. I love my mouth full of cock all the way to my tonsils. It's so large, there's no room to roll it around. It's a mouth full. I slide my mouth back to the head, juices are flowing from the little hole on the tip, I swallow. My mouth is full of his leakage. I slide my mouth up and down his erection. It's getting harder and harder, I know what is coming any second. I move the head to my wide-open mouth. I don't want to lose a drop, timing is perfect. He lets out a wild moan. I attempt to swallow every drop, it's not working, cum overflows my mouth and drips down my chin. I swallow mouthful after mouthful, there is no keeping up. I love the cum as it drips down my chin and to my body below. It's all in a days' work. The cookie business is wonderful, and fun as well, even on a rainy day.

I sit up between my customers as both heads are shaking. Both do a "wow" almost simultaneously. "Amanda," says Tom, "you are an amazing girl, unbelievable. How old are you, nineteen, twenty?" "No, I'm only eighteen." "Going to State?" "Yes, that is where my cookie money goes." "Amanda, you told me cheerleading camp." "Oh George, you caught me. Us cookie sellers have to have a great sales pitch, right?" George smiled. "Yes, that is true and you do have a pitch." He slid his cock back into its cage. "Well, guys, should I send you an invoice for my service?" Thomas jumps in quickly, "No I have cash!" "And so do I Amanda, you are too funny."

I hop out, arrange my panties and pull my shorts and top onto my body. "Tom, want to give me a number to call for a reorder." "Ah, no, go through George." "I'm always looking for new cookie customers so let your friends know. George, I will call you soon." I climb on my bike and pedal toward home.

My watch says one-fifteen. Wow, a quick story Amanda, find it now!! I park my bike and in the door I go, Mom and Dad sitting at the kitchen table. "Amanda, wetter than you anticipated?" Dad asks. "Oh no Dad, weather is perfect, I love the rain." "Why are you back so quickly?" A huge smile as I wave two fifty-dollar bills in the air. "Wow, what is this?" "I rode down the highway a long, long way and stopped at only two houses. They were so impressed that a young girl would be out on her bicycle on a rainy day to raise money to go to camp, they each purchased ten-dozen. Of course my new line; give them to your customers and friends."

"Amanda, I am so proud of you." Mom hugs me, and stares into my eyes. God I hate to lie, but what could I do? "I love you Amanda. You are amazing, you make me so proud." Dad was sweet, he knew me too well. "Yes Amanda, you do have a way, you are amazing." "I love you Dad." He knew something wasn't quite right.

Oh well, I'm out of cookies, my panties are wet, my ass has been fucked and swallowed a huge load. What more can there possibly be? Time for me to shower this rain off my body and plan for tonight's (birthday) celebration.

The boys are home. "Guys, what a game!" "Thanks for the note Amanda." "Wow Josh," as I put my arms around him, "I was so proud to tell my friends you're my brother." Johnny is shaking his head, "And how about that cheer squad? We added the major support!" We laugh. "Yes, you did, I was proud of you as well. I love you guys, I'm so glad you're my brothers."

I go to my room and lay on my bed with my music softly playing in the background and drift off for a rest after a tough day in the business world. Hopefully, tonight I can get Bargain Bob's attention and learn about the true business life. Will Ty be working? Has he shared with Chef Telly his Sam's experience? And oh God that Steve Hunt guy as Elvis, I'm so excited. "Amanda, its five o'clock, get yourself moving." "Yes, Mom, thank you." I slip on shorts and a top, go out to let Bandit run for a bit. The rain has left. The sun is peeking through. "That's my buddy." I put my arms around his neck, he licks my face and gives me his sexy smile. "Go get it boy!" Off he goes, he's fed and I brush his coat as he eats his dinner.

CHAPTER 43

Josh's Birthday

OK, it's time to work on my wardrobe for the evening. What would Elvis want to admire on me. No - no - maybe that, no, this doesn't work today, no could be . . . Yes! This is perfect. It's a tight black stretchy cotton skirt that shows my every move with a long sleeve red spandex turtleneck top. And oh yes, it maximizes my breasts. They're getting a bit larger, or is it my red top? No, they are definitely growing. No socks, no thigh highs. My legs are so tan and soft, why cover them? Red, four-inch heels, yes, perfect. Make up, Mom won't complain tonight, it's a family affair. Eye lashes, a bit of shadow, mascara, red lipstick, oh God, it's nearly time to takeoff! Out my bedroom door I go. "Oh Amanda, look at you! Wow!" Josh and Johnny compliment. "You do look very nice honey, although I don't care for the makeup." "Thanks Mom."

Uncle Ken has arrived. We file to the van and are off, we'll pickup Marianne on the way. Josh and I are in the far back seat leaving room for Marianne. Josh climbs out to let her slide between us. "Marianne, you look ravishing as always." "Thanks Josh." Everyone said his or her hellos. Marianne's long blond hair is so shiny. She is wearing a short black skirt and a black button up stretchy blouse. Her breasts and cleavage are not to be missed, she has just enough buttons open for maximum exposure. God, how I want to have breasts like that.

I immediately told her of my Sam's experience as we all three laughed. "We'll see if that conversation comes up this evening." "What's in your bag Amanda?" "I have two-dozen cookies for 'O'La Lay.'" "Oh yeah, I thought he wanted a truckload?" "Yes, he did." We laugh again. We pull in front of Cadillac's. There are lots of cars. Dad is searching for a parking space. Of course, it's Saturday night

and Elvis is on stage. We locate a parking place one block away, perfect. We all are looking stunning as we walk down the street and Marianne turns and looks at Josh. "Gosh I forgot, Happy Birthday! Oh, and great game last night. You were awesome, you animal, you." "Yes, it certainly was a birthday game not to be forgotten," Josh agrees. We walk through the glass and brass doors and over the marble floors. The brass ceiling shines. Wow, I forget how beautiful Cadillac's is. "Do you have a reservation for the Shiels for seven?" asks Mom. "Yes, good to have you back," says Stephanie. Her blond hair is perfectly in place with a beautiful happy smile.

The bar area is mostly empty. The restaurant is full to capacity with the exception of our large eight top table, which is by the dance floor with a large shiny brass rail dividing it from the seating area. Elvis is singing a lovely slow song, the dance floor has several couples dancing to his music. Our table is beautifully set - brass chargers, flowers, a bottle of wine in the center; all so elegant. I look at the walls above the rows of booths on either side. Two feet higher, photos, I missed them last trip. They appear to be pictures of our Capital City from the early nineteen-hundreds. I must have a walk and look them over before the night is finished.

Nicole is our server this evening. She is smiley and bubbly telling us the history of Cadillac's. The stories are told a bit differently this evening. Some things we hadn't heard from a couple of weeks ago. She takes drink orders. Marianne and Josh are laughing and seem to getting on quite well. John is chatting as well. Mom and Dad are facing the dance floor and holding hands. They are getting up to dance to Elvis's song, "I can't help falling in love with you". This is so perfect, the four of us are facing the bar area. I like to see who is coming and going. I like to know what is happening or perhaps going to happen. No sign of Ty on this very busy night. I'm sure he's helping get food out in a timely manner. Chef Telly, of course, is doing chef duties. A bit early for "O'La Lay" and Bargain Bob I suppose. I look briefly over the menu it all looks so great. "What are you considering for dinner?" I ask Marianne and the boys. They are thinking along my lines. I loved the Caddy buffet so much and it looked fantastic coming in the door. Our drinks arrive, Mom and Dad return to their seats, and we all place our orders. Elvis continues to sing his heart out, and is now tossing stuffed bears. OHHHH, Dad has caught a big white fluffy bear, the table applauds. He hands it to Mom. She has a huge smile and gives Dad a kiss and hug. I didn't miss this one, my cell phone camera caught it. I forget I have a camera with me most times. I must use this more often. I continue taking photos. "Closer Marianne and Josh, come on Johnny, get in the picture, Uncle Ken, Mom and Dad." I continue capturing memories.

Salads arrive for Mom, Dad and Uncle Ken. We walk to our Caddy buffet. Where to start; a salad I suppose. The three follow my lead; such a large selection, easy Amanda, I tell myself; I must keep room for dinner. Now back to our table. "How are your salads?" I inquire. "Very nice," answers Mom, the others are nodding with food in their mouths. Josh and Marianne are chatting comfortably, with John adding a word occasionally. It's great, Marianne and Josh, a perfect pair it seems. Although, it somehow makes me a bit uneasy.

Here comes Ty through the kitchen doors, as I look over Elvis and his glitzy costume, Ty spots us. That big smile appears. "Amanda!" I give him a hug. "How is everyone? Welcome to Cadillac's, great to have you with us this evening." He shakes Dad and Ken's hand and the boys as well. "Everything OK so far?" "Great," Dad and Ken answer. "Anything I can get you?" "No, Nicole is taking very good care of us." "Let me check the crowd and I'll return to check on you." We thanked him. "Amanda, will you be bringing up your favorite restaurant story this evening?" Dad asks, with his big smile. "When the opportunity arises, that is my plan." "I can't wait," says the birthday boy. I hold my soda in the air, a big table "O'La Lay," it's huge fun. Here comes dinner as Robert sweeps away salad plates and empty glasses. Another round of cocktails arrives, compliments of Ty. That was very sweet. Ty is back with a glass, soda it appears, we "O'La Lay" to the birthday boy. "Happy birthday Josh." Ty remembered, that was very good. Prime rib, steak and some exotic chicken dish for Mom. The aroma has my mouth watering, time for food. The four of us slide our chairs away. Let's see, a little fish, a little beef and just a bit of creamy chicken. Perfect!

The bar area is beginning to fill. Yes, "O'La Lay" has arrived and is doing an "O'La Lay" at the far end of the bar with a group of smiley happy folks. They are clinking their glasses laughing and hugging one other. One just wonders what brings all that on. By gosh, Bargain Bob is early, no, it's eight o'clock, he's right on time. He and "O'La Lay" give brotherly hugs to one another, as Bob shakes hands with the guys and hugs the girls. It seems like too much fun.

Oh my goodness, the Mayor and his wife are walking through the door! Bob is right there and gives his wife a kiss and pats the Mayor on the back as he shakes his hand and enters in deep conversation. I want to know what people like this talk about, it eats at me. I want to know how the real world works - soon! Bob has moved on shaking hands and greeting costumers as they walk through the doors, while chatting with folks leaving. "How was your dinner?" I can read his lips. Many stop and chat, he always smiles back and acknowledges all. He seems so pleasant.

The fish and the chicken are delicious, all the food has been great. I love this place so much. The dining room is clearing out a bit. Elvis still singing his heart out to the crowd. He is passing out leis, hanging them around our necks. We all thank him. Amazing, he has been performing for over an hour and not taken a break. Bob gets his money's worth from Steve Hunt, that's for sure.

"O'La Lay's" cookies, I must not forget. Speak of the devil, "Amanda, Marianne – hello!" - with his huge Caribbean smile. I get up, he gives me a huge hug and kiss. Marianne jumps up and receives the same. "Good to see you guys," as he shakes hands all around. "Happy Birthday Josh. I read about your game last night. You go boy!" We all laugh. He holds his cocktail high in the air, "O'La Lay" to Josh. The whole group clink their glasses with a huge "O'La Lay!" Ty is back as "O'La Lay" slid a chair near Marianne. Josh will have some competition.

I walk back to the buffet, just one more little piece of that chicken. Ty follows me

as I get near the Caddy buffet and whispers, "I want to tell you a secret." He walks toward the bathrooms. We get to the fountain, he looks around, takes my hand and pulls me to the storage area and closes the door behind him. His mouth is all over mine. I return his kiss. His hands are massaging my ass. He has pulled up my skirt and squeezes my ass through my panties. I feel his hardness all over my pussy, it feels good. He quickly unzips his pants. His cock is out and he is rubbing it all over my crotch. I let him go for now. I may need him to help get a visit with Bob tonight, I'm hoping. I reach down and stroke his hard cock. I decide I will play a little. I bend down and give it a kiss and a lick. I now stand up and guide it under my panties and let him slide it over my pussy. God, it feels so good. I would love to get fucked. "Ty, I must get back to the table. I was busted by two of my group last time." "Oh please Amanda, let me cum for you!" "Perhaps you can meet me later Tyson, you play your cards right and we'll see." I pull back and peek out the door, it's clear. I hustle out as he was putting it back in its cage while it continued to roar.

Back with my chicken, Ty is close behind, "O'La Lay" is telling Marianne, Josh and John stories. He is entertaining, it's so cute. Here comes Chef Telly. He gives me a friendly smile and a hug while telling Ty, "Wow, what a rush, it's finally slowing down. We've been backed up for hours, we made it with no returns tonight!" Ty shakes his hand. "You guys were rockin'!" "Good job Chef," "O'La Lay" tells him.

CHAPTER 44

Ty Busted

"Chef Telly, has Ty told you about our trip to my favorite restaurant last Sunday?" "No, I haven't seen him until tonight. He is normally only here on busy evenings. Why, where did you go?" "Well," Ty takes a deep breath, he has our tables' full attention, "we went to Sam's Club." "You what?" fires Telly with a cocky grin. "Chef, let me finish, that's exactly what I thought, but it turns out to be amazing." "At Sam's Club? Ty, what were you smoking?" "Chef, knock it off, let me tell you the story, OK?" "Go! I'll shut up." We all listened very intently as Ty told of his Sam's Club restaurant adventure. He begins to tell of his experience, our table listened closely. They could barely contain their smiles. Chef Telly was shaking his head with his mouth wide open. He could not believe what he was hearing from Ty, who is generally a very bright guy! Ty finished his story. "I'm telling you Chef, it was amazing. I learned so much!" "Tyson, let me get this straight," says Chef. "For a twenty-five dollar membership fee, you eat all year, bring your family along and eat all you want!" "Yeah," Ty replied. "Bavarian, wild goat cheese, Laredo style, sweet melon and Russian meatballs…all exotic, and you must tongue them?" I'm biting my lip to control my laughter that wants to burst out so badly. "Tyson, their silly meatballs are in cartons. They are not exotic and you eat them just like you do anywhere!" "No Chef, I'm telling you it was not like that, it was exotic meatball weekend." Telly is shaking his head from side to side. "And Ty, you believe of a riot on Saturday night at Sam's Club as well?" "Yeah, it was on TV 6 news." "Ty, my wife never misses the news, you think I wouldn't hear if they were rioting at Sam's Club?" Ty is rolling his eyes and shrugging his shoulders. "And let me get this straight, you also believe when the riot squad shows

up in uniform with guns the greeter asks for a Sam's card?" "Well, I did wonder about that."

Telly continues, "And the greeter had been demoted to a chef?" Finally, laughter could not be held back any longer, the whole table roared. "O'La Lay" fired out the biggest "O'La Lay" ever! Our table "O'La Lay's" and the roaring continues. Ty is looking around and finally turns to me, "Amanda, it was all a joke?" I looked down to hide my grinning face. Telly is shaking him around with both hands while wagging his own head back and forth. Tyson finally speaks. "Telly, I'm telling you it was so realistic. They all had exotic stories and all so dedicated to the concept! Amanda, how could you possibly be so convincing? And the chef's, God, you got me!!!" Telly and "O'La Lay" were going wild with crazy laughter. My family is trying not to embarrass him any further. "Amanda, you are amazing. How you could possibly pull off this complex joke? I feel totally stupid." "No Ty, we put a lot of effort into it, it's not stupidity, we were just good!! Well, the gig is up, I win. I'll make it up to you Tyson." Of course he had gotten what he needed last week anyway!

Our tables are cleared. Mom and Dad are dancing. Oh my, Marianne and Josh are going to dance a slow song. How nice! "Come on, Johnny, dance with me?" "I'd love to Amanda." He whispers in my ear, "Sister, you are the most beautiful and amazing woman Cadillac's has seen tonight." "You're too sweet John." "I love you," as he kissed my ear.

At the bar I see Chef Telly and "O'La Lay" in Bob's ear. Bob is shaking his head. They are rolling with laughter. I only guess as to what that conversation is about. Uncle Ken is talking to a lady that appears to be a bit older than him. She is handing him a flyer of some sort. They seem to be having a very serious conversation. She has a nice, friendly smile, a bit over weight, not fat. Her attire is not totally Cadillac style. She is talking, they are laughing, and she is pointing around the restaurant at various features. Ken is asking her to dance. Yes, they are walking to the dance floor, how nice. The song has ended. Elvis shouts, "Ladies and Gentlemen! Please stay right where you are. This is Bargain Bob's favorite song. I've learned it for him. Let's have a round of applause for Bob who created this facility for all of you tonight." The room applauds. I looked toward Bob, he slides his hand in the air with a wave while shaking his head. I don't think he cares for the spotlight. I wonder why, his face is on TV continuously. You would think he loves the attention on himself. Elvis says, "My song to Bob," as he begins to play the "Hawaiian Wedding Song". Wow, I don't believe I know it. I've listened to Dad and Mom's music for years, the title however, I don't recognize. It's a beautiful Hawaiian song. I guess the title told me that, such a romantic tune. It's about a couple on their wedding day. I whispered to my brother, "It is a beautiful song." He smiled. "Yeah, it's very nice."

CHAPTER 45

Conversation with Bargain Bob

Bargain Bob is on the dance floor. His favorite song, I guess he had better dance to it! He is dancing with a blond with long wavy hair, well-dressed, a silk skirt that shows off her lovely shape and nice legs. She's probably a cousin. Bob is dancing his way to our space. "Hello, Amanda, so good to have you back," he says with a polite smile. "You are beautiful as ever. Amanda, would you come to the bar in a bit? I would like to talk to you." "Of course, and Bob, I love your song." "Honey, I'll tell you the story and where it comes from." I smiled. John and I finished the Hawaiian wedding dance, "Thank you Johnny, so much."

Marianne and Josh are smiling. He is holding her hand. Uncle Ken announces, "Everyone, this is Rhonda. She is Bob's marketing director here at Cadillac's." Everyone introduces themselves, as Robert, our busser, gets Rhonda a chair. Well, isn't that nice. I'm still not certain why Uncle Ken is such a loner these days. I look to the bar. It has mostly cleared away. Bob is sitting with the blond. I excuse myself and tell Mom and Dad where I'm going and why.

I make my way to the back of the huge ornate bar, so shiny, lighted glass blocks and tall gold brass stools. The bar is a work of art in itself. "Amanda, thank you for coming over. This is Pam, one of my favorite cousins. I have fourteen, but she is my favorite." I smile at Bob. "I'll bet you tell that to all the girls." "Oh no, I wouldn't do that, right Pam?" She grins, "Right Bob," as she winked at me. "I am his favorite," and gives me one more wink. She excuses herself and I slide into her stool. "Amanda, I'd love to buy you a cocktail. I imagine that we'll have to wait a

year or two." "Sadly yes," I replied. "Honey, I'm going to wait. That's a Bargain Bob guarantee." "I'm holding you to that Bob." "May I be to the point?" "Of course Bob." "How in the hell did you suck Tyson into your outrageous scam? Sam's Club of all places!" I smile and shake my head. "It just popped out of my mouth two weeks ago, after meeting Ty. He's such a pleasant person, so well-mannered and would never offend anyone. I decided to take his unoffensive nature to the limit. Bob, you do not know the detail we created to suck him right in. I wasn't certain it could possibly come off as perfectly as it did. The detailed stories all of these Sam's employees told him, I may have been convinced myself!" Bob is laughing. "I seriously doubt that little girl. Ty also believes you have a fiancé. Amanda, if I remember correctly, you're not through high school." "You remember too well and I'm going to work here once I've graduated." "Is that a promise?" "It's definitely a strong maybe, Bob." "It amazes me that you are in high school and could get the best of Tyson. He is a very bright guy, how? I realize it was an elaborate scheme, but girl, you had to make the scheme work. I can be very theatrical myself when I want to. My sister, she is much better than I and I'm not convinced we could have pulled that off." Bob continues sipping on his Tanqueray and Tonic. I watch the bar lady automatically refill it. He doesn't ask, they keep a full one.

"Amanda, what are you going to do with your life?" "You know I don't feel comfortable calling you Bob. I won't call you Bargain Bob, can I call you Uncle Bob?" He smiled and shook his head, "Amanda, I would be honored to have you be my favorite niece." I am blessed! "Great, Uncle Bob! One day I will be very wealthy, drive beautiful American made cars, live in a mansion, and travel at my will." "Amazing girl! How will you make that happen?" "Uncle Bob, I have no clear answer, it will not be a husband providing it. I will never marry!" "Why in the world do you feel that way?" A deep breath, "Uncle Bob, I wasn't put on this earth to spend my life with one person. I love people, not just a person. When I'm wealthy, it will be because I made my fortune. I realize I can't do it alone, I will find help. It will not be with a husband and I do love your Hawaiian wedding song. The music is beautiful. I never want the dedication that song suggests to one person." "Amanda, that is amazing. It has taken me my whole life to figure that out and you feel it at such a young age. Honey, when I was young, I loved to be in love . . . It was such a huge rush, it was all I could think about, it controlled my mind and soul. It was on my mind, day and night." "Was it love?" "I thought so at that time. Amanda, it didn't last long, so much great fun and the thrill, soon it was gone. It fades so quickly. I've been married three times. I believed all three were forever. I realize now nothing is really forever. Sure, many people stay together and attempt to believe it's this beautiful love, that's the reason they remain married for twenty, thirty, forty or more years. It's mostly bullshit. Most are not happy, they are stuck…they need the security. Here you are a kid and you don't need that shit. What are you doing with your life now: this week, tomorrow?"

"Uncle Bob, many things, most of them would blow your mind." He smiles. "I'll give you a very simple one, I have a cookie business." "A what?" "You heard me. I

bake cookies and go door-to-door selling them." "You bake cookies?" "Well, sort of. I've sold twenty-dozen the last two Saturdays in a couple of hours. I sell them for five dollars a dozen. My profit is four dollars and twenty-five cents a dozen. That is an eighty-five dollar profit for a few hours on a Saturday and the tips are amazing Uncle Bob." "What do you mean tips?" I take a deep breath. Do I tell him? "Anyway, Uncle Bob eighty-five dollars sure beats the chump change babysitting brings. I'm just now getting my business organized. Soon I will spend more time selling and it could go right through my little roof." "Where do you bake them?" A deep breathe. "The truth?" "Yes, Amanda." "I buy them at the Dollar Store." "Oh my God! You - you how did you begin to make this happen girl?" "I was looking for a business. While visiting the Dollar Store, I noticed bags of two-dozen chocolate chip cookies for a dollar. I bought some boxes and I sell them a dozen at a time. The customers don't know whether I really bake them or not. I'm raising money for cheer camp. I have a very good sales story."

"Amazing, when I was your age, I would go door-to-door selling ink pens. Ten cents, six cents profit. Oh, honey, you may be my clone! Amanda, you are a rare breed. It must cause you some unusual problems. You being a beautiful female, things will come your way. You have many advantages we males are not blessed with. I have a strange feeling you know that at even at your young age. Most never know their whole life! I would like to spend some time with you Amanda," he handed me a card. "Don't lose it, they cost a lot of money!" Wow, a row of Cadillacs in front of Cadillac's and his smiling face on the corner. "Uncle Bob, what a great business card." "Yes," he agreed. "It's very difficult to throw a photo like that in the trashcan. Remember that my girl, I mean niece…Your business card, make it personal, have your photo doing what you do in full color, of course." "I can see it now, my business card: 'Cookies by Amanda,' with me in my cheerleader skirt." "Are you a cheerleader?" "No, we don't have athletics at our school! Maybe when I go to college." He laughs. "You are amazing, I may learn from you. That number rings directly to my office. I see your Mom and Dad coming this direction. Within a week, let's sit and talk. I'll send my limo to pick you up if necessary, I'll let your Dad know." He approaches Mom and Dad. I slide off my stool. Dad and Uncle Ken are shaking Bob's hand, I'm not sure what is being said, but Dad and Uncle Ken are beaming. I hear Dad saying, "Yes Bob, she is something. I would be honored to have you mentor her. I think she needs someone who understands the business world in her life. Perhaps she'll take you to Sam's Club for dinner soon!" "Ken, that story I won't soon forget. I can't believe this little queen put that together. Tyson is in his thirties, and this kid totally scammed him – wow, amazing!"

"Honey, here are your cookies," says Dad as he hands me the bag. "Oh gosh, they're for 'O'La Lay.' Oh no, he's gone." "You sold cookies to 'O'La Lay'?" "Yes, he ordered two-dozen. He wanted a truckload, I was not capable. My ovens weren't large enough." Uncle Bob hands me ten dollars. "I'll get them to him. I may try your famous recipe myself! We must get you to cheerleader camp young lady!"

My plan had worked so perfectly. I had nailed Don Juan's ass. I got a nice little

fuck in the storage room. Pulling the Sam's Club skit off so well was so much fun. I have a new confidence and know my Sam's scenario has brought me a new uncle. This is so important, I believe.

"Amanda, next Sunday, come to my house, we'll sit by the pool and talk. Ken knows where I live, he is welcome to come along. My home phone is on the back of the card if you may have any questions, my niece. By the way, Ken and Robert, Amanda is my favorite niece. I have dozens of cousins but only one niece." I am smiling so big, he is just so cute and so full of it. This will be much too fun. "Yes, Uncle Bob, about one o'clock?" "Great Amanda, I'll call if there are any changes." We all said our goodbyes. "Rhonda," Bob waives his arm as she is telling Ken farewell, "how about a press release to the media explaining the Amanda cookie story?" "Of course, Bob. Give me some facts!" "Rhonda, this is Amanda. Rhonda does our marketing here at Cadillac's. She puts out press releases, many times they bring a tear to my eye. They are so beautifully written. I have an unusual feeling she will be doing press for you in some capacity in the future." "O'La Lay" to that as I make a fist and punch Bob and the others. "Amanda is my niece, Rhonda." "Like your cousins, right Bob?" she smiles. "Sort of I guess, anyway, she's one of kind; you will soon see that!" "Amanda, good to hear you are part of the family." That was music to my ears. Part of this happy family - wow! What a night. Somehow I feel right at home.

CHAPTER 46

Marianne's My Girl

Josh is holding Marianne's hand as we walk down the street. Why does it bother me just a bit? I love my brother so much. I guess I consider her my territory. I know he has no idea. I may have to mark my little blond territory very soon. In the van as we drive along Marianne and Josh are chatting. I feel bad, but I believe I have a right to be territorial as I put my hand on her bare leg and gently rub my fingers back and forth. She smiles. "Amanda, I missed you tonight. Josh has taken very good care of me." I slide my hand up to her panty line and tickle the blond pubic hairs poking through. She spreads her legs for my hand a bit. Josh sees my aggressiveness, as a shocked look comes over his face. I slide my fingers over her clit, she takes a deep breath and leans her head on my shoulder. Her mouth is open. I passionately kiss her. Oh God, my poor brother. I feel this has to be done! Uncle Ken and John could see us if they turn around. I am well aware, but it makes no difference. I've fucked Uncle Ken and sucked my brother, so whom can they report to, nobody! Mom and Dad are in serious fun conversation way to the front. I feel safe. I continue sliding my hand over her pussy. Her legs have spread a bit more. It's a short trip to Marianne's home. Time is short. I slide myself to the van floor. She slides a few inches down the seat. My mouth is on her pussy licking through her panties. I quickly pull them aside and bury my mouth in her blond pussy. Her juices, God, they taste like she looks, sumptuous. My tongue is wildly working her, I want her cum now! She is attempting to keep herself calm and quiet, she must, she knows. She gently pumps my face, she whispers a quite OHHHHH. It was there. I licked and swallowed all, every drop. I pull her panties over her pussy and move up to my seat. Her head is turned in my direction. I give her a kiss. "Amanda, I love you," she whispers. I hoped Josh heard that. I have no problem loaning my girls, but don't

get carried away. Hmmm, I amaze myself, earlier I wanted to fix them up. I guess I'm not ready to give up my girl.

I look at Josh. I couldn't tell if his look is passion or disgust. Is he angry? I'm not certain. He'll be fine, a girl must control her little world and her people, that is my motto. How do I handle Josh? First, I must try to understand his feelings.

We pull into Marianne's drive. I give her a kiss as she says good night to Josh and the rest of the family. On the way home it appeared that Josh had developed a bit of an attitude. Was I wrong? I love my brother so much, but he can find his own woman. I would have no problem letting him fuck her as long as I was involved. Don't just slide in, that upset me. Is this my problem? Perhaps, it is puzzling. Is this how men feel about their women? I must talk to Dad or Uncle Ken soon. I'm really not certain if I could tell this story. I'm sure Uncle Ken had seen my display of affection.

Walking up to the house Mom and Dad are in such great spirits. Uncle Ken, John and Josh - no one seems to be talking. "Uncle Ken, Rhonda seemed very nice." "Yes, she is very lovely and loves life. I'm going on home. No painting for me tomorrow Robert." "Taking a day off?" asks Dad. "Yes, I need a break."

"Josh, are you OK?" "I'm fine Dad. I'm just tired." "Seems you and Marianne got along very nicely." "Right, Dad," as he closed his bedroom door. "John, what is wrong?" He shrugged, "Who knows Dad - too much fun, that's all." "Good night," as Dad is listening to messages, "Damn." "Robert, what's wrong?" asks Mom. "They want me at the shop tomorrow, a major problem." "I guess it's OK. It's double time." "Anita, my buddy Ron is coming over tomorrow afternoon. I have trouble catching him on the phone quite often. If he comes by, let him know I will be here by five-thirty." "Robert, I'm going shopping tomorrow, I won't be home, and the boys are at Ferris's." "Amanda, will you be here?" "Yes, I plan on it." "Amanda, his name is Ron, a very happy sort of guy. If I can't catch him, can you entertain until I arrive at five-thirty or so?" "Sure Dad, no problem, anything for you." I hug him. "I love you." I give Mom a big hug, "Good night. I am so happy to have a new uncle, Mom." "Amanda, Bob could be very good for your world."

I go to my room, close the door and turn on my music. I soon realize I'm unable to sleep. I can't get what I did to my brother off my mind. I know my problem. I'm so controlling, why? I felt earlier in the night they would be good for each other. I'm not prepared to give her up yet, maybe never! I love her, I love her pussy. I'm not in love, but have love for her. How can I spin this to Josh without him needing to know that I'm going to be happy first and then "you" if it fits my world? I slip on my panties and a top. Tap, tap, tap. "Yes?" a gruff voice answers. I open his door, walk to his bed and sit on the edge. A night-light is dimly lit his room. I see his outline lying on his bed. "Amanda, what?" "I suppose you're upset with me." "No shit sister!" "Joshua," I take a very deep breath, "I did it for you!" "Oh yea, right Amanda." "Josh, it was your first night with Marianne, you're not in love, you like her so what? Your heart is not broken, just your silly pride. Before it went any further, I decided I needed to show you how we felt about each other. You needed

to know she is mine! I loaned her to you for a few hours, be happy for the time I gave you. Don't be greedy. If you want to fuck her, I can arrange that, although I will be there as well, watching and partying. Borrowing is all you get for now. Someday, that may change, when it does, I'll let you know. Do you understand?" "I understand, you worry me sister!" "Not to worry brother, my world is exactly where I need it to be. Borrow my girls with my permission only. Even better, find your own and when you do, Josh, is it OK if I borrow her occasionally?" "Amanda, you're sick." "Josh, you can watch! Yes, I love my sick state. I was going to help make it up to you with a blowjob tonight, you're in no mood. I can see that. Josh, get your shit together, my birthday brother." I walk out and close the door. I always say it is much better to take the offense and go right after them. God, how I hate to defend myself.

I watch all the beautiful girls at school, at the mall, and walking down the street. Do they go through these silly situations? Do any of them attempt to control their destiny or simply live their lives? Was I too hard on Josh? Does he understand? Maybe. He'll get over it soon. He's not likely to hit on Marianne again or any of my other girls for that matter. It's all good!

CHAPTER 47

Bwana Ron

Sunday morning, I'm up at nine forty-five. Late for me. "Morning Mom." "Good morning, Amanda. Sleeping in this morning?" "Yes, a big night I guess. Where are you shopping?" "Twelve Oaks," she replied, "some new work clothes, I have quite a list. Two of my co-workers and I are going. I'm leaving very soon. I work a three-day shift starting tonight. I'll be home Wednesday." "Oh Mom, I hate that." "It's OK, absence makes the heart grow fonder, honey." "I know Mom. I'll miss you so much." She gives me a hug. "You're a good daughter, you make me so proud." "Thanks Mom." "I'm off, see you later in the afternoon." "Pizza tonight Mom?" "That would be great. The boys have some sort of function at seven o'clock tonight. So pizza at six or so?" "OK Mom." "Bye." I guess the house is all mine for a while.

I eat a little breakfast, slip on shorts and a top and out the door. "Bandit, how is my best dog today?" He's smiling, that's good. "Go get it," as I toss his ball. I find the perfect spot for tanning and drag out my chaise. It's nearly noon, so the sun will be just right. I must get to the Dollar Store for more cookies. I should count my money that I have stuffed in my shoebox. I must have several hundred dollars by now. Maybe I'll do some shopping someday soon. Then again, why should I? I have bushels of sexy outfits. Shoes! That's what I'm going to work on - hot sexy shoes. No Good Will, a nice shoe store is in order.

I go to my room to look for the perfect swimsuit. This little bikini is just right with the little tie on top, the mirror says yes. I fluff my pubic hairs. They are poking out all around the legs, yes, that's fine. Now it's out the door to my sunny space, and to let my Bandit out of his pen. The sun feels so good and my tan is hold-

ing up well for the little sun I've gotten recently. "Where is your stick? That's a boy, go get it." Oil all over, I love how it makes my skin shine, I love the oily smell. Soon it will be over, fall is approaching. Although, certain years I lay out in January, it's sometimes in the seventies. Other years, it may snow. Oh well, no need to worry. I can't control the weather. I chose to concentrate on what I can control, which I'm finding is most areas of my life. I'm sure Bob will have some positive input in that area. I'm so happy to finally become acquainted. I can't wait until next Sunday at his home. Did Uncle Ken commit to going? I don't remember, oh well. "Bandit, come back here," a car pulls into the driveway. He doesn't bite, but he is very intimidating. "Come boy."

A man is climbing out, no need to move. He has noticed me in my lounger. I wave him over. "Hi, I'm Ron, is Robert around?" "Oh yes, you are Dad's friend." "Gosh, he did not get a hold of you?" "Oh, my phone is shut off, I haven't checked my messages." "He was called to work, he will be home a bit later. I was nominated to entertain you. I sing, I dance, I play the harmonica. Which would you like first Ron?" A huge smile comes across his outgoing face. "A dance would be great." "Ron, as soon as I am rested, I'll do that dance." He pets Bandit. "God, he's big and so friendly, I was afraid to get out of my car." "I'm Amanda." "It's a pleasure to meet you Amanda. Your dog is so beautiful." "Thank you, he's my buddy." "He's so clean. You must wash him every day." "No, no - when Dad goes to the car wash, he puts him in the back of the truck and runs him through." "Really?" "Oh yes. It costs six dollars and ninety-nine cents for the truck and the dog. It's a great deal, although Dad does splurge." "Really? How?" "Well, for fifty cents more, they have a machine that gives him extra soap and conditioner and goggles to wear. That's why his coat shines as it does." "Wow, I have never heard of a wash like that." "I have three large dogs. I'm going to run them through. God, I hate washing them." "I know Ron, so does Dad." "Which car wash is it?" "Oh, they all offer that service Ron." "Wow, you learn something everyday." "Be sure and get the extra soap. It does make a big difference. It's also fun to watch. Just picture it Ron, Bandit all soaped up, with his goggles on and those big brushes gently pounding his coat. Ya know Ron, when I wash him here he hates it. But get him to that car wash. I don't know why, but he sure loves it. And now he gets to go through that huge dryer. It almost blows him out of the truck. He's tough though as he holds right on with his happy smile. Dogs must be at least sixty pounds or they tell you no." "Of course, all of mine are big enough," says Ron, "God, I can't wait to run them through. This is going to save me so much time." "Ron, you know what else?" "What?" "The three guys that do the final towel dry offs, they will buff your dog all up and for only fifty cents more! They then clip his nails and brush his teeth! Be sure to use that service as well, it's quite the value. You have to bring your own toothpaste Ron. Don't forget it." "I've never brushed my dog's teeth." He inspects Bandit's teeth as he pry's Bandits jaws apart. "Wow, they are bright and shiny." "Yup, we use Pepsodent, that's best for dogs. I read that on the Internet." "I'll get some tonight, the taste doesn't bother him?" "No, he seems to love it. I think he

realizes how it freshens his breath. They take the power sprayer and hit his mouth very quickly. He loves that the best, I believe." "That's amazing. I'm so glad you let me know about this." "If you think of it Ron give me a call and let me know how it works for your dogs." "I'll do that Amanda."

"Do you mind if I snag a beer from my car?" "Grab two Ron." "No, one is enough for me." "Ron, after the money saving tip I've given you, could I have a beer please?" "Ya, ya, God, I'm sorry. I'm just so excited I lost my manners." He comes back with two Coors Lights and pops them open. "Here you go Amanda, you going to college?" "Yes, State." "That's cool," as he sets at the front of my lounge. "How long have you known Dad?" I ask. "Oh, several years. We have a beer once in a while." He continues to pet Bandit while attempting not to peek at my little bikini suit. It isn't working. I caught him and gave a smile. "What a beautiful tan you have." "Yes, thank you, I work on it often." "That red suit goes so well with your tan." "Thank you Ron." "Ya know, most people call me Bwana." "Really?" "Yes, a very good friend of mine nicknamed me and it's stuck." "For what reason?" "You know, I'm not sure. He has little nicknames for everyone. We used to hunt and fish together and chase wild women many years ago. Of course, we were kids at that time, sixteen-years-old, long time ago."

"Those were the days. Now, he's very wealthy, I see him on TV everyday." "Really, who?" "Good ole Bargain Bob!" I gasped, what is the chance in a million years this guy would know my Uncle Bob? Oh my God. "Amanda, you OK? Have you seen a ghost?" "Bwana, my family and I were at Cadillac's last night. I talked with Bob for a long time. He is now my uncle." "Wow," Bwana turned and gasped, "You're not a cousin?" "No, I was immediately promoted." "Bob has good taste. You can be my niece as well." "OK, Uncle Bwana." He laughed and slapped his leg with his open hand. "I like you. You're all right," as he peers at my bikini again. "Ready for another beer Amanda?" "No, Bwana, I'm fine." He trucks to his car with Bandit right behind him. He pops open another Coors.

"Yup, Bob and I go way back." "First time I met him he wanted to kick my ass." "Why?" "I was hitting on one of his women. He was a little skinny guy, I was twice his size and he was going to whip me good. I was hitting on one of his girls but ya know what? They were all his girls. Everywhere I would go I would hear about Bob who drove a car called the 'Fugitive.' I was tired of that shit. He came to the roller rink to settle the score. I could skate, he couldn't, so I avoided him that afternoon. The look on his face, wow! He was pissed, he wanted blood, my blood! I got the hell out of there. Two weeks later I saw him in his car the 'Fugitive' setting in a female hot spot parking lot. I bit the bullet and pulled up beside him. We worked it all out and have been buddies thirty-plus years. Ya, I knew all three wives. His kids are like my kids. He's a good guy, unusual but good. He always worked his ass off. He got me a job at the factory where he worked. Course he left that job for his furniture business and got rich. Me, I work and live day-to-day like the rest of the world and love it. Got a great wife, my kids drive me crazy, what do you do? Be happy, do some drugs, drink a beer. I quit bitching years ago."

"Wow, that's awesome." "When I really get down I tell my wife I'm going down by the Nile and slug rats." I cracked up. "And what does that mean?" "It means it's time for a cocktail." I smile at him. He's a good guy. He and "O'La Lay" should hang together. "Do you know 'O'La Lay?'" He rolls his head and smiles, "Everyone knows 'O'La Lay', Bob brought him here in a canoe years ago." "Oh, my God. I love those stories. Do you know Chef Telly?" "Amanda, we're all family; of course you know one you know all of us, that is how our family works, girl!" "OK, I get it." "Bwana, I need a small beer." "Only one size honey," as he trucks off to his car. "Here you go," he hands me another beer.

Bwana is checking out my bikini very closely. I begin to feel my first beer. It's quite relaxing. I spread my legs just enough to make Bwana uncomfortable. It works. He's gulping his beer and attempting to be very coy. "Bwana, you can look, it's OK," as I spread them a bit wider. "Oh, God." He is embarrassed. "Don't be embarrassed, Bwana, your wife would be ashamed if she thought you were not looking at a pretty little lady with a hairy pussy, right?" "Oh God." He's at a loss for words. This is too much fun. "Bwana, this is what happens when you force me to drink too much." He sighs and rolls his eyes, "Amanda, I need more to drink. Will your Dad get home soon?" "Soon Bwana." "You save him a beer," as he goes for another. "Bwana, I'm going in to use the ladies room. I will return." "O'La Lay!" He smiles. I have a plan in mind. I go to my room and lay four pairs of panties on my bed and go back to the sun and slide to my lounge. "I got a small one for you, Amanda." "Thank you Bwana," as I put my knees in the air and open my legs wide, while giving him a smile.

"Do you ever go deer hunting?" "Yes, two times, both with Bob." "Really? Did you shoot a big one?" "No, never have shot a deer. Bob, he shoots two or three buck year after year. He always gets them, not sure why that is. He has photos in his office of every buck for thirty years, deer, rabbits, and muskrats as well. He's quite the outdoorsman. He taught me how to fish. Now, I'll out fish his ass any day, not in the old days. He would always kick my ass. Great memories Amanda. If you have half the memories I have of my past, you'll be blessed." He sure is giving my crotch his blessing. "Bwana, could I ask you a favor?" "Sure." "I'm going to visit my boyfriend tonight and I can't make up my mind which panties to wear. You appear to be a very good judge of sexy lingerie. I want to look my hottest tonight, could you help me decide? Would that be asking too much of you?" He looks around at the sky, the trees, and the moon. "I'm a busy guy. Got stuff to do, I like you. Yeah, I could help you out." "Perfect, Bwana, come with me." He grabs one more Coors and is going to bite the bullet, just for me, of course.

He follows me to my room. I point to the panties neatly lined up on my bed. "Which pair do you like . . . the yellow lacey ones, the white, pink, or the red thongs?" He's shaking his head as he stares at my red bikini again. "This is tough Amanda," as he chugs his Coors. "I think," he hesitates and looks at my bikini again. "Maybe I need to model them for you? Do you suppose that would help your decision, Mr. Bwana?" He agrees shaking his head with a semi-embarrassed smile.

I can't believe I'm embarrassing this big, macho guy. "Sit down." I take him by the arm to my chair. I hate to make so many trips changing. "Do you mind if I change right here?" His shorts have become a circus tent. He is attempting to keep his hands over his embarrassment and naughty cock. He wants to slap it and tell it to be good. He finally answers, "Ah ah, that would be fine." I stand at the end of my bed facing him, untie my string top and let it fall to the floor. He gasps. I tickle my nipples as I face him. "Bwana, you like hard nipples and little titties?" "Oh, God, yes." He chugs his final swallow of Coors and puts his can on the floor. I slowly pull my bikini down. "Bwana, close your eyes." "Oh yes, of course," he tightly closes them. I give my bikini bottoms a kick. They land in his lap. He opens his eyes, looks in his lap and back to my exposed hairy pussy. "Bwana, you opened your eyes! You're a very bad boy." I sigh. "You've seen my pussy. You might as well keep your eyes open." I pull the yellow pair over my hips. I walk slowly toward him and back. "What do you think?" "Aah, yah, those are great. Wow, ya." I face him and pull them off and kick them his way. My toss is a little short. His eyes glance to my jungle. I slide on the pink lacey pair. "Oh, yeah. I like those a lot." He smiles, looking at his empty beer can. I twist in a circle and wiggle my hips. He is getting very brave. He sniffs my bikini bathing suit. "Do you like them, Bwana?" "Oh God, yes, Amanda." He kisses them passionately. I love it when guys sniff my panties or in this case my bikini. I take two steps closer, pull my pink panties down and kick them in his lap. The bikini is gone immediately. He kisses the new arrival. I move back to the bed and pull the white ones over my hips. I love these. Lace around the waist and lots of lace around each leg, the fit is perfect. I walk directly in front of the Bwana. "How about these?" He drops the pink ones to his lap. I turn for him so my round ass is right at his nose. "They are so soft and silky, you can touch them if you like." Both his hands massage my ass. God, I love the feel of his strong hands rubbing all over my tail. I slowly rotate back and forth. "Amanda, these are winners. That is my vote." I turn and face him. He slides his hand between my legs. "Amanda, they are getting wet." "Oh, I'm so embarrassed!" I give him a wink. That cracks him up. "You are amazing girl." He continues massaging my wetness. I put my hands on my waist and slowly slide them off and hand them to him. Right to his mouth they go. His eyes riveted on my hairy bush in front of his face. I slide my hand over my pussy. "You like that, Bwana?" "Oh, God." "Do you like to suck pussy, Bwana?" "Yes!" "Be a good Bwana and lay down right here." I point to the floor. He quickly lies on his back. I turn and slowly lower my pussy to his mouth. His tongue immediately goes to work. "Oh yes, Bwana you do eat pussy so well!" I ride his face. I feel my juices leaking. I slide my ass to his mouth. I want his tongue inside me. His tongue is so very long, in and out, in and out. I ride his face. God, I wish I had a camera. I want videos of myself. I want to see what I look like – sitting on men's faces. Yes, with my savings, a video camera in my room, at my tree, in my living room. Wow, yes! Sammy could help me. "Oh . . . suck my ass, Bwana. You're such a good boy." I lift off his mouth. He sits up. "Wow, unbelievable . . . how embarrassing, Amanda, I got to take a piss."

I laugh, all that beer, as he walks down the hallway.

I have to be possessed. My body follows him. The door is partially open. I peek in. He's standing over the stool with a huge erection pointing up. Is that how guys pee? No wonder the toilet seat is sometimes wet. The walls and ceilings will be wet is my thought. He stands with a smile on his face, while shaking his head. It is gradually dropping. It may become easier to hit the large target. It drops a bit more. I can't believe my possessed body is watching. Here it comes, a heavy stream flowing to the pool of water below. It sounds like a jungle waterfall as it crashes to the lake below. Whoa! Why is this so exciting, watching this man take a piss? The stream is heavy coming from his huge cock. It has me so excited. I do not understand this. Why am I aroused? My pussy is dripping. My mouth is watering. The stream is slowing. Am I out of control? I open the door. He jumps back, startled. I drop to my knees and turn his cock to my mouth. He is still dribbling a bit. I don't care. It leaks on my face. I open my mouth. It's disgusting. I'm so excited. I lick the final dribbles from his cock. It doesn't taste like piss? I wonder why? I continue massaging his head with my mouth. It's growing so quickly, larger and longer. His hands are pulling on the back of my head while he is pounding my open mouth. His cock is rock hard. I know what is coming any second. "Oh, oh my God Amanda, oh my God girl!" he cries as cum fills my mouth. "Swallow it! Swallow it!" he yells. He gives it one last big push as I swallow every drop. Way too much fun!

The sun is still so warm. I go outside to enjoy and take it all in. My tan body soaks it up. I feel so good. Bwana decided he should hit the road. He'd talk to Dad another day. He has time to get to the car wash today. He thanked me for the dog wash tip. I thanked him so much for helping solve my panty dilemma. "Any time Amanda, any time at all. Always happy to help out!" he yells as he drove away.

Why that bathroom scene turned me on so much I have no idea! I'm sure however I will do it again. Imagine, a video for me to watch of some of these fun activities. Amanda, you are so smart sometimes! I have to come up with a plan on how to make my home movies happen. I'll work on that very soon.

I soak in as much sun as possible. It's getting late. "Come on Bandit, a few more tosses." He's happy and ready for dinner and a nap. Hmm . . . me too.

CHAPTER 48

A Talk with Dad

I take a shower and lay on my bed. I wonder if Bwana is getting his truck washed. What will he have to say about that? I feel there are only certain people who would possibly believe a story like that. Why is that? My Dad or Uncle Ken would laugh in my face. Of course, I would not tell them something so ridiculous. Someday, Amanda, you're going to tell the wrong person, you'll be the joke. Not really, I would simply admit I was trying to catch them!

I hear the front door open and close. No time to nap now. "Hi, Mom." I give her a hug. "Can I help you with your bags?" "Oh honey, yes, please." We drag in her bags. "Did you get some good stuff, Mom?" "Oh yes, it was a worthwhile trip." "Did you stop at the Dollar Store and get some fresh baked cookies?" "No, Amanda. I could have. Someone didn't mention it." That was enough knowing Mom would have done that for me. I hug her again. "I love you, Mom. What time do you leave us tonight?" "Around seven. Honey, could you help me put these bags in my room please. Pizza at six-thirty would be great. Dad and the boys will be along. It's four forty-five, I'm going to shower and rest for a bit." "OK Mom." She gives me a hug and we haul her wares to her room. Dad arrived soon after. "Hello, Amanda." "Did Bwana make it over?" "Yes, he stayed for a while, we had a nice visit, he said he would see you soon." "Sorry I missed him." "I think he was cool with it, Dad." "You took good care of him, right?" "Of course I did Dad." "He's a funny guy." The boys come through the door. "Pizza at six-thirty guys?" "All right," shouts Johnny. Josh acknowledges also. He's still holding a bit of a grudge it appeared. I went to Josh, put my arms around him. "Hey, I love you big brother." It was going to take awhile, I could feel that. Our six-thirty pizza arrived right on time. Mom is up and

ready for her new patient. She finishes pizza dinner and we would see her Wednesday. Off she went, the boys soon behind her.

Dad turned on the television and sits in his big chair. I join him. "Amanda, at last we have an opportunity to talk. What is it, honey?" "Oh, Dad, I don't know where to begin. There are so many things happening in my life I don't understand. Life is so puzzling." "Amanda, at your age that is to be expected. Of course I do hear tidbits and you may be moving a bit too fast." He shakes his head. "What are you saying, give me an example, Dad." He was puzzling me. "I guess we could start with my brew chugging buddy from several weeks ago, Amanda the show you put on for that old fart. He could have had a stroke." "Oh God, he told you?" "Yes, what you did to your brother last night!" "Oh my God, Dad, how would you know?" "Amanda, I'm not as dumb as I look! I do have a mirror. Your head disappeared Amanda! The look of ecstasy on your friend's face, what was that about?" Wow, how do I handle this one, no spin here with Dad. He knows me and how I am. "Dad, she is mine, only for now. I'm not ready to let her go off with someone else, not yet. I felt it was the best of the evils. I drew a line in the sand for them both. If either of them cross, they will be evicted from my life forever." "Amanda, you don't mean that." "Yes, Dad, I certainly do. Dad, keep in mind the chances of them crossing my line is very remote. I know them both very well." "Is that your control factor?" "Yes, Dad."

"Amanda, I'm concerned that your hormone imbalance, or whatever you have, will someday get you in a situation you may not be able to find a way out of. You are so young, so territorial. That really concerns me, honey." "Dad, it's me, it's who I am. I will not change. It's me. I'm comfortable with how I handle my life. As far as Josh, I will somehow make it up to him. Yes, I hurt his pride, Dad." "The picture is much larger." Dad sighed, I knew his concerns, they are mine as well. Dad did not need to know that. "Yes, your brew chugging buddy, I did put on a show he'll not soon forget. He got to see it all," I'm laughing. "Amanda, why would you do that, show him your body?" "Oh God Dad, if you only knew some of the things I've done! Dad, I love men looking, smiling, touching and fantasizing about what they want to do to me. It excites me." "That will not change?" "I don't want it to. I love every second of it. Is that wrong? You tell me, Dad!" "Wrong, I don't know. It's not normal." "Wait a minute Dad. It's right and normal for a man! I'll bet when you were my age if you could find women that loved looking at your body, you would do your best to show it whenever possible. Don't you lie to me Dad. Isn't that true?" He took a deep breath, "OK, yes, it's true. I would try to show occasionally. Not much interest I found very soon. That does not make it right, Amanda." "Dad, this is different. A man showing his private places intentionally would go to jail I suppose! A woman casually letting her skirt slide up her leg I doubt will see jail time." "Amanda, it's not proper." "Dad, neither of us will win this debate I can see that."

"Honey, there is something I need to share. You obviously have some sort of a hormone imbalance. As I shared with you earlier, at one time your Mom was the

most sexual, wild beautiful thing in this country. She was very controlling. Men lined up, she had it all. She was much like you. Amanda, she was concerned when you were born that it would pass to you. Honey, I don't believe she has any idea that remote possibility has come to pass. Please, Amanda, be smart. She must never know. I'm afraid she would quit her job and follow you daily. You would never leave her sight. She got into such a serious situation with her sexuality. A story I likely will never share with anyone, it was so traumatic. It changed her life, thank God. She would never have fallen for a bum like me." "Oh my God, Dad, you have to tell me!" "Honey, I can't. Please don't ask! My concern is you. How do we keep you under control my daughter?" "I can't imagine what I could possibly do to cause myself a traumatic problem."

"Honey, your mother didn't either. No one plans these things. You can't. When you live that life, shit will happen. Maybe not today or tomorrow, but Amanda, the dangers are everywhere."

I understood what he was sharing. Would it change my life? No, I would be very careful. "Dad, why do people get married, other than for the purpose of raising a family?" "Amanda, mostly for love and being dedicated to one person. That is the only person you want in your life and you live happily ever after." "Does it work?" "I suppose." "Are you and Mom . . . happily ever after?" "Yes, we do love one another." "Dad, your life seems so boring. Of course, you have your family. But Dad, all you two do is work, eat and sleep. During my little life, Cadillac's is the only time I've seen Mom really smile and hold your hand. If you're so damn happy, why don't I see that? You love I suppose, but is that enough?" A heavy sigh… "You make it enough, I guess." "Why? I can't imagine it Dad, living for years in a house with one person and a bunch of brats." I sigh, "Dad, my life will be so different than you and Mom's. Will there be love and dedication to one person? No way, not in my lifetime! I want many. I want to learn, I want to teach and share with the world." "That's a beautiful dream Amanda." "Yes Dad, we must dream it first. Ya know Dad, I'm going to make you and Mom a promise right now! I love you and Mom so much for bringing me into this world. For loving me and trying to understand me, I will make it up to you. I will find a way. I don't know how, Dad I will someday take care of you and Mom like you could never imagine." I walk over and wrap my arms around Dads neck. I look in his eyes, a tear running down my cheek. "That I promise you Dad. I love you so much!" "Oh, Amanda, what do I do with you? You are one amazing girl. I'm always there, never be afraid to tell me anything. I may not always agree. Two sides sometimes are better." "I will, Dad. I love talking to you. Thank you for being my father . . . OK Dad, time to lighten up a bit here. There are two pieces of pizza left, one for you and one for me." We said "O'La Lay" as we toasted our pizza together. We chatted a bit more and I said goodnight.

After pizza I retired to my room. That was a very intense conversation. I got busted with Marianne. Wow, I must be more careful. God, Mom could have caught me! What traumatic situation could have possibly happened to her? Learning more

of her amazing sexuality once upon a time, I'm understanding a bit more about myself and where my sexual thoughts and actions may have come from. Somehow I'm convinced there is so much more to my possessed sexuality.

CHAPTER 49

Beach Party Soon

I awake to a new day. In the bathroom I realize, oh crap, my period. Thank God, it slows me down for a couple of days. My sex life really isn't affected. I simply won't let anyone kiss me in that area for a couple of days. Oh, well.

I put on a red checked skirt with a white button up top and white knee-high socks, make up, and out to my bus, it's right on time. "Good morning Ray. My bus is looking good. Did you wax it just for me?" "Of course, Amanda." "How was your weekend, Mr. Ray?" "Just fine, thank you."

My boys have my seat. They are so excited to see me. It's so cute. "Amanda, we both missed you." "Thank God, Amanda, you're here. Your beach party is getting close." "I'm so ready," said Sam. "Me too," Roy added. "Yes, hopefully we will have sunshine guys." "We've each invited a friend, but have no commitment yet." "Lots of room guys!" "Great, Amanda," Roy slides his hand up my tan leg. Sam joins him. It's so nice to keep my boys happy. They keep my pussy in such good shape. It helps me to know I am alive and well. "Guys, don't get me all wet. It's my period today. Be careful." I'm not sure they knew what that meant, although they did slow a bit.

"Good morning Amanda." "Morning Mr. Jackson, did you enjoy your weekend?" "Well, it went downhill after Friday; hard to top that evening." "Yes, I hope it was fun and entertaining for you." "Did your cousin and her friend survive as well?" "Oh, yes, they're perfect."

At lunch, Ebony joined us. She's so sweet. I invited her to my beach party. She was elated and said she would certainly be joining us. We chatted a while. Back to class, no memorable events.

At home, Josh was still a bit standoffish, but slowly coming around. Dad fixed dinner. I gave everyone a big hug. After kitchen cleanup Josh half-hugged me. It's a start. In my room now, I decide to call Bri. "Hello, Bri?" "Oh, Amanda, it's so good to hear your voice. How was your weekend?" "Much too good, Ms. Bri." "Oh? Stories to tell Amanda?" "Oh, God, you don't want to hear. I did finally meet Bargain Bob and actually had a conversation. He has invited me to his house on Sunday." "Wow that's great. I hear he's quite the ladies man." "Could be, I see women around continuously. I don't see him chasing them around the bar as some of his friends love to do. I really want to get to know him. I want to learn, Bri. You ever feel that way?" "Yes, sometimes I do." "Are you on my bus this week?" "Not likely it seems." "I miss you. We'll get together soon?" "Yes Amanda, very soon. Your birthday beach party is coming quickly." "Yes, it is." We chit-chat and say our bye-byes.

My phone rings. Caller ID says Carl Kosto. Hmm . . . the name sounds familiar. "Hello?" "Is this Amanda?" "Yes." "What color are your panties?" "Oh my God, Jack, are you still alive?" He laughed. "You recognized my voice after three months?" "No, but no one else has ever asked that question." He laughed. "Amanda, I lost your number I had scribbled on a scrap. While cleaning my car interior, I came across it crumbled under my seat. I've wanted so badly to visit you again. Soon perhaps." "Jack, I certainly thought perhaps you didn't get your money's worth." "Oh no, I certainly did. I've driven your road several times to no avail. I have your number and will be calling soon." We did our goodbyes. Hmm . . . Carl Kosto. The name is very familiar, but Jack works fine. Finally, a call from Jack.

Next on the list to call is Sunny. "Hello, Sunny, Amanda here." "Oh, so good to hear from you, girlfriend," she continues, "I think of you much too often after Friday evening. Amanda, you're on my mind." "I miss you, Sunny! I fantasize about rubbing my hands and mouth over your beautiful ass." "Amanda, don't you get me going. I'm horny enough without your sex talk, quit," she giggled. "I just met you Sunny and I love you way too quickly." "I feel the same. Amanda, can I jump through your window sometime and have you all night? I'll go home early." We laugh. I knew it easily could happen. "Sunny, I want you soon." "OK . . . yes, girlfriend! I'm yours for the taking." We said our bye-byes, time for some sleep. My soft music playing, I drift away, my girls on my mind.

Off to school, typical quiet Tuesday, very uneventful. Life has become such a bore. Everyday bus antics are boring the hell out of me. I love my boys although it's getting rather old.

Mr. Jackson's class was entertaining, watching his eyes not leave the Amanda show. He was quite amusing. Mr. Jackson moved behind his desk and sat down. My entertainment became quite apparent as he slid his chair to the desk and continued his teachings. I love what I can do. I'll wear my panties again tomorrow.

"Bye, bye Ray, Ray. Are you getting excited about my beach party? I can't wait to see you in your little swimming suit," I say as I hop off my bus. No homework as usual. I never understood why many of my classmates carry piles of books home.

I seldom do. My grades are perfect. Are they disorganized and can't get it done in class or mostly slow? I'll think on that one.

"Come on, Bandit." I let him out to play. "Yes, I see your stick. Go get it." Around our beautiful lawn we go, tossing and chasing after it as he gives me his big smile. "Come on, back to your house." He runs into his pen.

The light is flashing on the phone. A message from Mrs. Sampson canceling my Thursday babysitting and requesting a week from Friday, the fourteenth of October, the day before my birthday. I guess that works. We will not leave for the beach until eleven o'clock. I will confirm with her. I quickly clean up the kitchen and tidy up a bit.

The phone rings. "Hello?" "Amanda, please." "Yes, this is she." "Amanda, your Uncle Bob." "Well, hello. What do I owe this pleasure?" He went on to tell me Sunday was not going to work after all. My heart sank. Business obligations, etc., Thursday evening he would like me to visit Cadillac's for the opening of their Cadillac Idol contest. Likely it would be a slow night, a great night to chat and get to know his niece. "Uncle Bob, I'm so excited." "My limo driver lives only five miles from your home. He will pick you up at six-thirty and return you." "Perfect Uncle Bob." Wow, how things work out for a reason, after Sampson's canceling a bit ago.

How great. What do I wear to Cadillac's? My head is buzzing! I need something classy, but sexy for my limo debut. I begin digging through my closet. Not to worry, there is lots of time to figure this out.

Dad has prepared a lovely dinner. Josh is warming up to me a bit. The ball game is away Friday night. Josh's team are underdogs, but he says they're ready. He's all fired up. John lets him know they will cheer them to a victory. "Will you be attending the game Amanda?" asks Dad. "Probably not, it's fifty miles away." The boys understand, I never miss a home game.

CHAPTER 50

Our Government

Another good night's sleep and off to school. "Morning, Ray." "Hello, Amanda." I brush my hip gently on his shoulder as I pass down the aisle to my boys. Some little fun talk and a tickle or two and the bus stops in front of our school.

"Good morning, Mr. Jackson. Is this a big day for our class?" "Of course it is Amanda. If you'll stop your antics I can stand and teach my class, girl!" "I'll try my best to do better, Mr. Jackson." "Amanda, PLEASE, no better! I'll have to leave the classroom," as he gave me a smile.

I spend lunchtime with my boys and Ebony. She's a regular at our lunch table. We are getting on so well. Hopefully I will soon get her in with the rest of our little group.

Later in class we are discussing federal and state government. Mr. Jackson is explaining who causes the financial pains our governments are dealing with and what causes these problems. He explains when layoffs, overtime, and fewer sales to consumers bring less money it is problematic because tax revenues decrease dramatically, while government spending remains the same. I raise my hand. "Yes, Amanda?" "I suppose when revenues are less, our politicians would realize they must cut back as well." "Yes, you would think so, wouldn't you? Somehow it doesn't happen, spending continues and the voters, the lobbyists, the persons who have gotten them elected believe they cannot operate with less. The hundreds of programs they fund have difficulty cutting back their resources." I raise my hand again. "Mr. Jackson, I watch the news regularly and understand many of our elected officials are doctors, lawyers, all highly educated, but most have never been in business themselves. How could we expect them to come to work and run the state

and federal economy, which essentially is a huge business?" "Exactly, you're right on target, Amanda. I think we covered this earlier in our class. It is so worth discussing. Let's hit on it again before we move on. Politicians know how to spend, but don't budget well. Again, they attempt to please their constituents, and of course, they want money for multitudes of reasons and quite often get it. Although, many times the money is not there so we borrow it. Deficits go higher and higher." "Mr. Jackson, let me ask you this. Let's say we elect you as our senator tomorrow. You're an intelligent, educated, smart guy. Now you are running a huge company with millions of dollars to spend. It's not your money at all. You didn't work for it. Do you spend it as if it was yours and you earned it, or do you purchase and fund programs, because it must be spent? You, of course, must help your supporters who elected you."

"A very valid point, Amanda. What happens is similar to winning the lottery. Say you win five hundred thousand dollars, do you spend it like you earned it or do you purchase many items you never would consider if you worked for every dollar and saved and saved? We all know what we would do when we win the lottery, we would go on a spending spree! It's the nature of the beast. That's precisely what we are dealing with." I raise my hand again. "Yes?" "How do we change? It seems very unlikely!" "True! Possibly a terrible Depression would change these ways is my guess. Because then, all would be lost. We start over again. The bloated economy is gone. We must feel pain before we change. OK class, think about that. It is true in all of life. Pain is what causes change." "Mr. Jackson, I, and the class I'm sure, are seeing the picture. I have a great idea that would save our government millions, maybe billions of dollars." "OK Amanda, what would that be?" A big sigh, "our federal government encompasses fifty states. Each state collects their own revenue mostly, and each pay their own bills and each suffer when the economy slows down. Why not channel each state's revenue to one location and let that location distribute all revenues back to each separate state by population, and eliminate forty-nine state governments, saving American taxpayers billions? An example, if a businessman has ten stores, and each store does their accounting separately, it costs five hundred dollars per store each month for this service. If all revenues go to a base and accounting is done together with all bills paid from that location it would save four thousand five hundred dollars a month. The bills are still paid and at a substantial savings, and this on a very small scale. Use this same process for our states. Does this make any sense?" "Yes, Amanda, it seems it does. Of course, now we have millions of unemployed people."

Someone else raises a hand. "Yes, Johnny." "Buy them all out. Give each two years salary, which could easily be done from the huge savings. They start a business. Our government receives more tax revenue. If they choose to blow it, I guess they wash dishes or work elsewhere." "Buyouts, that may be a very good solution," agrees Mr. Jackson. "Unemployment would increase dramatically for a period of time and yes, many would be flat broke in a short time, they will have spent their two year buyout bonus. So we solve one problem and have created

nother. You see, it is difficult to find any solution to solve a problem of this magnitude."

The bell rings. "Good discussion, class." I stroll up to Mr. Jackson and lean on my desk corner. "That was very good, Amanda. I believe the class was interested." He is looking at my short skirt. He slowly slides his hand over his crotch. Mr. Jackson smiles as he notices my stare. He slid his chair closer to his desk. God, he unzipped his slacks! I slowly slide my skirt up and touch my pussy as I look around the room. It's empty. I'm so disgusting. I know. I don't care. I want his cum, every drop, now! Am I crazy? Yes. I spread my legs wider as I glance around the room and toward the open door once more. "Take it out, Jack." His desk is positioned so no one would see me behind his desk on the floor if someone did unexpectedly walk through the doorway. He pulled it out. It's standing like a flagpole. My mouth was waiting. He slowly stroked his hard shaft. One more look around. I drop to my knees and crouch under his large desk. Oh, yes. My tongue slides slowly up the full length of his pole. "Oh, Amanda, you had me so hard yesterday," he whispers. "God, I love looking at your hairy pussy. You drive me wild." His cock head is in my mouth. I slide my tongue slowly down the full length of his shaft and lick his balls one at a time. I roll them around my mouth. He is stroking it while I massage his testicles with my tongue. He begins to groan. I know that groan. My face will soon be sprayed with his sperm. Oh God, gobs are flying, my hair, my forehead, I open my mouth. I feel it pounding my tonsils. My tongue is lapping up the final squirts. "Wow! I needed that Mr. Jackson," I look to his face from behind the desk. Amanda, you're amazing. Thank God there's only one of you. The world couldn't possibly handle two." I peek over his desk. It's clear. I run my finger over my face and slide as much into my mouth as I can recover. I feel gobs hanging from my hair and dripping from my forehead. "Amanda, let me wipe it out of your hair." "No Jack, leave it. I love cum in my hair."

I head for my bus. God, will Ray be waiting? He's trained, I believe. A few students in the hallway, I raise several eyes, they could not help but notice gobs of white stuff hanging on my wavy locks. I smile and keep walking.

CHAPTER 51

Ray Ray

"Oh, Ray Ray, I'm so sorry. I ran into a friend and had to help him out," as I boarded the bus. I haven't seen Ray smile in awhile, but I got his attention today as he stared at the cum hanging from my hair. "Amanda, would you help me out today?" he asks. Wow, I'm amazed, I'm still so horny. "Ray, whatever I can do!" He smiled. I know where my bus would be heading in a bit! I slid between my boys while raising some eyebrows as I walk down the aisle. "Amanda, what is in your hair?" inquired Sam. "I don't know Sam." He slides a gob out. "Ahh, Amanda, it's cum." "Really? How in the world did that get there?" "There's more!" Roy pointed out. "Isn't that the strangest thing, guys? I can't imagine!" Somehow the boys weren't terribly convinced. I'm not all that theatrical, I guess. I know I could have convinced Ty. The boys are kissing my pussy. I let them give it a very good work out. I want to be ready for Ray's massive cock. They soon are off the bus.

Once all the stops are through Ray pulls the bus to my big tree. I lean my hip on Ray's side. One hand is sliding up and down my thigh. I'm fantasizing about his huge weapon. God, how I wish I could get it up my ass. That's out of the question. That could never happen, it would tear me apart. If I wasn't a virgin, it could be handled. Oh well. He turns in his seat, unzips his pants and hauls out his monster. I'm on my knees. He is running his hands through my cum soaked hair. My mouth is rolling around its head while licking at his large wet hole. He is kissing my hair. God, he sucks the cum from my long waves. That excites him and me as well. He continues pulling my cum covered hair strands through his mouth. I look up. "Thank you, Ray. Please clean me up," I massage his huge balls, one at a time. They fill my mouth fully, they are so huge. I'm learning how much I love men with big

balls, a big cock is a positive as well. I want to slide the monster in my ass so badly. Amanda, forget it. Not possible, as I come back to reality. I slide the head back to my mouth and begin working it feverishly. The head is all I can fit inside my wet mouth. It's rock hard. Ray pounds the head a bit deeper. He's groaning and shouting, "Amanda, take it, honey, take it!" It shoots wave after wave. I'm vigorously slurping and swallowing, attempting to keep up. I'm on a mission. I vow I won't lose a drop. God, it tastes so good. I lick the last glob as I squeeze it out and slide it down my throat. Wow, why does squirting cum satisfy me? I guess some tramps are easily pleased. I stand up. "Oh, Amanda, thank you so much!" "Ray Ray, I like to take care of my drivers. I will need to do some shopping soon. Fifty dollars should be enough within the next couple of days. If I need a ride, I'll let you know. Bye-bye. I'll walk from here." I open my bus door and hop out. Wow, I needed that, two great cocks and two nice loads. I should be fine for a day or two. My hair is a little damp. The cum is mostly gone. My Ray takes such good care of me.

"Bandit, go find your stick." We play for a while. I go to my room and crash on my bed. It's been another fine day. Who should I send my government consolidation concept to? Seems like a great money saving solution. The problem is the politicians really don't care. They get their checks weekly regardless I suppose. To them, it really "ain't broken." When they someday have to take a pay cut or two, that's when we will begin to see some major changes. That would bring them to a realization of our broken government. As Mr. Jackson says, a bit of pain is needed for serious changes to occur.

We had a nice evening at home. Mom is back from her three day job. She was very tired. Dad and I helped with dinner and did dishes as she went to her room. She is at home for a day or two at least. Not sure of her schedule. Josh is becoming a bit more sociable daily, thank God. I love him so much. I don't like to have him upset.

I go to my room and lay my clothes for tomorrow night. I'll wear a stretchy white skirt, a silky pink blouse, pink high heels and big hoop earrings. Why don't I wear earrings more often? They look so great. I pierced my ears two years ago and somehow overlook doing the ear thing. I'll work on that. I could wear dark thigh highs. No, they cover my tan and my legs are so soft and perfect without. I drift off as I anxiously await limos, Cadillac's and Uncle Bob.

CHAPTER 52

Cadillac's and Uncle Bob

Thursday comes and goes. My evening is dominating my thoughts. I ignore my chance to debate with Mr. Jackson and the class. I'm becoming fonder and fonder of Ms. Ebony. She could be a keeper. She is like me in too many ways. She wants something in this life and will not settle for mediocrity. That is the case with Bri, Marianne and Sunny. I love all three so much but for other apparent reasons.

Roy and Sam are quite childish for teenagers. The few serious conversations we've had though do tell me that they will amount to something one day. "Bye-bye Ray. Thanks for cleaning me up yesterday. Did you brush the cum out of your teeth?" Silence, Oh God, I embarrassed him. "Well, thank you, Ray. You're my best bus driver." I skip down my drive. A quick play with Bandit and in the house I go.

"Hi Mom, you look much better today." "Yes, thank you Amanda, I'm all rested." I give her a hug. "I love you, Mom. You're my favorite mother." "Thanks a lot, Amanda. Are you excited about your big night?" "Oh, yes. I'm a bit nervous, although I won't let Uncle Bob know, you can bet on that. Mom, he intimidates so many people. I've noticed that when I've been around. Why do you suppose that is?" "Yes, he does. I'm really not certain. He is somewhat quiet, most of the time. It may be his appearance."

"He remains very mysterious to a large degree and normally tells exactly what he thinks." "Amanda, there is so much more to this guy. He listens more than he talks normally and will chop you off in the middle of a sentence if he doesn't agree. He will tell you exactly why he believes you're wrong, in his opinion, of course." "Mom, how do you know these things? I've never seen you talk to him." A sigh "Let's just say Bob and I go back many years. Some very difficult times I'm not

prepared to share. Amanda, please leave it alone. It's something I really don't want to discuss, OK Honey?" "Of course, Mom." I hug her and go to my room. Wow, what is that about? Is there a connection with her traumatic experience that Dad shared with me?

The limousine is pulling into our yard. It's huge! Long, black and shiny with Cadillac's in large gold letters on the side. Wow! And it's for me. How can this be happening? I pinch myself. Ouch, it's not a dream. I kiss Mom. She's happy to see me so excited. I walk out my door. The chauffer is standing beside the long vehicle with my door open. "Good evening, Amanda. I'm Alan." He was tall, at one time a very handsome guy now showing a bit of age and walks with a bit of a limp. I bend over and peek in, crystal glasses, liquor bottles, neon lights, music softly playing and it is immaculate. "Alan, can I sit with you? I don't feel comfortable in this huge car all by myself." "Of course," he answers. "I like company." He closes the door and opens the passenger door for me. I slide in. Away we go in my limo.

"Alan, how long have you been a chauffeur?" I politely ask. He smiles. "Couple of years, I guess. I'm a jack-of-all trades," he went on. "Bob and I go back thirty years or so." "Wow, that's a long time." "Yeah," he laughs, "it is. Bob is probably one of my best friends. We've had our ups and downs over the years. I think we've learned from each other." "Do you do things socially with him, Alan?" He laughs, "In the old days, yes. Cottages, Bob's of course, hunting, fishing, drinking, chasing women, and playing basketball." "Basketball?" I asked, "You look like a ball player. But Bob?" He laughed again. "Bob certainly is not an athlete although he loved basketball at one time. He's a scrappy bastard. He's half my size and would try to push me around on the court. One day he got so upset with me he thought he was going kick my butt. Of course, it wouldn't have worked quite that way. I'd have laid him out. When he's pissed he doesn't think about size advantage." He was laughing again. "The best times we have these days is probably deer hunting." "Bob is a hunter?" Bwana had mentioned that fact, no reason to let Alan know I had heard. "Oh, yes. He shoots deer yearly, sometimes three or four bucks. Many of us get skunked year after year. I sometimes don't understand myself how that happens. He sees things most hunters don't, I guess."

"He really doesn't miss much." I'm smiling. I understand more and more of his intimidating self. We pull to a parking space in front of Cadillac's. Alan whisks my door open and walks me to the door. "Hello, Amanda. Good to see you tonight." Stephanie is so personable. It always amazes me. "Bob is expecting you," she points down the bar towards him sitting with a group of people. I see a table set up with the same attractive blond sitting behind it I'd met a few days earlier, signing up singers for the contest. Pam, I believe, is her name.

I walk to the half-full bar. Bob spots me. "Amanda, you look so ravishing tonight." "O'La Lay" is sitting as well. I receive a big hug and happy smile. I'm introduced to Tim and Geri, they were the tall couple I'd seen several weeks before. There was also another jolly kind of balding guy with a mustache. He seemed to be a pleasant sort of guy dressed like a farmer. Not sure why. He seemed kind of out

of place for Cadillac's. His name was John. I also met a guy by the name of Jerry, who Bob called his dad. I doubt he was. He wasn't much older than Bob. Several of the group, including Bob, was not drinking alcohol. Bob appeared to be drinking Mountain Dew. Bob tells one of his friends sitting beside him, "get up, you're in Amanda's seat." He promptly jumps up, "Sorry Bob." "Everyone, this is my favorite niece, Amanda. She has become family, treat her accordingly." Geri said, "O'La Lay" and they did their thing. It was cute. Sitting in the midst of this, would it be as much as I hoped? We'll see. "Amanda," says "O'La Lay," "you left Marianne home, why's that?" "A long story you don't want to hear, I'm sure!" "Yes, I hate long stories," as he bends over with a laugh! Bob spoke up "I didn't invite Marianne for one reason: I want to spend some time with my new niece so you guys go sing, listen or have a cocktail. We got work to do." They laugh and began to slowly fade away. Geri asked as she was leaving, "Bob, should we save your stool at the front bar?" "Let someone borrow it, but I reserve my option on two stools." "OK Bob."

"Amanda, what would you like to drink?" "Mountain Dew would be fine." He waved and pointed to his glass. Boom – it was in front of me. "Amanda, this is Simone. She's my sweetheart." Simone was a very attractive girl with a deep, somewhat exotic appearance. There was a lot hidden in that girl. I felt it, as Bob spoke of her she beamed. I could feel the respect coming from her. "Simone manages my bar. Notice everything's perfect? That's my Sim." "Amanda, don't you call me Sim, only Bob gets away with that. I hate it. I think that's why he uses it!" She's so cute. I like her. "Amanda, I am amazed, as we talked last week about your Sam's day with Tyson, it has been the talk around here all week." "Poor Ty, he will never live that down." "Where does one come up with a story and scheme like that?" I laugh. "My friend, Linda, who works giving away little samples, complains continuously about the customers who stop in with their families and actually seem to have dinner. She gets very upset. I get a kick when she chats about her work. So why not play with it. Ty was my mark." "That is too funny Amanda," says Bob.

"How is the cookie business looking this week?" "Oh, Uncle Bob, after I sold out Saturday, I still haven't gotten back to the Dollar Store for a new supply." "Amanda, do you have friends who are young and aggressive like yourself?" "Yes, I do." "Do you suppose they are hungry like yourself and are capable of searching until they find success?" "Yes, I believe so." "Your cookie business intrigues me." "Really?" I ask. "Yes, would you entertain an idea that takes it a step or two further?" "Uncle Bob, I'd love to listen!" "OK," says Bob, "let's buy a semi truck full of goddamn Dollar Store chocolate chip cookies and get very serious. You could work seven-days a week, every night after school and Saturday and Sunday. What do you think?" My brain is clicking. He is watching my eyes, which show my shock and disappointment as I contemplate his plan. I come back to reality, he is laughing so hard, like, I got you! I guess he sort of had me although I don't really understand his joke quite yet. "I'm having fun with you, my niece. OK for real. What if we put together a formula for a true, tasty, beautiful cookie? Something people truly love and better yet, make it a health cookie. We add collagen to the recipe. Any health

conscious or aging person knows of collagen. There are many foods that contain that health ingredient. Are you ready? Here it comes girl! Chef Telly will create a recipe. We get your friends, perhaps your family on board, selling Health cookies. We can likely sell them for the same price and have a product people love and want more of! You personally will not make four twenty-five a dozen but Amanda, you and your family could be selling hundreds of dozens. You'll make much more on the volume plus your friends will make a great profit. We pay Cadillac's for producing the product and baking costs of course and a small profit to us. Your friends make good money. You make money from each dozen and you teach them the ropes." I am analyzing the concept. He talks much too fast.

"Uncle Bob, let's say that five dollars a dozen works. What do you think, a dollar to bake including ingredients, a dollar to Cadillac's, a dollar to me, and two dollars a dozen for my crew, we have a great product, not a Dollar Store cookie?" "Yes, that's my thought." I look at him with such admiration. "I think we can make this work, Uncle Bob." "I love how you think." "Wow, this could be huge! Hundreds of dozens!" "I'm not finished Amanda. What do you think of the name 'Collagen Health Cookies by Amanda?'" "Oh my God, I love it!" "And honey, on the box in small print 'feel young, stay healthy.'" "Yes!" "Glad you like it, here is the best part, you ready?" "Yes, Uncle Bob." "Beg me, come on, beg me." "Oh, please tell me Uncle Bob." He is laughing. He doesn't do that often. He is laughing out loud. "OK, here we go. We take them to schools, churches, non-profit organizations, which sell them for fundraisers. We're talking thousands of dozens of Health cookies." "Wow, Uncle Bob that is amazing! Can we do this?" "Yes, we can." "Oh Uncle Bob, I am so excited. Can we start tonight? Where is Chef Telly? We need him right now!" He is laughing. "Honey calm down. Telly will be along. We'll chat with him about collagen and what he can do with it. In fact Amanda, let me do that tomorrow. Now my niece, are you ready for the biggest kicker?" "Uncle Bob, there cannot be more!" "Oh Yes, Amanda. The Internet! We're focusing here the web, going nationwide with our Health cookies. It's new, it's original, and it's healthy. Now multiply that by fifty states. We're selling them to schools, churches, and nonprofits everywhere." "Oh, my Gosh, the potential is unlimited. Uncle Bob, that is the most amazing plan in the world! Wow!" "Amanda, 'O'La Lay' works for GM. He runs their computer system worldwide. We get him on board and put together a mind blowing website that is capable of grabbing the world with Amanda's Health Cookies." "Oh, Uncle Bob, chills are running up my legs and down my back. Can I say this, Uncle Bob?" "Of course." I whisper in his ear, "This may be better than sex!" Bob laughs out loud. "My niece, you are an amazing girl. Honey, please don't tell your friends. Let's plan a meeting with them. 'O'La Lay' and I will present the concept in detail soon!"

"Uncle Bob, next Saturday we'll all be together. Could you join us?" "Amanda, I'll make it happen. Where will you be?" "We will be at the beach on Lake Hagadorn, celebrating my birthday." "'O'La Lay' and I would not want to miss that." I give him a big hug. "Uncle Bob, you're the best! I love so much how you

think. This is an exciting business opportunity for you, Cadillac's, my friends, and me. This could easily be huge." "Amanda, that is true."

The Idol singers are now competing. "Such great talent," I tell Bob. "Sim, I'm ready, a Tanqueray and Tonic. Sim, Amanda and I will soon be business partners." "It sounds great Bob. I couldn't help overhearing the conversation!" "Uncle Bob, while I'm thinking of it, would you please come to my class at school and discuss the local business conditions?" Bob rolls his eyes, "Yes, they may not want to hear what I have to say, but of course, I'll be there." "Good, I'll discuss it with my teacher. He says you are a legend in the area." Bob chuckles. "Yeah, right." "Uncle Bob, can I tell you a story?" "Honey, of course. I do my best not to do all of the talking. It's your turn Amanda." "Uncle Bob, you talk when you have something to say. You don't talk just to talk as most seem to do." He laughs. "Amanda, still most don't listen. Most have no idea what I'm attempting to share. It's OK, I'm quite used to it. It's one of the many things that make me very strange. My girl, ya have me talking again. I must be drunk. Sim, get this gin out of here." She reaches for it. "Sim, you want to lose that hand?" He shouts. Sim was kidding, I guess. She had me fooled. She gives him her loving smile. She is so sweet. "Amanda, sorry for all the interruptions, your story, please." "Uncle Bob, this happened a short time ago. It changed my life, how I think and live." "Wow, honey that is intense. What?" I at last had his full attention. I sigh very deeply. "I have not told this to any of my family. I couldn't. I'm not certain I can even now. I thought I could a few minutes ago." "Honey, go on, please." Someone is tapping on Uncle Bob's shoulder. He didn't look, "I can't talk, go away!" He devastated the poor girl as she walks away. Bob is waving to Stephanie. She walks to him. "Yes, honey," she says. "I want no company. Let the other hostess know your job for now is to keep cousins, friends, and family away. Tell them I'm visiting with my daughter I haven't seen in years. I want no visitors, got it?" "Yes, Bob, I'll take care of it." Obviously, as I knew, this is not a good place for serious conversation. "Amanda, I am sorry. We have it handled."

"Uncle Bob, have you ever had an unusual situation occur in your life that moved you so dramatically that you know your life had changed forever? You didn't wonder, you knew!" Uncle Bob smiled and shook his head. "Yes Amanda, several times over my years." "Do those things happen to most people?" "No, Amanda, sadly they do not. Most folks are so tied up in their little tunnel vision lives. They miss the important learning experiences one really needs to learn and grow. They do not begin to understand how huge the world is. They are caught up in their own little world. Look around here at Cadillac's, great, dedicated, loving, hard working people." "That is so beautiful. Where does that take them in life?" "Most will struggle to survive. It will never cross their minds, how do I climb out of this? They become complacent and remain with that lifestyle forever. Most have no vision, it's very sad. Look around at all the beautiful folks, most will remain in a lifetime rut. There I go again, dominating the conversation. Amanda, what occurred that you would ask such a question?"

"This would be silly in most people's lives, Uncle Bob. I'm going to attempt to share with you something that happened thirteen days ago. I am in my room

elaxing on my bed. It was mid afternoon. Something slammed into my bedroom window. I got up and looked out. On the ground was a beautiful red male cardinal. He was seriously injured. On a branch nearby was his mate. She was very concerned as she watched his every move. His head was moving, as he lay in the grass. Him and his mate are looking at one another. His eyes were weakly blinking. She flies to his side. It was unbelievable Uncle Bob, he was dying. She knows he is leaving her soon. They nestled together. She is consoling him. I could see he was telling her not to be sad, be strong as they reminisced about the good life they'd had together. She lays her head on his as his eyes close for the last time." I look at my Uncle Bob. A tear is running down his cheek. Now, my tears are falling as well. He puts his arms around my neck as I hug him. "Something about the whole thing brought me to a realization Uncle Bob, and changed my life. Thirteen days ago I vowed to love my family, my friends and let them know how much I care. I never let a day go by without telling Mom, Dad, and my brothers how much I care. Any of them could be gone tomorrow." Another tear falls from his eye. Simone is standing behind him. "Bob, are you OK?" She is asking while rubbing her hands on his shoulders. Stephanie walks up, "Bob, what is wrong?" "Girls," Bob shakes his head, "I'm fine. Thank you girls. Thank you for all that you do here at work and how much you care. I love you both." They're stunned, this is not Bargain Bob. They hug him and he looks back at me. "Amanda that is a life-changing story. We forget to appreciate and love what we have, I understand. It is taken for granted much too often. Yes, I love my people. Do I tell them? No, I don't. I must try harder. Stephanie, Sim, insist Amanda tell you her bird story." They look puzzled as they agree to hear the story soon. "Go on girls, back to your jobs, I'm fine. Amanda it's awesome to witness such a thing and be capable of applying it to your own life. Most do not have that capability. It is simply learning from what we see daily and growing from those experiences and applying them to our lives. Most would have looked out the window and said, 'Oh a bird hit my window, too bad' and continue about their daily routine. Thank you for sharing your story Amanda, hopefully you will share it with your family soon."

"How is your Mom these days?" "Very good, thank you. Why do you ask?" A big sigh; "It's a long story Amanda. It's like your bird story. I could not tell it without breaking down." Big tears are rolling down his face again. "Uncle Bob, I'm so sorry." I'm grabbing bar napkins from the bar. I'm in shock. There are so many questions I realize will not be answered. Stephanie is back at his side. "Honey, what can I do?" she is asking. "Stephanie, it's a very unusual night, I'm fine," as he wipes the tears from his eyes. Uncle Bob hugs me again. "Amanda, thank you so much for being my niece, we have so much in common. For now, let's focus on Cookies by Amanda. Telly will put an earth-shattering recipe together. We'll be at our birthday beach bash to talk with your friends. I'll call you before the fifteenth to confirm."

He waves to Alan for the limo. It is nine forty-five, time to be home on a school night. "Uncle Bob, thank you so much for listening to me. I certainly had no

intention of creating tears." "Honey, it's all good. Memories we both will someday look back on, this night sitting here, the night I bonded with my niece. I realize my life has taken a new turn. Isn't it amazing how these things happen? Look out world Amanda is coming out!" Alan is at my side. He walks me to the car, "Front or rear?" he inquires. "Front is fine Alan, thank you." The limo glides through the darkness. Alan asks, "Amanda are you OK?" "Yes, I think so." "It appears you and Bob had quite an intense conversation." A sigh, "Yes, we did Alan. Do you know my mother?" "Yes, I do." "How?" Alan hesitates, "It's something we don't talk about these days." "What? How do you know my Mom?" Alan is shaking his head. "Amanda, I do not know the whole story." "What story? I'm not getting out of this car until you talk!"

He sighs and gently shakes his head. "Many years ago Bob had a terrible accident. He was hospitalized for a long period of time and then sent home to recover. Your Mom was sent from the hospital to help him rehabilitate. She spent the majority of her days and nights with him for a three-month period, they became very close. That was apparent as I visited Bob regularly. I'm not sure what transpired, no one talks. It ended with much heartache." "Alan, thank you so much I will never tell a soul." "I appreciate that Amanda. Again, it is an issue that is never discussed, OK?" "Yes! OK, let me out and you can have your car back." He opened my door. I gave him a hug. He is such a kind and gentle man.

Gosh, Mom is still up! "Mom, I love you, what a night!" "Did you enjoy yourself Amanda?" "Oh yes Mom, I did." I'm caught. I'm not sure how much I should talk about Bob. Some things had to be told. "Mom, Bob and I are going to be partners in my cookie business." I told her our vision, Health cookies and all. She seemed to be happy; "That sounds like a very good plan, Amanda."

In my bed with no music my mind is going over the events of the day and evening. Concern is not the word, it's much past that. What transpired many years ago? I refuse to let myself dwell on the situation, but it nags at me. Was this the past of Mom's traumatic situation Dad refused to share? He said that was before they were married, perhaps he was off a couple of years. One would have to believe of some kind of connection. Amanda, quit, now! It makes no difference! It does not affect your life, leave it alone. Let's concentrate on today's business and Health Cookies by Amanda, it has a very nice ring to my ears. My eyes are getting heavy I quietly drift away.

Friday came and disappeared quickly. I met with Mr. Jackson, flirted a bit and confirmed Bargain Bob's classroom visit. We discussed and decided early November would be perfect, just before the presidential election. I am really looking forward to his insight on the race.

CHAPTER 53

$\mathcal{S}unny$

Ray handed me his envelope as I leave my bus. That was good, like I need the money, but soon I will have video cameras everywhere. I continually dream of watching my friends and me having good fun, to see myself in action, whoa. Later that evening while having dinner, Dad gets a very devilish look on his face. "Amanda, I saw my buddy Bwana Ron today and guess what?" "Oh," I smile as I hang my head. "Amanda what did you do?" Mom asked. I shrugged my shoulders very innocently. "Anita, she told Ron to take his three dogs and run them through the car wash while in the back of his pickup." "Of course Ron knew better?" smiles Mom. "You would think so. He now feels like such a jerk. He not only went to one after getting turned down, he went to two more asking them for extra soap for his dogs and about getting their teeth brushed. Amanda, you must stop picking on our friends." "Dad it is just good fun. Who would believe Ron, Tyson, and your brew drinking buddy would believe my nonsense? I'm teaching them Dad." "You see, Tyson doesn't eat at Sam's anymore and I'll bet Bwana will wash his dogs himself." Mom and Dad are shaking their heads. "Amanda what do we do with you?"

Dad moves outside to do some trimming on the lawn while Mom and I clean up the kitchen. "Mom, are you happy?" "Of course Amanda; my life is perfect!" "In what way, Mom?" "Honey in many ways. My family whom I love dearly, my home, which we are so blessed to own, my work, I love my work. And, honey, there really isn't too much more." "Mom, I sometimes worry that you're really not totally satisfied with your life." "Amanda I certainly am. I once had my days in the world and the limelight. I wouldn't go back for any reason. I am completely content. My life, again, is perfect." I leave it at that and give Mom a hug and I'm out the door.

I play with Bandit for a while and pull some weeds with Dad. How I hate pulling weeds, it's nasty and dirty. My nails turn to trash. Oh well, thank God I don't volunteer often.

The sun is below the horizon. Low clouds far away offer a spectacular color show. I leave a note congratulating the boys on a great win. I hope they win. I have confidence. I hug Mom and Dad and think of bird day and how I would miss them if they were gone. They both again assure me they were not going anywhere and did ask of bird day. I told them again we would talk when the time was right, they understood.

Off to my room with my music, a pencil and pad of paper in my lap. I'm thinking about Cookies by Amanda. I jot down a church list, a school list, charity organizations, and a large business list. Over the weekend I will be at Josh and Johnny's computer and print it all out. I will work on our presentation to my group of friends. I will fire them up, I will have them visualizing great money prospects and learning of the business world to lead them in the proper direction. I can do this. I make more notes to myself. This must be done properly starting with a healthy cookie that is delicious. Should I help Telly with a recipe? We'll see.

Cookies! Oh my God! I must call George! I got so caught up with Healthy cookies I forgot to buy inventory! I'll tell him my oven broke down with no service until next week! "Hello George, it's the cookie girl." "Amanda, thank you for calling! God, I need cookies!" "Oh George my oven is broken down." "Oh, I see. I need ten-dozen more." "I have two others that would like ten-dozen each as well." "Our customers love them." "I'm so happy George. It looks like it will be next week before I can deliver." "I suppose the cookies could wait. If we pay you, could we come visit and we will take our delivery when your oven is repaired?"

Hmm . . . This is a tough one. I haven't been fucked in a while, a cock in my ass does sound very good. "The same one hundred dollar bonus from each as before George?" "Of course, honey." "Let me call you tomorrow George." "Amanda, I need a visit badly. You promise you'll call?" "Yes, I will, there's no guarantee on a meeting." "Oh Amanda please, I need you. I want to touch and taste you so badly. I'll give you a hundred dollar bonus." "Hmm . . . that sounds fair. I'll call you tomorrow George. Be near your phone early in the afternoon. Bye-bye." How does a girl turn that party down?

Four hundred dollars goes a long way toward my video equipment. I wonder what the cost will be for all that equipment. Let's see, where will I need cameras? In my room, the living room, the bathroom and my tree area, eleven cameras total. Audio that I can turn on or off and a screen for play back, and motion sensors. Sammy will give me prices Friday. Four hundred dollars would certainly help.

I must get a good night's sleep. I'll make the decision in the morning. I've got him now. If I choose to wait I can always get four hundred, the price will never drop. I was very satisfied with three hundred, but four hundred it will be from this point forward. They do drive a hard bargain.

I awake early. Time to get myself up and around. The clouds on yesterday's horizon are hanging over our heads today, no rain as of now. "Good morning Mom

and Dad." "Good morning Amanda, how was your night?" "Just perfect! The boys are where?" "Off to Ferris's very early." "Tell me the game was won." "Your note was perfect, the boys could not figure how you knew." "The score Dad?" Twenty-eight to twenty-seven, the opposition missed the final field goal. Guess who knocked the ball from the air?" "Josh! Bless his soul!" I shout. "He must be elated." "Yes, he was still on a high this morning. Too funny, he really could not figure how you knew." "You didn't tell, right Mom?" "Of course not, I do keep secrets." Yes Mom, I've heard that.

"Bandit, it's time for breakfast." I could read his mind: 'Thanks Amanda, although steak and eggs is what I had in mind, but this crappy dog food is fine.'

Back in the boy's room, the computer at my command. It's spitting out all sorts of pertinent information with lists of the churches, hundreds of them, and schools, and dozens of various charity organizations. All prime candidates to raise money with our Health cookies. This is perfect! All these organizations looking to raise money and this health issue has become so huge, this business can't miss. All my friends will be making money. It has to be me who motivates. I can do that. I'm a tramp, a very motivated tramp. That's a good thing, isn't it? "Yes." All my little family is so much like me in many ways, not just sexually. I believe they all will not settle for mediocrity in life. I'm so looking forward to my birthday beach bash. It will be way too much fun. What I will unveil financially will totally shock them all. I take a deep breath, I need to calm down. First, I must get my proposal together.

I will call uncle Bob early in the week to update him on my progress and let him know two o'clock would be perfect for the unveiling of our proposal. I'm sure I will let the cat out of the bag to some of our potential employees or partners, only because I'm so excited! I look over my computer printouts. There are hundreds of potential large customers. How do we attack this business, knocking on doors one at a time to begin, I suppose? I laugh to myself. Imagine the potential for Bri, Sunny, and Marianne raising money for cheer school, oh my God. If any one of them came knocking at my door dressed as I did when I made my calls. I'm picturing Sunny standing in my doorway. "Hi, I'm raising money for cheer camp," as she shakes her little ass and presses her large breasts against her hot tight top. "Oh God, ten-dozen please. Come on in while I search for money…" Yeah, "O La Lay" to that as I give myself a smile.

God I wish she were at my door right this second. I have five hundred, maybe a thousand dollars. I'm not sure how much. It would all be hers if I could have her for a minute or five, OK, ten minutes. Yes, she can sell cookies I have no doubt. This could be way too much fun. While helping make my friends become wealthy, we will control the world together. I can't wait. I've got myself so fucking horny. I'm going to call George. I know he's so disappointed my oven is on the blink. I'll deliver his cookies soon.

"Hello George, Amanda." "Oh honey thank you for calling as you promised." "George, I appreciate your little bonus, you know my cookies are so great. Could you possibly convince your friends to each kick in that little bonus you offered as

well? I will add extra chocolate chips. I know they will be so happy with my cookies. George, nine-thirty tonight in our spot would be perfect, bring some beer. I love long neck bottles. Coors Light would be so much fun for us all. Be sure and tell them how great my cookies are with regular chocolate chips. I'm so excited! Should I call and confirm, George?" Wow, I'm so out of breath after that long spiel! "No Amanda I'll work it out with the guys. See you at nine-thirty with Coors long necks." "Bye-bye George."

Oh my God, as I hang up the phone, I am struck with a fantastic idea! Let me call Sunny. "Hi Sunny!" "Oh hi Amanda, how are you girl?" "Just perfect. Big plans today Sunny?" "No boring." "Come spend the night with me." "Oh gosh that would be great. Let me find my father and get permission. He may want to meet your parents." "Of course, that's great. I would like to meet him as well. I can make a very good impression!" "I'll bet you can." She laughs. "I'll call you right back."

"Hello." "Oh hi Amanda! I'm so excited!" "Dad or Mom will drop me off at three o'clock, is that too early?" "That's perfect. The sky is clearing a bit, bring your sun stuff and something really hot for tonight. I have a huge surprise for you." "What Amanda?" "Surprise, surprise." I gave her directions and hung up. Yes!

This could be so much fun. I will tell Sunny, the first friend to know of our new venture. Of course I will let her know our new venture should not be as risqué as my little rendezvous tonight, but that would be their decision. I certainly would not encourage my girls to have that much fun. Gosh, tonight I have her little ass in my bed for the whole night. Life is so perfect!

My little cookie party at nine-thirty, wow! When I show up with Sunny, oh my God, George and his friends will cum in their pants when they see my hot little bitch. Quit it Amanda! My panties are feeling damp. Tough it out! Save yourself! I'll let her know we'll be having a beer or two. Gosh I hope she likes Coors. I'll give her a hundred dollars of my cookie money. Amanda, you are so good. Generous too!

I'm fantasizing, seeing a cock running in and out of her shaved pussy, her legs spread, begging for more. Amanda quit it, you're going to cum in your panties. Now, what shall I wear to my party? Shorts, a little skirt? I could sneak out my window, in just my panties and a little top, perhaps? A little early, if it was totally dark I may. I'll save that for another day. This little yellow nylon little girl's skirt is perfect with a white stretchy top, white knee socks, white lacey panties and big yellow earrings.

The clouds are fading and the sun is peeking through. Once I see a bit of blue sky, my experience is soon there will be lots of blue. I think the blue grows.

I find the perfect sun area on our beautiful green manicured lawn. "Yes, come on Bandit, you drag that chaise lounge and I'll get this one." Guess he didn't hear me. Fine, I'll get it myself. Throw your own stick you lazy deaf dog. Yes, the sun has arrived! The mugginess is fading. "OK Bandit," I give up and give it a toss, "go get your stick, you lazy dog."

In the house I search for the perfect suit. Yes, yellow is my color today. God this

bikini top is so tight. My breasts seem to be growing daily. They will be like Mom's very soon. Yes, my bush curls from under my yellow bikini bottoms. Just as I like, as I twist and turn in the mirror. I'm looking good and this is my night! I have towels, lotion, Mountain Dew and all lotioned up. The sun is not perfect, but comfortable. A car is pulling in the drive, yes, it's Sunny. I walk toward the car and quickly pull my bikini bottoms down to cover my exposed bush. Sunny and I give each other a hug. "Amanda, this is my mom." "Hello, Mrs. Harrison. Thank you so much for delivering my favorite friend. I promise to take very good care of her tonight." "Are your Mom and Dad home?" "No, they're not, shopping I believe." "Would you like me to have them call you when they arrive?" "Yes, Amanda that would be fine." She hands me her business card. "Sunny, call me if there are any problems. I'll pick you up in the morning late, if that is OK Amanda?" "Oh, yes, that will be fine." "Bye girls, have fun tonight." "Bye Mom!" "Bye Mrs. Harrison." She drives away, I put my arms around Sunny and give her a kiss on the mouth. She whispers, "I love you Amanda." I give her a smile, "Come Sunny, let's get you changed before our sun leaves us." She lays her bag on my bed. "Wow, such a nice big room, a queen size bed. Are you expecting company?" "In my dreams Sunny, and my dream has been granted!" My mind is racing, God, she will be undressing. I am sitting right here. She lays her suit out and pulls her top over her head and unhooks her thirty-four-C bra, out they bounce. "Sunny your breasts are so perfect and beautiful." She smiles and puts a hand under each and shakes them for my pleasure. "Sunny quit that, I'm saving you. I'll have you all night in my bed." I'm fighting to control my urges. I want her so badly. She slides off her shorts along with her panties and steps forward. "Amanda I want your mouth in my pussy now." "Oh Sunny, I have plans for you tonight that are going to blow your mind, trust me. I want you horny and I want to watch your passion, you must attempt to control it for now!" "Amanda, I want you so badly right now!" she says with the cutest smile. God I love this girl. "Trust me Sunny, save it! Let's go sun for now."

Our passion put aside, we're on our lounges. Bandit is running wild, Sunny has a new friend. "Do you have a boyfriend Sunny?" "No not really. There are several that may say otherwise, but no steady thing. I avoid that steady stuff." "You do know my brothers of course?" "Oh yes, not well. That Josh, he's the king, two great games. He's a good guy it seems." "Yes he is. I'm very proud." Keep his hands off my Sunny and we'll be just fine. "Can I tell you something sexually personal Amanda?" "Of course!" "Do you know how many times I have thought about you after seeing you come out of the theater with cum dripping down your face and your hair?" "Really?" "Yes! That was the most exciting thing I have ever experienced. You excited me so much." "Why?" I asked. "I'm not sure, but I fantasize about something like that happening to me." "Sunny, are you a virgin? That's a silly question I guess, my tongue was buried in your pussy." She laughed, "No, obviously I'm not. What you did to me last Friday was incredible. I have never cum like that in my life. I've read and heard of these things, but Amanda to experience that with you . . . I will always be your Sunny." "The guys you've been with, why

no climax?" "Only one guy and only four times, a kid from out of town visiting my neighbors. He would cum as soon as he stuck it in, pull up his pants and go home. I suppose I was just a fuck to him." "Of course, he meant zero to me as well. I want to be more active. I seem to intimidate the boys."

"Sunny, I understand that completely. Look at you, you are a bombshell. Fuck those little boys, go for the men. They don't cum in their pants." "Yes, I want cum dripping off my face," she whispers to me. "Amanda, one day after my little friend left, he tossed his condom in the grass." "I picked it up and put it in my mouth." "Oh my Gosh I was so excited as I licked his cum from inside the condom, I loved it. I want the real thing!" "Sunny I'm happy you are so passionate. I relate so well." "Tell me some stories Amanda." "Oh I will. Now, are you ready to hear my surprise?" "Yes of course, tell me!" "No, beg me!" "Quit it Amanda. I'll shake these titties in your face." "OK, OK, I'll tell you. Let's see, where do I start? I have a business, selling cookies. I have several customers who love my cookies and they enjoy me as well. Tonight, we are meeting some of my customers!" "Where?" she blurted. "Down the road I have a secluded place. We'll go out my window at nine twenty-five." "They are bringing us a beer or two and also will give us a little tip. You will receive one hundred dollars. You do nothing but show up."

"Of course, I will be fucking them and how I love that!" "Seriously Amanda? Are you kidding me or what?" "No Sunny I'm not. Of course you could just wait in my bed. I'll only be an hour or so and I'll have you the rest of my night." "Amanda, I wouldn't miss this. I dream of these things. But with you, it happens. How do you do this? I watched you suck your teacher off and I only fantasize about these things" "Sunny why fantasize, you can live them all. Make it happen. Live your fantasies!" "I'll learn Amanda, please bear with me." "Sunny, I will never leave you. You may have to share me, it's OK. I will always love all of you." "Remember the football game last week, when you stood behind me and rubbed your hand on my ass? I was never so excited in my life. God, what you do to me! I wanted you right there, right on the football field. It would have been so fun letting both teams watch!" "Sunny, I love how you think. We will have so much fun, we'll start tonight and you'll get a hundred dollar tip." "Geez Amanda, I've never had that much money."

"My girlfriend, I have a business plan. Bargain Bob and I are working on a plan that will make us rich." "Ya right, Amanda, Bargain Bob's the only rich one, how do you know him for God's sake?" "Sunny, that's a story in itself. You will meet him at my birthday beach party." "Are you serious? Bargain Bob? We'll actually see and talk to him?" I love the reaction to this guy, just because he's been on television for years and has done well, people seem to consider him a celebrity. Then again, I did stalk him and put this elaborate plan together and embarrass one of his employees. Sometimes I forget that. How the world works amazes me! "Sunny, yes, we have put together a plan. Our group, hopefully, will become very seriously involved. Do you have dreams of living the good life someday Sunny? Or are you satisfied with mediocrity?" "Amanda, if I get my hands on something workable, I'll work like a dog. I will live the good life. I do not want to depend on

a man for anything other than a good fuck and, girl, with you I don't need that." We laugh. "Sunny, let's keep them around for our fun and entertainment." "How about financial gain?" Sunny asks. "OK, let's vow right now to stick with only the guys with money in their pockets and see how much we can transfer to ours." Sunny is bouncing in her lounge. "Oh God, you worded that so perfectly. You're amazing Amanda!" "Let's make that happen." "Amanda, you must give me a clue on your plan. Your party is a week away. I won't sleep this week!" "OK." I briefed her on my cookie business as well as my side income from it. I let her know they are my cookie customers this evening, of course, not telling her I was making the big money. "Why would I deliver product later if my oven was broken?" She was laughing so hard. "You and your stories and your ability to sell Dollar Store cookies as your Amanda product…You amaze me." "Sunny, keep in mind, it's all in the sales pitch and of course pretty girls certainly go a long way in many households." I go on to share Bob's insight to where our health cookie business could feasibly go.

I have her interest. She's a very bright, motivated girl. She's so excited and has grasped the bigger picture. It's amazing how one can motivate. This is what our team will be about. No lazy bastards or bitches on our team. Sam and Roy pop into my brain, can those two be motivated? I really don't know. I'll know very soon! If not, Bob will have his team of motivated bitches. Look out world! Amanda's Health Cookies are about to strike! I can't wait until Saturday!

"Sunny, do you ever worry about getting pregnant?" "Of course," she says. "Don't we all? I'm on the pill, but it still concerns me." "Occasionally the pills do not work I've heard." "I want no children ever and, God, an abortion, the pain, the idea, the principal. I take my pills regularly." "That's good Sunny." "How about yourself Amanda?" "I have no worries and no pills." "How?" "I'm a virgin." "Oh my God, how can that be?" "Sunny, it's true." "I love cock in my ass and mouth, I'm not sure I'll ever let any male inside me and have to worry of pregnancy. I'm like you, no kids in my life!" "Wow, cock in your ass? Doesn't it hurt?" "The first few times yes, as long as you take it slow and he's not hung like a horse, it's perfect. I keep myself so clean always. It's amazing the situations that arise to receive a good fuck." "Wow, I want to try that. Do you cum?" "Oh yes, of course. I have no idea what you girls feel with it inside you. I try not to think about that and enjoy what I do." "Amanda, you are so smart. If I had a choice that is exactly what I would be doing." "Sunny, can I ask a personal question?" "Of course." "Why do you shave your pussy?" She laughs. "My Mom insisted several years ago. 'These days you must be proper and for cleanliness purposes' was her story." "So Sunny, would you let it grow for me?" "Amanda I would do anything for you." "I lean over and kiss her shoulder." "Sunny, I love the hair on my pussy so much. I can't wait to bury my face in your blond bush." "Amanda, I feel my blond hairs growing as we speak!" Thank you my girlfriend!"

"OK Bandit, give us your stick." He has been waiting very patiently taking in all this boring girl talk. He looks at me with a look that says: "it's about damn time you girls stop yakking," and then he charges off.

The sun is fading. It's time to go in and get cleaned up. I'm hoping I can convince Mom to have pizza night. I decide to go for it. I call and order it for seven-thirty. I'll tell Mom to put her pots and pans away. I'm treating tonight. Where are Mom and Dad? I don't remember where they were going. The boys will be home and starving as well. Better order two large ones with lots of meats and cheese. "OK, one more toss and you go back to your house, Mr. Bandit." No painters today. I believe they're getting lazy!

"Sunny, go ahead and take your shower. I'm going to pick up the kitchen quickly." I flip on Fox news and see our presidential candidates battling it out. The kitchen is all shiny again. Yes, Mom and Dad are pulling in with groceries and many bags. I rush out to help. "Mom, Dad, I lost you guys." "Yes, gone a bit longer than we planned. A big sale at Kohl's. Dad and I picked out some new rugs and curtains for the living room and got groceries." "Pizza tonight Mom, no cooking." "That sounds fabulous Amanda, thank you so much." In the car were countless bags of groceries. "Mom, are we having company, all these bags?" "No, I'll fill the freezer. You know how I dislike shopping." "Mom, Sunny is spending the night with me. Here is her mom's card, please give her a call and introduce yourself." "OK, where is Sunny?" "Showering." "I don't believe we know her." "She is new in my life Mom. You will love her. She is going to be a partner with Uncle Bob and me. Dad, you and Uncle Ken getting lazy on our paint job?" He smiles, "Maybe. Ken went with Rhonda to an art fair and I took the day off. So, yes, I am getting lazy I suppose." Sunny joins us. Wow, she is wearing a beautiful blouse and tight gray slacks. Her blouse is unbuttoned just enough to create some fantasy. I introduce her. Mom asks many questions. Sunny answers her so quickly. She's so bright and well spoken. I can see Dad is quite impressed. "I see you being part of the family, Sunny," he says. She beamed, that was so sweet of Dad. Wait till the boys get a look at my girl! "The boys are later than normal Dad." "Yes Amanda, they went with the Ferris's to pull the docks and close their northern cottage. I expect them quite soon." "I don't want them missing pizza time." "Honey, our microwave works just fine and no, you cannot eat their share!" "OK, fine Dad." We laugh.

"Come on Sunny, let's put down Mom's new rugs and pull down the old curtains." An hour later curtains are hung, rugs are down and pizza at the door. "Right on time. Mom, your choice of color is perfect. You've made our house shine." I give her a hug and Dad as well. "Good shopping! Dad, you should take Mom to the mall more often." He smiled with pride. Dad gave her a hug and a kiss. "Anita, you're amazing." Dad can be sweet occasionally. I'm sure bird day has added something!

The pizza is perfect and Fox new is still on the television. The news is just the same old stuff, Obama, McCain, talk, talk, talk. Soon the election and we can begin bashing the winner for all our problems I suppose. I suppose all those all-day news stations must talk about something!

We're off to our room as we listen to my music. "Good night Amanda, we're going to bed very soon as well." "Thank you for dinner Amanda, we'll see you girls in the morning!" "Good night Mom. Good night Dad. I love you both."

CHAPTER 54

Cookie Delivery

Music is playing softly in my room. We're ready to party. Oh God, I'm so excited. "Let's do this, I will tell my cookie customers you are my friend and want to watch. Do not let them touch you. You talk, tease, show off, and follow my lead. I want them to want you so badly they may pay a bit more. Any extra money we collect will be yours. Let's see just how crazy you can drive these three men without them touching your body." "Amanda, you sure this will work?" "No, I'm not sure. I've learned a few things about men. I would bet my life's savings they will be going berserk." "That's cool Amanda, as long as I get fucked tonight. I'm so horny. I want to taste cum right from the spout." "We'll see what we can do! Remember, follow my lead, you are there only to watch."

"I'm going to shower. You're all cleaned up in and out, right Sunny?" "Oh, yes, I catch on very quickly. You shower. I'm going to get dressed and add a touch of make up." Off to the bathroom, thirty minutes later on my way back to my room. "Hello Josh and John, a long day?" "Hey, Amanda. Yes, the Ferris's worked us long and hard." "I have someone I want you to meet." I open the bedroom door. Sunny was walking away from the mirror working on her makeup application. I look at her and choke. Oh my God, I was uncertain if I dare show her to the boys. She took my breath away! She was wearing the most body clinging and fitting turquoise, soft silky shorts I had ever seen. They fit her so absolutely perfect. Her ass, beautiful legs and midriff took my breath away. She wore a long sleeve white soft-brushed cotton turtle necked top. It fit so tight, her breasts were begging to be caressed. Her nipples poked through the light cotton material, protruding out at least a half an inch. She wore white knee socks and large turquoise earrings. Her long blond hair

shined. "Sunny, come meet my brothers."

She had applied her make-up and eye shadow that enhances her beautiful blue eyes. She stepped into the living room, the boys both chewing on pizza turn to her. God, it was hilarious. Josh immediately choked on his. John's mouth dropped open as pieces of pizza fell from it. Sunny smiled as she watched the boys attempt to regain their composure. In a low sexy voice Sunny asked, "How's the pizza guys?" They look at one another and now back at Sunny with an embarrassed smile. Josh broke their silence. "Sunny, Amanda has many beautiful girlfriends, my God, you top them all. You are stunning. You are beautiful, I'm sure you hear that constantly." "You know Josh, I don't. People perhaps think those things, but they seldom are spoken. So thank you, a lady likes to know she's appreciated. You should do that more often in your travels Josh." "Sunny that is very good advice, could you go back to Amanda's bedroom so that I can finish my pizza without looking like a total jerk," says Josh with a smile. We all laugh.

She turned and walked toward my room. No pizza in my mouth, thank God. I would have choked as well. The boys and I look at one another. I think I have a very nice ass, but looking at Sunny, my God she does know how to show it. I look at the boys, "Don't cum in your pants guys." John smiled, "I easily could Amanda. How did you score her?" I laugh. "It's a story I'll share with you someday. When I tell that one, I guarantee you will both cum in your pants. "Goodnight boys," I hug them both. "Love you, my best brothers," and off to my room.

I sat on my bed and watch her finish applying her mascara and eyeliner. "Sunny I could easily stay right here and forget our fun plan." "No Amanda, it will be great fun! I'm going to broaden my horizon on this night watching you." We laugh again. My little yellow skirt seems rather boring with my girl along. It will be so much fun making them beg. I'm certain they will.

It is nine-twenty p.m., already dark outside. It's funny how I really don't remember exactly what time darkness takes over. "Amanda you are so hot, that skirt, that top, you're long tan legs. Look at your beautiful eyes . . . OK, let's stay right here." "Cut that out, Ms. Sunny!"

Out the window we slide, across the side yard toward the road. "Bandit, be good OK? No bark." He was much too busy admiring Sunny's ass to speak let alone do a bark. He watches as we walk past without a sound.

We arrive at my big tree. The car windows are down. I hear our cookie customers laughing and talking. I walk to the car with Sunny at my side. "Hi ya George. How is my favorite cookie customer?" "Now that you've arrived Amanda, perfect and you've brought a friend! How nice Amanda." "Yes, she just loves my cookies she wanted to meet some of my customers. Hope you don't mind if Sunny hangs around for a while." "God no, this is Bert, and Max in the back seat." "Hi guys!" Both doors front and back swing open. "Coors Light, just as you ordered Amanda." All eyes deciding which of the scenery to be ogling first. Sunny slipped into the back seat, leaving the door open as Max handed her an open Coors. I'm getting ready to slide over Bert. He gently pulls me toward himself. "Amanda, please

sit on my lap." He and Max both are very handsome fellows much younger than George, late twenties or early thirties. I spread my legs a bit and slide onto Bert's lap facing him. He'd opened my Coors and handed it to me. This was a little uncomfortable, drinking my Coors while facing him. "Bert, I would like to sip on my Coors for a bit and chat with my George." "Oh, of course." I arrange myself between them.

"Sunny, how is your beer?" "It's terrific girl!" She and Max are laughing and chatting. George hands me an envelope. "Cookie money Amanda, give me a call when your oven is back in order. I'll drop by and pick up our cookies." I slide the envelope to the dash. A hand is caressing each of my legs, very slowly creeping upward and gently massaging my thigh. "Oh you boys, don't you dare get my little pussy hot, OK?" "Amanda," Bert whispers, "we're not like that." I feel four fingers, two on each side of my panties sliding ever so gently over my clit. I spread my legs a bit, my skirt is over my thighs. I slide down in the seat, each of my hands caressing their hardness through their slacks. I lift my hand and take a sip of Coors and slide it into the holder. "Guys, cocks out please." They quickly slide zippers down. Two erect cocks spring into the air. "Sunny are you behaving?" I inquire. "She sure is," Max replies. "What do I do with this girl?" "Max, she is an observer tonight, she is rather shy. Sunny put your head on my seat and pay attention to my two customers." Her head is beside mine. I feel her tongue caressing my ear, God how I love her. I have a cock in each hand, slowly stroking them up and down. Two hands passionately are massaging my wetness. "Amanda, you're so wet," whispers Bert. I lay my head back, Sunny's mouth is moving closer. I've wanted her kiss, her touch, her feel, the whole afternoon, finally, we let the boys watch our passion. Our mouths find one another. I roll my body to the side in my seat and wrap my arms around her neck. My ass is half in the air, four hands massaging my hot body. I love these hands on my ass and sliding up and down my crack to my clit. Bert is lifting my top as my mouth continues its passion on my girl's beautiful face. I lick and kiss her mouth, her cheeks, and her perfect nose. I pull away from my Sunny. I must take care of my customers, they certainly could be buying cookies elsewhere I suppose!

I slide onto Bert's lap. His long cock is sliding over my wet pussy through my panties. His mouth is passionately sucking my plump lips. I suck his tongue into my mouth. He rolls it over my teeth, my tongue, and back to my lips. His passion is so intense. His hand slides over my hot pussy once more. I reach my hands down and slide my panties to one side. With the other hand I slide his hardness to my back door. I slowly lower my hips. "Sunny, I want you to watch." Her head is center seat immediately. I want her to watch Bert bury it in my ass. I want her to watch me ride his hard cock. I look to her eyes as she takes a deep breath. "Max, if you promise to give Sunny a nice tip, I'm going to let you massage the most perfect ass in the world." She watches Bert's cock sliding inside me. "God, yes, whatever she needs. Sunny, can I massage your ass? I will tip you very well." "OK, Max, only because I like you." Max's hands finally get the opportunity to massage her beautiful roundness though her skimpy silky turquoise shorts. She slowly rotates

her ass back and forth for Max. She's so sexy. "Oh my God," Max is talking out loud. "Sunny, could I please kiss your beautiful ass? Please Sunny, a few kisses." "A few might be OK," she answers. Bert's shaft is half-way inside me. I very slowly work it down, Sunny staring at his hardness working its way deeper inside me. I lean over, my mouth again on hers. I feel her passion. Max must be gobbling, licking, sucking her turquoise shorts. He's moaning with pleasure. I'm pumping up and down on Bert's cock. He is wildly shrieking, "God, Oh My God, I'm cumming, I'm cumming!" My mouth is on Sunny's passionate face, licking, sucking her mouth all over. I feel the sudden jerks of his cock as it explodes and shoots his semen deep into my interior. I slam my ass down once more, the limpness will arrive very soon. Poor George, my favorite customer is taking it all in as he wildly strokes his penis. He doesn't seem to be doing any complaining. He knows how damn good my cookies are and I'll be delivering them very soon. Bert's cock has wilted inside me. I slide off his lap. I whisper to Sunny as I slide my mouth away. "Stay right here." Max is begging from the back seat, "Sunny could I please pull them down a bit? I want to taste you so badly." "No, you keep licking my shorts. Remember, I'm a spectator Max." I watch her wiggle her ass in his face. He continues to beg, "Please Sunny, a few licks on your bare ass." "I don't think so Max. I'm not like this. How big is that tip you referred to Maxi?" I'm watching, I want to suck George, but this is so amusing I can't take my eyes away. He pulls out a wad of bills and hands her a hundred-dollar bill. "Please let me taste you." "Make it two hundred Max and I'll let you fuck my ass once you get it all salivated up." He hands her another hundred-dollar bill. Good girl, as I watch him slide down her turquoise shorts and panties while she leans ever so seductively over the car seat. I can't pull my eyes away. I watch him bury his face in her ass. She is moaning with pleasure while pumping her ass all over his hot mouth. God, I need to get George off. I want so badly to see Max's cock slide into her ass. I whisper to her, "No cock until I do George, OK?" "Yes, yes!" She says as she pumps her ass and her pussy on his mouth.

George is so patient, although he has not missed a lick. He's appreciating all the action. His cock is rock hard. I know what that means as I slide it deep in my mouth. God he is groaning so quickly, up and down I go, bobbing my head wildly. His hands are on the back of my head pounding my mouth. I want to suck his balls, too late, it's shooting. He groans, "Oh God, yes, oh yes, yes!" My mouth is flowing over. I don't want to let a drop get away. No room to squeeze the last drop. My mouth is full of his hot juice.

I focus my attention to the back seat. Sunny has obeyed my orders, her head still on my seat back. Max is still relentlessly sucking and licking my Sunny. I shake my head back and forth. My lips move toward hers, she opens her mouth for my kiss. My lips now on hers, my mouth opens. George's load slides into her mouth. She is shocked as she receives his semen and lets it slide down her throat. Oh my God, the passionate kiss that followed, I will never outlive.

I look over the seat. She is allowing Max to rub his hardness over her ass. How I want to watch his cock slide inside my girl. My wish becomes reality, his cock

head opening her door. I know what it's like, it fucking hurts. I press my mouth back to hers and whisper, "Relax Sunny, relax." She nods. She grimaces with pain as the head opens her door. She sighs. I whisper, "Give it a minute. Max, take it easy," I command. He understands. He gently slides his cock head slowly around her rectum. He slowly presses forward. She feels the head slide into her ass. He applies more pressure, it's sliding very slowly. She's rocking back and gently riding his shaft. I press my mouth to hers. God, the passion, I'm so blessed to have found this woman. He is pounding her ass with his full cock. He moans, "Oh sweet Jesus, Sunny, I love your fucking ass! God I love your ass," as he squirts deep inside her. He pulls it out, "Sunny here cums the rest." He shoots the balance of his load wildly over her beautiful ass. Sunny is rubbing the slimly goo over herself. What a turn on for me. Where is my camera? "Guys, let's have a Coors. This has been too much fun!"

This has been very hard work. Selling cookies is not so easy some nights. God that Coors tastes damn good right now! I want so badly to do an "O'La Lay," but I would have to explain. I just drink my beer. "Sunny, how is my girl?" "OK Amanda. Watching was fun, thanks for allowing me to party with one of your customers." "You are so welcome. Bert, George, you are so quiet, cat got your tongues?" "Amanda you drained me. Wow, those are some great cookies." "Yes it's true George." "Are we out of beer or what?" Sunny asks. "Of course not." Bert hands one over the seat. "Is the party over guys?" I ask. "This is the most fun I've had in years. George, thank you so much for telling me of your cookie girl. Amanda, I want you so badly, it may not go back up after Sunny stealing all of my passion. Amanda, could I get a dozen free cookies next time?" I knew what he was insinuating. He'd paid two hundred dollars and is soon getting great cookies, but the bonus didn't quite materialize. "Yes Max, I'm yours. Let George know how to find you and I'll make a special delivery just for you." "Amanda you are special and Sunny, oh my God!" His head is wagging back and forth as we climb out. I grab my envelope off the dash and we say our goodnights. The two of us each grab a Coors and wonder away. I put my arm around my girl.

"Amanda, that was so much fun. Is cookie business like this always?" "It is what you make it Sunny. Our new business will be a bit more professional and organized." "I'm sure we executives will have our fringe benefits." Sunny is holding her two one hundred-dollar bills in the air. "My God, look at these beauties. The memories are not to be forgotten Amanda. Just leaning over the seat, having Max beg to touch my ass, how would you know he would beg and offer money to touch me? My silly boyfriends have touched me so many times. I enjoy it as much as they do and now, money?" She waves her tips in the air. "Sunny, stick with me. Those silly little boys are a waste of your time. When they do occasionally get it, they become cocky and tell all their buddies of their conquest. Most are good for only two or three strokes at best! The men are happy to help with our overhead." We have a big laugh together. "Shhhhh! We need to sneak past Bandit, my great guard dog." We sneak past his sleeping body and climb through my window.

CHAPTER 55

Sharing Sunny

Great, everything is as we left it. Music softly playing, lights off, my night-light dimly lighting the room. I slip off my skirt. Sunny pulls her top over her head. Her pink lacy bra, her cleavage, my passion rises. I stare at her beauty. I want to ravage her body now! I choose to enjoy watching the show. She pulls her turquoise shorts over her hips and down to her knees; they drop to her feet on the floor. She kicks them, they fall in my lap. She knows what she is doing to me. I put my mouth on the crotch of her shorts. The faint scent of Max's cum fills the air. One hand goes to my soaked panties as I flick my clit. My passion is rising! She unhooks her lacy bra, her tits bounce into the air. Oh my God, I'm cumming! No, not yet. Oh God, it's too late. I want to scream, Aaaaaa! Sunny knows what's happening. She moves quickly to me, pushes me backward on my bed, rips off my panties and buries her mouth in my bush. Oh God, oh God. I love this woman, this passion for her, how is it possible? She's driving me wild! She groans. I spread my legs wider, my hands on the back of her head, pumping my pussy. "Oh God, oh God, Oh Sunny," I'm cumming again and again. "Oh I love you, Oh Oh Oh!!" She looks at me with a passionate stare, "Oh, my Amanda." Oh God, I need my camera, I want to see this beautiful look over and over, the passion in her face, her eyes. I will never forget this night. I reach for her, she climbs my body, my mouth on hers. "Amanda, I love you." Her passion has no control. I roll her to her backside. Her huge tits, finally they are mine. My mouth attacks her nipples, she is moaning with pleasure. "Oh, Amanda, Oh my girl." "Oh Sunny, I love your breasts, God I love them. I need your pussy in my mouth now." I move quickly to her private area, her juices everywhere, my sheets soaked with her wetness. I press her legs toward her head.

I want her ass, I want to taste Max's cum. My tongue slides inside her back door, deeper in and out. I spread her legs wider, my tongue at its full penetration. I smell a faint odor of his cum. That bastard came so deep inside, my tongue is at a loss. I continue sucking and kissing as I move back to her pussy, her legs spread so widely. She's moaning. "Shhhh, Sunny, we don't need Mom or Dad visiting tonight." I continue lapping and kissing and sucking her pussy as it pounds my face. "Oh Amanda, it's yours, it's yours." I lap every drop. Oh I love her juicy pussy, her cum, God I love her. Our bodies wilt. "Oh, God, what a night." "I'm exhausted. I blame it on that damn Coors." I close my eyes and drift off to sleep, my face resting between her legs.

I awake, a pee call. I move my head, a puzzled moment, where am I? Oh yes, my Sunny. I kiss her pussy and a quick lick. Off to do my duties and slide back into bed, pull back the covers and arrange my Sunny. She hops out and walks out my door, a pee call I suppose. I fantasize, God, how I'd love to have my brothers catch her walking down the hallway and see her nude body. I could picture her breasts bouncing freely as she struts down the hallway.

I watch her in my dimly lit room, as she climbs back into bed, slides under the blankets and puts her arms around my body. We passionately kiss one another. Her skin is so soft. I want to lick her body from top to bottom. Our eyes close as we drift to Cookie land.

I awaken. It's morning, my arms clinging to my girl. I open my eyes to Sunny's smile. She is gazing directly into my eyes. "Good Morning Amanda. Thank you so much," she whispers. "Last night was amazing. Thank God for the Capri." I gently squeeze her body and kiss her lips. Time for another pee, quickly I hop up. I take a shower and return to my room.

Sunny is in my robe and says, "My turn." "Bath towels in the closet Sunny." "OK." I make my bed, get dressed and go to the kitchen. "Good morning boys, no work today?" "No, a day off, we'll mow our lawn today." "Where is Mom?" "She has a two-day shift." "Oh, and Dad?" "Uncle Ken and Dad are painting." "Great, let's get this house finished, right guys?"

Sunny walks into the kitchen. "Morning John and Josh," in a low sexy tone, she's aware Dad is not in the house. Her blond hair shining, lipstick glowing and the white shorts as provocative as last night's attire, not to mention her tight pink button type tennis shirt. I am so disgusting, how does this girl give you hot flashes looking at her body? The boys are immediately ready to cum in their shorts "again" after jerking off last night is a certainty after meeting my Sunny! The boys attempt to be cool as they eat their breakfast. "Sunny you look so beautiful this morning." "Thank you Amanda, I must look my best for the Sheils family!" "We do appreciate that," adds Josh. Sunny stands at the counter with her back facing us. Both boys' eyes locked on her body and ass as she pours cereal. She is wiggling her ass back and forth. I'm sure she must know she is driving the three of us into a sexual frenzy. She is wearing pink panties under her white shorts. The lacy pink is clearly visible. "Sunny, sit down before I attack your beautiful ass." "Amanda, you should not talk that way, you could destroy my image with your brothers!" "Sunny, they

know what a tramp I am, it's fine!" She turns toward us with her bowl in her hand and spreads her legs, it's the sexiest stance. "Sunny, have you had some model training?" asks John. "Thank you for noticing, yes, three years. Someday modeling will be my career." "Sunny, I didn't know that! You certainly will be the best girl." "Thanks Amanda. Come to modeling class with me someday." "Yes, I would enjoy that Sunny."

The boys continue their gaze while attempting not to be too obvious. "Don't you guys love her huge breasts?" I asked as both quickly look away. "No one talking?" "Amanda, you love to embarrass us." "John, it's a very simple question right?" "Yes, I do love her breasts." "Well, thank you John. I enjoy them as well," says Sunny with a sexy smile. "What do you enjoy the most Josh, her tits or her ass?" "Amanda!" "Josh, it's OK, we're all family! Sunny, turn and show Josh your ass." Before Josh could interrupt, she quickly turned and slowly waived it back and forth. "Josh, you must look!" He finally looked as Sunny was peeking over her shoulder while running her hand over her buttocks and slides her hand to her ass as she gently massages herself. John couldn't quiet himself. "Sunny, you are the most beautiful woman I've seen in my life." She turned and smiled. "Thank you, you haven't seen much yet!" "Sunny, Josh is very upset with me. A week ago we had a problem. Would you help me make it up?" "Amanda, your wish is my desire." "Are you OK Josh?" He rolls his eyes, "Yes, don't embarrass me!" "I wouldn't think of it big brother. Sunny, unbutton your blouse please." Her hands moved to her top button, slowly one at a time until her pink lacy bra was fully exposed. "Isn't she cute guys?" Both together, "Oh God, yes!" "Tits or ass guys, take a vote?" "Ass," blurts John. "Come on Josh vote," says Sunny. "God, I love one as much as the other," he finally admitted. "You guys want to make a deal I ask?" "Amanda, what is the deal?" asks John. "Show Sunny your cocks and she will show you her ass." John immediately stands up, unzips his pants, he was not going to miss this opportunity. He pulls it out, it was erect. "John that is nice, please play with it just for me," says Sunny in a seductive voice. He obeys and begins slowly stroking it. Josh is getting brave and stands up, unzips his shorts and hauls it out. Sunny is all smiles, "You nasty boys." She turns, puts her back to us and leans over the counter, rolls her ass back and forth and slides down her shorts and lets them slip to the floor. Her pink lacy panties cover her perfect ass. "Johnny, come help me with my panties please." She steps back and rotates her ass back and forth. John steps to her, two fingers on each side of her lacy lingerie and slides them down over her hips and lets them drop to the floor. Sunny slides her fingers after wetting them over her ass hole. She slides them in her pussy while caressing her ass hole with the wetness from her pussy. She reaches behind for John's cock and gently strokes it. She is sliding it up and down her crack top to bottom. The pleasure on his face, where is my video equipment? His look is priceless!

"Oh, John, I want your cock in my ass." She guides it to her perfect ass. I see the juices secreting from his hardness, his virginity is about to disappear. He is pressing, she is moaning. I know the pain she is experiencing. The head slips in,

Sunny groans. I feel her pain, it will soon subside. He gently presses deeper inside her. She is rocking back on his cock, deeper it slides. He slowly slides his rock hard cock in and out. Four strokes, now five, "Oh, oh, oh, Sunny, I love your ass, Oh God, you've got my cum." She is rocking backward and moaning passionately. "Oh Sunny," as it wilts so quickly. "Josh get up there." I didn't have to say it twice, thank God, as I subdue him from ramming his erect cock inside my girl. "Are we going to be friends again?" I ask. "Yes, Amanda, Yes." "OK brother; Sunny, tell him what you want." "Josh, fuck my ass, now! I want your cock in my hot ass!" Her door wide open; Josh rams it deep inside her. She is pumping back, "Fuck me Josh, fuck me." "Oh God, I am cumming, I am cumming." This is so exciting! His breaths are very deep, his hot wet juices are dribbling down Sunny's buttocks. Yes, I think Josh and I can be friends once more.

A car is pulling in and parking in our drive, "Oh God, Sunny it's your Mom, she's early." Sunny pulls her lacy panties over her fucked ass, pulls up her shorts quickly and buttons her blouse. "That was great, guys." She hurries to my room and grabs her bag. I give her my hundred-dollar bill and passionately kiss her lips. "Amanda, I love you too much." "Sunny, thanks for taking my brother's virginity. You were so perfect for them this morning." "Amanda, taking it in the ass is great fun. A bit more time, I could have cum for your brothers." "Oh Sunny, I want to lick your ass so badly." "Amanda, come out to my car and Mom can watch. I'll lean over the hood and you can suck and lick me." She's so cute, I should take her joke one step further and lay her ass over the hood and watch Mom's eyes pop! But no, I am trying to be so good. I'll leave that one alone. She says her goodbyes to my brothers and hustles off to her waiting car.

Back to the kitchen, Josh is shaking his head. "Amanda, wow, how do you make these things happen? Why do these beautiful girls love you so much? You are amazing!" He and John both give me a perfect hug. "Neither of us can begin to understand how you do it, we love you so very much little sister! You made a promise and made it happen!" "Amanda, could we borrow Sunny again?" asked Josh. "She is my dream woman, a loan would be fine." "Oh, we'll see, you must be very good brothers. I think you two need to find a couple of those hot college girls and let me borrow them occasionally!" "I will keep your request in mind. Amanda, where were you two last night? I knocked on your door at nine-thirty, no answer. I peeked in at an empty bed." "Oh, we went for a walk." "Amanda, an hour later you had not returned!" "Joshy, you don't have to know everything!"

I go back to my room after attempting to quiet Josh's wondering mind. Do I need a lock on my door? Ah, what good would that do? He'd get Dad to check on me and with no answer he would break down my door. Oh well, Josh is manageable and even Dad. Mom would be my concern. I promised Dad she could never know what a tramp I am. What would she do if she knew? Ground my little ass, punish me, how? Would I let her know that I am aware she has many hidden secrets herself? Wow, hopefully I never have to deal with that situation. It certainly could be mind altering, perhaps for both of us, ahh, no worries for this moment.

CHAPTER 56

Monopoly

I plan to sun for a while this afternoon. My mind flashes back to Sunny. God, she is so hot! I am amazed how excited I became as I witnessed my brothers sticking their cocks inside her. I flash back to Sunny standing dropping her shorts and spreading her legs for them both. I believe I was as excited as my brothers! Damn it, why did her mom have to show up? I was next in line. I wanted so badly to bury my face in her beautiful ass and lick as much cum as I could swallow and feel her passion. How I wanted my brothers to watch my hot little bitch cum. Amanda, certain things you have no control.

Sunday flew by, I hung out in the sun, and chatted with Marianne and Bri. No bus ride again this week for Bri. Damn, I need her soon. Marianne is doing well, she misses me as much as I do her. She did make reference and questioned me concerning Chad once more. "Amanda, he has not been to my room for weeks, thank God. Tell me girl, why?" "Marianne, be happy with the satisfaction your problem has been resolved, why ask questions?" "Amanda, I'm not quite as dumb as I look, I did not make the connection as he picked us up a couple of times and now I'm realizing he is never coming to my room again! You are a devious little tramp, aren't you?" I laugh so hard, "Oh Marianne, I love you. I'd rather be called your problem solving tramp." "Amanda, that works just fine! I love you." We say our bye-byes.

Jack called again. This time I recognized his true name on my caller ID and pick up the phone. "I am wearing yellow bikini panties that are very lacy," I say with a seductive voice. He cracked up. "Amanda, I want to visit soon. My schedule is still upside down. Soon, can I visit and play with you?" I assure him I would do my best to be available as we say our goodbyes. I'm not certain why I think of his seductive

looks and his hands all over my body that early evening. Was it evening? God, I don't remember the time of day. It was my first experience; perhaps that's why it excites me so.

He has no idea that I know his true name, I suppose. Of course he must realize I have caller ID. Although he couldn't be aware that I have realized he is our newly elected city council president. I saw his photo in the paper with a story on my Jack. He is a real go-getter, according to the news story. He owns a large grocery store in our city. I supposed with his demur he was living the high life. It certainly does pay to read and keep up with current events. Good girl Amanda, somehow I am excited to show him some of the new tricks I've learned since our last encounter.

It's a quiet week leading up to my beach party, perhaps I am saving myself. I've talked to my girls several times making final plans. My boys each have a friend joining us. Bargain Bob confirmed two o'clock is great for him and "O'La Lay" to meet with my beach gang. Ray Ray is picking us up at eleven a.m. sharp on Saturday morning. Ebony is so excited to meet all my family. I've invited Josh and John. They are attempting to arrange to mow Sunday at the Ferris's. I would love to have them along. I've advised Josh to bring his own woman. He laughed, "Amanda, no, I want to borrow one of yours, after receiving your permission of course!" I knew he was trainable, "Yes!"

I've made our reservations for Cadillac's on Saturday night, at eight o'clock. We may need a nap after sunning the day away. Uncle Bob did mention our cookie factory was coming right along!

Friday arrives and passes so quickly. "See you eleven a.m. Ray. Wear a sexy bathing suit OK?" "Yes, of course, Amanda." "The weather is to be perfect. We'll get you all tanned up, OK?" "Ya, ya, ya! Bye-bye!"

We are all so excited. Yes, my brothers will be joining us. Perfect, that makes, let me count, twelve including Ray and myself. Uncle Bob and "O'La Lay" will be joining us later. All my notes, I can't forget to take them along. I believe my new family will be very excited about our new business plan. I don't know what to expect with this wild and crazy gang. Of course, no alcohol, I don't see how I can make that happen. Yeah, I do have buyers. Ray, I could never ask! Uncle Bob, would I consider drinking with him around? If I insisted, Ray could get us beer. No, I can't even consider that! He could be in serious jeopardy if we were busted. This is a tough one. We'll see, what's a beach party without a drink or two? A difficult call, perhaps it won't come up!

Josh's game is tonight, away again. They're the favorites tonight for a change. My birthday is a few hours away! "Brothers, win one for me!" as Josh and Johnny are walking out the door, "Yes Amanda, we're going to give 'em hell, just as you would." "We're both so ready for your party tomorrow," Josh added. "It's going to be so much fun guys. I'm so happy you're joining us, also tomorrow night at Cadillac's. I can't wait to celebrate!" "Amanda, you live like you are twenty-one now, what more do you have in store?" asks Josh.

The boys are off, he is so right, what will a new year bring? My God, this year

has been amazing! What will I find to humor my little world and myself? Only God knows, and I'm still not certain he gives a shit about Amanda and her antics.

OK, Bandit's all taken care of. Mom won't be home tonight and Dad will stop and have a cocktail or two this evening. It's six p.m. Sammy will arrive in an hour. God yes, my party should begin tonight. Maybe I'll do some Mic Ultra with Sammy. Do you suppose he remembers? They don't forget when it comes to entertaining a tramp. OK, showered, I put on mascara, a touch of eye shadow, and lipstick. I dress myself as hot as ever, a red little polka dot silky skirt and a sleazy bra! Oh yes, my pink with black lace crotchless panties; how perfect is that? They may help me to drive a better deal on my video equipment. Pink knee socks and pink hoop earrings, a peak in the mirror. Oh God, Sammy will cum in his pants! Sammy is pulling in my drive. I leave a note for Dad and congratulate the boys. Yes, it's my birthday, certainly a win tonight.

Out the door, "Hi Sammy." "Amanda, you have outdone yourself, look at you." In a low voice, "Amanda, may I say something?" "Yeah Sammy." "Your breasts have grown in the few weeks since I've seen you and God you're more beautiful." "I'm getting older Sammy. My birthday's at midnight." "My gosh, Happy Birthday Amanda!" "Do we celebrate your birthday on our way home?" "I hope so Sammy!" "I'll have the Mic Ultra ready!" "O-O-O-O-K! Sammy, in your business do you sell video recording cameras, microphones, monitors, TVs, DVDs, and editing components?" "Yes, that is my business Amanda." "What do you suppose it would cost to cover three rooms and two outside areas? A total of twelve cameras with motion sensor audio that can be turned off and on. I also need a thirty-two inch TV, DVD and VCR." "Installed, Amanda?" "Yes, Sammy." "Ball park, ten thousand, give or take." "Could you possibly meet me Wednesday at ten a.m. at my home for a bid?" "Of course, I'd be happy to. I'll give you the family discount."

We pull into Mr. Sampson's drive. His house is amazing, his beautiful lawn is picture perfect. We walk in the front door and I'm quickly greeted. "Amanda, you look so cute tonight. You are growing up so quickly." "Thank you Mrs. Sampson. Hello Sandy and Andy." "Hi Amanda, can we play Monopoly tonight?" "Oh, we'll see, you two want to beat me don't you?" "Yes, and we will Amanda!" "OK, we'll see." "Amanda, here is my cell number," says Mrs. Sampson, call if there are any problems. The kids are to be in bed by nine-thirty. We have a house party this evening. It could be after midnight before we return. Please let the dog out at eight or so to do his outside business, if you would. Let's see, yes the two cats are fine inside. I think that covers it Amanda." "Great, and you two have a good night. You look gorgeous tonight Mrs. Sampson." "Oh thank you. Sam, you all set?" "Yes dear," out the door they go.

"Come on Amanda, let's play Monopoly." "OK, you two set up the board and get the bank and real estate cards ready, OK?" "Yaeeeee, we're going to take all your money Amanda." "OK guys and gals." I clean up the kitchen and polish while they're getting the game ready to go. "Come on Amanda, we're ready for you." "Are you two going to gang up on me?" "No," Andy says, "I always beat Sandy!" "No

you don't, I won last game." "OK, one game in six, I'm still the champ." I slide to the dining room table. "OK, pick your little board rollers." "We've got ours Amanda." "OK. Good. I've got the fire truck, and I'll need that anyway." "Why?" asks Sandy. "I'm going to be ON fire and burn your houses and hotels, that's why!" Oh they find that so funny. "But ya know what kids? I won't really need the fire truck." "Why not?" asks Andy. "Because, I'm going to let them burn." "Oh Amanda, we'll burn yours down, you just watch." "OK kids, I'm going to ask one question before we start." "What Amanda?" "Do you want me to let you win and teach you about Monopoly as we go, or should I play for real and take your money?" They both cheered, "Play for real Amanda." "OK, you asked for it, you two are pros, give me the dice, I'll go first!"

I roll a nine, Connecticut Ave, one hundred twenty dollars. "I'll buy it." I pay Andy and he gives me my card. Sandy rolls a three, Baltic Ave, sixty dollars. "OK, I guess I'll buy it." I hate to spend my sixty dollars. Andy hands her a card. Andy rolls a six, Oriental Ave, "OK, I guess," one hundred dollars and he takes his real estate card. "Andy, I'll give you two hundred for Oriental Ave, right now." "OK Amanda." I give him two hundred. He is so excited. "Ha, Ha Sandy, I made two hundred and you spent sixty dollars already." I can see this will be fun tonight. My roll - a two, St. Charles Place for one hundred forty dollars. I hand my money over and get my card. "You got doubles, Amanda, roll again." "Oh OK, oh only a three. Virginia, one hundred eighty dollars. I hand Andy my money and he hands me my card. "Amanda you're going to run out of money and we'll win as they both laugh." "That could be Andy, I was broke when I arrived, and I'll be broke maybe when I leave!" Andy's roll, he lands on States Avenue, one hundred forty dollars. He hesitates and says, "I guess I'll buy it." He sticks one hundred forty dollars in the bank and gets his card. My roll, I land on chance. "Oh Amanda, might go to jail, ha, ha, ha." Take a ride on the Reading, collect two hundred if you pass go. "Sorry, no jail guys." "Andy hands me two hundred for passing go. "Keep it Andy and give me Reading Railroad." They each pass up property purchase opportunities. "OK my turn again." I land on Vermont. Yes, a monopoly for me!

"Amanda, you're losing." I count my money. Eight hundred and change left. I hand Andy seven hundred fifty dollars. "What for Amanda?" "I need three hotels for my monopoly." "Amanda, you're broke, ha ha ha!" "But Andy, I'm not hungry, I'm OK." He didn't really get it I don't think. I arrange my hotels. They take turns rolling the dice and buy an occasional property, they are saving their money. Andy lands on Chance, advance to Boardwalk. "Are you going to buy it?" asks Sandy. "No, it would take a lot of my money." My roll again, Pennsylvania Railroad. I scrape my final dollars together and mortgage one property and pay. "Andy, give me my card," he does. "Amanda you're broke." "I'm still not hungry Andy." They both look at me like God she's so stupid, who taught her to play this game. Sandy rolls, she lands on Connecticut with my hotel. "Oh Sandy, thank you for choosing my hotel to stay tonight, six hundred dollars please!" "Amanda, you'll take all my money." "Oh Sandy, I enjoy attractive young ladies staying at my hotel. I'll buy you

a cocktail tonight!" "OK Amanda, you know I can't drink! Give a better room rate hotel queen." "Sorry Sandy, but thank you for staying at my hotel," Sandy forces a smile. Andy now lands on Vermont Avenue. "Oh Andy, I love handsome guests like you at my hotel, only five hundred fifty dollars tonight. Andy it's a great deal, all my rooms are half off tonight. You are going to be such a good customer, I can see that…five hundred fifty dollars please." "Amanda, you're taking all my money." "OK Andy, I'll make you another deal. Give me only three hundred dollars and States Avenue you bought for one hundred forty dollars." "That's a great deal for me, Amanda." He hands me three hundred and his property. My turn, I count my money. "Let me have six houses, here's six hundred dollars." I lay my houses neatly on my three monopoly properties. Around we go, now they buy very little property, they are saving their money. Soon one is staying at my hotel again, the other is renting my house. My houses soon become hotels, now they're both broke. I have all their money. "Amanda, did you cheat?" asks Andy. "No you sold me your properties, didn't you?" "And I made money on them Amanda." "Not enough I guess." They both are looking very grumpy. "Did you both pay attention to what I did?" "Yes, you spent all your money." "No, I invested my money, that is how life works in the real world. You buy things that return you money. You must spend first and it grows, that is called investing. With this game, buy, never pass a property up, never! Mortgage, do whatever is needed. Tell me guys!" "Never pass a property up, right Amanda?" "Yes, that's right." Sandy and Andy are staring at each other. "Wow Sandy, I guess Amanda knows how to play Monopoly after all." "Come on Amanda, let's play again." "Uh, no, it's nine-thirty, get ready for bed. You two play Monopoly with your friends, do like have showed you, and you'll be the champions." "OK Amanda, you are cool even though you took our money to stay in your run down hotels!" They chuckle. "Yes Sandy and Andy, they are all a little shabby, but you know what, you two low life customers paid me to stay!" "Amanda, you're so bad." Laughing, "Yes I am. OK, get ready for bed." "Yes Amanda, the Hotel Queen," they giggle as they trudge away. I tucked them in, they were so happy to learn about Monopoly. I had fun picking on them, they took it very well.

CHAPTER 57

Mr. Sampson

I sent their dog Cocoa out for a late run, put the game back in its box and wandered through the house. Great, the room with all the cameras and screens was unlocked. I don't know much about video stuff, what was here certainly seemed very professional. I looked around again. There were cameras on the ceiling, several screens, a sofa, a small bed, TV, monitors. He was probably a movie buff, although I saw no movies. Not what I have in mind at all for my rooms. My cameras must be smaller and not visible, something no one would ever notice or suspect. Oh well, I close the door, go into the other room and watch TV after letting the dog back while I plan my big day.

Two more hours! The big birthday will arrive! Funny, I don't feel any older. You probably don't feel that until you are much older like twenty-five or thirty. I suppose then I'll really feel it!

Midnight is here. The big day has arrived! I think I'm somewhat of an adult. What kind of a year will it bring? God, haven't I done it all, what's left? I'm sure I'll find something to keep myself entertained.

I'm thinking of my beach party with all my friends together on the beach, that should be an experience. Having a beer or two would be great. How can I make that happen? I hate when things are not in my control. My business presentation is weighing on my mind, it will be so important. Uncle Bob's involvement with all his business knowledge, how can this one miss? My whole family, making lots of money, that's my plan. They must first choose to work. I believe they all could be very dedicated to a good business concept.

The door opens, it's twelve forty-five a.m. "How was everything Amanda?" "Oh,

just perfect." "Kids were good?" "Oh yes Mrs. Sampson, you should be proud, they are so well mannered. I love sitting for them." "You must have played Monopoly." "Oh yes, they taught me some good tricks, they love that game so much." "They play with the neighbor boys all the time, although they only seem to win with each other. The neighbors take all their money, they complain to me constantly." "Come on Amanda, let's get you home." "OK, Mr. Sampson." "Honey, I'm going to stop by the office for some paperwork, no need to wait up." "OK Sam, I'm going on to bed. Be careful, you've had a lot to drink." "I'm fine." "Good night Amanda, thank you so much." "Bye-bye Mrs. Sampson."

I slide into my seat and close the door. We pull out of the drive. Sam opens a Mic and hands it to me. He is sucking one as well. "Happy Birthday little girl." "Thank you." "Let's celebrate," he slurs. I haven't seen him intoxicated before, tonight was my night I guess. My first birthday beer ever, that is, on my birthday. God, it tasted so good. Sam's hand was caressing my leg. "Come, sit by me birthday girl." I hesitate, oh heck why not? I slid closer. I could smell the hard alcohol on his breath. I guess I have no problem with a drunk as long as they are not dangerous. "Amanda, your legs are so soft. You excite me so much." He takes my hand and rubs his crotch with it. I continue massaging as he lets my hand go. Yes, I guess I do excite Sammy, it was apparent with his hardness as I continue stroking his slacks. "I need another beer Sam." He takes my bottle and tosses it out his open window and hands me another and tosses his empty as well. "Man, those beers are going down so smoothly," he exclaims. He continues sucking on his longneck. His hand has found my crotchless panties. "Amanda, your pussy is so fucking hairy, it drives me wild. You like that?" he inquires as he continues fumbling with my pussy. "Oh yes Sammy, you have a touch when you are drunk." "Drunk? You little bitch, don't talk to me that way." "Calm down, Sam, just having some fun." "Have fuckin' fun with your boyfriends, not with Samuel Sampson!" "Sam, you better run me straight home I think." "Bitch, I'll let you know when you'll go home, you got it?" He pulls by my big tree and shuts off the ignition. He unzips his slacks, "No foot massage tonight Bitch. My lotion is going somewhere else." Hmmm, this certainly could be a dangerous situation on this night. I'll suck him off and walk home is my plan. I slid my mouth on to his cock. "Yeah you little cock-sucking whore, that's what Sam needs, a fucking cock sucker tonight." He pulls my head by my hair, "Tell me you're Sam's cocksucker!" "Sam, I'm your cocksucking bitch." "Yes, you are," as he slams my head on his cock and rams it in and out of my mouth. "You like that cock, don't ya bitch?" as he lifts my head off by my hair. "Yes, Sam, yes I love your cock. Cum in my mouth." "No fuckin way." He pulls me up by my hair and pushes me to my back on the seat. He tosses his bottle out the window and buries his face in my pussy. "Spread those legs whore." As disgusting as it sounds, I was enjoying his degrading language, it was exciting me. His mouth on my pussy, told him the story of my excitement. My juices were running freely to his open mouth. He was pushing my legs yet farther apart. "God, that's good pussy. Bitch, I want that pussy tonight you fuckin whore." He attempts to climb on me. "Sammy, I love it doggy

style." "Well turn your fucking ass over, whore!" I move toward the dash and move to my belly and stuck my ass in the air. "Suck my ass you bastard!" I scream at him. He liked that. His mouth is buried in my ass. My plan is to eventually stick his cock in my ass. If I handle it slowly I doubt he will know the difference. Amanda, this is very dangerous territory, although I believe I am in control. Now going through my little birthday mind, this is going to be the best birthday present ever, a ten- thousand dollar fuck. My video equipment is being paid for. Sam will be very surprised come Wednesday, surprise, surprise! Until then I must get through this alive!

"Bitch, I want you to know what a man feels like in your fucking hairy pussy. Right Bitch?" "Oh yes Sam, I want a real man." "Well Bitch, you got one tonight." Yuk, I can feel his drunken drool soaking through my top, what a girl will do for a few pieces of equipment! His voice is barely audible as he slurs, "I want to give ya somein to mumber on your birthday, you fuckin exhibitionist whore." Hmm . . . That did have a great ring to it, a very good line. I reach back and massage his cock. I guide it up and down my crack, it is highly unlikely he will even know what hole he is fucking! "You ready for a man, Bitch?" "Oh yes Sammy, please fuck this bitches pussy." I slide it to my back door, he presses, the head pops through. "God your pussy is so fuckin tight. Oh God, how I love tight pussy." He is ramming me with all he has. "Oh Sammy, I love your cock in my pussy, God I love it. Fuck me, fuck me!" I am earning my ten thousand dollar equipment package at this very moment! Is it the language, is it his drunkenness, or is it simply cock fucking me? Of course, my ten thousand dollar package certainly does brighten the picture. Only I know that could easily be only a down payment! "Sammy, please, I want to feel your cum squirting all over my ass, please! Soak me with your fucking cum!" "Oh is that what you need Bitch? I can help with that order, yes I fuckin can. Ohhhhh, take that Bitch." I feel his cum shooting all over my crotchless panties on my hairy pussy. "Oh Sammy, it's so hot, please rub your cock all over my pussy, my ass, let me feel your cock." "Yaaaa, you like that you fucking slut." "Oh yes Sammy I do, wow!" Sammy is wilting away. He is slumped in his seat. I arrange myself and sit back up. I look at Sam, God – he is passed out! I shake him, he mumbles. Oh well, where is that beer. Oh, it's a twelve pack and eight left. Sammy doesn't appear to need another right now and the fucker didn't pay me for sitting tonight. Oh well, I'll collect on Wednesday.

I grab the remaining eight and walk to my house. My window is unlocked if need be. I don't want Dad claiming my brews. I peek in, no Dad. I'm sure he's been sleeping for hours. I slip through the house to my room after grabbing a plastic zip lock. I rub all the semen I can find, not already soaked into my crotchless panties. Crap, how I'll miss this pair, as I write MAS and lock them up. I lay on my bed feeling my fucked ass with my fingers. Sammy is going to be so pissed when I break the news of my video equipment deal that will arrive straight from his warehouse. I'll assure him of course, he can stop over and we'll make a great movie together. Sam, Sam, you can talk your dirty language if you choose. Geez, I hope he

doesn't die in his car tonight. That would be a real bummer! Of course, Mrs. Sampson would still want to pay. Something like this getting out could very easily ruin a happy funeral. Sandy and Andy would feel so bad knowing their Dad had raped the Hotel Queen on her birthday. Well, if he dies, we do have a solid back up plan.

Oh yes, beach party tomorrow! Woo, Hoo! God how I love being old! This is going to be a fucking great year, join me and see! "O'La Lay."

Growing Up Amanda - II Coming soon!

Wow! What will a new year bring: I'm using and practicing what I have learned, and living it to its fullest. Can there possibly be more? My next year will shock even myself. My connection with Uncle Bob, wow! I couldn't imagine in a thousand years where that could possibly take me, and Sammy, oh my God, who would ever have guessed! My video equipment was solely for my pleasure, where that takes me is shocking! God, you will laugh, you will cry, it will tear at your sexual core, as it does mine! My world will rock yours. Come travel with me for another year. I realize I am not your normal kid. Somehow sexual adventure seems to follow me wherever I go, why is it? I'm a kid, I don't begin to understand why. You know by this time I'm doing my best to avoid this type of terrible pleasure. Although, I do admit occasionally, I can be a bit creative for a naïve teenager. Follow me for another year, do you suppose you can keep up? Happy traveling. Bye-bye!

Yours truly,
Amanda